SKINNER'S MISSION

SKINNER'S
MISSION

Quintin Jardine

headline

First published in 1997
by HEADLINE BOOK PUBLISHING

First published in paperback in 1997
by HEADLINE BOOK PUBLISHING

13 15 17 19 20 18 16 14 12

ISBN 0 7472 5043 X

Typeset by Palimpsest Book Production Limited
Polmont, Stirlingshire
Printed in England by
Clays Ltd, St Ives plc

HEADLINE BOOK PUBLISHING
A division of Hodder Headline PLC
338 Euston Road
London NW1 3BH

This book is dedicated to the town of L'Escala,
which allowed me the peace and quiet to write it.

ACKNOWLEDGEMENTS

The author's thanks go to:

Jerry Joyce
The late Chic Murray
Tom Shields

1

'This is just the sort of thing that can happen when you sell a dodgy Ferrari.'

Six heads turned towards the doorway. The white-coated scene of crime technicians stood automatically to attention. They shone like spectres in the white glare of the temporary floodlighting, which was reflected also by the puddles which covered much of the floor of the burned-out showroom.

The man, white-clad like the rest, gazed slowly around the ravaged shed. The scene took him back to the aftermath of an urban riot to which he had been taken by the Los Angeles Police Department, during a month-long international police symposium visit in California, from which he had just returned. He counted, spread around the area, the skeletal shells of eight motor cars. They rested not on tyres, for they had melted into the floor, but on bare wheel hubs.

'Relax, ladies and gentlemen,' the newcomer barked, at last. 'I'm only paying a visit.' He looked, automatically, at the oldest of the men in white coveralls. 'Where's Chief Superintendent Martin?'

'He's through the back, sir. With the ME.'

The big man nodded. 'Thank you, Arthur.' His eyes

roamed slowly and carefully once more around the gutted area. He smiled, grimly. 'What d'you think of the show so far?'

'You can rule out accidental causes, sir. Or spontaneous combustion. This was very deliberate, sir. Good old-fashioned low-tech arson, with nothing fancy about it. The blaze had several seats, but from what the firemen told me about its spread, I'd say they all went up at the same time.

'We've still got some poking around to do, but I should be able to draw you a picture in a wee while.'

'Don't draw it for me, Inspector. Chief Superintendent Martin's in command here. Like I said, I'm just passing through.'

The red-haired man nodded, sagely. 'Very good, sir.' He paused. 'But it's still good to see you back.'

Deputy Chief Constable Bob Skinner grinned and accepted the Inspector's proffered handshake. 'Thanks, Arthur. Between you and me, and anyone else who's listening, it's bloody good to *be* back, even at half past two on a pissy awful late winter's morning in Seafield, even with the north wind blowing the rain off the river and carrying the smell of the sewage works along with it!'

He glanced around the showroom once more, smiling grimly. 'Not an insurance job, then?' he said, in a mischievous tone.

The other man laughed, with the same grim gallows humour as Skinner. 'Not unless the man who puts in the claim fancies doing fifteen years for his trouble. Insurance jobs nearly always start in the main fuse box, or with something inflammable accidentally falling across an electric fire.

'Whoever did this just walked in and set the fucking place on fire!'

The DCC nodded. 'And some very high-priced motor cars in the process.'

'That's right, boss. According to the ad in yesterday's *Scotsman*, a red Ferrari, three Beamers, at least two Porsches, a classic Mercedes sports car, and a very rare Maserati.'

'Funny,' said Skinner, 'for all the things that we've tried to nail Jackie Charles for, I never fancied him for dealing in hot motors!'

His smile vanished as he glanced again at the Inspector. 'So why do we need an ME? Young Sammy Pye only told me about the fire when he called. All he said was that Mr Martin thought I might like to come along.'

He could see the man shudder beneath his loose, white tunic. He nodded his head towards a blackened, empty doorframe, at the rear of the showroom. 'That's through there, sir.'

Skinner frowned. 'It's not Jackie, is it?'

'I had a good look at it, sir, but for all I could tell it could have been my father-in-law's pet greyhound . . . except I think that it only had two legs!'

It was the DCC's turn to shiver. 'I've been trying to lock up that wee bastard Charles for just about all of my police career, but I wouldn't wish that on him.' His voice dropped. 'I hate fire, Arthur. It gives me the creeps, especially when I see how easily and how well people burn.'

'I know what you mean, boss,' said Inspector Dorward. 'I go to crime scenes practically every working day. It's my job. Mostly they don't bother me, except where there's kids or fire involved.

'D'you remember that one last summer out in East Lothian, when that bloke was burned alive. Your wife was the Medical Examiner. Some job she has, eh! I don't know how she does it.'

Skinner frowned. 'She's a tough lady, is my wife, but I'm glad she's not here. Who was the poor bastard on call for this one?'

'Doctor Banks, sir.'

He tugged awkwardly at his vast white overall suit. 'I suppose I'd better go and join him, then. Give me a shout when you're ready to draw us that picture of what happened here.'

'Will do, sir.'

Picking his way carefully through the blackened, soaking debris on the floor, the DCC walked across to the doorway at the back of the showroom. He had almost reached it when suddenly it was filled by a stocky, wide-shouldered blond man, the thickness of his build emphasised by his protective suit. The tinted contact lens which he wore made his vivid green eyes shine oddly in the bright light.

'I thought I heard you, boss,' said Chief Superintendent Andy Martin. He stepped back, allowing Skinner to enter the small, blackened room. Although the door had burned away to ashes, its frame and the lower half of the walls which partitioned the chamber off from the rest of the unit were constructed of steel sheeting. They, the substructure of a large metal desk, and four filing cabinets, had survived the blaze. The twisted, charcoal-black figure which lay at their feet had not.

4

The duty Medical Examiner was crouched over the body. He looked up for a second at the newcomer, giving him the briefest of nods. Skinner responded with a grunt. He disliked Banks, and had often questioned his thoroughness, even on occasion his competence. However he had always stopped short of having him removed from the list of police surgeons, mainly because he suspected that if he took the step he might be accused of acting under his wife's influence.

The only other living person in the room was Detective Constable Sammy Pye, the most junior member of the small personal staff which Andy Martin maintained as head of CID. He stood, silent and pale in the corner of the room.

'You didn't mention this added attraction when you woke me from a sound sleep, Sammy,' said the DCC. 'All you said was that there had been a call after a major fire at Jackie Charles' showroom, and that Chief Superintendent Martin thought that I might like to join him.' He grinned. 'Did you think that if you mentioned an immolated stiff, I'd have decided to stay in my bed!'

The young man reddened. 'No, sir. But . . .'

'Leave the lad alone,' Martin intervened. 'None of us knew about the death until we got here. All that our fire brigade colleagues said to us was that they had a suspicious blaze down here in Motor City, and would we like to come along.'

'When were they called out?'

'Around nine. This building isn't seen easily from the roadway. A passing motorist spotted the glow from the flames once they broke through the roof.'

'And when did the fire service call CID?'

'About an hour ago, just before we called you. This was some fire. They had gas tanks, paint and God knows what all in this place. It took the lads four hours to put out the blaze completely, and until they could be sure that the petrol storage tanks underneath us weren't going to blow. As soon as they were able to take a look inside they realised from the pattern of the damage that they were dealing with a crime. But I don't think they had found the body when they called us.'

Skinner nodded. 'Fair enough. But how come you're here? You're Head of CID. What the hell do we have divisional offices for? Haven't I taught you anything about delegation?'

'No,' said Martin, cheerfully. 'Not a single, solitary bloody thing! All I'm doing is following the example you set when you were in this job.' His soft smile faded. 'But seriously though, I've got a standing order in place that anything involving Jackie Charles is reported immediately to my office. Like I heard you say to Arthur Dorward, he's been Number One on our target list for years, or at least since Tony Manson got killed.'

'And you want the glory of banging him up?' Martin looked at him sharply, surprised. 'Only joking, Andy!'

'As a result,' said the Chief Superintendent, heavily, 'when the night duty man in Dave Donaldson's office logged in the Fire Brigade report, he did the right thing and phoned Sammy, who takes the night calls for me.'

Skinner smiled sympathetically at the young man. 'We've all had to do night telephone duty in our careers, son. But I'll tell you a strange thing. The higher up the tree we get, and the more we have willing lads like you to shield us from the middle of the night

6

calls, even so the fucking phone seems to ring more and more.'

He looked back at Martin. 'So what about Jackie? Has anyone called his house yet, to see if he's in?' He pointed downwards. 'Or are you assuming that we're looking for a new public enemy Number One?'

'The Fire Service phoned him as soon as the blaze was reported. There was no reply, but there's a Porsche outside, with Jackie's personal number, "N1JJC", on it.'

The DCC frowned. 'I see. Still, let's not jump to conclusions. He could have left it here for a service.'

'Sure, but then again . . .' Martin looked at Skinner, very slightly askance.

'To answer your question, boss, I haven't sent anyone out to his house yet,' he said. 'I know you're as interested in Charles as I am. That's why I told Sammy to call you, even before I knew there was a body involved.

'Hope he didn't wake the baby,' he added.

'No. Master Jazz sleeps through the phone these days. Just as well. I'm in deep enough shit with the wife as it is.'

The Chief Superintendent looked at him, sharply once again, but decided that it was not the moment to follow up the remark. Instead he said, 'I thought we might go to the Charles place together, sir, to pay a call on Jackie, or possibly, probably even given that car, on his widow.'

Skinner sighed. 'The lovely Carole, eh. I haven't seen her in years.'

'You know her?'

'Too right I know her! Years ago Jackie and Carole used to live in Gullane, not that far from me. There he was, living the life of a respectable young motor dealer,

7

and there was I, a young blood in the CID, knowing that he was one of the biggest villains in Edinburgh, and a part of the team that was trying to put him away.' Again, Martin glanced at him in surprise.

'It was more than a wee bit embarrassing at the time. A couple of times Myra and I were invited to parties, and the Charleses were there.'

'What did you do?'

'I stopped going to parties. Eventually the Charleses moved up to Edinburgh, but by that time Myra was dead, and I wasn't getting party invitations anyway.'

'Eh?'

Skinner nodded. 'Don't look surprised. A single man, especially a widower, is a very awkward guest at married couples' parties. All the guys watch him like a hawk around their wives.'

Martin stared at him. 'I'm single, and I've never noticed that.'

'Aye, but when were you ever stuck for someone to take to a party? Anyway, enough of my past. Doctor, how's the sift through the ashes coming along?'

The middle-aged Banks pushed himself awkwardly to his feet. 'That is more or less what it is. All the features and genitals have been obliterated, most of the flesh has been reduced to ash and what's left is roasted.'

'Could this be Jackie Charles, the owner of the show-room?'

'Yes, Mr Skinner, it could. But it could also be just about anyone else on the surface of the planet. I will need to open the body up before I can even tell you the gender of the victim. As for identification, that will have to be done through dental records. Even that might be difficult, since most of the fillings in the teeth seem to have melted.'

Skinner looked closely at the body for the first time, and felt his stomach lurch. Apart from the blackened, grinning skull, there was nothing that was recognisably human.

'Do what you have to, Doctor, as soon as you can.'

'Sir.' Sammy Pye spoke without moving from his corner. 'You won't see it where you are, but there's a wedding ring beside the body.'

'Pick it up, then, Constable, and let's have a look.' The DCC glanced at Martin. 'Who says I can't delegate?' he muttered.

Taking a deep breath and holding it, the young Pye bent over the black, stinking, sodden mass, and picked up a small, approximately round object with his thumb and second finger. He held it up for Skinner and Martin to see, then placed it on the DCC's outstretched palm.

'A man's ring?' asked Skinner.

'Could be,' Martin replied. He produced a torch from his tunic and shone it on the band. The fire had distorted it until it was almost oval but it still gleamed in the light. He picked it up and shone the beam around the inner surface. 'Bugger,' he whispered. 'No inscription, only a hallmark.'

'Even that might tell us something. Come on, let's get out of here and leave Doctor Banks to his work.'

The DCC led his two colleagues back through the showroom and out into the forecourt, which was lined with undamaged cars, all high-value used models, if less costly than those which had gone up in flames. The policemen stood there, protected from the drizzling rain by their tunics, and looked down Seafield Road, the recognised heartland of motor car retailing in the City of Edinburgh, at the lighted logo towers of more than a dozen car dealerships, which advertised among them almost every manufacturer in the marketplace.

'Quite a set-up,' said Skinner quietly. 'You want any sort of car, odds on you can get it here. Twenty-five years ago there was virtually bugger all on this road but for whisky bonds, the bus depot and the Dog and Cat Home.

'Now there are God knows how many millions turned over on this strip every week in the year. And you could argue that Jackie Charles started it all.'

He broke off and turned to Pye. 'Right, Sammy,' he said. 'It's oral examination time. What can you tell us about Jackie Charles?'

Alarm at the snapped question showed in the young Detective Constable's eyes, but for no more than a second. Then he nodded, and it vanished to be replaced by cool confidence.

'John Jackson Charles, sir,' he began, as if reading from a page in his mind. 'Known to all his friends and associates as Jackie. Aged forty-eight, and born in Edinburgh. He was an only child and his parents were thoroughly respectable middle-class people. His father, Martin Charles, was sales manager with the main Ford dealer in the city until he retired twelve years ago. Mr Charles senior is seventy-seven years old. He and Mrs Charles senior, who is seventy-five and who has always been a full-time housewife, now live in a cottage in St Andrews owned by their son.

'The Charles family lived in a small bungalow in

10

Corstorphine, and Jackie was educated at the Royal High School. He left school at eighteen with a clutch of Higher passes, but didn't choose to go to university. While he was at school his father had given him holiday work at the Ford dealership, and when he left, he insisted on starting there full-time.

'He was there for three years, until there was a row. The directors of the business discovered that he'd been dealing privately in used cars, often selling to customers who had come into the Ford showroom. Jackie was sacked, and his father might have been too, only his bosses were persuaded by Jackie that his dad had known nothing about his illicit sales.

'Not unnaturally, Charles moved out of the family home after that incident. He bought a semi-detached house out in Penicuik, and began to deal from there, selling to private customers, or locating and supplying specific cars to the trade.

'He did that, apparently successfully, for three more years. Then all of a sudden he went up in the world. He opened up, in this very showroom, the first car dealership in Seafield, and at the same time he and his new wife moved from Penicuik to a villa on a new development, Muirfield Park, in Gullane.'

Detective Constable Pye paused, and looked at Skinner. 'I'm sorry, sir. That's as far as I've got with the file so far.'

'That's fair enough,' said the DCC. 'I didn't expect you to have memorised Jackie Charles' complete life story, but you've done pretty well. Let me fill in the rest for you.'

He paused, as Pye looked at him, in relief. 'In those

11

days,' he began, 'before computer storage and analysis, the business of criminal intelligence wasn't anywhere near as sophisticated or as high-tech as it is now, but it existed nonetheless. Fair or unfair, secondhand car dealers were among its priority subjects, and so when Jackie Charles made his big move it stood out like a sore thumb. My team became even more interested when our routine investigation showed that Jackie wasn't renting his new showroom. He had bought it for a hundred and twenty grand from a dealer in domestic heating oil, who had anticipated the collapse of his market.

'The showroom had plenty of stock too, much of it bought for cash at auction in the month before the opening. My people did their sums. The showroom and the new house were mortgaged to an extent, but we worked out that Jackie must have laid out over a hundred thousand in cash.

'We had a guess at the profit that he might have made in six years of trading, but it fell well short of that, and the Inland Revenue were happy with his tax returns. So we looked around, and we came up with a theory.

'Around a year before Jackie Charles made his big move upmarket, there was a major robbery in Edinburgh. One of the biggest industrial employers, a company called Indico, had its payroll snatched in broad daylight from an armoured van on a back road out in Sighthill. Five men in two cars stopped it and blocked it in. They were dressed SAS-style and were armed with shotguns, handguns and sledgehammers.

'They smashed their way into the cabin of the truck, hauled out the driver, put a gun to his head and forced him to unlock the back door. The security guard inside had a go as soon as it was open. One of the gang shot him in the legs with a sawn-off. Afterwards the man had to have a leg amputated.'

Skinner paused, to make sure that Pye was following his narrative. 'Indico had a big payroll,' he went on, eventually. 'The gang escaped with almost half a million pounds. None of it was ever recovered, and they were never caught. Six months after the event, an informant gave us the name of someone he said had driven one of the cars. The man named was Douglas Terry, the manager of one of Tony Manson's saunas. He was picked up, but he denied any involvement and of course, a couple of girls from the sauna came forward and gave him an alibi.

'My squad made the reasonable assumption that Tony Manson was behind the robbery, and that he had done his usual efficient cover-up. But then a few months later, Jackie Charles spent all that money, and the case was reopened. Us guys in the Serious Crimes squad took another look at the staff of Indico, the company which had been robbed. We had already investigated everyone in the accounts department who might have known about the movement of cash, but couldn't find a thing.

'This time we looked at former staff as well. We found that a young book-keeper had packed in her job three months before the hold-up, and we read her resignation letter. It explained that she was leaving to work in her boyfriend's business. When she worked at Indico, her name was Carole Huish. By the time we read the letter, she had become Carole Charles.'

Young Pye's eyes widened, but Skinner held up a hand, seeing Inspector Dorward approach. 'You can read the rest for yourself, Sammy.' He turned towards the newcomer. 'Yes, Arthur. Are you ready to draw that picture for us?'

The man nodded. Like the others he had pulled up the hood of his tunic against the rain. 'As ready as I'll ever be, sir.

'Like I said earlier, this was a low-tech job. The arsonist used petrol as his fuel, good old four-star. Some of it was in cans near the office door, some of it was in the tanks of the cars in the showroom.'

'How was it triggered?' asked Andy Martin.

'The old-fashioned way, with petrol-soaked rope as fuses. We've found traces of what we think is hemp residue leading from the showroom doorway right up to the tanks of the Maserati, the Ferrari and the two biggest BMWs, and to a pile of what we reckon are melted oilcans, beside the empty office doorframe.

'Whoever did this set up the fuses, stood in the show-room doorway, lit them all, closed the door behind him and buggered off.'

'But wait a minute,' said Martin. 'All that couldn't have been done silently. Surely the victim in the office must have heard?'

'Not necessarily, sir. We found a melted radio in the office with the volume control turned up pretty high.

'But even so, take a look at this.' Dorward held up a bright brass object, with a darker piece of twisted metal protruding from it.

'It's the lock from the office door, as we found it among the ashes. It's been turned, and the key is on the outside.'

Martin stared hard at him. 'So your evidence in the witness box would be that the victim was locked in,

14

before or after the fire was set, yet could have been unaware of it until it was too late.'

Dorward thought for a few seconds. 'Yes, sir,' he said at last. 'That's what I'd say under oath.'

'Yet the arsonist knew that the poor sod was in there,' said the Head of CID, 'because he turned the bloody key!'

'Which makes this,' muttered Skinner slowly, 'not an insurance job, or a fire-raising by someone with a grudge against Jackie Charles, but cold-blooded premeditated murder, possibly with the man himself as the victim.'

He looked at Martin. 'I think, Chief Superintendent,' he said heavily and grimly, 'that it's time that you and I paid a call on Mr Charles. Unless, that is, we've seen him already this morning!'

2

Skinner had been brought to the scene by a patrol car, and so they set off for the Charles home in Martin's Mondeo, with the Head of CID at the wheel.

'I never knew you were on that Serious Crimes team, boss,' said Martin.

'What? The one that turned up the Carole Huish connection? I thought I'd told you that.' He smiled in the dark.

'I was a young DC, twenty-three, younger even than Sammy Pye. Myra and I were just married, and living in a police flat in Clermiston. We were there for about a year and a half before we bought the cottage in Gullane, through a guy my dad knew. Myra was well pregnant when we moved in, and Alex was born just a couple of weeks later.

'Salad days those were, but they didn't last long.' The big man shook his steel grey head, as if to clear away a memory.

He looked round at Martin and he grinned again. 'Christ, Andy, were we full of ourselves on that squad, when we linked Charles to Indico.'

'How did you follow it up?'

'Roy Old and I . . . he was a Sergeant then, poor Roy

. . . were told to go and talk to her. Archie Gillespie, our gaffer, decided that he would send out a couple of junior guys rather than fire off the big guns too early.

'We interviewed her at the showroom, the very one we've just left. She handled all the paperwork for the business in those days. That was the first time I had ever met her or Jackie. We were told not to put the wind up her, just to tell her that we were interviewing everyone connected with Indico, and it had taken us that long to get around to former staff.'

He laughed out loud. 'That's what we were told, and that's what we told her. By God, but she was a cool one, was Carole, even then. Jackie wanted to sit in on the interview, but she just fluttered her eyelashes and shooed him away. Roy Old did the talking at first, just like we'd been ordered. "Nothing to worry about, routine enquiry," all that stuff.

'When he asked her if she had knowledge of the payroll delivery route and timing, those eyelashes stayed rock solid. She didn't bat either of them, not one bit. She just looked at Roy and said, "Yes". That was all. And I knew right then that she had come up with the information for the robbery and that Jackie had set it up.'

He tapped his strong, straight nose. 'It came off her in waves, her self-assurance. You know how people react, Andy. Everyone who's asked a question like the one Roy asked her – especially, in my experience, those with nothing to hide – will show some sign of discomfort, or alarm, or downright panic. Not Carole. When she looked Roy dead in the eye and said, "Yes", she was as good as saying, "So fucking what, you're never going to prove anything, and all three of us in here know it."

'Then she gave me the look as well; and she got to me. The red mist came down. I could have blown my CID career right there. I forgot Gillespie's orders. I gave her the Evil Eye, as hard as I could, and she didn't flinch. I've met maybe half a dozen people in my life that I couldn't stare down. Carole Charles is one of them.'

He paused in thought. 'Her husband now, he isn't. He knows I've never been able to nail him for anything, but he reckons that one day I probably will, and for all that he's a ruthless, clever wee bastard, he can't look me in the eye for long.

'Yet that morning, twenty-three years ago, she did. And you know what, Andy, she was gorgeous with it. As I looked at her I realised that she was giving me the eye, and that I fancied her. There I was, with a new wife, starting to get a hard-on over some bird who was simply taking the piss out of me. That made me feel guilty and angry all at once, and all of a sudden. I stood up, and I looked around the showroom. With my John Henry bulging my Y-fronts, I pointed a finger at her and I said, none too quietly, "A few other people knew about the payroll too, but you're the only one with a husband who's just spent a hundred fucking grand on his business."

'That brought Jackie over, and it scared the shit out of Roy, who knew Archie Gillespie better than I did. He hustled me out of there, and told me to write up a report that showed we had followed the Gaffer's orders. So I did, but I finished it with my personal opinion that we need look no further.'

Martin looked sideways at Skinner, as they sat at a red traffic light. 'What was the outcome?'

'I got my arse kicked by Gillespie, in front of the whole team. Not because of the report, but because of Jackie Charles. He was so confident that he made a joke of it to his father. He told him that because he had borrowed to invest in his business and because his wife had worked at Indico, they were being accused of being Bonnie and Clyde.

'Charles Senior was in the same Masonic Lodge as Archie Gillespie, and over their next handshake he complained to him about me. So my Superintendent told me out loud – very loud – that if I ever wanted his job, I'd better learn fast about the limits of delegated authority . . . in other words about obeying fucking orders!

'Archie took over the enquiry, of course, and *because* Martin Senior had tried to use the Masonic thing, he went for Jackie with everything he could. Gillespie knew from the off that I was right, but the Charleses were too cool, and too well covered.

'We firmed up on a theory eventually, although theory it remains to this day. We discovered that Jackie had sold a couple of cars to Tony Manson. Our hypothesis was that he, and Carole, had dreamed up the Indico job, and that Jackie had taken it to Manson. Terrible Tony had supplied the men and the shooters, and he and Jackie had split the proceeds.

'You know the story from then on. There have been fifty-seven armed robberies from regional and sub-Post Offices around Central Scotland in the last twenty years, and thirty-four raids on small town banks. All that improved criminal intelligence that I was talking about earlier has led us to believe that Jackie Charles has been

19

involved in funding most of them, in the same way that Tony Manson backed him in the Indico job.

'We know also that he is the money man behind just about every loanshark in Edinburgh and Midlothian, that through nominees he owns half the minicab licences in the area and that by a process of straightforward extortion he has a financial interest in the rest.

'We know all that,' said Skinner grimly, in the dark. 'But we've never been able to prove it, because people are too frightened, or too well rewarded, or just hate us too much to co-operate with us.

'On top of that,' he growled, 'national police intelligence sources tell us that Jackie Charles has been responsible for supplying out of town wet contractors, or hit-men as Joe Punter would say, to take care of local difficulties around Britain. They say that he's a member of a Magic Circle of organised criminals, connecting London, Manchester, Liverpool and Scotland.'

The DCC glanced across at Martin. 'I've had two failures in my career, Andy. There have been just two guys I couldn't nail: Tony Manson and Jackie Charles. Tony's dead; now maybe Jackie's gone the same way.

'Maybe, finally, through all that he's upset someone enough to have a wet contractor brought in on him.' Skinner looked out of the window of the Mondeo as it drew up at the foot of a long driveway which wound up towards an impressive villa just off Ravelston Dykes Road. 'Let's go and find out.'

The two detectives climbed out of the car. Skinner checked his watch in the glow of a sodium street lamp. It was 3.25 a.m. He turned up the collar of his trademark black leather overcoat to protect himself as best he could against the rain, which had grown heavier since they left Seafield, and followed Martin up the herringbone-patterned red-brick driveway.

No lights showed in the house, but the door of the double garage was raised. Inside, dimly they could make out the shape of a car. They had almost reached the house when they were blinded, their approach triggering a 500-watt halogen security light mounted over the garage door.

Cursing softly and shielding his eyes from the glare, the Chief Superintendent took a torch from his pocket and shone the beam towards the blackness of the garage doorway. It illuminated the rear of a gleaming new Jaguar XK sports car, registration number 'CHC 1'.

'It's as if Carole left the garage open for Jackie coming in, and went to bed,' said Skinner, quietly.

'Let's find out,' said his colleague. He stepped up to the front door, under its stone vestibule, and pressed the bell, leaning on it for several seconds. The policemen took a few steps back, out into the rain, and waited, looking at the upper windows. They were out of the arc of the movement detector attached to the halogen light; after a few seconds it winked out.

'Cocky bastard,' growled Skinner. 'So confident that his security's minimal.'

Martin was almost ready to ring the doorbell once again, when a light went on in one of the upper windows, to their right. Behind the damask shade they saw the silhouette of a figure peering out into the pitch-black garden, looking around but failing to spot them. Eventually the windowframe swung open slightly, and a disgruntled, sleepy voice called out . . . a male voice.

'Christ, Carole, have you lost your bloody keys?! And what the hell are you doing coming in at this time anyway?' At once, both detectives recognised Jackie Charles' clipped voice, and his well-groomed accent. They had heard it often enough, yet it carried a frustrated, peevish tone that was new to them.

Martin took a full, deliberate step sideways back into the arc of the security light, triggering it once more. 'It isn't Carole, Jackie. It's Chief Superintendent Martin and DCC Skinner. We need to talk to you, now. Come down and let us in, please.'

Jackie Charles' tone changed at once. 'God, Bob Skinner, you always were a tenacious bastard. Now you've got this one at it. Have I got to write to my MP to stop you lot harassing me?'

'Your new MP's a friend of ours, Jackie,' said Skinner. 'I don't think she'd listen to you. Anyway, this isn't harassment. Like Andy said, we *need* to talk to you.' He laid heavy stress on the word, and his tone was an unquestionable command. The window closed.

Less than a minute later, the front door opened, and Jackie Charles held it wide for them to enter. He was wearing a blue silk dressing-gown, over matching pyjamas, with Morland leather sheepskin-lined slippers on his feet. He was a dapper man, around five feet eight, but with a stocky build which made him appear shorter. His dark hair, heavily flecked with grey, was expensively but traditionally cut, and looked neat even in the middle of the night, as it swept back from his temples and from his forehead.

He pointed them towards the living room. 'You know the way,' he said, dryly. 'You've been here before.'

The policemen stepped into a room to the right of the hall. They took off their overcoats and threw them on an occasional chair beside the door, then crossed the room and stood with their backs to the fireplace. Charles followed them and bent to ignite a living-flame gas fire.

'Where is your wife, Mr Charles?' asked Martin, formally, as the dapper man sat in an armchair.

He frowned up at him. 'She'll be staying over at her pal's place, I suppose.'

'What's this pal's name?'

Charles shrugged. 'Donna something or other. They go to a yoga class two nights a week. Other nights they go out on the town together. When that happens and Carole has a few too many she'll crash out there.'

'Often?'

He shrugged his shoulders. 'Fairly often, but it doesn't bother me. Carole and I have our silver wedding coming up soon. We've got no secrets.'

Skinner turned a laugh into a snort at the words. Charles looked up at him sharply. 'What's all this about anyway?' he snapped.

'Why isn't your car in the garage?' Martin went on.

'Carole will have taken it. She preferred it to the new Jag I bought her. Less hairy around town, she said.'

'Are you certain of that? Were you here when she left?'

Charles shook his head. 'No. I was at Ibrox last night, as the guest of one of the finance companies that I use to provide hire purchase for customers. I was picked up from here at five, and I wasn't dropped off again until around one. Listen . . .'

Martin cut him off. 'Was your wife doing anything else last night, other than seeing her pal?'

23

He nodded, quickly. 'Yes, but why . . . ?' He frowned.

'We'll get to that,' said Skinner. 'Answer, please.'

'Okay,' said Charles, testily. 'She was going to the showroom yesterday evening. Carole's been a working director of our car business from the earliest days. She's familiar with every aspect of it. We have a book-keeper there, but Carole's the finance director of the company, and she goes over the management accounts, regularly and often at short notice. She told me that she would be going there at seven, after the salesmen had finished, and that she'd be meeting Donna after she had finished her check.'

'Would she have driven on to meet Donna?'

'Possibly, but she could have called a taxi; I don't like our cars being parked in town overnight.'

'We can check that,' said Martin quickly. Too quickly. For the first time genuine alarm showed in Charles' face.

'Come on,' he said, insistently. 'What the hell is this about?

Skinner sat down in an armchair opposite him. Old, but often-remembered horrors come back to him, and for the first time in his life he felt sympathy for the man who had been his target for so long.

'Jackie,' he said, gently, 'someone torched your showroom tonight. They totalled the place. When the firemen had it controlled, and went in to clear up, they found a body.

'From what you've said, it could be Carole.'

Charles' jaw dropped open. His eyes widened. The colour left his face. His mouth worked trying to form words, but nothing came out.

24

'Jackie, we need to trace this Donna woman. Where does she live?'

The man shook his head. He turned his head away, so that neither policeman could see his eyes. 'I don't know,' he said quietly.

'What's her second name?'

'I don't even know that.'

Skinner paused. 'Well, where's Carole's yoga class?'

'Marco's, in Grove Street. Two nights a week.'

'Okay, we'll start there. But first, I want you to look at this.'

Standing up, he reached into the pocket of his jacket and produced the wedding ring found by the body. He stepped towards Charles and held it out for him to see. 'Could this have been Carole's?'

The man turned back towards him to look at the buckled band. After a few seconds he held up his left hand towards Skinner and Martin. The two policemen looked and saw that he wore a wedding ring, a close match, for all its distortion by the fire, in width and shade of the one which lay on Skinner's palm.

'We bought our rings together,' he whispered at last. 'I have fairly slim fingers, so they were interchange-able.'

Skinner closed his fist on the gold band and touched the man on the shoulder. 'Sorry, Jackie,' he said quietly.

'Appreciated.' The reply was almost lost in a cough, as Charles struggled to regain self-control.

Andy Martin hesitated for a moment, before speaking, formally once again. 'Mr Charles, can you give us the name of your wife's dentist.'

The man stared up at him for a few seconds, with an

25

expression of growing horror as he realised the purpose of the question, and as his imagination went to work.

'His name,' Martin asked again

Finally, Charles nodded. 'John Lockie.'

'Where does he practise?'

'Eh? Oh, in Inverleith Row.'

'Have you been his patients for long?'

Charles shook his head, and shrugged his shoulders, as if he was trying to focus. 'Carole and I have been his patients for twenty years,' he said, at last.

'Thank you. We'll contact him as soon as his surgery opens this morning.'

The man pushed himself to his feet. 'Is there anything I can do?'

Martin shook his head. 'I'm sorry, there isn't; you just have to leave us to our work. We'll do our best to trace this woman Donna, but at the same time, if the body is that of your wife, we'll work to confirm it as quickly as possible.'

'You're alone here, Jackie, yes?' asked Skinner.

'Yes.'

'Do you have any live-in help?'

'No. We don't go in for them.'

'*In case they see or hear too much,*' the hard-nosed policeman in Martin almost muttered, but he recognised that Skinner had declared a truce in the battle to nail his number one criminal enemy. Instead, he said as sincerely as he could, 'Would you like us to send someone to be with you?'

From the midst of his grief, the real Jackie Charles shot him a piercing, proud look. 'You must be fucking joking!' he said.

Bob Skinner, in spite of himself, smiled. 'Okay,' he said, 'but remember, until you hear from us again, do nothing.' He looked the man hard in the eye, and as he did he saw that the shock was fading, to be replaced by a burning anger. 'You understand me,' he repeated, with emphasis, 'nothing at all.

'We'll be back to see you as soon as we can, with good news or bad. And when we come back, we'll want to have a much longer talk.'

3

Bob Skinner and Andy Martin sat in an all-night greasy spoon café just off Leith Walk, beloved of coppers, Chinese waiters and other night people.

Coffee steamed in great white mugs before them, and four freshly-baked rolls, crammed with fried egg and grilled bacon, lay on a plate in the centre of their table.

Skinner looked around at his unpretentious surroundings. 'D'you remember, Andy, the last time we were here? You were a Sergeant and I was in your job. I was a simple widower with no greater burden than a teenage daughter, and you were a bachelor boy, footloose and fancy free.

'Now I'm a hudden-doon married man, and you're engaged to said burden.'

Martin smiled. 'Come on, Bob, you never thought of Alex in anything like those terms.'

The big man across the table shook his head. 'No, of course I didn't. Watching her grow into a woman has been the great continuous joy of my life so far.' And then, his face darkened. 'I just wish that Myra had been around to share it with me.'

'Sure you do,' said his friend, softly, 'but she wasn't. She died, man, eighteen years ago.'

Skinner nodded. 'That's right, she died. And through all those years, no-one, not even you, not even Alex, ever realised how much I missed her.'

He looked up, his eyes piercing. 'You want to know the truth? I still miss Myra, just as much as I ever did. Here I am, I'm married to Sarah, something that I never really imagined in all those lonely years. We have the son I always wanted, wee James Andrew Skinner, and he's a cracker too. My daughter's graduated and engaged to be married, and my best pal's sorted himself out in the process.

'I've got all that going for me, and guess what?' He tapped his chest. 'In here, a great part of me is still torn up with grief and longing for Myra, who's been gone since Alex was four years old.'

Suddenly he reached across the table, grasped Andy Martin's hand, and squeezed it, hard, momentarily. 'Yes, Andy; as you said, Myra died. just like – let's not kid ourselves – Carole Charles did tonight. Villain or not, my friend, I feel for wee Jackie. I've worn the shoes he's in this morning.

'Eighteen years ago someone tried to kill me, and Myra died instead. Tonight, as I see it, someone tried to kill him, and Carole got in the way.

'You're going to find out who killed Carole, and put him away for life. And I'm going to find out, finally, who sabotaged my car and killed Myra. They might have been poles apart as women, with vastly different moral values, but they both deserve the same justice, Andy. Everyone does.'

The younger man nodded, but there was a look of doubt in his eyes. 'I agree with you one hundred per cent about Carole Charles, but . . .'

29

'But what?'

'Well there's Sarah to consider, isn't there. I was there, remember, the night you got home from hospital four months ago. I remember how she reacted when you said to her what you've just said to me. I remember the argument and the atmosphere between you. All of a sudden you became a couple I didn't know.'

Bob looked across the table, chewing on a mouthful of egg and bacon roll. 'You saying you agree with Sarah?' he mumbled.

'Come on, man. You two are going to be my in-laws. Ask me to referee if you like, but don't ask me to take sides between you. What I'm saying is that I can understand what Sarah feels, especially after what you said a minute or two ago.'

Andy looked over his shoulder to ensure that there were no eavesdroppers, but the café's only other occupant was seated on the other side of the room, deep in an early edition *Scotsman*. He leaned forward and said, almost in a whisper, 'Look, you had a terrible experience last year. You were stabbed, and Sarah sat by your bedside for a couple of days not knowing whether you would live or die.

'Then you had to have hypnotherapy, and all sorts of deeply buried experiences were turned up, including the one from the scene of Myra's death. Now, on the basis of that recovered memory, you've decided that she was murdered, and you've announced that you're on a mission to find her killer.

'On top of that, you've just told me that you miss Myra as much as ever. You think Sarah won't have picked that up? Or have you told her too, straight out?'

'Don't be daft! What d'you take me for?'

'For a confused man, and maybe for an obsessive.'

'What do you suggest I do about it?'

'I suggest that you try to think objectively. Okay, a long time ago you suffered traumatic amnesia. Now you believe that under hypnosis you experienced a complete recollection of the scene of your wife's death. Maybe, just maybe, you were wrong about the details at least. Why not focus on that possibility, and get your life back in perspective?'

Bob shook his head. 'It's not a possibility, Andy. I'm not wrong. You want to try regressive hypnotherapy, mate. It's a virtual reality helmet, only it isn't playing a movie or a game. It's replaying your life.

'Remember, son, I was at the scene of the accident where Myra died. That was one of the things that Kevin O'Malley showed me in his treatment. I arrived not long after the Mini Cooper S – the car I would have been driving, not her, on any other day – hit the tree. I knelt beside the car and I looked inside.

'I looked at every detail of that car. Myra's handbag with her Chanel bottle broken. The bag of chocolate raisins that I had left on the shelf, strewn all over the place. The Cooper's front end smashed in, and most of the car's works in the passenger compartment.' He paused and looked Martin straight in the eye.

'And the hydraulic brake fluid pipe, cut about halfway through. Not broken, not snapped, but cut so that the fluid would leak out, until all of a sudden, with no warning, the car would have no brakes. I looked at all that, and being a bloody good Detective Sergeant, I made a mental note of every detail.

'Then, when there was nothing else in the car that I hadn't inspected and logged in my mind, nothing else to distract me and when I couldn't avoid it any longer, I looked at my wife and I saw her, covered in blood and glass, with her chest smashed in by the steering column, and her face wrecked by the wheel.

'I looked at that scene, I went into shock, and the trauma closed my mental notebook, closed it tight until Kevin O'Malley reopened it for me four months ago.'

He looked across again at his friend, and Martin saw a plea for understanding in his eyes. 'There's no mistake, Andy. I don't think it's even possible to dream things up under that sort of treatment.

'The trouble is that Kevin told me that once the memories were opened up I'd be able to live with them.' He smiled sadly and shook his head. 'He was wrong about that one, though. I've carried every detail of that scene at the front of my mind ever since, and it won't go away.'

His voice grew even quieter, and became hoarse. 'But there's something worse. I can remember too, the way Myra was when I kissed her goodbye that morning. How beautiful she was, how much I loved her, and how horny I got every time I took her in my arms. It wasn't just Alex or you who didn't know how much I missed her. Neither did I.'

His gaze dropped to the table. 'Sarah and I don't have sex any more, Andy. Two months ago we had a huge fight. In the course of it, she told me that when we were in bed, I was making love to someone else, and just fucking her as part of the process. Know what? She was right, and we haven't touched each other since.'

Martin shifted in his seat, embarrassed by the rev-
elation. 'Bob,' he said hesitantly, 'have you thought
about going back to Kevin O'Malley for more treatment?'

Skinner gave a short, harsh laugh. 'The only time
anyone'll get to look inside my head again will be at a
post mortem. There's only one course of treatment that'll
do me any good, and that is to track down the evil bastard
who cut that brake pipe.

'I've been itching to start my mission, as you call it,
since the day I got out of hospital. I'd have begun a month
ago, but when I was signed off the sick list, I found out
that the Chief, silly old bugger, had booked me on a
month-long crime symposium trip to Cali-fucking-fornia
without consulting me.' He shook his head. 'Imagine,
sentencing me to thirty days in LA without the option.
We had words, I'll tell you. First time ever, but we had
words, did Sir James and I.'

He paused. 'Now. Am I going to have words with
you too?'

Martin frowned. 'I hope not. But think for a moment,
will you, about what it is that you're asking me, your
Head of CID, to support. We've got ten major crimes
on our hands, not counting the new imperative we've
been landed with this morning, and you're asking me
to commit resources to an investigation opened eighteen
years late, on the basis of no evidence other than a single,
uncorroborated recovered memory which, as your lawyer
daughter told you, the greenest advocate could demolish
if it was given in evidence.

'What do you imagine the bean-counter back at HQ
would make of that? Do you see the councillors on the

Police Board agreeing that it would be a proper use of resources?'

'It's got fuck all to do with the councillors,' Skinner growled. 'And the day the bean-counter gets in my way, I'll shove his beans up his arse, while they're still in the tin!' Then he paused, and nodded an acknowledgement.

'Still,' he said, reluctantly, 'I take your points, every one of them. I wouldn't dream of asking you for man-power or other resources. This investigation will be conducted by my office alone, and my first priority will be to prove that my memory is accurate.'

Martin looked relieved. 'Thanks for that, at least,' he said, then his expression changed as a sudden thought struck him.

'Here, speaking of your office, you've got a decision to make, haven't you?'

Skinner nodded. 'Aye, that's right. With Maggie Rose promoted DCI, I've got to find myself a new personal assistant.'

'You created your own problem. It was you who promoted her.'

'Aye, I know. But losing Alison Higgins the way we did forced me to make some changes that I'd have preferred to leave for a year or two.' He smiled.

'I've got someone in mind though.' Martin's forehead furrowed into a frown of curiosity, in which Skinner detected a hint of apprehension. 'Don't worry,' he added. 'it isn't one of your people . . . although I'd like to give young Sammy a run in the job one day.

'I'll do something about it today.'

He drained the last of his coffee. 'I'll be available to you as well, whenever we need to go back to see Jackie

Charles. In all the circumstances you'll want to lead this
investigation personally, but having seen him together
once we should both be in at the follow-up. Bring
McIlhenney along if you like, though, with continuity
in mind.'

He glanced at his watch. 'We should have something
from Mr Lockie in a couple of hours. Meantime, you can
drop me off at home, then have yourself a shower and
a shave.'

'And sleep,' said Martin mournfully. 'What about
sleep?'

Skinner smiled and looked out of the window of the
greasy spoon, into the black, wet, late winter's morning.
'You're forgetting,' he drawled. 'I've been in bloody LA
for a month and this is only my second day back. As far
as my body's concerned it's still a beautiful evening.'

4

'If the fire was that strong, then for once I don't blame Banks for reserving his opinion.'

Sarah Grace Skinner was not the greatest fan of her professional colleague, but she nodded in grudging approval as Bob described the scene of the blaze and the discovery of the body.

'Once the pathologist has a look inside, though, he'll be able to tell the gender right away. Add to that the fact that Mrs Charles has been with the same dentist for twenty years, then if it's her you should know as soon as he sees her records.'

Bob nodded. 'I expect so. On top of that there are the wedding rings. Jackie gave us his. Our lab people will look at the hallmarks under a microscope. If they match, that'll back up the identification.'

He gave a small involuntary shiver. 'What a subject to be discussing when I'm holding my only son, for almost the first time in a month.'

He thrust James Andrew Skinner, known by one and all as Jazz, high above his head. The child squealed with delight. 'Boy,' said his father, 'but you've grown since I've been away.' He looked sideways at his wife. 'That's what annoyed me most of all about Jimmy booking me for that American trip; the fact that I would miss a whole month of this fella's first year.'

'He missed you too,' said Sarah with a smile, looking in her full-length bedroom mirror and adjusting her grey business skirt. 'I had nothing but "Da-da-da" out of him every time the phone rang. I think he's held back his first steps so that you would see them.'

'He's ready to walk, you think?' he said, surprised. 'I mean, he's not a year old yet. Alex didn't stir off her arse till she was about sixteen months.'

'Asse,' Jazz shouted, gleefully, relishing the sibilance of the sound.

'Bob! I've told you to watch what you say around him. He's like a parrot!'

'Sorry, sorry, sorry. Bottom, Jazz, okay? Bottom, bottom, bottom!'

'Bmm! Bmm! Bum!' the child mimicked, his strong voice rising in a triumphant crescendo.

'Oh no! Look pal, let's just concentrate on the toddling bit, okay?' Bob lowered the baby on to his feet beside the bedroom chair, watching him as he took a grip of its arm with his chubby little fingers, then releasing him to stand upright, with only the chair's support.

'I see what you mean,' he said. 'Any day now.'

He stood up and turned his wife to face him, his hands on her shoulders. 'And how's his mother getting on? I haven't had a chance to ask you since I got back. Still enjoying the University job?'

She looked up at him seriously. 'There was a time, not so long ago, when you wouldn't have had to ask me that question. You'd just have known. We used to be closer than Siamese twins, Bob. What's happened to us?'

He dropped his hands from her shoulders and his face screwed up in exasperation. 'Jesus Christ,' he said softly, 'I've been accused of a few things in my time, but being knocked for not being telepathic any more, that's a first.

'I've been away for a month, remember. In your homeland.' His voice rose, and Jazz frowned up at him, with a child's keen awareness of changes in tone or expression.

Sarah nodded. 'Yes, I realise that, but before you went away . . .'

'Before I went away, during the day you went to give your lectures, and I went to the gym, building myself back into something like I was before I was knifed, so I could go back to work as if nothing had ever happened to me. But at night you never talked about your work. Christ, you never talked about anything.'

She shot him a hot look. 'No, because I knew there was only one thing you really wanted to talk about: my predecessor, Myra, and your newly-discovered obsession with her death, or rather, with your guilt.'

She saw his jawline tense. 'What do you mean, my—'

'Don't . . .' She held up a hand to stop him '. . . let's get into this now. Or ever again, even!

'Okay. You ask me about my job. Fine, I'll tell you. I hate it. I don't know why I ever took it on. Ego probably, the idea of having a chair, and being a Professor at my age. The reality is that it chills me to the bone. All those young faces, either thirsting for knowledge, or more likely putting in their specialist lecture time and waiting for the boring cow to finish. I stand up there every day and I feel unreal. I'm a doctor, and a damn good one, yet I've allowed myself to be turned into a dictating machine.'

'What do you mean "turned into"?' he snapped.

'Don't mess with me. I know what happened. The Principal asked Jimmy Proud if he could suggest anyone for the course, and you and he put your heads together and came up with me, because you thought it would give me more holiday time to look after the baby.

'You manipulated me, Bob.'

He looked at her with pure scorn. 'Rubbish! Jimmy came to me and asked if I approved of his putting your name forward, and we *both* came to you and asked you. And you said "Yes". That's how it was.'

She shook her head. 'I did that because the way you looked at me made it quite clear that was what you *wanted* me to say. Not because it was what I wanted to do.

'Still,' she acknowledged, 'I said "Yes". As a consequence, during all that time you were recovering, I'd come home every night quivering with frustration. But you never even noticed, because your mind was on something – no, someone – else.'

They were both dimly aware of the staccato, staggering movement at their feet, yet they were staring at each other so fiercely that neither reacted to it, until each felt strong little fingers grip their clothing at the knee.

Only then did they look down, to see Jazz, beaming up at them in his delight at his first steps, which they, in their anger, had missed.

5

The mountain was still there, waiting to be conquered: the pile of essential papers, reports, proposals, personnel files, correspondence and other assorted documentation, piled high in the in-tray on his big rosewood desk, waiting for his scrutiny and his note of approval or rejection.

On the previous morning, his first full day back at the police headquarters building in Fettes Avenue since his stabbing four months earlier, and since the unwanted American trip for which Chief Constable Sir James Proud, his well-meaning commander and friend, had volunteered him, Skinner had wilfully ignored the heap. Instead he had chosen to pay a surprise visit to Superintendent Dave Donaldson, and his deputy Chief Inspector Maggie Rose, to congratulate each on their promotions.

During the DCC's absence, but on the basis of his advice to Andy Martin, the two had taken over command of CID in the force's Eastern Area, a great sprawling land-mass taking in a part of the city of Edinburgh, and all of rural East Lothian and Berwickshire.

He had filled in the day being taken by Rose, his personal assistant until her step up in rank, on a tour of the many CID offices for which Donaldson and she were responsible. In one, at Haddington, he had seen a face from the past, and had made a private note.

There was a gentle knock on the frame of the open door behind him. 'Good morning, sir.' He turned with a smile. Ruth McConnell, his secretary, stood there, with the morning's additions to the paper pile clutched in a folder in her hand. She was devastatingly attractive, with a slight pout to her lips which seemed to add value to an almost permanent smile. Her glossy brown hair hung past her shoulders, and her legs did the job for which they had been designed as well as any Skinner had ever seen. Ruth was one of those women who would never put on a long skirt if there was a shorter one, fresh and pressed, in her wardrobe.

'Welcome back,' she said. 'You are going to stay here today? The Chief's back from his ACPO meetings, and he was hoping to see you.'

'He could have been seeing me for the last bloody month,' Skinner grumbled, but with a half-smile.

He moved behind his desk and pointed towards the coffee filter on a table by the far wall. 'If that stuff's hot, pour us a couple of mugs and pull up a seat.'

Ruth nodded. A minute later she was seated before him, rearranging the mountain of work into a series of categorised hills.

'This *is* all essential stuff, Ruthie?'

'Yes sir, I'm afraid so. I filtered out as much as I felt able, the Chief took on a hell of a lot, and Mr Martin helped where he could, but all of this is stuff we all thought you'd want to see.'

'Fair enough. I wish I'd been able to keep Maggie here till I got back, but that would probably have cost her

her promotion. I couldn't have left Donaldson without a deputy for that long. And of course, I couldn't break in a new PA in my absence.'

He paused, reached into the breast pocket of his jacket, and produced a slip of paper, which he handed across the desk. 'Now I'm back, the gap will be filled without further delay. I want you to pull that officer's file for me right away, and to arrange an appointment in this office, for four this afternoon.' He paused.

'Now, let me spend half an hour on this lot, and then I'll go and see the boss. I expect I'll have to go out with Andy Martin later on this morning, but other than that you can tie me to the desk for the rest of the day.'

She raised her right eyebrow, only for an instant, and very slightly, but it was enough. 'Get away with you, woman,' he shouted, with a grin, 'and let me be about my work!'

As his secretary swept rhythmically out of the room, closing the door behind her, Skinner leaned back in his leather chair and looked around him. As much as he hated paperwork, he enjoyed the room in which he did it. It looked out on to the main driveway up to the headquarters building. He had always liked to be able to see what was happening in the world around him, and to feel a part of the comings and goings of the day. As he looked down at the Chief Officers' parking area below him, he saw the Chief Constable's black Vauxhall Omega roll into the space beside his own white BMW. Sir James Proud climbed out laboriously, in uniform as always, his silver braid, and silver hair gleaming against the dull March morning.

Having not seen Proud Jimmy for over a month, it

struck Skinner suddenly that his commander, friend and patron was looking older and more tired than he had ever seen him. 'He was without a deputy for a bloody long time,' he mused in a whisper to the empty room. 'Must have been quite a strain.

'Even dafter then, that he should extend it for an extra month by sending me to something that Willie Haggerty in Strathclyde was bursting to attend.' He thought back and remembered Sir James' uncharacteristic insistence that his force should put one over on the much larger West of Scotland constabulary.

Thrusting the thought from his mind, he took a last look around his office before settling down to work. It was comfortably furnished, and well decorated, in slightly old-fashioned hessian. The paintings on the walls, all originals, were his own. His favourites faced his desk. One was a big, blue, arrogant cockerel, painted in oil by Rhoda Hird, an East Lothian painter who lived close by his cottage in Gullane. The other was a colourful, slightly bewildered torero with a lazy right eye, and the expression of someone who carries the certainty that one day, something very bad is going to happen. It was the work of Miguel Morales, a Catalan artist with a burgeoning reputation. Skinner had bought it on a whim, and on a credit card, one night in a bar-cum-gallery in Spain.

He smiled again, nodded 'Good morning' to his two old friends and settled down to work.

He was almost through his allotted half-hour when Ruth buzzed him through. 'It's Sir James. If you're clear, can he come in?'

'Sure,' said Skinner. 'I'm a captive here.'

He had hardly spoken before the door, rosewood to match his desk, swung open. He stood up in automatic deference to a senior officer, and to greet a friend. 'Bob,' said Proud Jimmy, 'you don't know how good it is to see you back behind that desk.'

Such was the sincerity in his voice that Skinner spluttered in his surprise. 'Christ, man, that you can say that! After you sentenced me to a month on the most useless jolly I'd ever seen!'

'Och, Bob,' said the Chief, suddenly mournful, 'you're not still angry about that?'

'I never was angry, Jimmy, just astonished. It was a waste of time, and we both know it. Not blowing my own trumpet, but if I had to go there it should have been to teach, not to sit on my arse and be lectured at for a month. The FBI are sincere guys, but they've got no real coppers left. Joe Doherty was the last of the breed, and now he's out of it.'

He shook his head. 'But look, that's history, let's not discuss it any more. We've got more than that to worry us.'

'I agree, Bob,' said Sir James. 'But my decision was wrong, and in hindsight I have to admit that much to you. It's just that we thought . . .'

Skinner's eyes narrowed and his brow furrowed. 'What do you mean "We"?' he demanded. 'Was Andy Martin in on it, or Jim Elder?'

Alarm showed clearly in the Chief Constable's eyes, but the moment was broken by a diplomatic cough from the doorway. 'I'm sorry, Mr Skinner,' said Ruth McConnell, 'but Chief Superintendent Martin asks if you could join him right away. He said that it's time to pay your second call on Jackie Charles. We have a positive identification of his wife as the body in the showroom.'

'Okay,' said Skinner. 'I'm on my way.' He moved out from behind his desk. The Chief Constable stepped aside, almost eagerly, to make way for him, with a sigh which sounded to his deputy like one of relief.

6

Martin Charles was with his son when the two police-men arrived. Skinner had asked Ruth to telephone the Ravelston villa to warn of their arrival, and the old man had opened the front door before they had even made it far enough up the brick driveway to trigger the security light.

He led them not into the main reception room, but to a smaller apartment to the left off the hall. It was small, and furnished only with two expensive leather recliner chairs, a cocktail cabinet, a nest of occasional tables and a huge television set with cinema-style speakers set around it.

As they entered, Jackie Charles was seated with his back to the door, watching a repeat showing on a satellite channel of the previous evening's football match at Ibrox, the one which he had been watching in person as his showroom had exploded into flames. Martin had already confirmed with his hosts that Charles had been in their party, and that he had been collected from and delivered to his home by a hired limousine.

Mr Charles tapped his son on the shoulder. 'John. The police are here.'

Charles used a remote control to snap off the television picture, in the same movement which brought him to his feet. He was freshly shaved, and neatly dressed in pale grey slacks, a blazer with gold-crested buttons, a white shirt, and a silk tie that was almost luminous in its blueness.

'That's it, is it?' he said in a calm, measured tone. 'You've identified her.' Not a question: a statement.

Skinner nodded. 'I'm afraid so, Jackie.' Beside him, the old man buried his face in his hands. 'We didn't really expect anything else, did we?'

The man's square shoulders slumped for the merest instant, then straightened once again. 'No,' he said. 'When she didn't show up at home by nine I knew for sure. When she did stay at her pal's, Carole was always back by then, bright-eyed and bushy-tailed, without a hint that she'd been rat-arsed just a few hours before. Yes, she had great recuperative powers, did my wife.' He smiled, grimly.

'This morning I sat through in the kitchen, waiting for her. I made coffee for two. I got the cereal bowls out and fetched the milk off the step. I put the eggs on to boil at twenty to nine, and defrosted some rolls from the freezer. I sat there hanging on to whatever doubts I had left, counting down the minutes, and finally the seconds to nine o'clock.'

Jackie Charles patted his father on the shoulder. 'As soon as nine struck, I knew that there was no possibility that it could have been anyone else in the showroom last night. I phoned my father and told him what had happened.'

He looked up at the two policemen. 'Would you like some coffee? Don't worry, it hasn't been stewing since half past eight. I made some fresh stuff.'

Skinner and Martin nodded.

'Okay, let's go through to the kitchen.' Martin Charles made to lead the way. 'No, Dad,' said his son. 'I need to talk to the officers alone. Once I've done that, I'll have to pay a call on Carole's mother. You can come with me then.'

Skinner and Martin followed Charles out of the television room, across the hallway and into a spacious Smallbone-fitted kitchen, with a lime-washed table and four chairs in an alcove at the far end. The policemen sat down, side by side, as the bereaved husband poured coffee into white Wedgwood cups.

Skinner looked around. 'Real Edinburgh upper-class,' he whispered to Martin with irony in his tone. 'You'd never guess he's a bloody gangster.'

The man laid cups before them, and took a seat opposite. He was pale, and grim-faced, but undoubtedly he was in control of himself – the cold, hard Jackie Charles they both knew. Clearly he had come quickly to terms with his loss.

'Right, gentlemen,' he said, briskly. 'What do you want to ask me?'

'There's something we have to tell you first of all,' said Martin, quietly, 'though maybe, just maybe, you've worked it out for yourself given the circles in which we all know you move. We believe that your wife's death may have been more than a tragic accident in consequence of a wilful fire-raising.

'We believe that the fire may have been, in fact, an attempt to kill you.'

Jackie Charles looked at the policeman, his face dark with sudden rage. The smooth, civilised shell within which he normally lived had vanished in an instant. 'What makes you say that?' The sound was a hiss.

'The door to the office, where your wife died, was locked. From the outside. Your car, with its very distinctive and very well-known registration number was parked right at the entrance to the showroom. Someone walked into the premises, set the fire, quietly, though maybe not so quietly since the radio in the office was on quite loud, but very efficiently. Then he turned the key in the office door and lit the fuses, leaving you, as he thought, to burn to a crisp among your rare and exotic motors.'

Charles' lips were drawn back, his mouth set as if in a snarl.

'Tell us,' asked Martin, 'how was the office constructed? Did it have solid walls? It was a shell when we got there.'

The man shook his head. 'The door was solid wood, but the upper half of the walls were glazed, to let in light during the day.'

'Clear glass or opaque?'

'You couldn't see through it, not to recognise someone.'

'But you could make out a figure inside?'

Charles nodded. 'Yes, and obviously in the evening the office light would be on.'

'But the showroom lights would be switched off?'

'That's right.' The man's face was impassive, set in a cold, hard stare.

'You're not surprised, Jackie, are you,' said Skinner. 'For twenty years you've been telling us you're a respectable business figure, and most of Edinburgh has believed you. Yet when we tell you that someone has tried to murder you but killed your wife by mistake, you accept it as fact, without the slightest twitch of an eyebrow.'

Charles glared at him, playing unconsciously with his wedding ring, but said nothing.

'You might think that we wouldn't care,' he went on. 'That we'd have a "Live by the sword, let them die by it" sort of attitude. Well, we don't. Never have. This is our city and we'll have no fucking swordsmen running around in it.

'We might think that you're an evil, pernicious, murderous little shite, and that your late wife was probably your partner in crime as well as life, yet still we're going to investigate her death as vigorously as if it was the Lady Provost who had died in that fire, and you were sitting opposite us wearing your gold chain of office.

'So with that in mind, we have a number of questions to put to you. The rest of this conversation is formal, and will be taped.' He produced a small recorder from his pocket, switched it on and laid it on the table.

'First of all,' said Martin, 'tell us something about the car business. What were the showroom hours?'

With a visible effort, Charles seemed to master his anger. 'Variable describes it best,' he said. 'But midweek, we're always closed by seven, at this time of year at least. The mechanics work nine to five though, with occasional overtime on Saturday mornings.'

'How many salesmen do you have?'

'Two fulltime. Mike Whitehead and Geoff Bailey. They've both been with us for a while; Mike seven years, Geoff five. They're good guys.'

'You get on well with them both?'

'Of course I do, or they wouldn't be there. They

specialise in selling quality cars. Any clown can sell a used Fiesta to someone who can only afford a used Fiesta, but discerning people, people with cash, need to be given confidence in their buy, and to be persuaded that they're investing in a good set of wheels.'

'You don't owe either of them commission money, or anything like that?'

Charles shook his head vigorously. 'No, they're paid as soon as the customers' cheques clear and the HP money comes in. No, you can forget Mike and Geoff; they are trusted friends.'

'What about your book-keeper?'

'The girl we have now, Amy Innes, is fine. Carole chose her. We had difficulty a couple of years back, though, with her predecessor, Carl Medina.'

'What sort of difficulties?'

'Not to put too fine a point on it, he was at it.

'There were sundry purchases unaccounted for. Carole reckoned that he was topping up his salary. I couldn't be bothered setting traps for him or anything like that, so I just sacked him.'

Skinner looked sharply across the table. 'How'd he take it?'

'Badly, at first. He threatened me with an industrial tribunal.'

'What did you threaten him with, Jackie?'

Charles looked at him coldly, with a flicker of a smile. 'I never threaten people, Bob.'

'No,' said Martin, 'but you know a man who does. So I guess Medina didn't go to tribunal.'

'No. He could see what the outcome would have been.'

'I'll bet! Have you seen or heard from him since?'

Charles shook his head. 'Not directly. But I had a letter a couple of months ago from another dealer, the Renault chap in Gorgie, asking for a reference.'

'What did you do?'

'I declined to provide it, of course.'

'Of course,' said Martin, dryly. 'Did you have any other employment problems at the showroom? With mechanics, for example?'

'None at all. All our people are paid above the union rate, they all have overtime opportunities and they've all been with us long-term.'

'Customers? Any disgruntled punters come to mind?'

Charles looked offended. 'Mr Martin, I don't have any disgruntled clients. I deal in quality motor cars, and they tend to be reliable. I give good warranty terms, and I never quibble about putting any problems right.'

'I'll know where to come for my next Ferrari then,' said the Chief Superintendent, with a smile. It vanished as quickly as it had appeared.

'You said that you had two full-time salesmen. Who else is there?'

'There's me for a start.' His expression changed, betraying more than a touch of smugness. 'I can still out-sell anyone on the lot, as the Americans say, and I like to prove it. I go down to Seafield for a few hours on most days. Very occasionally, my father will spend some time on the forecourt, just to keep his hand in, as it were.

'But that's all. No-one else on the selling side.'

'When you go in to the showroom, is it at any set time of the day?'

'In the afternoon normally.'

'And you stay until . . . ?'

'Until we close. If I'm there, and I am on most days, then I'm the chap who locks up.'

'When would you leave, normally?'

'Once I've checked over the day's documentation, addressed and stamped the finance applications, locked away late cheques and new tax disks, seen that everything was in order in the workshop, and maybe made a couple of phone calls about interesting cars advertised for private sale; once I've done all that it's usually about nine o'clock.'

'So the murderer could have expected you to be on the premises at the time last night's fire was started.'

Charles nodded. 'If he knew anything about me, yes,' he said quietly.

Andy Martin leaned back from the table. 'Right, Mr Charles. So much for the dealership. Now let's talk about your other interests?'

'Which ones?'

'Let's start with loansharking, shall we? Could your heavies maybe have leaned on someone, or someone's family, just a wee bit too hard? Can you think of anyone on your books who's facing a doing, or worse, and might have decided to head it off?'

As Skinner and Martin looked across the table, they saw the professional mask with which they were so familiar descend across Jackie Charles' face. 'I don't know what you mean,' he said quietly, looking Martin, but not Skinner, in the eye.

'Okay,' said the Chief Superintendent. 'Let's have a go at the taxi business. You own, through front companies, forty-two per cent of the minicab licences in Edinburgh and around, and you extort protection money from the holders of the other fifty-eight per cent, or at least from those who don't want to wake up to find their vehicles with no tyres or windscreen.

'Have you had any threats arising from those activities?'

'Send a copy of that tape to my solicitor, please, Mr Martin, so that I can sue you.'

The Chief Superintendent ignored him. 'How about your betting shops? You own five. You must have a few big losers.'

Charles shook his head. 'I don't allow credit to those who can't afford it and my staff have orders to bar people if they think they might be losing too much.'

Martin laughed. 'Okay, Jackie. So far you're Simon Pure, without an enemy in the world. Only it seems bloody obvious that you *do* have an enemy. Could it be an associate from outside this city? Do you have information which might have made you dangerous to someone?'

'What associates, Chief Superintendent? What information?'

Suddenly Skinner leaned forward and picked up the tape recorder. He switched it off and put it back in his pocket. 'Okay,' he said. 'Enough of the ritual dancing. Let's get on with our job, Andy.'

He stood up, Martin rising with him, and looked down at Charles, fixing him with his gaze. 'This may be a waste of time, but I'll warn you anyway, Jackie. Don't get in our way here.

'If I'm given the slightest evidence that you know

who might have done this, and are keeping it back from us so that you can take your own revenge, then I'll charge you with withholding information. I might not get a conviction, but imagine what it would do to your social reputation around town.'

'I should fucking care!' Charles' face was set rock-hard as he spat out each word. He stood up. 'When can I plan my wife's funeral?' he asked coldly.

'When the Crown Office says that you can. I don't know yet when that might be; but in the meantime just don't be planning to bury anyone else!'

7

'D'you think he knows who did it, Boss?' asked Andy Martin as he turned off Comely Bank towards the head-quarters building.

Skinner, in the passenger seat, shrugged his shoulders. 'You can never be sure with Jackie, but I don't think so. I'll tell you one thing though: we'll have started him thinking.

'We'd better find that guy Medina before Jackie. Otherwise, guilty or innocent, he's liable to find himself being cremated by a blowlamp from the toes up!

'You're in charge of this investigation,' he said, 'but you'll need more than your own staff.'

'That's right,' said Martin, holding his pass out of the window for inspection by the officer on the main car park gate. 'The crime was committed on Dave Donaldson's patch, so he's up for it. I've called him and Maggie in to see me at midday.' He glanced at the Mondeo's digital clock. 'They should be here by now.'

'Mmm,' muttered Skinner, thoughtfully. 'That reminds me. Andy, when's the next Senior Command Course at the College?'

'Next September. Why?'

'Because I want Maggie on it. She's come up through

56

the ranks nearly as fast as you have ... it's been faster than I intended for both of you, but you can never foresee the way things will work out. She's got Command Corridor written all over her, and we should prepare her for it.'

'What about Donaldson? Won't he be huffed if we send her?'

Skinner shook his head slightly. 'He's got it in him too, but he's more openly ambitious. He'll see you lined up for the next ACC slot, when Jimmy finally hangs up his baton, or if Elder moves somewhere else ... which he won't, with only seven years left to retirement. He'll have figured out that, by that time, Maggie'll be ahead of him in the queue. We've got a woman High Court judge in Edinburgh now, and Maggie will be this force's first woman ACC.

'Believe me, in a couple of years, Dave'll be looking for chief officer rank with another force. He'll get it too. He's a good tactician, is Donaldson.'

Martin steered his car into his allotted space, near the building's basement rear entrance. 'I'll bear that in mind,' he said. 'Now I'd better talk tactics with him myself.'

'Aye, and I'd better run our Chief Constable to ground. There's something I have to sort out with him.'

But when Skinner returned to the Command Suite, he discovered that Proud Jimmy was locked in the safety of an Appropriations Committee meeting, a task which would have fallen to Skinner had he not been returned so recently to active duty.

'He should be clear around four thirty, sir,' said Gerry, the Chief's secretary. Like Ruth McConnell, whom Skinner shared with ACC Elder, he was a civilian.

The DCC thanked the young man and stepped across the corridor, looking in on Ruth to announce his return.

'I got this for you, as you asked,' she said, holding out an orange folder, the colour which denoted personnel files. She smiled what seemed her usual smile, but Skinner wondered for an instant whether, within it, he could see the faintest hint of disapproval.

He put the thought from his mind as he sat behind his desk and opened the file. He recalled the last occasion on which he had seen it, at a promotion board the year before, and remembered the very attractive, dark-haired woman with the huge, wide brown eyes.

He looked down at the file and saw those eyes smiling up at him, from the photograph clipped to the first page. He read sections of the report's summary aloud, in a murmured tone.

'Detective Sergeant Pamela, known as Polly, Masters, promoted and transferred to Haddington six months ago, after a short spell in the press office.

'Late entrant to the force four years ago, then aged thirty. Born in Motherwell,' Skinner grunted at the connection with his own home town, and that of his late first wife, 'educated at the local schools. Religion Protestant. Degree in marketing from Strathclyde. Worked in-house for an insurance company in Glasgow, and latterly for a consultancy in Edinburgh.

'Parents still alive, one older brother, one younger sister. When aged 24, married David Somerville, in Motherwell. Divorced four years later, and moved to Edinburgh.

'Exemplary service record. Passed Sergeant and Inspector examinations at first opportunity. Good reports from senior officers in every posting.'

Skinner laid the folder down at the side of his desk. He smiled as he remembered his question to WPC Masters at her promotion interview.

'What made you chuck a lucrative job, in which you were well qualified and experienced, and the Vauxhall Cavalier which undoubtedly went with it? What made you do that to put on one of these stiff, itchy uniforms and pound the streets in thick-soled flat shoes, carrying a damn great side-handled baton as your only protection against the real possibility that someone is going to come at you with a weapon?'

And her answer, in a clear, strong West of Scotland accent.

'I did it because I wanted a career where what I did made a difference for the better in the way people live, rather than one in which I used my skills to persuade them to buy products which were no different from any other on the market, and which were probably bad for them in the long run.'

He tapped the folder. 'Could be, Sergeant Masters, that you're the one.'

8

Two potential chief officers sat opposite a third, across Andy Martin's desk in the CID office suite.

Martin sat with his back to the window in the plain magnolia-painted room. Behind him Detective Superintendent Dave Donaldson and Detective Chief Inspector Maggie Rose could see the sharp, crenellated tower of Fettes College, many of its classroom windows lit, as the minds of its privileged students were illuminated through the dull day.

Donaldson, a year or two older than the Head of CID but still in his mid-thirties, was a tall slim man, with relaxed, friendly eyes, an easy smile, and a taste for suiting which had earned him the nickname 'Flash' among his junior officers. He gave off a powerful air of self-confidence which in many another job with less stringent promotion criteria would have been enough in itself to mark him out automatically as a high flyer; looking at him across the desk Martin had a sudden vision of his colleague selling Ferraris on Jackie Charles' forecourt.

However, the achievement of high rank in the police force is based on more than self-belief, and the Chief Superintendent's recommendation that he be promoted into the vacancy as Eastern Area CID commander had been based on an impressive service record which showed no hint of recklessness, and a clear-up rate on investigations under his charge which matched even Skinner's, and his own.

Maggie Rose was impressive in a different way from Donaldson. Her red hair was a good indicator of the core of her personality, but outwardly she was a calm, thoughtful woman. Her clothing tended to emphasise the quiet side of her nature, although Martin thought that it had become slightly more flamboyant since her marriage to Special Branch Inspector Mario McGuire.

One of the great strengths of Maggie Rose, the one which had drawn her first to DCC Skinner's attention, was the fact that she never offered a view that had not been considered carefully, with all the risks analysed and all the consequences measured.

That was why Skinner had taken her on to his personal staff, and it was why he had concurred with her appointment as Donaldson's deputy with a degree of reluctance.

And that may have been why Martin was looking at her, although he addressed his questions to them both.

'Given the breadth of Jackie Charles' known, or at least suspected activities,' he said, 'this investigation is going to be intricate, to say the very least. What would you two say our priorities should be? And do either of you see any short-cuts we might follow?'

'Well,' began Donaldson. 'I'd say . . .' He stopped in mid-sentence. 'Sorry, I shouldn't jump in all the time. Mags, you're the strategist on the team. What do you think?'

'*Good command skill,*' thought Martin, with a glance at the Superintendent. '*Assess your subordinates' strengths, recognise them publicly, and make use of them as much as you can.*'

Rose sat silent for a few seconds, looking at Donaldson as if searching for anything patronising in his tone, but finding nothing.

'Given what we've heard, sir,' she began, 'the first thing I'd say is that I agree with the Boss. We have to find this chap Carl Medina, on the basis of Charles' statement.

'But the second thing I'd say is that I wouldn't hold out too many hopes that he's our man.' She nodded towards Skinner's tape recorder which lay on the desk, which Martin had just replayed. 'His was the only name that Charles actually volunteered during that interview. It occurs to me that if he thought for one second that Medina was his wife's murderer, he'd have kept it to himself, and done something about it himself.'

She paused. 'We all know that Jackie Charles is a criminal. Yet he's never been caught, and is only associated with crime through whispers from touts that we've never been able to corroborate or present in evidence. People like Jackie Charles, if they were straight, would make great personnel directors. They know people, inside and out. They have the same skill as the most senior police officers in recognising strengths and weaknesses, and they take precautions to ensure that those strengths or weaknesses never become threats.

'There was a gangleader arrested in France a couple of years back. They reckoned that he had ordered at least fifty murders of associates simply as a precaution.'

She paused and looked at Donaldson. 'Go on,' said the Superintendent, fascinated.

'I've studied Charles. He is a very shrewd, ruthless man. He told us that Medina was suspected of stealing from him, and that the only thing he did about it was to sack him. That alone tells me that he regarded Medina as a nonentity. I don't believe the story about the industrial tribunal; not for one second. Jackie simply threw that in for effect.

'He thought that Medina was just a pipsqueak, stupid enough to try to steal a few quid from him. If he had thought that he was the sort who would set fire to even a single car out of revenge, then Medina wouldn't have been sacked, he'd have fallen off a high building, or would have been a hit-and-run victim.

'Jackie threw us that name as a bone, to set us on a false trail, while he starts his own investigation. We can warn all we like, but we won't put him off pursuing his wife's killer.'

'Unless he did it himself?' mused Donaldson, aloud.

'Yes,' said Rose, 'we have to keep our minds open to that possibility. We've had no information that Charles has ever personally harmed anyone, but he has caused it. His closest associate, other than Carole, is, as we know, one Douglas Terry, the same man who was a suspect in the Indico payroll robbery. He went to work for Charles a couple of years afterwards and they've been as thick as thieves . . . now there's a simile for you . . . ever since.

'Terry's official job is general manager of the betting shops and taxi businesses. But we know that he is the middleman into the loansharking and that, in every respect, he's Jackie Charles' fixer. His name and Jackie's are linked inextricably.

'Okay, we know that Charles was at Ibrox. But if he had wanted Carole dead for any reason he'd have told Terry, and Dougie would have seen that it was taken care of, specifically while Jackie was in a very public place.'

She looked across at Martin. 'What do you think, sir? You saw Charles.'

The Chief Superintendent shook his head, slowly. 'We can't discount the possibility, but I don't believe it. Neither does the Boss. When we gave him the news that Carole was probably dead in the fire, he was genuinely stunned, and he wasn't acting. The second time we saw him, he'd worked out what had happened, and guessed that he'd been the target. He was quietly incandescent.

'So, Maggie. Any thoughts on priorities?'

She nodded her red head. 'Yes. One, trace Carl Medina and bring him in for questioning.

'Two, go through the books of the car dealership for anything that might point us in the direction of someone with a grudge. Unlikely, I admit. I don't think that Jackie's legitimate business will give us any leads, but it has to be done.

'Three, interview all of Charles' known close associates, beginning with Douglas Terry, to see if we can pick up the slightest hint of anyone from whom Jackie might have been under threat.

'Four, start pulling in the loansharks, at random. Lean on them until they cough up names of their biggest debtors, just to make us leave them alone.

'Fifth, start pulling in his taxi drivers, off the street, to see what they might have heard. While we have them, check their driving licences, insurance situation, criminal background, everything else. If we find anything to show the person to be an unsuitable or illegal driver, we can go back to the court to have that particular licence removed.

'Sixth, start interviewing the other taxi owners. Look for special grudges against Charles, and look for any hint that some of them might have got together to put a stop to his extortion.

'Seventh, pull in every known gangleader in Edinburgh. Not just because we have an opportunity to make a nuisance of ourselves, but to see if any of them have heard anything from outside Edinburgh, about Charles being in trouble.

'Eighth, using Special Branch, explore the criminal intelligence network throughout the UK to see whether that throws up any leads.' She paused and looked at her colleagues, from one to the other.

'That should be enough to go on with.'

Andy Martin leaned forward across his desk. He smiled in admiration yet again of Rose's thoroughness. 'I agree with all of those, Maggie, and I see the theme that runs through them. This isn't just a murder investigation. It's an opportunity at the very least to interfere with Jackie Charles' illegal business interests, and at the maximum, to make it too risky or difficult for him to carry on with them.

'So let's pursue all of those lines of investigation. Use what manpower you need, but report to me at every stage. Neil McIlhenney and Sammy Pye, from my personal staff, are at your disposal too.

'The first thing to do is find Carl Medina. The second is to get into the books of Charles' legit businesses.'

He paused, and took a deep breath. 'But the third . . . and this is another priority . . . is try to find his other records. Jackie's criminal business is too extensive for it to have been conducted all in his head, or in Carole's, or in Douglas Terry's. Somewhere there have to be records, maybe bank books and evidence of cash deposits and movements.

'We've worked for years in the belief that if we could find the nerve centre of his other business we'd have Charles by the balls. Twice in recent years we've had tips that there were books kept in properties belonging to his companies.'

Martin frowned. 'In each case when we got our search warrant and got in there we found unfurnished apartments and empty safes. It was as if they had known we were coming. I want you to listen out for more whispers in the course of this investigation. We might be in luck next time.'

He paused. 'The big complication in this investigation is the husband of the victim. You're right, Mags. The DCC can warn all he likes. He could even take the guy into a small, dark room for half an hour. But it wouldn't make any difference.

'Jackie Charles will be after the man who killed his wife. He will run his own investigation alongside ours. If we can't stop him, we might as well make what use of him we can. So from this time on, keep an eye on him, and on Douglas Terry.

'You never know where the two of them might lead us.'

He stood up. 'I've asked our press office to call a media briefing for one o'clock.' He glanced at his watch. 'That's in five minutes.

'Royston's line has been melting all morning, but I told him to hold fire until the Boss and I had seen Charles and I was ready to make a statement in person.

'Let's go to meet the press, and start a few hares running.'

9

'Your four o'clock appointment is here, sir.' Ruth's tone over the intercom was neutrally formal. It was the one which she used on the odd occasion on which the DCC summoned an errant officer for a reprimand.

'*God. I hope she's told the woman what this is about,*' he thought to himself, fearing that she had not.

His supposition was all but confirmed a few seconds later when the door opened and Sergeant Masters entered briskly, in a sharply pressed uniform. She stood stiffly in front of his desk and saluted, looking nervous, her eyes unnaturally narrow. Her hair had grown since he had seen her last, and she had struggled to fit it inside her cap.

Skinner smiled broadly as he rose to his feet, returning her salute clumsily. 'At ease, please, Sergeant. Take a seat.

'What is it?' he asked. 'Don't you like CID?'

The expressive eyes widened. She shook her head at first, then nodded. 'No, sir, I mean, of course I do, sir. I mean . . . oh God.'

He smiled again, moving from behind his desk, to the low leather chairs which surrounded his coffee table. 'I'm sorry if I've confused you or embarrassed you,' he said. 'Come on and sit over here, and calm down, this is nothing to be nervous about.

'I didn't go into detail when I asked Ruth to make the appointment, but I should at least have made it clear that I didn't expect you to come in uniform. You're not on parade here, so take off that damn silly hat.'

Sergeant Masters sat where he indicated, arranging herself neatly, and tugging her uniform skirt down to cover her knees. She removed her cap and shook out her hair. 'Then may I ask, sir, why am I here?'

Skinner nodded. 'Of course, and we'll get to that, but let's have a chat first. It's Polly, isn't it?'

To his surprise, she hesitated, 'Well, sir, that's what they call me at the station, and it appears on my record. It's a nickname I picked up at school, and it's followed me ever since. Actually, I was christened Pamela. That's what my parents call me and that's what I prefer . . . if I'm given the choice, that is.'

He grinned. There was something about her style which set him at ease, at the same time as he was trying to unbend her. There was nothing pretentious about her. Her expression was open and honest, and her voice was clear, with no trace of a Sunday accent. 'Fair enough,' he said. 'I understand, although I'm the opposite, myself. Anyone calls me Robert, other than my nearest and dearest, my hackles start to rise. Pamela it shall be.'

He looked at her, appraisingly, for a few seconds. 'Do you remember, Pamela, that outrageously loaded question that I asked you at your Promotion Board?'

She smiled, for the first time since she entered the room. 'Oh yes, sir. I worried for ages afterwards in case you thought that my answer was just trite interview bullshit.'

Involuntarily, as if she had drawn it from him, Skinner smiled back. 'And was it?'

She shook her head vigorously, serious again. 'Oh no. I asked myself the same question over and over again, before I left my marketing job . . . incidentally sir, it was a top-of-the-range Sierra, not a Cavalier. If I hadn't believed my answer then, I'd be a director of the consultancy now; driving a Scorpio, probably.'

'And earning more than me, no doubt,' he said. 'You've had six months in CID since we met last, six months with the duties of rank as well as its privileges, such as they are. Is your view still the same?'

Her head cocked to the side as she thought about his question. 'Basically yes, sir. I think it's a bit less simplistic now, less idealistic. I'm coming to understand that helping people live better lives can sometimes mean locking them up for thirty years. But I think that my reasons for being in the job are still positive.'

'You've come to it,' he hesitated, '. . . forgive me . . . later than most. Can I ask you, has that limited your career ambitions?'

'I don't know that I have defined career ambitions, as such, sir. I've never thought in those terms.'

'Well, think about them now, Pamela. Take your time, while I pour us some coffee. Sugar?' She shook her head as he stood up.

A minute later he resumed his seat, placing a white cup and saucer before her. 'Well?'

'Okay. My career ambition, sir? I would like to be

promoted to the limit of my competence, not one grade above it.'

'Like too many people you have observed in the police force?' he asked, with a grin.

'No, sir,' she said, quickly, but not too quickly. 'Not too many in the force, but quite a few in other places. When eventually I retire, I would like to think that I have made a positive contribution all through my career, and not got in the way at the latter end.'

'Fair enough. Now can I ask you, indelicately, about your private ambitions. You're divorced. Why?'

'David was involved with someone else. I left him and moved to Edinburgh.'

'Are you in a relationship at the moment?'

'No, I'm not. I've had enough of those for a while, I think.' Suddenly the brown eyes narrowed again. 'Sir, is this about me and Alan Royston? If it is, I admit that we had a relationship for a time. It didn't work out, but it didn't even occur to me that it might have been improper, or against regulations. It began after I moved into the press office; it wasn't the reason for my being transferred to it.'

Skinner was taken completely by surprise. 'Pamela, I didn't even know about your relationship with Alan Royston, nor do I care. The force press officer is a civilian, and you are both single people. What you do or did outside the office is none of my damn business. Listen, the only time I care a stuff about my officers' sex lives is if there is a chance of them affecting performance on the job . . . and don't misunderstand my meaning!'

He paused. 'Look, I'd better get to the point here.

'You know DCI Rose? She was with me when I saw

you yesterday at Haddington.' Pamela Masters nodded briefly, intrigue replacing the concern in her eyes.

'Well, before her promotion, Mags held one of the most important jobs in this force. She was my personal assistant.' He pointed to the piles of paper which still rose from his desk. 'As you can see, I am badly in need of a replacement.

'I'm looking for someone who is mature, responsible, intelligent; someone who is capable of broadening my outlook on most issues and of contributing original thought when asked; someone who does not draw back from using initiative and where necessary from taking decisions; most of all, someone with whom I can get on, and who can put up with me and my occasionally short fuse.

'This isn't a competitive interview situation. There are no rules about how I fill this one. The job's yours if you want it.' He smiled, as he saw her mouth drop open in surprise.

'There's no promotion involved,' he said. 'Recently the post has been filled by a DI, but that doesn't mean a thing. What I will say is that if you spend time in my outer office, even a short time, and make a go of it, you will be seen as being on a fast track.'

He stood up, and Pamela Masters followed his lead. 'Take twenty-four hours to think about it. Talk to Maggie Rose, if you like. She'll tell you about my dark side, as far as she's seen it. If you turn me down, no-one will ever know and it won't affect your prospects in any way; but I'd like to think that you'll be with me first thing on Monday morning.'

He began to escort her towards the door, but she

stopped. 'I've thought it over, sir. I appreciate your permission to speak to DCI Rose, but I always like to trust my own instincts.

'Can I ask you two questions?'

'Sure.'

'What time do I report on Monday, and should I be in uniform or plain clothes?'

10

Skinner thought that he could catch traces of Pamela Masters' perfume hanging in the air a good ten minutes after his office door had closed behind her.

After she had left he had buzzed Ruth and had told her to make arrangements for her transfer from Haddington CID to his staff. Next he had dictated memoranda for typing next day to Andy Martin, and to Dave Donaldson, as line commander, to advise them of his decision.

He had just finished his memo to Donaldson, and had turned his attention back to his paperwork when he was interrupted by Ruth, on the intercom. 'Sorry, sir, but you asked me to call you whenever the Chief got back.'

Sir James Proud had barely settled behind his desk when Skinner rapped on his door and slipped into the room. 'Yes Bob,' he said, as ingenuously as he could, 'what can I do for you?'

The DCC frowned down at him. 'You can continue our conversation of this morning. I'm your second in command, yet you let slip that you had discussed my trip to America with someone before deciding to send me. If it was my other boss, the Secretary of State, that's understandable. If it was another Chief Constable, say Jock Govan, fair enough. Now if it was Jim Elder or

Andy Martin, while I could live with that, I'd feel like chinning them for not mentioning it to me afterwards.' He paused.

'No, no, Bob,' said the Chief hurriedly. 'Don't say anything to Jim or Andy!'

Skinner looked at him, curiously. 'What's going on here? Why are you on the defensive about this?'

Proud Jimmy fidgeted behind his desk. 'D'you remember?' said his grim-faced Deputy. 'I said "If you want me to go on this thing, you'll have to order me." And you said "So be it." Now it seems that you had set it up with someone else.

'I want to know who that was. No, I *demand* to know who it was.'

The Chief swung round, in his swivel chair, shaking his silver head as he gazed out of the window across the force playing field.

'Oh dear,' he muttered. 'Oh dear, oh dear, oh dear.'

11

'Let me go over this again, because I still can't believe it!'
Bob Skinner was almost shaking with rage, and had failed
entirely in his resolve to keep his voice below a shout.

'You went to my Chief Constable, and you asked him
to send me on a trip which you knew I would hate, and
which you knew would take me out of the country for
a month. You had the unbelievable temerity to interfere
in my professional life, and to keep it totally secret
from me!

'Do you realise that in the process you compromised
the relationship between Jimmy and me, and put the
poor guy in the impossible position of having to choose
between the interests of friends?

'Do you realise that you persuaded or bullied him into
behaving unprofessionally, and put him in a position in
which I would be justified in making a complaint against
him to the Police Authority?

'Now *why* . . .' he roared the word, '. . . did you do
that? How in Christ's name were you *able* to bring
yourself to do that?'

He loomed over Sarah, his face as dark as hers was
pale. His black leather overcoat lay crumpled on the
floor on the far side of the kitchen, where he had

thrown it as he had burst through the door to confront her.

But she stood her ground. 'I told him what I believed,' she shouted back. 'That you were going back to work too soon after sustaining such a major injury, and that I was afraid, you being such a stubborn, reckless character, that you might put yourself in a physical situation where you could do yourself long-term harm.'

'That's a bloody lie!' he bellowed, his rage unabated. 'You knew the shape I was in a month ago. I was back to full fitness.

'How did you find out about the bloody thing?' he barked. 'Christ, I didn't know about it till I was told to pack my bags.'

She looked up at him, her hair ruffled and her eyes blazing. 'Andy told Alex about it. He said that he was on the short-list to go, but that the Chief would probably send Jim Elder. Alex mentioned it to me. I saw it as a way of making sure that you took care of yourself properly and didn't put yourself at risk.'

'No!' he shouted at her again. 'That's a lie, a lie, a lie. I've been lied to over the years by real experts. You're a bloody amateur. Now, you *will* tell me the truth!'

She broke away from his glare for the first time, and turned her back on him, leaning over the kitchen work-surface, gripping it as tightly as she seemed to be holding on to herself.

At last, she could hold on no longer. She spun round to face him. 'Okay, Goddammit!' she screamed, her voice suddenly coarser, her accent more American. Her face was flushed, suffused with anger.

'I did it in the hope, the vain fucking hope, that in the month you were away you might forget about this stupid, blind obsession with solving what you imagine to have been your first wife's murder.

'For the three months before you went away, we couldn't talk about anything but it would come round to Myra. Why the Goddamn woman even found her way into our bed!' Her right hand flew up, and she slapped him across the cheek, leaving a vivid red mark.

'She must have been one great lay, Bob, because you were thinking eighteen years back when you were screwing me, moving differently, doing things you'd never done before. Did she really like that? Was she really that wild?'

'Yes,' he said, quietly now, but just as angrily, and with a cruelty which Sarah had never seen before. 'Yes, she bloody was.'

'Yeah, I guessed she must have been, because eighteen years on she still has you by the cock!' She began to sob, and to punch him, hard, on the chest, with both fists, until he seized her by the wrists.

'I thought it was guilt-driven at first, this crusade of yours,' she said. 'That you were chewed up by remorse because it should have been you in that car, not her. Then I realised that it was more, that when she was alive you were completely in her power, and that somehow Kevin O'Malley had awakened not just your memory of her death, but of the hold she had over you.'

She looked up at him, tears streaking her face. 'Now it won't leave you, Bob, not until you have the strength to will it away. But you don't, you bastard. You don't want to. You're wallowing in your memory of her. You're putting our marriage and our future to one side, because of a ghost.

'That was why I used Jimmy, to have you sent away, in the hope that over those thirty days you would come to your senses, and would start missing *me*, not her. But the minute you walked through that door, when I saw the Chanel Number Five that you had brought back for Alex, I realised that nothing had changed.

'In fact, it's worse than ever.'

She drew the back of her hand across her eyes and squared her shoulders. 'Straight choice, Bob. Her or me. Dead or alive. Past or present. Stay or go.'

As he looked down at her, he felt his anger leave him. But it was replaced by something else. During the years of his widowhood, there had always been Alex as the focus, the pivotal point of his life. Yet he knew that with a strong mother there to rear him, Jazz would never need him in the same way

Until that moment, he had never felt real desolation, never realised that it was palpable, never realised that it could consume the soul, not until that very moment as it engulfed his.

'How can I stay, Sarah?' he said, quietly. 'When my life is built on trust, and when you've proved to me that I can't trust you any more?

'You say Myra had a hold over me, but that's absolute crap. You don't know anything about how it was between the two of us.

'You look at me and you say I'm obsessed. Sure I am: with justice. I always have been, and I always will. But from where I'm standing, you're obsessed too: with blind, irrational jealousy, so much so that you've resorted to deceiving Jimmy Proud, my friend, so you could manipulate me and control my actions and my life.'

Suddenly he smiled, but it was full of sadness. 'Forget the rights and wrongs. The fact is that now, when each of us looks at the other, neither of us is seeing the person we married. You agree?'

She looked him in the eye, and nodded.

'So tell me, Sarah, my wife,' he said. 'How can I stay?'

12

Finding a needle in a haystack is rather easy, if it is the only one, and if the searcher has a sufficiently powerful magnet.

There was no Carl Medina listed in the Edinburgh telephone directory, but a single call to DVLC in Swansea uncovered one licensed driver of that name in the city, living at an address in Slateford. A subsequent check with the City of Edinburgh Council Finance Department revealed that the Council Tax for that address was paid by one Angela Muirhead, by monthly instalments, remitted from an account at the Clydesdale Bank in Charlotte Square.

Dave Donaldson pressed the entry buzzer at the smart, newly-built block of flats and waited. But no voice came from the small speaker in the casing, only the hum of the lock being released by remote control.

The flat, listed 'Muirhead/Medina' beside the buzzer stud, was on the third floor of four. There was no lift, but Donaldson and Maggie Rose took the stairs at a trot. Number 3c was at the end of a long, narrow hallway, heavy with intermingling stale cooking smells which made the detectives' stomachs churn. The front door had obscure glazed panels, top and bottom, but no bell, only a letterbox with knocker attached.

It was six thirty, and the flat was dark inside. DCI Rose rapped the knocker, three times, hard and loud. After only a few seconds the hallway behind the door was lit up, and a tall figure approached.

'Have you lost your keys, Angie? They're not hanging up in the . . .' The voice, muffled at first behind the closed door tailed off as it opened, in a classic mixture of surprise and alarm as the man saw the two officers on the doorstep.

'Carl Medina?' asked Donaldson.

The man nodded. 'Aye, that's me.' For all his Hispanic surname, his accent was pure Edinburgh, and his features and his fair, thinning hair, swept back from a high forehead, betrayed no Latin connection. He was a strikingly handsome man, around thirty years old, but he seemed, if anything, Nordic in his ancestry. Maggie looked at him, thought of her swarthy half-Italian husband, Mario, and was struck by the vagaries of genetic inheritance.

'Superintendent Donaldson, DCI Rose, Edinburgh CID,' her colleague announced. 'We'd like a word. Can we come in?'

'Aye, if you like,' said Medina, with a sigh.

The two detectives stepped into the flat. Closing the front door behind them, Medina pointed them towards a room at the far end of the hall. As soon as she stepped into the sitting room Rose's eye was caught by the late edition *Evening News* lying on the small couch, and by its front page heading, '*City Woman Dies in Fiery Hell*'.

'What can I do for you?' he asked.

Rose picked up the tabloid and held the front page towards him. 'I think you know.'

Medina said nothing, but gave a brief nod, his gaze dropping to the grey-carpeted floor. He pointed the detectives to the two soft, cream-coloured armchairs on either side of the couch, on which he sat down himself.

'We'd just like a chat for now,' said Donaldson. 'Later we might want you to make a formal statement, but we'll cross that one when we get there.

'Is this your permanent address?' he asked.

'Aye.'

'You live here with Miss, is it, Angela Muirhead?'

Medina shook his head and smiled, for the first time. 'That's Ms. Angie's very definitely a Ms.'

'What does she do for a living?'

'She's a civil servant. She's personal secretary to some high flyer, in the new place down in Leith.'

'Where is she now?'

'Her boss works all hours. She's no' usually home before seven.'

'Where do *you* work, Mr Medina?' asked Rose.

'I don't, as I'm sure you know by now.'

'Did you apply for a job recently?'

Medina glanced across at her, sharply. 'I apply for jobs all the time. I hate that bloody Giro, Miss . . . er, sorry, I didn't catch the name.'

'It's Rose,' said the DCI quietly. 'Let me be more specific. Two or three months ago, did you apply for a job in the motor trade, with a Renault dealership?'

'Aye.'

'What was the job?'

'Book-keeper. Unqualified accountant. That's what I do.'

'What was the outcome?'

He glanced at her, a sour expression crossing his face. 'I'm still drawing the bloody Giro, amn't I.'

'Do you know why you didn't get the job?'

Medina looked away from the officers, towards the wall. 'Oh aye,' he said, heavily. 'One day the recruitment people said it was as good as mine, the next I was told that my last employer's reference was, quote unquote, "unsatisfactory". That wee bastard Jackie Charles!'

Donaldson leaned forward. 'Come on, Mr Medina. You were sacked for dishonesty. Surely you couldn't have expected Mr Charles to give you a reference after that?' He paused. 'You do admit that, don't you?'

The fair-haired man laughed bitterly and rose to his feet. 'Oh sure, I admit that I was sacked. But it had bugger-all to do with dishonesty. Carole fell out with me. It was her that put the boot in with Jackie.'

'Come on, man. It's easy to plead the innocent now. But you backed off from your threat to take Mr Charles to an industrial tribunal, didn't you.'

Carl Medina looked down at him, in what seemed to be genuine surprise. 'I never mentioned the word Tribunal, far less backing off from one. I knew there was no point.' As the man paused, Donaldson glanced at Rose and saw a brief smile flicker around the corners of her mouth. 'Listen, Superintendent,' he went on. 'I was accused of nicking small amounts of cash, here and there. That was nonsense on two counts.

'One, if I *was* bent – which I'm not – I'm too good an accountant to do anything as obvious as adding up a few columns wrong. Second, for all you CID people may believe, there's no cash flowing through a business like Jackie Charles Motors. No-one buys a Ferrari for readies these days, not even a lottery winner. It's all cheques, in and out.

'The only way to make a bit on the side is through backhanders from insurance brokers and finance houses. That doesn't happen much, and when it does the sweeties don't get anywhere near the book-keeper.'

'So what did happen?' asked Donaldson.

'Carole fiddled the books herself, showed them to Jackie and said I did it. She told him to sack me. That was that. I haven't worked since.' Medina gave a weak smile, devoid of humour, and flopped down once more on the couch, shaking his head.

'But why didn't you go to a tribunal, if you'd been fitted up?' asked Maggie Rose.

'Like I said, there would have been no point. It would have been my word against Carole. Not just that either; I knew enough about Jackie Charles to realise that it would have been a bad idea.'

'What did you know about him?' snapped Donaldson.

'Oh, things I'd heard. Not so much about Charles himself, but about that guy who works for him in his other businesses, Dougie Terry. He used to come around the showroom every so often, to see Jackie.'

'What had you heard about Terry?'

Medina paused. 'I work out a bit, in the gym at the Commonwealth Pool. I met a guy there once – about five years back, just before I started working for Charles – who told me that *he* knew a guy who did odd jobs for cash for Terry. We were just bullshitting, ken, about how you could make a few quid out of the bodybuilding. I was talking about Arnold Schwarzenegger, but this guy started on about Dougie Terry.'

'Did this man describe the sort of odd jobs he was talking about?'

He nodded. 'Aye. He said they involved breaking people's arms and legs: even, on occasion, breaking them so they'd never be right again.'

'Did he mention anyone specific?' Rose cut in, softly.

The man hesitated. 'Aye, he did. Mind you, at the time I thought it was crap. I thought it was all crap until I saw Dougie Terry. This guy mentioned a footballer, a lad named Jimmy Lee, played for the Jam Tarts. He had a bad gambling habit, and he was rotten at it. He owed a bookie a stack of cash, far more than he was making, and the Hearts didn't exactly look like winning the European Cup that year.

'One Saturday night, after a Tynecastle game, Lee was on his way home in Wester Hailes when he was jumped in the hallway of the building where he lived.'

'I remember that case,' said Dave Donaldson.

'The whole of Edinburgh remembers it. The boy's kneecaps, and both his ankles, were smashed to bits. He'll never walk right again, never mind play football. The guy I met at the Commonwealth Pool said that the guy *he* knew had been involved in it and that it had been set up by Terry, to settle the boy Lee's score with the bookie.'

'Can we put some names to this story, Mr Medina?' asked Rose.

'I don't know the guy's name. Working out you see people to talk to, between exercises, like, but you don't usually get to know them.'

'Have you ever seen the man since that conversation?'

'Once or twice, but not in the last three years or so. He just stopped coming to the Commonwealth. Maybe he ruptured something. That can happen to the real keen guys, like this bloke was.

'Could you pick him out if you saw him again?'

Medina nodded. 'Sure. I don't remember much about his face, other than that it was red and sweaty and that he had a big moustache, but he had a big vulture tattooed on his right shoulder. That was a one-off, and no mistake.'

'Maybe we'll take you on a tour of the gyms and health clubs, Mr Medina,' said Donaldson, suddenly and sharply. 'But let's get back to the point here, okay?

'You've said that Mrs Charles made false allegations against you, and had you sacked. You've told us that she fell out with you. You were the company book-keeper, and she was its finance director. If you were good at your job, as you say, why would she just "fall out with you"?'

'Carl?' The voice came from the hallway. All three heads turned and looked towards a slim, dark-haired woman as she appeared, framed in the doorway. She looked tired, concerned, and not a little puzzled as she frowned at them. The two men stood up, and Medina moved towards her.

'Angie, love,' he said, helping her out of her heavy, navy-blue woollen coat, 'these people are CID officers. There's been a death at the place where I used to work. The boss's wife was killed in a fire, and they're treating it as murder. It's in the *Evening News*.'

Angela Muirhead looked at the detectives. 'But why come here? It's been years since Carl worked there.' She turned to Medina. 'How long is it since you were made redundant, Carl, two years now?'

The man looked at Donaldson, a plea in his eyes. 'Look, Superintendent, can we finish this later?'

The detective shook his head. 'Sorry, we either finish it here or you come down to the station with us right now, and we do the whole thing again, formally and under caution.

'I think it best if Ms Muirhead knows the truth anyway, don't you?' Without waiting for a reply he looked at the girl. 'Mr Medina wasn't made redundant. He was sacked, so his former employer tells us, on grounds of dishonesty. Mr Medina denies that. He says that his boss's wife, the victim in last night's fire, fell out with him and made up evidence against him.

'When you came in we were asking why she would do that. So, Mr Medina?'

The man looked from Donaldson to Angela Muirhead, who stared back at him, her frown deepening, then to Maggie Rose, who sat silent, returning his gaze, and finally back to the Superintendent.

'Okay,' he said at last, in a hard, bitter tone. 'Carole Charles made a pass at me and I turned her down.'

'Sure she did,' said Donaldson, his voice dripping with sarcasm.

'She did!' cried Medina, insistently. 'She liked the young lads, did Carole. She was always flirting when she came into the office. It was nothing that anyone else would notice, just the odd wink, the odd suggestive remark. It used to piss me off a bit, but I was hardly in a position to do anything about it.'

'Except resign?' said Rose.

'Exactly, Chief Inspector, and I wasn't about to do that. Angie and I were saving up for a new house, and jobs were even less thick on the ground then than they are now. So I put up with it. Anyway, Carole was nearly twenty years older than me. I thought it was all a bad joke.' He paused.

'Finally, one night I was working late, getting ready for the auditors, when she came into the office. We were the only people there. She came straight round the desk, pushed the books to one side, pulled up her skirt and sat on my lap, straddlin' me.

'She just went straight for my fly. She said, "I'm going to have you, son. No more messing around. This is your big night." I'll never forget it. All the time she was laughing at me.' He looked across at Angela Muirhead, who stood staring at him, her right hand gone instinctively to her mouth.

'What did you do?' asked Rose.

'I just lifted her off me, and sat her down, on her bum, on the desk. I said, "No way, Mrs Charles. I'm sorry, but I'm not daft enough to fuck around wi' the boss's wife." I zipped myself up and I walked right out of there.' He paused, and looked again at his fiancée.

'I didn't know what to expect when I went in to work the next day. But nothing happened, or was said. In fact, I didn't see Carole for a week after that, till one afternoon she came in. She didn't say a word to me. She just started going over one of the purchase ledgers, one I hadn't opened for weeks.

'After a few minutes she picked it up and went to see Jackie. Next day he called me in to see him. He said that Carole had caught me on the fiddle, and that I was fired. He said he was sorry, because he had always liked me, but his wife was adamant that I had been in the till and that was it.'

'Did you deny it?' asked the red-haired Chief Inspector.

The man shook his head. 'What was I going to say? "Look Jackie, your wife made it up. She's in the huff wi' me because I wouldn't shag her." No, all I said was, "She's wrong, but too bad." Then I cleared my desk and I went home.'

'Where were you yesterday evening?' asked Donaldson, quietly.

Angela Muirhead answered. 'He was here.'

'All evening?'

'Yes,' said Medina. 'Angie got in just before nine. I had the dinner ready to heat up.'

He smiled, then gave a soft laugh. 'Look, I didn't go anywhere near that garage. I'm not the vindictive type. But if I had wanted to sort out Jackie or Carole, I'd have taken a copy of something she left lying around in the office one day.'

'What do you mean?'

'I don't know what it was for sure, but it wasn't about the car business. It was a ledger and it showed cash movements in and out, with dates, sources and recipients of payments, but with initials, not names. I scribbled a few notes at the time. It occurred to me afterwards that if I'd stuck the damn thing under the photocopier, I might have been able to use it to hang on to my job.'

'Or you might have lost a lot more than that,' said Maggie Rose, bristling inwardly, all of a sudden, with excitement. 'You don't still have those notes, do you?'

'I might have. I've got lots of old junk in my briefcase. I'll have a look through it. If I find anything I'll let you have it.'

'Okay,' said Donaldson, sourly. 'If you do turn up these mythical bits of paper, bring them with you to the

St Leonard's police office at four o'clock tomorrow, and ask for me. But be sure you turn up then even if you don't find them. I'd like you to make that formal statement we mentioned.'

He nodded to Rose. 'That's enough for tonight, though, Maggie. I imagine these two will have some talking to do. Let's leave them to get on with it.'

Angela Muirhead showed them to the door. It had barely closed before Rose looked up at Donaldson. 'That was an interesting half-hour, and no mistake.'

The Superintendent's eyebrows rose. 'You thought so? The only thing that I could hear was a liar covering up the Porky Pie that he told his girlfriend when Jackie sacked him for cooking the books. Redundant, indeed!

'As for the stuff about the man with the vulture tattoo; all that could just have been a half-hearted attempt to smear Charles.'

'Maybe lies, maybe truth,' said Rose, 'but for sure, Carl Medina's given us a few hares to chase. D'you think we should report this to Andy Martin tomorrow morning?'

'Aw, come on, Maggie,' said Donaldson. 'I know that Martin's in personal charge, but we don't want to go running to him with every rumour we pick up off an informant, or a guy like Medina, who's scared and tossing out crap.'

She stopped as they reached the top of the stairway. 'I agree that the story about the man with the vulture tattoo was vague and a bit fanciful. But these notes that Medina promised us, that could be something else again. We've been looking for years for anything that ties Jackie Charles to the illegal activities which we know he runs or bankrolls.

'Whether admissible as evidence or not, these scribbles that Medina says he made could be the first return we've ever had. Let me ask you something, Dave. If the Boss was running this investigation, would you hold something like this back from him?'

Slowly, the Detective Superintendent shook his head.

'Well,' said his deputy, 'in that case my advice is, don't for one second treat Andy Martin any less seriously than you would treat Bob Skinner.

'Unlike the Boss, Andy's famous for being even-tempered and imperturbable. But I've always had the feeling when something really does rattle his cage, the outcome could be spectacular!'

13

Bob Skinner sat on the low stone wall of his cottage in Gullane, looking out across the lamplit Goose Green. It was just after nine, but the rain and cold of the previous evening had been driven away by an unseasonably early warm front, and he was perfectly comfortable in his jeans, and a denim shirt.

Not much moved in Gullane after dark, other than in the constantly busy main street. The Green was still and silent, as silent as the house behind him. He looked across it and thought of long-gone summer days, his first in the village. He remembered sitting in the sun, on the same piece of wall, with Myra beside him and with their newborn daughter asleep in her pram.

He smiled in the dark as he remembered the outrage of the new parents when the August funfair had set up on the Green, with the loud music which accompanied its carnival rides, and his attempt to force them to turn down the volume which they feared would disturb their child.

The showmen had been pleasant and understanding. They had turned the volume down a notch and had promised that they would stop before darkness fell. 'But you wait and see, Mister,' they had said. 'After a couple of days your baby won't even notice that we're here.'

Of course they had been right. On the second evening of the fair, Baby Alexis had slept through the cacophony as if it had been a lullaby. In years thereafter, the showmen's arrival had been one of the highlights of her summer, and the carnival people had become welcome visitors and good friends. Bob smiled again, and if anyone had been there to see they would have called it wistful, as he recalled their shock on the day that they arrived to learn of Myra's death a few months before. The reality of their grief and the depth of their sympathy were still fresh in his mind. Had he accepted, all of his and Alex's rides on their swings and roundabouts would have been free that summer, but he had insisted on paying their way.

He looked across the Green, through his memories, and counted four cars mounted on its verge outside the rear entrance to the Golf Inn Hotel. That had always been a popular parking spot for patrons. When the Skinners had first arrived, those cars, almost invariably, would disappear after closing time, but after only a few weeks of their residence, once word had spread that the eyes of the law were upon their owners, most would still be there in the morning.

In fact, Bob had always mentally put away his warrant card as soon as he had driven into his home village, but his presence there, especially as he had risen through the ranks, had seemed to ensure that the patrolling constables were always on their toes. Now, as he sat in the dark and the silence, he saw a man emerge from the pub's back door, climb into one of the cars and drive away, up the Green and out, towards Erskine Road. He wondered to himself if standards had slipped since he had become, in the main, a weekend resident. He wondered too how long it would be before the village's sharper eyes and tongues would note that he was back among them permanently. Already that evening one pair of eyebrows had risen, a moustache had twitched, and a mental note had been taken when he had wandered alone into the Mallard and ordered a pint of Seventy Shilling and a bar supper.

Abruptly, he stood up from the wall, stepped clean over the garden gate, walked up the path to the grey-stone cottage, turned his key in the lock and stepped inside. As it had when he had arrived earlier that evening, still reeling mentally from his explosive confrontation with Sarah, the house seemed to greet him like an old friend as he switched on the lights.

It had seen most of the pivotal moments of his adult life. It was the home he had shared with Myra; the home to which he had returned after her death to try somehow to break the news to a four-year-old; the home which he had made for Alex as he had raised her to womanhood, for many years devoting himself to her to the almost complete exclusion of anything resembling a personal life.

Eventually, it was the place to which, with his daughter grown and gone to University in Glasgow, he had brought Sarah; the place where they had first made love, where he had made love in the truest sense of the word for the first time in more than fifteen years.

Sure, there had been the occasional date, the occasional invitation to dinner parties 'to make up the numbers', and on training courses, trips to conferences and on holiday in Spain – always far away from Gullane and his home with Alex – the occasional midnight encounter, flawed, fumbling, unsatisfactory: but mostly there had been nothing, save for parenthood and policing.

Although it might have been understandable, it would not have been true to say that Bob Skinner had walled himself up with memories of his late wife. There had been a block between him and the detail of those recollections, a barrier which lately had been smashed and swept aside. Of course he had grieved for Myra: he had missed her more than he would or could admit to himself. But he had looked at the past as if though a mist, as he had put everything from his mind but his work and the raising of his daughter. In each of the two pursuits, in anyone's judgement, including, unashamedly, his own, he had been outstandingly successful.

Now he stood at, or near, the pinnacle of his career. His daughter was secure too, her adult life mapped out before her. With his new wife and child, and with his power to do good through his work and his rank, he should have been the most privileged and contented of men.

Except for the memory: the razor-sharp recollection conjured by Kevin O'Malley's therapy from his subconscious, the picture that his mind had taken in that ravaged car, but which shock had blocked it from developing, and with it his certainty that Myra had died because someone had set out to kill him.

And with that memory had come all the others, in which he had been unable or had refused – even now he did not know the truth of it – to indulge himself. Recollections of his time with his first wife, thrusting themselves uncontrollably into his consciousness, intimate memories invading intimate moments. It was as if a spirit was demanding to be put properly to rest.

He had a chest full of ghosts in the attic.

After Myra's death he had gathered together those of

her personal effects which had not gone to her mother or directly to Alex, most of their photographs and personal memorabilia, and many of the teaching papers from her teaching career. Each item he had packaged, and put away in his old cabin trunk.

Finally he had come to the diaries which his wife had written, completely privately but assiduously, every day for as long as he had known her. Not once, while Myra lived, had he ever looked inside, and in death he had respected the only privacy which she had ever sought from him. So he had put them away too, all of them in the trunk, unread and unreviewed.

He had intended that one day he would give the collection to Alex, so that as an adult she could discover the mother she had never really known. But somehow, he had never quite got around to it, had never quite found the right moment. Since Myra's death, he had opened that treasure-chest only once, then closed it again, very quickly, as if he had been afraid a genie would jump out.

He climbed the stairs to the attic room. He switched on the light in the small, dusty store-chamber, and he saw it. It was a broad, grey canvas-covered box, with a leather handgrip at either end. Two wooden bindings ran round its circumference, securing the box by their steel grips, which could be padlocked but now were not.

It had belonged to his father, and once a year it had been crammed tight with clothes for the family holiday. When he was a child, and it was packed and stood on end, it had seemed huge. He had a vivid memory of standing before it and looking up, for at that time it was taller than him. Now it was just an old grey trunk.

He yanked the metal catches apart and raised the lid, hesitantly, as if he expected the box to give a sigh, or perhaps a snarl. It did neither; instead the dust rose up from its lids in clouds. Coughing, he looked inside. The contents were packed in boxes and brown envelopes. He scanned them quickly, until he saw a grey cardboard shoe-box, jammed against the side wall on the right, and slightly crushed. Carefully, he lifted it out and took off the lid. It was full of rolls of 8mm cine film, with their ends neatly tucked away.

One Christmas his father had been given a cine camera, projector and screen, by a well-meaning old aunt. Having no interests other than golf and bridge, he had passed the set on to his fourteen-year-old son. Bob had used it from that time on until video cameras of manageable size had become available. All of his later films of Alex had been transferred to video, but the shoe-box, this long-hidden cache, held all those he had shot of Myra.

He looked into a corner of the attic and saw the projector, in its box, and the screen in its cylindrical case. They too were covered in dust. Once Sarah had asked him about the trunk, and what was in it. 'Stuff of Myra's,' he had said, 'best left alone,' inviting no further enquiries. She had shown no interest in the cine equipment or screen. They had not been touched in years. Now, closing the trunk on the rest of Myra's life, Bob Skinner picked up his projector, blew some of the dust away, and carried it, the screen and the box of films downstairs.

He was concerned for a moment that the old apparatus might have rusted, but when he set it up on the dining table, and switched it on, the machinery turned as smoothly as ever and its bulb cast a bright rectangle, first on the white wall then on the screen as he unrolled it and clipped it in place in its frame.

He picked a roll of film from the many in the box, and looked at its label. 'Teacher Training College Graduation', he read. He put it away, took out another, and another, and another, seven in all until he found the one for which he was searching. 'Corfu Two', he read softly.

He fitted the film on to the upper arm of the projector, then fed it through the bracket, past the bulb, and wound its end into the receiving spool. Finally he turned off the dining-room light, and switched the motor on.

The screen flickered white at first, as the blank early frames went past. Then suddenly, in an instant, an image appeared, in close-up and in perfect focus.

One thing that he had never forgotten was how beautiful Myra had been. He could see it mirrored to an extent in her daughter, although essentially Alex's looks were a blend of her parents' features. He stopped the projector and she smiled at him from the screen. Her dark hair had been cut short for that holiday, and swept back. Highlights from the sun glinted in it. Her body was tanned honey-gold, and her skin shone with health. She was smiling at him, through the lens and through the years, with her full red lips, and with her eyes, her huge, brown, wide, tell-it-all eyes.

They were her best feature; the weathervane of her moods, an infallible printout of whatever was on her mind at any waking moment. Looking at her, even if he had not remembered, Bob would have known beyond

99

doubt what was on her mind back then, in Corfu, on their honeymoon.

He flicked the switch and the film rolled on. The scene widened as the zoom unwound and the cameraman backed off. They were on a terrace balcony with high walls on either side, and nothing in front but railings and the clear blue sea. On the deck were two white sun-loungers with blue cushions. Myra was spread on one, half-seated, half-kneeling. She was naked. He stopped the film again and gazed at her, feeling his tears come. The sun, high in the summer sky, gleamed on the Ambre Solaire which he had rubbed into her full firm breasts with their upward-tilting nipples, into her flanks, into her back, her legs, her flat, firm belly . . .

He flicked the switch again. In a single supple movement, she rose from the lounger, and turned, stepping towards the rails as if to lean over them. She was the same honey-gold colour all over, and her oiled buttocks bunched as she moved.

She turned again and came towards him, laughing as she approached, mouthing silent words, and sending even stronger signals with her eyes. Then a hand reached up – but not too far, as Myra had been five feet ten inches tall – and took the camera.

There were a few wild frames as the lens swung round, until at last a young man came into shot. He was tall, and tanned as deeply as she. Sun-oil gleamed on him also, on his forehead, his strong, straight nose, his high cheeks, and on his wide shoulders. His fair hair was cut short, and his blue eyes were creased by his smile. He looked as happy as anyone Bob had ever seen. He remembered. He had been.

The camera began to pan downwards, slowly, over his chest with its mat of tangled bleached-blond hair, over his tightly muscled stomach, past his slightly protuberant navel. The camera began to zoom in and the shot went out of focus, but not so badly that it was impossible to make out the big hand as it flashed up to clamp over the lens.

The screen was dark for a few seconds. When it lit up once more, Myra was seated on a high stool, at an open-air bar. She was clothed this time, but only just, in a short, clinging yellow dress with a halter-fastening, from beneath which the tops of her breasts bulged, as if trying to break free. She was still smiling, and her great brown eyes were still beckoning, beckoning him now as they always had.

The stillness in the room was eerie. The whirring of the projector cut the silence like a knife paring off a layer of butter. Above the soft sound he could hear the sound of his own breathing, slightly fast and rasping. And then, gradually, he began to fancy that below it, within it, he could catch the whisper of a second breath in the darkness.

He stared hard at the screen, and as he did the hair on the back of his neck began to prickle. He squeezed his eyes shut for a second, and when he opened them everything had changed.

He was still staring at Myra, but suddenly she was three-dimensional; Myra and Sarah mingled together as the film of his first wife seemed to shine and move around the form and features of her successor.

'I came out here to talk, Bob.' Sarah/Myra said coldly. 'To try to persuade you, to try . . . oh I suppose, to try and fight for you!

'Bad move, huh? Now I can see what I'm up against.'

He stood there, rooted to the spot, with his heart pounding heavily in his chest like a hammer. Struck dumb, he shook his head and squeezed his eyes shut once more. When he opened them, Myra was alone and two-dimensional once more.

In her Seventies honeymoon dress, she stepped down from the barstool and walked, smiling, lustily, towards him once more, as she had done in the scene on the terrace. As her image grew, and as Bob's confusion, his emotions, and his memories combined to overwhelm him, he fancied, but without certainty, that he heard the soft click of the front door, closing.

14

'Who was telling the truth, d'you reckon, Dave? Jackie Charles or Medina?'

'I'll give you a more solid answer once Maggie and I have had the guy in here for formal interview, and once he's forced to commit himself on the record, under questioning that's a bit tougher than he had last night.'

Donaldson looked across the meeting table in Martin's office. 'But my gut feeling is that I don't believe him. When we got there, he had read the *News* report, and he knew that Mrs Charles was dead. He's not Einstein, but he may have guessed that Jackie would have told us about him and that we'd be coming to see him.

'He could have dreamed up that story as a defence, or with an eye to recovering his reputation, knowing that Mrs Charles wasn't around to deny either it, or the allegation that she had cooked the books to fit him up.'

'That's true,' said the Head of CID, 'and there's sod all we're going to be able to do to verify it either way. Apart from the vehicle registration documents and a few other papers, that were kept in a safe built into the floor, all the records of the business were kept in the office filing cabinets. Although those were still standing, the heat of the blaze was so great that the documents inside caught fire.

'When Arthur Dorward's team opened them up all they found was sodden black ash. You and Maggie can lean on the guy Medina as hard as you like, but if he sticks to his story, invented or not, you're not going to be able to do a thing to disprove it.'

Martin shrugged his shoulders. 'Ach, it's a sideshow anyway. What about the big question? Could Medina have killed Carole Charles?'

Donaldson looked to Maggie Rose, seated alongside him.

'Means, motive and opportunity, sir,' she said. 'The means, petrol and towropes for fuses, were handy on the premises.

'Motive? Medina says he was unfairly dismissed. He did nothing at the time, possibly out of fear or out of caution, but when he missed out on a job because Charles wouldn't give him a reference, that could have been enough to provoke him finally to revenge.

'Opportunity? Angela Muirhead was about to give him an alibi, but Medina wouldn't let her. He seemed to go out of his way to tell us that she'd been out until just before nine. He could have done that to protect her, to prevent her from putting herself at risk for him.

'Let's assume that the truth is that Angie got home at ten to nine, and he was there. The opportunity question hinges upon whether he could have made it from Seafield to Slateford in less than twenty minutes.'

'I could,' said Martin.

'Aye,' came a mumble from his right. 'Provided there were no lampposts in the way.'

The Chief Superintendent looked sideways at Detective

Sergeant Neil McIlhenney, who grinned wickedly and said, 'Sorry, sir.'

'Leaving lampposts out of it . . . The first thing you'll have to find out is whether Medina has a car or access to one.'

'I have done, sir. I called Angela Muirhead at her office this morning. She confirmed that they have one car only and that she uses it to go to work. She had it on Wednesday evening. That leaves taxis. If he had picked one up in Seafield Road at eight thirty, he'd have been home by eight forty-five, before her.'

'Cutting it fine,' said Martin.

'Yes,' Rose agreed, 'but it's possible, and it means that he could have had the opportunity.'

'Agreed. So it has to be followed up. If he was picked up, unless he was daft enough to book one of Jackie's minicabs, it would have to be a black taxi that he stopped. Put people on to checking them all, now, but get round the mini-operators as well.'

He looked across at Rose, then at Donaldson, then back at Rose. 'Gut reactions, please, having seen Medina. Could it be him?'

Donaldson nodded his head, slowly. 'I could believe that,' he said, almost grudgingly. 'I could just about see him having the bottle to do it.'

'I don't agree,' said Maggie Rose, forthrightly. 'I don't see this man having the ruthlessness to do something like that. The fact is, I believe him. At heart he strikes me as a basically honest chap, who loves his girlfriend. Although I agree we have to investigate him as a suspect, I'm inclined to accept his story, even the bit about the man with the vulture tattoo. If he brings those notes with him

105

when he comes to see us this afternoon, we'll know for sure.'

'Let's see,' said Martin. 'From what you've told me, my own view hasn't changed. Jackie Charles threw us Medina like a sprat to keep us busy. But if Medina's other information leads us anywhere Jackie may live to regret it.'

He glanced around the table. 'Which brings me to the way forward. Every investigation has to have a clear objective, and this one is catch the person who murdered Carole Charles.

'However we have peripheral matters being thrown up already. If we're given information, it has to be followed up, even if it doesn't appear to be related directly to the main goal. Let's get our organisation right to ensure that we can do all that.

'Dave, I want you to concentrate on the main thrust of the investigation, chasing vehicle sightings, possible taxi pick-ups, people with grudges along the lines we discussed earlier. With Charles' books reduced to ashes, your next priority is to interview Douglas Terry and to investigate him. Whenever someone tries to kill a general, the first suspects are always the soldiers behind him.

'Once you've done that, if we're still looking, work though that list of priorities we discussed.

'While you're pursuing those lines of enquiry, I'll ask the Boss . . . since Special Branch reports directly to him . . . to brief Brian Mackie and Mario today and start them looking for possible leads from outside the city.'

He turned to Rose. 'Maggie, I want you to follow up on the side issues as they come up, starting with the man with the vulture tattoo. See if you can find out if he does exist, and if he does, then find him. I remember the Jimmy Lee case too. In fact I was involved in the investigation. I'll never forget the X-rays.

'Lee swore blind that he had been mugged by a gang of Hibs casuals. We even found a Hibs scarf dropped at the scene. But the thing was, the Hibees were playing in Aberdeen that day, and all of the likely suspects were still on the supporters' buses, driving home down the M90, when the attack took place.

'If Mr Vulture can give us a lead, even if it is five years late, nothing would please me more. Mind you, Maggie, you should still ask Medina why he didn't come forward with this story at the time.'

He looked up again at Rose. 'When he brings in those notes, if he does, let me see them. I'll take a view on what we do about them at that stage.'

He nodded sideways, to where Neil McIlhenney and Sammy Pye were sitting. 'Use what resources you need, but Dave, I want you to work closely with Neil, and Maggie, you take Sammy. Like the Boss, I believe in tight core teams of people who know each other and work well together.

'So, crack on, and remember, keep me in touch all the time. No surprises, please. I hate surprises.'

Martin stood up from the table. As his colleagues followed his lead and made to leave, he stopped Donaldson with a touch on his arm. 'Dave,' he said, picking up a sheet of paper from his in-tray. 'I got this just before you arrived. There'll be a copy for you at St Leonard's. It's a memo from the Boss.'

'What's it about?' asked Donaldson, puzzled.

'Let me read it to you. It says:

DCC to head of CID, copy to head of Eastern Area CID.

   As you will know I have been without a personal assistant since the promotion of DCI Rose. With your agreement, I propose to appoint Detective Sergeant Pamela Masters to the post, effective immediately. While in the past my PA has been a Detective Inspector, Sergeant Masters is in my view an officer of considerable potential who will benefit from a spell in the Command Corridor.

'That's it.'

'Mmm,' said Donaldson. 'He wants Pretty Polly, eh! Fair enough. I've got a good DC out there I can promote in her place. Nice of him to ask for our agreement, though.'

Martin laughed. 'That's Bob doing his best to consult with the two of us. But make no mistake, he isn't asking for our support, he's telling us we're going to give it!'

'Still,' he mused, 'a Detective Sergeant. Is Masters that good?'

'She's only been in the rank for six months. From what I've seen, she's bright, and very keen. But I wouldn't say she'd ever be Chief Constable material.'

'Maybe not, but she must have something. Time will tell what it is.'

15

Skinner was sitting at his desk, working his way silently through his paper mountain, when Martin stepped into his office to give him an update on the Charles investigation.

He listened in silence to the report, shrugging his shoulders once or twice, showing real interest only when the Chief Superintendent mentioned Medina's story about his notes from Carole Charles' mysterious ledger.

'What did Donaldson and Rose think about that?' he asked. 'Did they think he was making it up?'

'Donaldson thought he was probably at it. Mags believed him though.'

'What do you think the notes might tell us?'

'From what Medina said, they won't give us names. But they might give us a better clue of what it is we're looking for. If the guy is speaking the truth, and we're right about what he saw, then at least we know that we're on the right track: that there is a record of Charles' bent businesses, and the form that it's in.'

Skinner swung his chair round and looked out of the window. 'Tell you what I think,' he said softly. 'If Carole was carrying the ledger when Medina saw it, then it wasn't just for that night. I'd guess that Carole kept those books personally, and that Jackie never went near them or saw them.'

The DCC glanced back quickly towards Martin. 'He's

so careful that he'd keep them at arm's length from himself. He'd never let Dougie Terry hold them. He's an employee, not a shareholder and accountancy isn't his game anyway.' He stood up and looked across the headquarters approach road to the school beyond, studying the comings and goings. Ruth McConnell was hurrying up the pavement, back from her dentist's appointment. Alan Royston was hot on her heels as if trying to catch her up. Dave Donaldson, heading in the opposite direction passed them both, with brief nods.

At last he turned back to face Martin. 'So let's say that Carole had charge of the books. But where did she keep them? Not at the house, that's for sure, in case we ever did find a Sheriff soft enough to give us a search warrant on no evidence.'

'How about a bank safe deposit box?' asked the Head of CID.

'Possible, but too visible. I stick to the theory that the Charleses had a sort of head office in one of their properties, like we were told when we were given those two abortive tips. Remember, the ones where we turned up but the cupboard was bare.

'We gave up on that theory after the second let-down, but what if we were right? It's possible that the ledger was cremated along with Carole, but what if it isn't? It could be lying somewhere in Edinburgh, full of the evidence we need to nail Jackie Charles.

'If it is, then there will be only one person who knows where it is. That's Jackie himself. And my guess is he'll never trust anyone else to collect it for him. It'll be only a matter of time before he has to take the chance of picking it up himself.

'I know it's ifs and buts, Andy, BUT . . . Keep a specially close eye on the little fucker, just in case he shops himself.'

Martin was struck by Skinner's expression. There was a hard, mean gleam in his eye that he had never seen before. 'Christ,' said the Chief Superintendent, 'and here was me thinking that you were going soft on the guy.'

The DCC stared back, coldly. 'That was yesterday. He's had his moment. Now he's back in the pond with the rest of the piranha and I'm after him.'

Andy Martin had always been keenly attuned to his friend's moods. His forehead wrinkled in a frown as he sensed his underlying tension. 'Bob, what's up?' he asked.

Skinner's broad shoulders sagged, his grey-maned head dropped, and the anger left his blue eyes. 'I've moved out to the cottage, Andy.' He paused, as Martin gasped, surprise and concern mingling.

'I told you that Sarah and I haven't been hitting it off for a few months.'

'Yes, but . . .'

'Last night we had a Premier League bust-up, and it left us with nothing else to do but put some space between ourselves.' He slumped back into his chair.

Martin gazed across at him. 'God, Bob, it's got that bad?' Skinner nodded. 'What was the fight about?'

'Andy, I'm sorry, but I don't want to talk about it. Every time I think about it, I get so angry.'

'How long is this separation going to last?'

'I don't know. Maybe for good.'

'For Christ's sake, man, you can't mean that. This is you and Sarah we're talking about. There's nothing you two can't sort out.'

Bob shook his head. 'This is a different me, and a different Sarah, not the *Scotsman* couple of the month, as you called us once. She can't cope with my need to investigate Myra's death, I can't cope with her . . .' He stopped short. 'Never mind sorting things out, Andy, at the moment we're finding it difficult just to be in the same room as each other.'

'What about the baby?' asked Martin, anxiously. 'You can't just walk out on him.'

'I'll see the wee man every day, starting with lunchtime today. Longer term, we'll have to see how it goes, but the way it is just now, he's better off with his parents living apart than putting their arguments before his needs. Whatever happens James Andrew will cope.'

'And what about you? The loss of Myra has caught up with you, all of a sudden. When you stop to think about it, the loss of Sarah is going to hit you as well. Jazz is just a baby, and babies are resilient: but you, will you cope?'

He smiled. 'Oh yes, Andy, I'll cope; if it comes to it, like I did before, by focusing completely on my work. It may not make me a nicer guy, but the villains of Edinburgh – or maybe somewhere else – will come to regret it.'

'What do you mean, somewhere else?'

Skinner glanced across the desk. 'Sir William Green retires next year as Metropolitan Police Commissioner. Just between you and me, Andrew Hardy – yes, the Secretary of State for Scotland, no less – called me in to see him just before I went to America.

'He said that my name had come up in discussion, and he'd been detailed by the Home Secretary to ask me if I would wish to be a candidate. How about that, no experience in the top rank, yet I get an approach?'

Martin stared at him, his mouth hanging open in amazement. 'What did you say?'

'I said I'd think about it, and let him know when I got back. I had decided more or less to say "Thanks, but no thanks. I wouldn't fancy the change in my family's lifestyle". Now, things are different. The way I'm feeling, I'm swinging towards saying "Yes, please". I have to give him an answer next week, because they want to make the appointment before the General Election.

'I'm sure there isn't a cat's chance they'd actually give me the job, but the approach started me thinking. It's common knowledge that the Chief Constable's job in Strathclyde comes up around the same time. I just might have a punt at that.'

Martin held up his hands. 'That's big stuff, Bob, but don't do anything for the wrong reason, please. You have to take considered decisions on career moves like those, rather than just taking a punt, as you put it, because your private life has gone sour.'

'I know that, Andy. Yet all of a sudden I need a new direction in my life. Either of those jobs would provide that for sure, if I, and other people, decide I'm up to it.'

'*Which they will*,' thought Martin. He began to move towards the door. 'Look, there's a hell of a lot happening to you right now, more than anyone can expect to handle alone. If you'd like, I'll come out to Gullane and we can talk everything through, away from this place.'

Skinner nodded. 'Yes, my friend, I'd welcome that. But not just yet. There's someone I need to talk to, before I see anyone else. Do me a favour and ask her if she'll come out to see me, tonight.'

16

Neil McIlhenney and Dougie 'the Comedian' Terry eyed each other up with an odd mixture of animosity and amusement. They had met professionally several times over the years, usually after a robbery, a violent assault or, once or twice, a death.

Each encounter had come after Bob Skinner's intimidating cross-examination had persuaded, cajoled or simply terrified a suspect into letting slip Terry's name in connection with the crime for which the subject had been caught red-handed.

Every time, he had been brought in for interview. But the man had his own interview technique, as effective in its way as that of the DCC. Whatever the question, however it was put, be it direct or indirect, softly spoken or shouted, Dougie Terry never answered.

That was not to say that he was silent. Throughout most of his interviews he had told jokes; quick gags, one-liners. 'What's the difference between parsley and . . .', McIlhenney recalled, and had to suppress a smile. Occasionally he would lapse into a Chic Murray role. CID records still had a few interview tapes filled with the faultlessly replicated voice of the late, great, mystical Scottish droll.

Looking across the desk at Terry a memory jumped unbidden into the Sergeant's thoughts.

'*I was driving past a farmhouse, and I ran over a cockerel. So I rang the doorbell and told the farmer's wife.*

'"*I'm terribly sorry,*" *I said. "Can I replace it?*"

'"*Fair enough,*" *she said, "the hens are round the back".*'

Involuntarily, a chuckle escaped from McIlhenney's lips, making Detective Superintendent Donaldson look round sharply.

Eventually the police had given up asking questions. Whenever the Comedian was implicated, detectives would bring him in, put the allegation to him, switch on the recorder and sit back to enjoy the entertainment. When, occasionally, Terry was fresh out of jokes, he had other talents. One of the CID's most treasured tapes was known simply as 'Sinatra', a flawless forty-five minutes of the Maestro's best loved songs.

Once the performances were over, Dougie Terry was always released. He knew full well, as did the police, that no criminal case can be laid on the basis of an uncorroborated allegation. Once, Sir James Proud had suggested that he might be charged with wasting police time. 'How could we?' Bob Skinner, then Detective Chief Superintendent, had replied. 'His defence would be that it was time well spent!'

Terry's unshakeable confidence that there was never a case to answer was based on the fact that the police informants were almost invariably men with short memories. They had not forgotten what had happened on earlier occasions to those who had told tales. Two had been stabbed to death in prison, another slashed and

scarred for life, and three more simply beaten sense-
less.

'What'll it be today, gentlemen?' the Comedian asked
as the two policemen took seats at the side of his desk, in
his small attic office in Stafford Street, and as his secretary
closed the door as she left the room. Without warning, he
switched to Chic Murray mode.

*'My doctor asked me the other day, "Are you disturbed
by improper thoughts during the night?"*

'"Not at all," I told him. "I enjoy them, actually."'

'Now look . . .' Donaldson began, but before he could
go further he was interrupted by Neil McIlhenney, who
reached into a pocket of his overcoat and slapped half-
a-dozen large photographs on to the desk, under Terry's
nose.

'I thought we'd give you a laugh for a change, Dougie,'
he said, with a friendly smile. 'Take a look at those. See
that big black thing? That's Carole Charles. Remember
her? Middle-aged, very attractive woman? Jackie's wife?

'Some of these were taken in what was left of Jackie's
showroom, after the fire on Wednesday night; the rest at
the post mortem, when they had to cut her open to find
out whether she was a man, a woman or just leavings
from a barbecue. See there? That's a good close-up of
her jawbone. You can see her teeth.

'I was at the PM yesterday. It was like watching
someone dissect a lump of charcoal. I'm sure you'd have
sung your way through it, though.'

Dougie Terry stared wide-eyed at the photographs.
Beside McIlhenney, Donaldson heaved and turned away.
For a second, the Sergeant thought he was going to
be sick.

116

The ghost of Chic Murray had vanished. Terry turned the awful photographs over and pushed them, face-down, away from him. A sudden pallor had fallen across his broad, chiselled features, and his bright eyes had a shaken look, their confidence gone, for the first time that McIlhenney could recall.

'All right,' he said in a quiet flat tone. 'You've made your point. Get on with it.'

'Who did it?' asked McIlhenney, directly.

The Comedian stared back at him across the desk, and answered, for the first time in the Sergeant's career. A question with a question. 'Do you think that if I knew that I'd be sitting here talking to you bastards?'

'I'll take that as a "no", then, will I? Let me try another. Who's taken the hump at Jackie Charles lately?'

'How would I know? And why are you asking me, anyway?'

McIlhenney shook his head. 'Dougie, you're new to this game. The idea is that *we* ask the questions and *you* answer them.

'Let's try again. You are Jackie Charles' Vicar on Earth. While he ponces about as a fashionable merchant of fashionable motors, you are the general manager of all his downmarket businesses, the five John Jackson Bookmaker betting shops and the taxi businesses. Now, to your knowledge has Jackie upset anyone in those businesses, to the point that they would try to kill him? Straight answer, yes or no, and look me in the eye when you give it, please.'

Terry straightened up in his chair, tugging briefly at the lapels of his Hugo Boss suit. He looked McIlhenney hard in the eye. 'No,' he said quietly.

'Is everything in order in those businesses?'

'Yes, as far as I know.'

'You don't have a betting-shop manager who's been into the till and is about to be rumbled? Or a taxi controller who's been creaming off the takings?'

'No.'

McIlhenney looked sideways at Dave Donaldson. The Superintendent, still white-faced, nodded to him to carry on. 'This is all very new for us too, Dougie,' he said, 'your answering questions like this. We're not used to believing you. So just to be on the safe side, we'd like to have our experts look at the books and records of the businesses you manage for Jackie Charles.'

'Fair enough,' said Terry. 'If Mr Charles agrees.'

'He will, though. I mean, we're investigating his wife's murder.' McIlhenney paused. 'When we do that, Dougie, we're not going to find that you've been at it, are we? It wasn't you that tried to kill Jackie, was it?'

The man's jaw clenched. He seemed about to explode. 'Listen you . . .'

McIlhenney held up a hand. 'I know. I know. You're going to say that Jackie Charles is like a brother to you, and anyway, you're an honest businessman with a professional reputation and all that stuff.

'In that case, we won't bother to ask you about all the other things that we know you do for Jackie. There'd be no point in asking if somebody was after a share of the big money to be made out of the minicab business, or if somebody else wanted to take a percentage for funding armed robberies.

'If we did that, you'd just start telling jokes again, wouldn't you.'

Dougie Terry, his composure recovered, smiled at McIlhenney and sang the first four lines of 'My Way'.

The Sergeant applauded, silently. 'Pitch perfect, Dougie. The voice is as good as ever. Sorry we can't stay for more. We're off now, but do us a favour, will you? Make sure that all the books and records of Jackie's businesses are ready for our people by close of play today.

'Oh aye, and that includes the details of his property investment company, the one that holds those flats he lets out. Rent books and everything, so we can see what's occupied and what isn't. You never know. Damp housing can drive tenants to extreme measures!'

The policemen stood and made to leave. Donaldson was at the door when he turned. 'I wonder if you've considered this, Mr Terry. Hypothetically, of course. If Mr Charles did have criminal connections, and some of them were upset with him, you don't suppose, do you, that if they found they couldn't get to the organ-grinder, they'd come after the monkey instead?' He smiled, but in a way that was more threatening than anything else.

'Do you know the words to "Mack the Knife"?' he asked. 'Maybe you should add that to your repertoire.'

With McIlhenney at his heels, he stepped out of the office, leaving the Comedian at a loss for a punchline.

17

'Have you ever gone in for weights and the like, Sammy?' asked Detective Chief Inspector Rose.

'Me, ma'am? No, I've never fancied it. Running's my game; that and a bit of squash. I did karate when I was younger though.'

'You should start again. Join the club at headquarters; Mr Skinner helped start it years back. He still keeps it up; says it's the best combined physical and mental exercise there is.'

Detective Constable Pye nodded down the line of weight-training apparatus. 'That's right, ma'am. I reckon that the guys who go in for this sort of stuff are only trying to make up for other shortcomings.'

'That's interesting,' said Maggie Rose. She paused. 'My husband lifts weights. Have you met him? DI McGuire in Special Branch. Big bloke. I must tell him about your theory.' Sammy Pye fell suddenly silent.

Smiling still, the Detective Chief Inspector looked around the Royal Commonwealth Pool fitness suite. Although it was late morning, six men and two women were exercising on the machines, making their way through arduous circuits, working on a different group of muscles each time. The heavy smells of sweat and analgesic sprays mingled in the air.

'Hello.' The voice came from behind them. 'Sorry to have kept you waiting. I'm Simon Horner, the manager. What can I do for you?'

Maggie Rose shook the outstretched hand, introducing herself and Pye. 'We're looking for someone who used to train here,' she said. 'We don't have a name, but we do have a good description. A man with a big moustache, and a distinctive tattoo of a vulture on his shoulder. Does that ring any bells?'

Horner pondered for few seconds, clutching his chin as if it were an aid to concentration. 'A vulture, eh? We get a lot of tattoos in here. We had a burst of Pocahontases a year or two back, and a few Lion Kings before that. There's loads of snakes wound round daggers, eagles and other stuff. I've even seen a unicorn. But I don't remember a vulture.'

'When was your man here last?'

'Around three years ago, we think,' said Rose.

'Mmm,' said the manager. 'I was only appointed two years ago. Maybe you should ask my predecessor, Calum Berwick. He's down at Meadowbank Stadium now.'

'We'll do that.' The Inspector paused. 'If he can't help us find this man, how many other weight-training places are there in Edinburgh for us to cover?'

Horner shrugged his shoulders. 'I'm guessing, but if you count the other sports centres, private clubs, colleges, office and factory facilities, there must be upwards of a hundred.'

Maggie Rose sniffed the pungent air. 'Thanks,' she said, wryly. 'You've made our day.'

18

James Andrew Skinner cast himself off from the armchair which served as his leaning post, and stepped, teetering, tottering, towards his father, who was seated on the edge of the couch in the sitting room at Fairyhouse Avenue.

There was a look of triumphant achievement on the child's face as his forward momentum carried him almost at a run into Bob's outstretched hands.

'What a boy!' said his father as he caught him. 'Going on ten months and practically running! We are going to have to watch you like a hawk from now on. Aren't we, Tracey?' He looked over his shoulder at the young Australian nanny, who stood in the doorway.

'That's right, Mr Skinner. Now that he's found his feet, he'll be all over the house. I think it would be a good idea to have a gate fitted at the top of the stairs. I put him in his cot for a sleep this morning, and the little so-and-so climbed right out again and headed for the door.'

Bob nodded, hefting his son up to his shoulder. 'You do that straight away. Pick the nearest joiner out of *Yellow Pages* and ask him to fit something up right away, no later than first thing Monday.' He peered at the baby, nose to nose. 'Meantime, you stay away from the stairs, understand?'

'S'airs,' said Jazz, adding yet another new sound, if not quite a word, to his vocabulary.

The girl looked puzzled. 'Joiner?'

He smiled. 'Sorry, Trace. I suppose that's carpenter in Australian. Let Sarah know about it when she comes in tonight.' He hesitated. 'I'll be out at the cottage for the next few days. I've got some things to do, and I'm better off out there.'

He knew that he was not fooling the sharply intelligent girl, but she simply nodded. 'I'll get the phone book. Meantime, Jazz's lunch is in the kitchen. There's a sandwich there for you too. Corned beef. That all right?'

'Of course. Thanks, lass. You didn't need to do that. Maybe I'll come home for lunch more often from now on.'

He carried his son into the kitchen, fitted him into a high feeding chair, and began to spoon scrambled egg into his mouth. The child ate ravenously, demandingly. Bob's sandwich lay untouched on the table.

Father and son were both so intent on the serious business of lunch that each looked round startled when the door to the garden opened. 'Hi,' said Sarah, unsmiling until she reached Jazz. 'Hello, Big Boy. Got a new nanny, huh?' She leaned over to kiss him, and ruffled his fine fair hair. 'Mamma!' said Jazz, spraying yellow crumbs of scrambled egg.

Automatically, Bob reached out a hand to her. Nimbly she rolled away from his touch.

'Is this going to be the routine from now on?' she asked quietly.

He nodded. 'Whenever I can, I'll visit him at lunchtime. After work too, if it's not too late and it's okay with you.'

'It's okay, on one condition. That we don't discuss anything other than Jazz and any personal arrangements we need to make. I don't want to hear another word about Myra, or her death, or your Goddamn misplaced sense of duty and loyalty.' Her voice was cold and bitter.

'Yes, yes, yes,' he said quickly, to placate her. 'That's agreed.' A shout from Jazz took him back to his task. He fed the child another spoonful and looked up at Sarah. 'What are we going to do, love?' he asked earnestly.

'I don't know,' she said. 'And don't call me love until you can make me believe you mean it again. I don't know about *we*. I do know one thing that *I*'m going to do. In fact, I've done it already. I've quit my job at the University. Vacation starts on Monday. Next semester is all revision work for my students. I told the Principal today that if he can find someone to handle that, I'd like not to come back after the break.'

'How did he take that?'

She shrugged. 'He was disappointed, but he understood. I told him that my life was changing, that you and I had separated and that . . .'

He looked at her, taken aback. 'You told that f—' He caught himself at her frown, and fed Jazz the last of the scrambled egg. 'You told that old windbag. Christ, it'll be all over the New Club before the day's out.'

'Then maybe you'd better put in an appearance there, to confirm it.' She looked at him, a touch of sympathy creeping into her eyes. 'Bob, you'd better start thinking in those terms, because that's what's happened. That's the choice you, okay we, made, and it's only us, the two of us together, who can unmake it. Right now, even if you wanted that, I'm pretty sure that I don't.'

He turned and reached for the apple purée which Tracey had blended as Jazz's dessert. Keeping his voice as casual as he could, he asked, 'Do you want to formalise things, then?'

She shook her head. 'I don't see the need for that . . . not at this stage anyway. If either one of us decides later on that it has to be permanent, then we can get lawyers involved. Till then, let's keep it between us.'

On cue, and as if maliciously, the phone rang. Sarah picked it up. 'Hello. Yes, he's here.' She held the instrument out to him. 'It's Alan Royston.'

He took it from her. 'Yes, Alan.' As he spoke an image of Royston and Pamela Masters came into his mind, taking him by surprise.

'I'm sorry about this, sir . . .' The police press officer sounded hesitant. 'But I've just had a call from the Editor of the *Scotsman*. She's attending a lunch at the University, and she was told up there that you and Sarah have separated. I asked for her source, of course, but she wouldn't tell me who it was.

'I hate to bring this to you, but—'

Skinner cut him off short. 'Alan, tell the lady that my wife and I do not discuss private matters in the public press.' He paused. 'Tell her too that she should go back to her source and tell *him* that if I hear one more piece of gossip about this, then his life won't be worth the living!'

19

'Jimmy, don't blame yourself. There's no need. You were misled into doing something that you believed was in my best interests.

'Sarah and I have screwed things up between us. We've both been at fault, and now we need to back off from each other, to see if we can sort it out. And,' Skinner added, 'to let me do something that I have to do.'

He paused, looking across the coffee table at the Chief. 'Do you remember when my wife was killed?'

Sir James Proud sighed. 'Never forget it. I was ACC Operations then. I saw the report myself.'

'Can you remember how the incident was handled by the Procurator Fiscal? I was in a haze around then, but I don't recall there being a Fatal Accident Inquiry.'

'There wasn't, Bob, not a formal court hearing at least. The officers at the scene reported that it was a straightforward loss of control due to excessive speed; no eye-witnesses but no indication of any other vehicle involved. The post mortem confirmed that death was due to crushing injuries to the chest and would have been instantaneous.' He gazed at Skinner.

'I ordered the report completed and sent it to the Fiscal in Edinburgh.'

'Not the deputy in Haddington?'

'No, I sent it over his head. I went straight to the top man and told him I didn't see the need for a full FAI before Sheriff and jury, and that I didn't want one. He agreed.'

'Did you keep a copy of the report,' Skinner asked, quietly.

Sir James shook his head. 'No, I didn't. It was the Fiscal's property, not mine. I sent him the only copy.'

'And were there photographs with it?'

'There were, but I didn't forward them. I sent them back to the photographic unit. I imagine they were destroyed.'

Proud Jimmy looked anxiously at Skinner. 'This is part of what's between you and Sarah, son, isn't it?'

'That's the way she wants to see it,' said the DCC, choosing his words carefully.

The Chief hesitated, studying his friend's face. 'Bob,' he said at last. 'You don't want to get into this. Not after all this time. And you don't want to see that report. Take my word on it.'

'Ah, but I do, Jimmy. I do. I need to see it. You take *my* word on that.'

He stood up and left the room by the side exit. Across the corridor, his secretary's door was open. 'Ruthie,' he asked. 'Would you get me Mr Pettigrew, the Procurator Fiscal, please.'

'Yes, sir, but Brian Mackie and Mario McGuire are waiting in your office.'

'As soon as they've gone, then.'

Mackie and McGuire stood up as he entered the room, but he waved them to the comfortable seats around his low table. 'You'll have read something of the Carole Charles death, I take it,' he began, briskly.

'Yes, boss,' the thin, dome-headed Detective Chief Inspector replied. 'Only press reports, though.'

'My wife told me about it last night, sir,' replied the powerfully built, black-haired McGuire. 'She told me they interviewed someone yesterday.'

'That's right,' said Skinner. 'She and others are following it up today. But DCS Martin and I have a job for Special Branch too. We want you to consult your colleagues in the network around the country, and find out anything you can about anyone with a grudge against John Jackson Charles . . . a big enough grudge to make him a target for murder.

'We need a full report as soon as possible. Consult Andy Martin as you require, but let me know at once of anything you turn up. I'll be at my Gullane number over the weekend, or available on my mobile.' He stood up, almost jumping to his feet.

'That's it, go to it.'

He was buzzing Ruth as the door closed behind the two detectives. Within two minutes, she called him back. 'Mr Pettigrew on the line, sir.'

'Davie,' said Skinner, heartily, as she put the call through. 'How are you doing?'

'I'll be doing better when you give me someone for that fire in Seafield.'

The DCC smiled as he pictured the mournful, black-bearded face at the other end of the line. 'We will, Davie, don't you worry. With a bit of luck, and a bit of time, we might give you more than that.

'But this is about something else. How long does your office keep police reports on accidental deaths? What's the Crown Office rule on retention?'

'There's a certain amount of discretion on that,' said Pettigrew. 'In this office we keep them for at least twenty years.'

Skinner smiled in huge satisfaction. 'Excellent. In that case, I want you to do me a favour, by having some weekend reading couriered to me at Fettes Avenue by close of play today, under Eyes Only cover.

'I want to see the report on the death of my first wife, in a car accident in East Lothian, eighteen years ago.'

'I'll still have it,' said Pettigrew, hesitant, and clearly curious.

'I'll tell you why in due course, Davie. Meantime, it's just possible that you might have a call from my Chief Constable asking you not to let me see that file.

'If that happens, my friend, you're going to have to decide which of the two of us you'd like least to upset!'

20

'Big guy, with a Zapata moustache. I remember him all right. "The Vulture" was what we called him, in fact; on account of that bloody great tattoo.'

Calum Berwick smiled as he stood among the shining apparatus in the weight-training room at Meadowbank Stadium. It was less busy than the Royal Commonwealth Pool facility had been. Only four people were at work, but all were pressing heavy weights, concentrating so hard that none of them appeared to notice the group of three near the door.

Rose glanced down the room and saw, through the glass wall at the far end, a number of athletes pounding round the synthetic track upon which two Commonwealth Games had been celebrated.

'You get the serious people in places like this, the hard trainers, and you get the posers,' said Berwick. 'The Vulture was a bit of both. He could do his stuff on the apparatus okay, but he liked to strut around too, flashing the pecs at the girls, and running off at the mouth.

'I remember hearing him say once that he had the tattoo done when he was in the French Foreign Legion. He was a hard man, by his way of it, but I had him marked down as a bit of a wanker.'

'What age was he?' asked Maggie Rose.

'In his thirties, for sure, but whether early or late, I wouldn't like to say.'

'Can you recall his real name?'

Berwick made a face. 'I was afraid you were going to ask that. I've been trying to remember, but I don't think I ever knew it. There was no membership requirement up there. You just paid and lifted, paid and lifted, every time.'

'Have you ever seen him here?'

The manager shook his head. 'No. Not once. And I'd have remembered that bloody tattoo for sure, if I'd seen it.'

'Up at the Commonwealth,' asked Pye, 'did you ever hear him speak of anywhere else he might have trained?'

Berwick considered the question for a few moments. 'No, I can't say that I did. But the guy worked out a lot. Big circuits at least three times a week, daily at some times. I doubt if he'd be training anywhere else at that time.'

'Yet he just stopped turning up,' said Rose.

'So it seems, if Simon doesn't know him. He must have joined a club. A lot of the serious guys do. It can work out cheaper than here in the long run.'

'That's just great,' said the Chief Inspector. 'We'll have to start working our way round them.'

Berwick began to head for the door. 'One thing more,' Rose called out. 'Do you remember a guy named Carl Medina from your days at the Commonwealth?'

'Carl? Sure, he was one of my regulars up there. He comes here too on occasion, on the special unemployed concessionary rate. Nice guy, quiet. He's not a body-builder; just trains to keep fit.'

131

'Is he the sort of guy who'd have associated with the Vulture.'

Berwick shook his head, emphatically. 'No. He's the sort of guy the Vulture would have tried to impress.'

He escorted the two detectives to the stadium's foyer, waving them goodbye, as he trotted back down the stairs to his office. Rose and Pye stood alone in the big entrance hallway.

'Got that list of clubs, then, Sammy?' asked Rose, slightly wearily.

'Yes, ma'am,' said Pye. 'But before we start, there's something I wondered if we might try.'

'What's that?'

'Well . . .' The Detective Constable hesitated. 'This guy was a regular at the Commonwealth Pool until three years ago, then all of a sudden he just dropped out of sight.'

'So,' said the DCI, 'd'you think he might have re-enlisted in the Foreign Legion?'

Sammy Pye smiled. 'Maybe he did, ma'am. Or maybe he got lifted. Maybe he's in the nick.'

Rose looked up at the young man. 'That's good thinking, Sammy. I'm seriously impressed. Let's try the Prison Service. If we get lucky, we'll have saved ourselves a lot of legwork.'

21

'I wish we could put a tap on Jackie Charles' phone,' said Neil McIlhenney. 'We threw a few scares into Dougie Terry this morning. I'll bet the first thing he did after we left was get on the blower to his gaffer.'

'I hope it was,' replied Andy Martin. 'The two of them would have been expecting us to ask for clearance to look at his books for evidence of embezzlement and the like, but asking to see the records of his property company, that's different. That will have taken them by surprise, and that's why – you're right Neil, I'm sure that's what he did – Terry would have been on the phone to Jackie.'

'We don't need a tap to work that out. Charles certainly didn't bat an eyelid when the Boss and I asked for access. He didn't think it over for a second: just said yes.'

Skinner rose from the uncomfortable seat in Dave Donaldson's office in the St Leonard's Police Office. The building was new but much of the furniture had come from the old High Street station. Months after his stabbing and the major surgery which had saved his life, the DCC still found it painful to sit on hard chairs for too long. 'Anyway, Neil,' he said, 'it should never be made too easy for us to listen in on someone's telephone. We've never established reasonable cause or evidence sufficient for us to ask for wire-tap authorisation on Charles.

'If you could plug into his line, just like that, how would you know that I couldn't plug into yours?'

The big Sergeant grinned back at him. 'I wouldn't know that, sir. I don't know that you can't. But if you did, your ears would be sore in no time from listening to my Olive blethering on to her mates.'

None of the three others in the room had actually met Mrs McIlhenney, but the awe in which her husband professed to hold her had made her a figure of formidable legend among his colleagues.

'Seriously, though, sir,' said McIlhenney. 'It'd be worth hearing what the Comedian was saying to anyone right now. He didn't see the funny side when Mr Donaldson suggested that he might be a consolation prize for whoever failed to kill Jackie.'

Skinner's eyebrows rose and he looked across at Donaldson. 'Why did you say that?'

'To see if he runs, sir,' said the Superintendent.

'So far he's stayed put.'

'Then suppose that's because he's our fire-raiser?'

Skinner shook his head. 'He isn't. I don't believe that for one second.'

'What makes you so sure, boss?' asked Donaldson. 'Does Charles have some sort of hold over him that the rest of us don't know about?'

'Yes,' said the DCC, with the faintest trace of impatience. 'I've known this pair for twenty years, and I think he does. Three holds, in fact. They're called loyalty, friendship and gratitude. Terry's done a good job for Jackie over the years and he's been well rewarded for it. Look at the Jag, the big house in Torphichen, the expensive suits. He actually likes Charles, and Charles likes him. The guy's too loyal to have been bought.'

The Superintendent looked at him. 'Maybe that loyalty will go if we can find something solid to nail Terry with. Maybe he'll give Jackie up then.'

'Maybe he will. So let's hope that Maggie can find this guy with the vulture on his shoulder, or that we get something from these notes the man Medina is bringing in.

'Speaking of whom . . .' He glanced at his watch: it was twenty-three minutes past four. 'He should be here by now.'

'Can't be, boss,' said Donaldson. 'I gave specific instructions that I was to be advised the second he arrived.'

Andy Martin looked at him, then across to McIlhenney. 'In that case, gentlemen,' he said, 'why are you sitting here? Let's not await Mr Medina's pleasure. Go and bring him in.'

22

'Let me get this straight,' said Sonia Cunningham. 'You're looking for someone and all you know about him is that he may have a moustache and he still has a tattoo.'

'That just about sums it up,' said Maggie Rose, cheerfully.

Behind her desk in the airy office, which looked across towards the Gyle Shopping Centre, its car parks teeming with Friday evening shoppers, the Grade Four officer in the Scottish Prison Service Agency shook her neatly-coiffured head. She was in her early fifties, but her complexion was younger, her age hinted at only by the deep laugh lines around her eyes. They creased as she spoke. 'You've just described more or less the entire male prison population . . . and a few of the women as well!'

'But this is a very distinctive tattoo, we're told, on his right shoulder. We're hoping that you have a description of it among your records.'

'That's possible,' said Miss Cunningham, 'but it's a long shot. We list distinguishing marks, but we don't necessarily describe them. And we don't draw diagrams of their positions on prisoners' bodies.

'Still, you're welcome to look through our files. How urgent is this? Can it keep till Monday?'

The Chief Inspector shook her head. 'I don't think so. This relates to a murder investigation.'

'In that case,' said the woman, 'I'll give you each a desk and a terminal, and I'll have someone show you how to access the files.

'But be warned. You could be in for a long, boring and maybe, at the end of it, a fruitless weekend. Scotland's prisons have never been more full!'

23

McIlhenney pressed the Muirhead/Medina button and waited. After a minute, he pressed again. The speaker remained silent.

'Maybe he's turned up at St Leonard's,' said the Sergeant at last, more in hope than expectation.

'No,' said Donaldson. 'We'd have had a call on the mobile if he had arrived.'

'Then let's get in and have a look.' Simultaneously, McIlhenney pressed three other buzzers. A few seconds later an elderly lady's voice quavered from the tinny speaker.

'Yes?'

'Gas Board emergency,' said the Sergeant, quickly. 'Let us in, please.'

'Oh! Oh. Yes.'

There was a hum from the lock and he pushed the entrance door open. 'Where is it?' he asked Donaldson.

'Two floors up. Level three, flat C. This way.' He led the bulky McIlhenney towards the stairway, up the steps at a trot, two at a time.

When they reached flat 3c, the door was closed. The Sergeant, slightly out of breath, rapped the letterbox knocker, hard, shouting as he did. 'Mr Medina, are you in?'

The door swung open with the force of the knock. To his astonishment McIlhenney saw that its frame was splintered and that the keeper of the Yale lock was hanging awkwardly and loosely. He stepped into the gloomy hallway.

Carl Medina was in.

He lay on his back, a few feet from the doorway, slack-jawed, his dull glazed eyes staring at the ceiling with an expression of pure astonishment. At first McIlhenney thought that the man was wearing a particularly garish red tee-shirt, until Donaldson, behind him, switched on the hall light and he saw that the once-grey garment was saturated with blood, and until the stink of violent death attacked his nostrils.

'Ahhh, you bastard!' the Sergeant hissed. 'What's this about, then?'

Hardened to such scenes, he took a deep breath, leaned over the body and looked, professionally and dispassionately. He counted four large stab wounds in Medina's chest and abdomen. One of them had ripped open his belly, and several feet of twisted intestine had spilled out from the gash, like glistening, gory intertwined snakes.

He stood up and, as he did, he felt the bloody carpet squelch under his feet. 'Want to take a quick look round, sir?' he asked.

Donaldson shook his head. 'No. Let's play it by the book. I'll call the DCS, then the scene of crime team and the ME. We don't want to contaminate the site. Let's just wait outside until everyone else gets here.' He backed out through the front door.

As McIlhenney turned to follow, his eye was caught by a number of rusty brown marks on the beige carpet of the entrance hallway, and by a black plastic object lying in a corner.

'Mind your feet, sir,' he barked. 'Those marks on the floor look like bloodstains. And what's that?'

As Donaldson froze and stood stock-still, the Sergeant, wary himself of leaving fresh marks, tiptoed around the stains on the carpet and, carefully, picked up the black plastic sheet. At once he realised that it was a binliner. As he lifted it a number of smaller bags fell out, crumpled up together and streaked with drying blood.

'What the hell!' he exclaimed, holding the binliner at arm's length and turning it inside out. Holes had been cut in the top and in the sides. 'The clever bastard. He's worn this thing like an overall and the supermarket bags over his forearms and his feet, to keep the blood off his clothes and his shoes, and to avoid leaving any trace of himself.

'Once he was done, the bugger just stripped them off and walked away.'

'Maybe the plastic bags will give us a lead,' said Donaldson.

'Maybe,' muttered the Sergeant, with an edge of irreverent sarcasm in his tone, 'if we start by lifting everyone that's shopped in Safeway over the last few months.'

The Superintendent shot him a look which was intended to be reproving but failed, then produced his mobile phone from his pocket and dialled DCS Martin's direct line number.

McIlhenney listened as he described their discovery. 'No, sir,' he heard him say. 'It doesn't look as if the man had a chance. Somehow the killer got into the building and knocked on Medina's door. As soon as he started to open it he smashed his way in and attacked him.

'From the looks of it, any one of these wounds would have been fatal.'

He paused. 'No, sir, we haven't gone in any further than the front door. Yes, we'll wait for Arthur Dorward's team, and for you to get here.'

24

A chill ran through Bob Skinner as he looked at Medina's corpse. In another place, a few months before, with only a slightly different outcome he could have been lying like Medina, staring up into eternity with dispassionate, white-clad detectives working quietly around his body.

He gave a small shudder and the moment passed.

'Like you said, Dave,' he said. 'The boy didn't have a chance. Any guesses about how the killer got into the building?'

'All the entrances are secure, boss, but he could have done it like we did: pressed any bell and said he was the postman. Or, he could have been someone Medina was expecting.'

Skinner frowned. 'Don't fancy that. In that case the victim would probably have been at the door waiting for him by the time he climbed the stairs, and he wouldn't have been taken by surprise. He looks to have been quite a fit lad, too.'

He turned to Dr Banks, who was standing on the other side of the body. 'Got any idea of the time of death, doctor?'

Banks looked hesitant, as usual. 'Well, as you know it's hard to be precise.'

'Well don't be precise, man,' the Deputy Chief Constable snapped. 'For once, just fucking guess!'

The doctor flushed. 'Very well. Late morning, I'd say . . . but I won't be bound by that.'

'*No,*' thought Skinner, '*you won't. Yet my wife could give me the time down to the half-hour and probably tell me what the killer had for breakfast.*' Inside him, a river of loss threatened to burst its banks, but with an effort of will he contained it and turned back to his men.

'I don't understand this,' he said. 'We've only got one suspect as the orchestrator of this murder, yet he was the guy who put us on to Medina in the first place. Why would Jackie offer him up as a candidate, and then have him knocked off?

'Is the little shit so arrogant that he's trying to tell us he's more powerful than we are?'

He slammed his right fist into his left palm, the speed of the gesture startling Donaldson. 'If he is, then he's in for a nasty shock. Once and for all, I'm going to get this villain.

'Dave, you, Neil and Dorward's team comb through this place for those notes of Medina's. Don't worry about looking after his girlfriend. I've called Pamela Masters into action earlier than she expected. She's picking her up from her office, breaking the news to her and finding her somewhere else to stay tonight.

'Meantime . . .' he looked at DCS Martin, '. . . Andy, let's you and I pay that little bastard Charles a visit!'

25

'Chief Superintendent, Bob; if I'm all of the things which you have been on a mission over the years to prove that I am, then surely the fact that I'm still walking about shows that I have just a wee bit of intelligence.'

Jackie Charles looked at the two detectives coldly, with the self-assured expression of a successful general.

'If that is accepted,' he said, 'you can't think, surely, I would be so stupid as to mention my connection with this man Medina to you and then do something like this?'

Skinner stared back at him. 'Jackie, where you're concerned, I wouldn't discount anything. You're one of the most villainous bastards I've ever met in my life. You stand here in your fine house, waving your old school tie, and maintaining your honest business front.

'In reality you've been behind just about every crime in the book. If something had happened since yesterday to make you think that Medina was a danger, I wouldn't, for one second, put it past you to have had him killed. So far, that's our principal theory.' He walked over to the window of Charles' study, on the villa's upper floor, and looked out, westwards, over Murrayfield Golf Course.

'The question is, what could have happened to make you pop the boy. Try this for size. After our people saw Dougie

Terry this morning, he was straight on to the phone to you. That much I know. Telecom have confirmed that a call was made from his number to your mobile, around the time our guys left Stafford Street.

'I reckon that something could have been said during that interview which made you think that Medina was a risk after all. Something they asked for upset you, made you think that it might lead us to something which your former book-keeper might have seen in your wife's possession, and might have been able to identify in court, for all that the entries were in coded language, as being connected to you.'

He glanced at Andy Martin, then gazed back again at Charles, harder than ever, but the man stood his ground. 'Maybe Carole told you once that she thought Medina might have seen this thing. Maybe then you thought little of it. Maybe today you changed your mind.'

Jackie Charles leaned against his handmade desk and picked a piece of dark fluff from his coral pink Pringle sweater. Then he looked up at Skinner and said, quietly and with the same assurance as before, 'If that's your principal theory, Bob, then you'd better get another. Because I had absolutely nothing to do with this man's death.'

The DCC shook his head. 'No, no, Jackie, we're not letting you off the hook.' He looked out of the window once more. 'I'll tell you something,' he said, over his shoulder, 'although you may have worked it out already.

'I've got a reputation for being a bit volatile: short-fused, you know. But Andy here knows me better than anyone, and he'll tell you that I'm the most patient man in the world. When it comes to crime, I think long-term. I see criminals as my mortal enemies, and in pursuing them I never get discouraged, and I never give up.'

He turned and he smiled: a hangman's smile. He raised a hand, palm upward, fingers curling. 'I have this guiding principle, you see. I believe that if I'm patient, and if I wait long enough, then one day, God will deliver the balls of my enemy into my strong right hand.

'Be in no doubt: when that happens, I don't even try to resist the temptation to squeeze as hard as I can!' As he closed his powerful fist, tight, Jackie Charles, in spite of himself, winced.

He walked towards the door, Martin beside him. 'Your turn's coming, Jackie. It's coming soon. And when it does, I'll be using *both* hands.'

The two policemen hurried down the stairs and out of the house, to Skinner's car which was parked at the head of the driveway.

'Sir,' said Martin, formally, and with a touch of caution. 'You've had Charles in your sights for a long time now. We'll get him eventually, but as far as you're concerned, don't you think you're becoming a bit . . .'

'Obsessional, you were going to say.' The DCC shook his head and laughed. 'Christ, everyone's accusing me of that these days.

'This time, you might be right though. I'd forgotten how much I hate that wee bastard. I have done, I think, from the first moment I ever saw him, and I'm quite certain that I always will. In fact the cold-hearted way that he's accepted his wife's death has made it worse.

'I've got half a mind to take him down to the mortuary, and make him look at her body. Only I'm pretty certain that it wouldn't faze him one bit.

'Maybe you should keep me at arm's length from this investigation from now on, Andy, for everyone's sake, mine included. Keep me informed, but through Pamela, not directly. I'll try my best to steer clear of you.'

He switched on the engine and put the car in gear. 'Starting now. Time's getting on. I have something to pick up from headquarters, then I want to look in to say goodnight to my son.

'Last of all, I have a date with my daughter.'

26

It was another fine evening. The lights of Edinburgh shone brightly across the dark waters of the Forth Estuary as Bob gazed out of the dining-room window of the Green Craigs Hotel. Across the table, his daughter sat quietly, her coffee cooling in its cup.

'So that's the story, Alexis.

'That's why I'm out here, and that's why Sarah and your wee brother are in Edinburgh. Irreconcilable differences, you lawyers call it.'

Alex looked at him anxiously. 'Come on, Pops. Not irreconcilable, surely? You can work things out between you. Look, I know you think that what Sarah did was wrong, and if you force me to it, I agree with you.

'But you have to ask yourself why she did it. Surely it was for you, because she was worried about you and because she loves you.'

He looked back from the window. 'I wish it was as easy as that, sweetheart, I really do. You think I didn't ask myself why she did it? I did, and I asked her, and I saw the same answer both times.

'Sarah didn't manipulate your Uncle Jimmy for me, she did it for *her*, to stop *me* from doing something *she* didn't want me to do. Because that something involves your mother.

'I can't reconcile that with the Sarah I fell in love with and married. It's a part of her I didn't know was there. She looks at me now and she sees a different man, and that's true too. But . . .'

He paused and looked across at her and she could see the depth of his hurt. 'Alex, am I a selfish man?' he asked, quietly.

She looked at him and shook her flowing, wavy locks. 'Pops, you . . . and my fiancé . . . are the two least selfish men I know.'

'Well that's not how Sarah sees it. By her way of it I am selfish in my determination to investigate your mother's death. Yet when I try to explain to her that this is something that I have to do, she won't see it that way. She sees it as my own selfish mission.

'"Myra is dead. Let her stay dead." That's what she demands. As if I could bring her back to life!' He said it suddenly and bitterly.

He reached across the table and squeezed his daughter's hand. 'Come on. Let's go back to Gullane. There's something I want to show you.'

He paid the bill and they drove home, up the mile-long straight and through Aberlady. They sat in gathering silence. As Bob steered smoothly round the curve where Myra had died, it became unbearable.

'I miss her too, Pops,' said Alex at last, her faced framed in the amber glow of the dashboard. 'Every day of my life I think of her. All those years, when you were being father and mother rolled into one I still couldn't help missing Mum.' Her voice faltered.

'I never expected you to stop missing her, my darling,' Bob whispered. 'It's just that I did my best not to, myself. But now the dam has burst.'

The Goose Green was quiet as usual, as he parked in front of the cottage, beside Alex's Metro, and led her indoors.

The projector was set up on the dining-room table, a reel of film loaded and ready to run. He sat Alex down on a straight-backed dining chair and turned off the lights. 'I want you to see this,' he said.

The film flickered white at first then into life. Alex stared at the beautiful young woman in her strikingly effective bikini. As the camera shot widened and panned out she recognised Gullane beach, thronged with day trippers on a bright summer's day. The tide was almost full.

Her hand went to her mouth as she saw the toddler. The little girl, wearing nothing but a sun-hat and a smile, as she lurched and staggered in the sand, falling backwards, laughing, at her mother's feet.

The film rolled on. When it finished and Bob switched on the light, she was in tears. 'Oh Pops,' she said, quietly as he stilled the spinning reel. 'How beautiful she was. The photos don't do her any sort of justice.'

'No,' said Bob, quietly. 'They don't, do they. She was *alive*, your mother, in a way that very few people are. She was bright, funny, wanton and loving. She lit the place up. We had only lived here for a few years, but the whole village turned out for her funeral. Everybody.' He smiled. 'Even a certain wee man that your fiancé is currently trying very hard to lock up. I remember how touched I was by the turnout, and I remember noticing how shocked everyone was.'

He began to rewind the film. 'There are more movies of

the two of you together,' he said, 'and others as well. I'll have them all transferred to video, save one. That'll come to you after I'm dead.

'Meantime – and it'll be a long meantime, mind – there's something else I want you to have. It's under the table, out of the way.'

Alex looked down, and saw the trunk. 'That? It's the old box from the attic. The one you told me not to touch. You were so serious about it that I never dared.

'What's in it?'

Her father reached across the table and squeezed her hand once again. 'Your mother's life is in it. Everything about her. Her Highers certificate, her College diploma, her photographs, records of her teaching career, some of her favourite books, some of her clothes: I put them all in there after she died, in a sort of time capsule. With them, you'll find the diaries that she kept so faithfully all her years. Everything of her is in there.

'I could never bring myself to reopen it, save once. I should have given it to you a long time ago. I want you to take it now, away from here; through to Glasgow, not to Andy's.

'When you're alone, and only then, open it, and go through everything. Learn about your mother. Read the diaries. I suppose she was writing them for you, in a way, writing down all the things she did, that we did, that we talked about.

'When you've finished, you should decide what's to be done with everything that's in there. Whether you should keep it, to show your daughter eventually; whether some things should come back to me. Each of those decisions will be yours.'

He pulled the trunk from under the table and stood it on end. Alex heard its contents shift inside. 'Open the door,' he said, 'and I'll carry it out to your car. It's been gathering dust for far too long.'

'Okay,' said his daughter. 'I was going to stay tonight, if you wanted, but if you don't mind I'll go back through to Glasgow now. Andy isn't expecting me or anything.'

She hugged him as he stood there. 'Pops, I don't know what to say. But somehow, I think it was right of you to keep the box upstairs till now. I don't know if I'd have been able to handle it before. Even now, I'm not sure how I'll feel. I only know that this will be the most private thing I've ever done.

'You sure you don't mind if I go?'

'Not a bit, love. You do what you have to do.' He nodded towards a big brown envelope which lay on the table. 'Anyway, I've got some reading of my own to do.

'But not tonight, I think. That I have to keep for the morning light.'

27

The midnight oil was burning in the Scottish Prison Service headquarters. Maggie Rose and Sammy Pye sat before computer terminals at adjacent desks, in a big open-plan office, lit only by neon tubes over each exit and by the glow from their screens.

They were finishing the third round of coffees provided by sympathetic security guards, surrounded by the remnants of Burger Kings fetched by Pye from the Gyle Centre four hours earlier.

'You'd think, ma'am, wouldn't you,' said the Detective Constable, 'that in this day and age there would be a simpler tracing system than going through every individual file.'

Rose groaned her agreement. 'It would be nice, wouldn't it, if we could just key "Vulture" into the system and press a button. But no, we have to open and read every file. It takes so much time. How far d'you think we've got?'

Pye pulled up a notepad window. 'We're a quarter of the way through, ma'am, that's all.'

'And that quarter has given us three possibles to be followed up, of men listed as having large tattoos on their bodies.'

The Chief Inspector leaned back and switched off her terminal. 'That's it for now, Sammy. I'm cross-eyed. Let's knock off for tonight, and get back here for nine thirty tomorrow morning. The Cunningham woman was right. We are in for a long, boring weekend, and probably a fruitless one. I can see us slogging around those health clubs after all.

'Maybe I'll persuade my husband to come in to help us.' She paused. 'Wait a minute, I outrank him again. Stuff the persuasion, I'll order him!'

28

Alex Skinner sat in the mingling glow of a large red candle and of the gas fire.

The trunk looked even bigger on the floor of the tiny living room in her flat in Glasgow's University district. She stared at it, nursing a long-stemmed wine glass which she held pressed between her breasts.

She sat there for perhaps half an hour, motionless apart from occasional sips from the glass, doing her best to prepare herself mentally to lift the lid on her mother's life, as Adam Duritz sang, unnoticed, from her stereo speakers.

She was alone, as her flatmate had left that afternoon for Easter vacation. The weekend was hers, if she chose. She had intended to spend it with Andy Martin, but he had warned her that he was heavily committed to the Charles investigation.

For most of the life that she could recall, her mother had been a misty, mystical figure. Unknown to Bob, she had begun to hold secret conversations with Myra only a few weeks after her death, as a means of consolation, and of keeping the pain of bereavement under control.

Over the years she had kept her mother alive in her heart, as best she could. Now she had seen her again for herself, she realised that the mother she had made into an imaginary friend had been no more than a candy floss fantasy beside the real Myra, a woman whose vitality had proclaimed itself like a fanfare, even from the flickery old cine film.

She had remembered her hair, her face, her soft breath, her smell, but the power of her mother's personality had been beyond her comprehension at the time of her death. In the film shot on the beach, when she had taken over the camera, her father had seemed to be completely under her spell. Now so was Alex, once again.

She thought of the diaries. What would she see, through these windows into her dead mother's soul?

For a while, she considered going to bed, and leaving her reading for the morning, like her father. But a mix of daring and curiosity overwhelmed her. She switched on the overhead light, and opened the box.

Everything inside was in brown paper parcels, save for a pair of black high-heeled shoes, and a maroon-coloured tube containing, Alex guessed, her mother's College diploma.

She picked out one parcel. It rattled as she lifted it. She squeezed and shook it and felt the round surfaces of bracelets and necklaces. She replaced it and took out another which yielded to her touch, until she encountered a curving wire which she guessed to be the support of a brassiere cup.

She took out the biggest parcel of all. It was heavy and her touch told her that it contained a number of rectangular objects, tightly bound together. Eagerly she tore it open, and found inside a series of A4 hard-covered volumes, bound with yellow twine into two bundles. They were ordinary page-per-day, stationer's desk diaries, some blue, some black, some red, some green, each with the year in gold lettering on the front.

She looked at the bundles and counted seven in each; fourteen diaries in all, bound together in chronological order. Her mother had been almost twenty-eight when she died; she had begun to keep her diaries in her fifteenth year.

Alex took a deep breath and refilled her glass with Fleurie. Picking up the first bundle, she slid the first volume out without untying the twine.

She settled into her comfortable armchair, opened the diary and began to read.

29

'Some day this job might pay us back all the lost weekends it owes us,' said Detective Chief Superintendent Martin.

'Some day,' said Dave Donaldson.

'Some hope,' said Neil McIlhenney. 'Anyway, what if it did. Can you imagine a hundred and forty-two consecutive weekends, all strung together, of being dragged round the Gyle Centre by the wife, with the kids yapping at your feet?

'That's one thing about really bloody high-profile murders; they're great for getting you out of the way of drudgery.'

Donaldson laughed. 'How many kids do you have, Neil?'

'Two. Lauren's nine, and Spencer's seven.

'The things we do to kids, eh. Olive named the first one after a model, and she turned out to be wee and fat. The second one she named after a shop, believe it or not. We were rolling along Princes Street one day, with Lauren in the pram and Herself about ten months pregnant, when all of a sudden she stops. I thought she was starting there and then, like, but no, she was staring up at the Marks and Spencer sign with her mouth hanging open. "Look," she says, "isn't that a lovely name when you read it? That's what we'll call him." "Mark?" says I. "Okay." She looked at me as if I was daft.' He paused with a slow smile.

'I often think to myself how lucky it was that we'd made it that far along Princes Street. I'd have hated the poor wee bugger to go through life called Littlewood McIlhenney!

'How about you, sir? How many kids have you got?'

'Jane and I have four,' said Donaldson. 'Tony's seven, like your lad, then there's Janet, she's five, Stephanie, just turned four, and Ryan, eighteen months.'

'You should be on schedule for another quite soon,' said Martin, grinning.

'Don't joke,' muttered the Superintendent, sleek-haired and well-groomed even though it was just after eight o'clock on a Saturday morning. 'Jane's expecting in three months. Another boy, we've been told.'

'Maybe you should call this one Luke,' said McIlhenney. His companions stared at him, puzzled. 'As in "Luke, enough's enough, okay!"'

'So it is,' said Martin, laughing and shaking his head. 'Now down to business.' He glanced around the mobile incident room in which they sat. It had been set up in the car park alongside the block of flats in which Carl Medina had died. The Chief Superintendent looked across the table at the fourth man in the room. 'Arthur, would you give us a summary of what you found at the scene, please.'

'Yes, sir,' said Inspector Dorward. 'First of all, as you supposed, Medina was overwhelmed at once by an unexpected, violent attack. The post mortem is being held this morning, but that's just a formality.

'We've established that just before midday an old lady on the top floor answered a buzzer call from someone saying he had come to read the electricity meters. She let him in, but he never arrived.'

'Did anything strike you about the style of the attack?' asked Martin. 'Was there any trademark, any sort of signature?'

'No, sir. There was no frenzy about this attack. It was cold, calculated and very efficient. The perpetrator went there specifically to kill Carl Medina. After the killing the flat was searched. There were traces of the victim's blood all around, transferred by the plastic bags which the killer wore on his hands and feet.

'The search was concentrated in a specific area, among papers and notes kept by the victim. They had been ransacked. Of course, we have no way of telling whether or not the killer found what he was looking for.'

'Did our man leave any forensic traces?' asked Donaldson.

Dorward smiled. 'We went over that house all night, and didn't find a thing. Not a scrap.' He paused, as if for effect. 'Then we looked at the inside of the binliner. Nothing.

'Finally we looked at the four Safeway bags. Inside one of them, we found a fifth bag. It had eye-holes cut in it, making it clear that the killer wore this bag as a hood. Attached to it, on the inside, we found a single strand of hair.

'We've established already that the strand didn't come from the victim, or from his girlfriend. We've no way of establishing where it did come from, short of possibly testing every Safeway checkout person in Edinburgh.

'Right now, we can't tell whether the hair came from our killer. But when we find him, if it's his, it'll help put him away for life.'

Martin smiled. 'Wonderful, Arthur. We've actually got

some evidence; good old-fashioned evidence for your new DNA technology to work on.

'Arthur, you and I will go together to obtain hair samples from Jackie Charles and Dougie Terry. We'll promise them if we have to that if the tests prove negative the samples will be destroyed afterwards and that no DNA information will be retained.

'There isn't a cat's chance that we'll get a match from either, but let's do it just to keep the pressure on them.'

He leaned back in his hard chair. 'The Boss gave Jackie a good going over last night, but he still couldn't get near him.' He paused. 'In fact, the wee bugger almost had me believing that he didn't know a thing about Medina's death. That reminded me that we mustn't put all our eggs in one basket in this investigation.

'Where's the girl Muirhead?' he asked suddenly.

'Pamela Masters took her to a friend's place in Learmonth Terrace,' said Donaldson.

'Okay, you and Neil go along and interview her,' said Martin. 'As gently as you can, but keep it formal. You don't need to pull her in to St Leonard's, but make it clear that it's more than just a sympathetic chat. Ask her to tell you everything she knows about Medina. Then lean on her just a wee bit.

'You never know, Medina might have had a rival, someone who fancied Ms Muirhead, with or without her encouragement. And maybe, that rival . . .'

'Cut up rough, sir?' said Neil McIlhenney.

30

Alex awoke with a start. The room was hot and clammy from the Cannon Gasmiser, although it was burning only at medium output. The heavy curtains were drawn, and the reading lamp shone over her shoulder, its beam focused on the volume in her lap.

She shook her head, completely disorientated and still slightly woozy, and blinked hard. She looked up at the clock on the wooden mantelpiece, and saw that it showed five minutes before nine.

She stared at the curtained window, her confusion turning into slight alarm. Quickly she put the book to one side, rushed to the window, and threw the curtains wide. She cried out with relief as the light of the Glasgow morning flooded in. 'Thank the Lord for that. I thought I'd lost a day.'

And then the memories of the night before came flooding back. Supper with her father, the shock of the cine film, his presentation of the trunk . . . and her mother's diaries.

She jumped as the phone rang. For a moment she thought of letting it go unanswered, but finally she picked it up.

'Alex?'

'Andy! Morning, love. Where are you?'

'I'm at work. I thought you'd have stayed at Bob's

last night. I just called his number, but there was no answer.'

'No, I decided to come through here.' She hesitated. 'I've got some studying to do, some intensive reading. I thought I'd tackle it in a one-er over the weekend. You don't mind, do you? If it's any consolation, I've got my period.'

He laughed. 'After the conversation I've just had with McIlhenney and Donaldson that's a big consolation, believe me. Look the fact is, I'm going to be tied up for longer than I thought. Maybe I could come through there when I'm finished. You're alone, aren't you?'

'Yes, but . . .' she hesitated. 'I really have a lot of studying to do. I think I'm better left on my own. You go out with the lads, or whatever you used to do before you had me hanging around. Er, no. On second thoughts don't do that!'

She heard him laugh. 'Okay,' he said. 'I'll get by, don't worry. I'll see you when you're finished.'

'Okay. Bye. Love you.'

She put the phone down and wandered through to her small bathroom, peeling off her stale clothes as she walked. She brushed her teeth, and gargled with a blue mint mouthwash, before stepping into a lukewarm shower. Under the strong spray, she hunched her shoulders to send the water cascading down her back, then leaning back she pressed her arms together to channel it to where she felt most sticky.

Fifteen minutes later, in a clean white tee-shirt and panties, and munching a micro-heated croissant, she felt more or less refreshed. She settled back into her chair, and picked up the diary which she had been reading when she fell asleep.

It was the second of the fourteen volumes. The entries were meticulous, in a young but clear hand, with not a single day, or, it seemed, detail missed. Alex looked at the page, and remembered at once why she had put the diary down at that point.

April 21.

Sixteen at last, and what a day it's been. Mum and Dad were good enough – daft enough – to let me have my party on my own. Campbell came round early and gave me my birthday present. I gave him his, on the carpet in front of the fire. (Well, I'm sixteen now!) I timed him with the second hand on the mantelpiece clock while he was doing it. Seventeen seconds. That is not what it says in the books I've read.

Campbell is quite nice, but he's just like a dog panting around me, and frankly he's hung like one as well. A Chihuahua though, not a Great Dane. The boy Skinner, though, he's different! Quiet and broody, doesn't talk much, but those eyes of his say it all for him. He's supposed to be a bit straight-laced – according to Alice anyway – but I sense hidden depths there.

I sense more than that too. Bob and I had a dance tonight, me in my tight dress and him in his baggy trousers. That wasn't a gun he had in his pocket. It was a cannon!

Campbell didn't like me dancing with him, but what happened to him was his own fault. I've never seen anything like it. It was so exciting!! Then Bob stopped Big Zed in his tracks, with just that look.

What a pity! I'd have liked to see more. I think Bob was disappointed too, the way Zed chickened out. I only just managed to clean up the carpet before Mum and Dad got in. Imagine, sweet sixteen and they're fighting over me already!!

Alice says she thinks Bob's a virgin. She should know. He won't be for much longer, though, if Myra Graham has anything to do with it!

Alex closed the diary, flushed and flustered, feeling slightly embarrassed, slightly guilty. She fought it by thinking back to her own mid-teens. There had been no sex on the carpet on her sixteenth birthday, but with her father's looming and ominous presence, despite the fact that he had gone down to the Mallard for most of the evening, that would have been unthinkable; even if there had been a candidate around.

But there had been her dreams, her lusting and a certain amount of fumbling in the cinema. She thought back also to some of her conversations with her school intimates, and wondered how different these had been from her mother's discussions with herself in her diary.

Calm again, she opened the diary and read on. As she discovered, Myra's campaign to deflower Bob Skinner reached a successful climax after only seven days.

31

The morning air was fresh and not too cold as he ran past Fenton Barns, down the curving dip in the road, then, his stride shortening, up the climb towards Dirleton Toll.

He glanced quickly through the iron gate as he passed the cemetery, catching a quick glimpse of his wife's gravestone, but as always he ran on without stopping. The wind was strong from the west and the hardest part of the run lay before him as he began to pound out the two miles westward, back to Gullane. Cars rushed past him on the main road in both directions, some heading for North Berwick, most at that hour of the morning bound for Edinburgh.

He ran even harder as he took the curve at Archerfield and the village came into sight, punishing himself, forcing himself back towards the sort of pace he had been able to achieve before his stabbing, taking pleasure from the realisation that he was almost there.

Sweat was pouring from him as at last he turned off the Main Street, past the bakery, and ran up and across Goose Green, to finish his run as always by vaulting his garden gate.

He cooled down in the back garden for a few minutes, then unlocked the back door and stepped straight into the small shower. He had installed it when Alex was a child, for use when she returned from the beach. A full ten minutes later, naked and towelling himself off vigorously, he stepped out, and into the kitchen. Eventually he wrapped the towel around his middle, poured himself a large glass of orange juice from a container in the fridge, and walked through to the dining room.

The big brown envelope lay on the table, untouched since the night before. Suddenly, as he looked at it, steeling himself to open it, a memory burst unbidden into his mind.

Myra's sixteenth birthday party, in her parents' big house in Orchard Street.

His own sixteenth, a few days earlier, had been marked quietly and within the family, like any other. The Graham girl had treated hers as a milestone, and had summoned around twenty of her friends to its celebration, making the point in her telephone invitations that her parents would be absent on the night. He had known Myra since the early years of primary school. They had played together as small children but had become mere nodding acquaintances as the boys and the girls had been diverted into their separate pursuits. Now as adulthood beckoned the groups were being drawn back to shared pastimes.

He had gone to the party with Alice McCready, a neighbour, with whom, once a week, he shared the back row of the Rex Cinema. Myra's date for the night, he remembered, had been one Campbell Weston, a self-styled Romeo with a cultivated hard-man image but a soft centre. Campbell had been grinning and preening himself like a peacock as Bob and Alice had arrived, but as the evening went on, Myra had paid less and less attention to the spotty boy and more and more to Alice, and thus to him.

She had played her hand beautifully, he remembered with a smile, chatting to them both in the big breakfasting kitchen, frowning in disapproval as cigarettes were smoked, and beer was drunk. Gradually, the Beatles and Herman's Hermits had given way on the Dansette to Tony Bennett, and Nat King Cole. Gradually, the lights in the lounge had gone out. At last Myra had made her move.

'Alice, can I have a dance with Bob? For my birthday.'

Refusal had not been an option. Even before the hapless Alice had nodded he had been whisked through to the lounge, where the sofa and chairs had been pushed back to the wall to clear a space for dancing. He closed his eyes, and it all came back. The glow of the coal fire, the musky smell as youngsters groped and fumbled in the dark: and Myra, as they stepped out to dance, to become adults, to fall in love.

Nat Cole was singing 'There's a Lull in My Life' – in Bob's head, he was singing still – but the tempo of the music was unimportant. She had simply pressed herself against him and moved. He was tall, almost full-grown, and so was she. He remembered her fingers running though his hair, the lushness of her kiss, her tongue in his mouth, the firmness of her breasts, their warmth through his shirt, her right hand roaming, his sudden erection, her murmur.

And then the realisation as the music stopped that everyone in the room was staring at them. All at once Campbell Weston was there, his face contorted, tugging at Myra's shoulder, pulling them apart. He had pushed him away, but Campbell had lunged back towards him, swinging a wild, vicious punch.

Until that moment Bob Skinner had never hit anyone in his life, or even thought of it. All the way through school, there had always been something about him which had made him immune to bullying or victimisation. But his attacker had lost face before his crowd, and was in a corner.

He remembered how naturally it had come to him; swaying sideways to avoid the blow, countering in the same movement by slamming his right fist wrist-deep into the youth's midriff, driving the air from his lungs and the beer from his belly. He remembered his calmness in the heat of the brief encounter. He remembered the surge of unexpected, surprising pleasure as his attacker had collapsed, puking, to the floor. One of Campbell's cronies, a bruiser known for no obvious reason as Big Zed, had taken a threatening step towards him. He had simply smiled at him, nodding invitingly, only to see, to his secret disappointment, the thug back off.

Naturally, that had been the end of the party. The fallen Campbell, unable to walk unaided, had been carried off by his crew. Bob had offered to help clean up the carpet, but Myra had told him that she could manage. 'You take Alice home,' she had said, both of them knowing that she was telling him to tie off a loose end, so that matters between them could be put on an official and proper footing.

On that April evening thirty years before, the course of Bob Skinner's adult life had been set. Now he looked at the parcel on the table, whose contents told how, twelve years later, it had been shattered.

He picked up the envelope, tore it open and drew out

the report inside. It was enclosed in a stiff green folder, bearing the two-line heading 'Procurator Fiscal's Office. Fatal Accident Report'. Written on it in heavy blue, he saw a number, a date, and the words 'Mrs Myra Skinner'.

He opened the folder. The first document to meet his eye was a letter, to the Procurator Fiscal. He read aloud.

Sir

The enclosed is a report into the death of Mrs Myra Skinner in a road accident on the date noted.

No other vehicle was involved in the incident, and there were no eye-witnesses. It is the view of the attending officers that the accident was caused by a combination of excessive speed and freak road conditions.

Mrs Skinner was the wife of a serving police officer. Detective Sergeant Skinner arrived by chance at the scene before his wife's body had been removed from the vehicle and this has added to the natural shock of bereavement. It would cause him further suffering if he were forced to give evidence at, or even to attend, a Fatal Accident Inquiry, and if the full report was led publicly in evidence. It is my view that the circumstances of this death are so clear that an FAI is unnecessary.

I would be grateful if you would so determine and instruct accordingly.
    Yours faithfully
    James Proud
    Asst Chief Constable

Skinner turned the page. The second document in the file was a report by the first attending officer. He scanned it, silently.

'Constable David Orr and myself were on patrol near Ballencrieff in our traffic car when we were summoned to the incident by a call made by a passing motorist from the AA box nearby. We arrived within three minutes of receipt of the call.

On arrival we found the vehicle, a Mini Cooper S, registration number DRN 328J crashed against a large tree on the south side of the A198, at Luffness Corner. Agricultural vehicles had been working in the field to the north of the road and there was a large patch of mud on the carriageway.

Tyre marks through the mud leading directly to the vehicle indicated that it had taken the corner, skidded on hitting the hazard and failed to respond to steering. The distribution of the mud on the road indicates that the vehicle lost traction as a result of aquaplaning and consequently did not react to braking.

The severity of the damage caused to the vehicle when it struck the tree indicates that it was travelling at excessive speed.

On examining the vehicle, we found the driver, Mrs Myra Skinner, pinned behind the steering wheel. We searched for a pulse but found none. She had suffered lacerations to her face and hands, and the steering wheel was crushed against her chest. The angle of her head indicated also that she might have suffered a broken neck. It being impossible to remove her from the vehicle without special equipment, we awaited the arrival of the emergency services, and in the meantime took photographs of the accident scene in general and of the interior of the vehicle.

The fire and ambulance services had just arrived when another vehicle, a Triumph 2000, stopped at the scene, ignoring police signals to keep moving. The driver got out and rushed over to the crashed vehicle. I recognised him as Detective Sergeant Robert Skinner, whom I know to live in Gullane.

Sergeant Skinner became hysterical when he realised that the dead woman was his wife. He began to try to remove her from the car himself, and had to be restrained by the attending officers and the ambulance crew. A second police car was summoned to take Sergeant Skinner home.

In due course, Mrs Skinner's body was cut from the vehicle by fire service officers and removed by the ambulance for post mortem examination.

Constable Orr and I interviewed the motorist who had made the emergency call, Mr Nigel Steadman. He said that he was not an eye-witness to the accident, but that the Mini Cooper had overtaken him at high speed a few minutes earlier as he was leaving Aberlady. His formal statement is attached to this report.

This supports my conclusion that excessive speed and adverse road conditions were the cause of this fatal accident.

Signed

Trevor Haig, Sergeant

Skinner read on. Constable Orr's report, couched in the same police-speak, agreed with that of his Sergeant in every detail. He turned to the statement of the witness. 'Nigel Steadman, aged 41, of 12 Tayview Road, North Berwick,' he read. 'Wonder if he's still there?' He looked at the single page.

I was driving home on the evening in question, having left work early. I had driven through Aberlady and was just passing the end of speed limit sign, when I was overtaken by a green Mini. The car was driven by a young woman.

I was travelling at 35 mph at the time, and I would estimate that the Mini was going twice as fast as me. The vehicle was out of my sight before I had reached the end of the first straight out of Aberlady.

A few minutes later I reached the Luffness corner and saw the vehicle crashed against a tree. I stopped to offer assistance, but I could see at once that the driver was dead. I am an AA member and so I made an emergency call from the AA box a short distance from the scene.

He had to force himself to read the post mortem report. He had attended many in his career, and could picture the scene, with its awful sights and smells. For a second he thought of closing the folder, but, making an effort to disassociate Myra's face from the images in his mind's eye, he began to read.

The examination had been carried out by Trevor Hutchison, an experienced man whom Skinner knew and respected.

The body was that of a woman in her late twenties.

Examination showed superficial cuts to her face, hand and arms, several of which had windscreen fragments lodged in situ. The right eyeball was pierced by a glass fragment, which was removed.

The victim had sustained a classic whiplash fracture of the third cervical vertebra and the spinal cord was severed. This injury alone would have proved almost instantaneously fatal.

There were severe, also classic crushing injuries to the chest, caused by the steering wheel. The sternum was shattered by the impact and bone fragments were removed from the heart. The liver was ruptured and pierced by lower ribs in two places. These injuries would also have proved immediately fatal.

The victim sustained several non-fatal injuries. Both legs were fractured in several places, as was the right forearm. There was also a depressed skull fracture caused by impact with the windscreen frame.

Examination of the victim's brain and major organs showed no abnormality, and there was no indication that she had suffered any form of seizure. In my opinion she was aware and alert at the time of the incident.

A fully-formed foetus, male, eleven weeks, was present in the uterus. It was perfectly normal, and I do not believe that any complication of pregnancy contributed to the accident.'

The shock of it washed over him, chilling him suddenly to the bone. Cold sweat spread on his forehead as he dropped the folder, shaking. Proud Jimmy's warning leapt back into his mind.

'You don't want to see that report. Take my word on it.'

'No wonder, Jimmy, no wonder,' he sighed. 'For eighteen years you spared me the knowledge that I'd lost a son as well as a wife. What a decision for a friend to have to take. What a friend to take it.'

32

'Good morning, ma'am.' Mario McGuire, propped on an elbow, kissed his wife as she swam back into wakefulness. 'And where the hell were you last night? I tried to stay awake, but I don't think I made it past midnight.'

Maggie pulled him down towards her and moulded herself against his thick, muscular body. She ran her fingers through the hair on his chest, passing them gently over the scar from his old wound.

'I was with a young man,' she murmured. 'We were alone all evening. I got home around one, absolutely done in. I didn't think it, er . . . appropriate, to wake you.'

His big hand ran smoothly down her back and gripped her buttocks, squeezing them gently, pulling her even tighter against him. 'And what were you and this young man up to?'

'We were looking for another man.'

'What, isn't two enough for you?' He kissed the side of her neck, and gave it a sudden light bite, sending a shiver through her.

'This is a very special man,' she said. 'Carl Medina told us about him. He may have information which can tie Douglas Terry to a serious assault five years back, on a young Hearts footballer, Jimmy Lee.' Her hand moved down from his chest, until it found its pathway blocked.

'Indeed,' he whispered. 'I thought the Hibs casuals did that. So what's his name, this very special man?' He rolled her gently on to her back.

'I don't know. I only know that he has a big vulture tattooed on his right shoulder.' She reached up and bit him. 'Right there.'

He leaned over her, head still, eyes closed. His hand moved, very slowly, up the inside of her thigh, towards the warmth. She began to move under his touch. He whispered in her ear. 'Mulgrew. Evan Mulgrew.'

She sat bolt upright, her eyes suddenly wide. 'You know him?'

Mario rolled backwards, smiling at her surprise, looking up at her, smugly. 'I lifted a guy, name of Evan Mulgrew, a few years back from a flat in Brunswick Street. He was a suspect in an indecent assault case. We got there early doors and caught him in bed with his woman.

'I watched him as he got dressed. He had a big tattoo on his right shoulder. I was fascinated by it. Big vulture. Very realistic.'

'What happened to him? Did he get sent down?' Her voice was eager, excited.

'I don't know. I wasn't involved in the investigation. They just called me in as extra muscle to help arrest him. In the event he came like a lamb. If he was convicted, he'd have gone to prison for sure. I remember one of the lads telling me that the victim was a judge's daughter.'

Maggie jumped out of bed, evading his grab for her. 'What's the time?' she called over her shoulder.

'Quarter to nine.'

She grabbed her dressing-gown from its hook behind the bedroom door.

'Mags,' he said, more than a little petulantly. 'It's Saturday morning.'

'I know, but I've got to get back into the Prison Service computer, to see how it responds to the name Mulgrew.'

'But Mags, on a Saturday morning?' He was plaintive now. 'We always have French toast on Saturday morning.'

'It'll still be Saturday when I get home. Probably. Anyway, think yourself lucky. I was going to take you with me. You've just earned yourself a morning off!'

'And talked myself out of . . .'

'French toast!'

33

Pamela Masters was an early riser. She had done her aerobics routine, showered, dressed and made breakfast, all before the telephone rang at five minutes past nine o'clock.

She gulped down a mouthful of toast and apricot jam as she reached across from her perch on a high stool, to pick it up.

'Hello, this is Pamela.'

'Good morning, Sergeant. This is DCC Skinner.' A cold shiver of nerves ran through her. She slipped down from the stool and stood stiffly upright.

'Listen,' he went on, 'I know I said report on Monday, but there's something I want to let you in on, and to get started on myself; something that's been in the in-tray for far too long as it is.'

'He's got a nice voice,' Pamela thought, as her nervousness left her. *'I hadn't noticed that before.'*

'I'm at a bit of a loose end today, and I intend to go into the office. This isn't an order, and I wouldn't want you to cancel other engagements, but if you're clear would you like to come in and join me at Fettes?'

She glanced at her wall diary. It showed a hair appointment at 10 a.m., a lunch date at Jenners with a girlfriend, and a 3 p.m. date in the Royal Botanic Garden with an old friend of her former husband, who had called her out of the blue two days earlier. The rest of the day she had left free, just in case. It had been a long time since Alan Royston.

'Certainly, sir,' she said. 'When do you want me there?'

There was a pause. 'I want to call in to play with my son for a while. Give me a couple of hours, so let's say eleven thirty. Come straight up to my office.'

'Very good, sir.' From the other end of the line she thought she caught a faint chuckle.

'Oh, and Pamela, remember. Don't wear uniform this time, just come as you are. I hate formality at weekends. Come to think of it, I don't like it much at any time.'

34

The little flat was an unexpected find in the heart of the City. It was in the basement of a tall grey Victorian terrace with a small, unadorned but neatly swept courtyard to the front, but opening out at the rear into a large well stocked and lovingly maintained garden.

It would have been quiet on any morning, but at just after 9 a.m. on a Saturday, birdsong was the only sound to be heard.

Angela Muirhead was in the garden, sitting on a wooden bench seat, idly throwing scraps of stale bread on to the grass. As each piece landed, a finch, a sparrow or a tit would plummet down from its perch in the bushes against the boundary wall to snatch it up. Occasionally more than one bird would eye the same morsel and there would be a fight.

She looked up as the policemen approached. She was barefoot, wearing a bulky black sweatshirt, and grey cotton trousers. Her hair was tangled, she wore no make-up and her eyes looked heavy, and slightly puffy.

'Hello,' she said to Donaldson, dully, as recognition dawned.

'Good morning, Miss Muirhead,' the Superintendent replied. 'This is Detective Sergeant McIlhenney. He and

I are investigating Mr Medina's murder, and we have to ask you some fairly detailed questions.'

'Can we do it out here?' she asked. 'I don't like being indoors just now.'

'Okay,' said Donaldson. 'Let's sit at the patio table.' She nodded and led the way across to a small grouping of plastic furniture arranged on the paved area on to which the flat's French doors opened.

'This isn't an interview under caution,' said the Superintendent, 'but I'd like to tape it for convenience.' The woman nodded; he placed a small cassette recorder before her.

'What was your relationship with Carl Medina?' he began.

'He was my partner. We lived together,' she said in a voice that was almost a whisper.

'Could you speak up, please,' said Donaldson. 'For the tape.

'Were you intending to marry?'

She nodded. 'Yes, when we were in a position to start a family.'

'What was stopping you?'

'Money. Carl hasn't had a full-time job since he left the garage. Our idea was that if I had a baby, I'd go part-time afterwards, but with Carl out of work we just couldn't afford to lose half my salary.'

'What sort of man was Carl?'

'Lovely. Kind and gentle; quite serious, yet he could be funny when he wanted.'

'Did it come as a shock to you when he lost his job with Jackie Charles?' asked the detective.

Angie Muirhead nodded again. 'Yes, it did. He seemed to be getting on well there. He liked the salesmen, and the company liked him enough to give him the same Christmas bonus as they got.'

'Are you sure the company knew about the bonus?'

She looked up, offended. 'Yes, quite sure! There was a letter of thanks with it, from Mr and Mrs Charles.'

'When he was fired, he told you he'd been made redundant, yes?'

'Yes.'

'What did you think when you heard us say that he'd been dismissed for fiddling the books?' Donaldson looked at her, trying to read her expression.

'I didn't believe it,' she said, at once. 'Carl was on a good salary, and there were the bonuses. He didn't need to steal anything. I still don't believe it. After you left on Thursday Carl explained everything that happened. He said that he made up the redundancy story because he was too embarrassed to tell me what Mrs Charles had got up to.'

'You accepted that?' A harder tone came into the policeman's voice. 'He told you a respectable woman nearly twenty years his senior made a crude pass at him, and you believed it?'

'Yes. I believed it. I do still. The world's full of spoiled rich bitches.'

'And Carl would never have been unfaithful of course.'

'That's right,' she said, defiantly.

'How about you, Miss Muirhead? Were you faithful to him?' To the detectives' surprise the woman flushed, and looked away.

'Answer, please,' said Donaldson.

'Yes.' It was a whisper. 'Apart from one time.'

'When? Speak up, remember.'

'At an office party.'

'Your office?'

'No. Carl's, the Christmas before he left the company. It was at Mr Charles' house. Everybody had a bit to drink, and I got talking to Mr Charles. He seemed very nice and he made me laugh. It's a big house, and before I knew it we had sort of drifted away from everyone. There was a back bedroom. All of a sudden, I just felt out of it, completely gone, absolutely helpless. I've always suspected there was something in my last drink. When he came on to me, I knew what was happening, but . . . I was just numb; couldn't speak, couldn't do anything.' Her voice was barely audible, but instead of interrupting her, McIlhenney picked up the tape and held it close to her. 'He did it, then he helped me into a bathroom, and left me there.' Her eyes were filled with tears.

'And afterwards? You didn't think of making a complaint?'

She shook her head, helplessly. 'How could I? I mean, I'd let him, hadn't I? Oh I felt so dirty, yet if I'd said that my drink had been spiked, who'd have believed me?'

'We would have, love,' said McIlhenney, quietly. 'But proving it would have been another matter.'

'Did Charles contact you again after that night?' asked Donaldson.

'No. Never. Not once. A few months later, Carl was fired. I haven't seen Mr Charles since that night at his house.'

'Did you ever tell Carl about the . . . encounter?'

'Of course not. I was afraid to.'

'Why? Because of what Carl might have done to Jackie Charles?'

She shook her head, vigorously. 'No. Because of what it might have done to us,' she said vehemently.

'When Carl was made redundant, I thought that it might have had something to do with it; that perhaps Mr Charles was scared I'd tell him, and that in turn he'd tell Mrs Charles.'

Donaldson took the tape from McIlhenney, and looked at it to check that it was still running. 'Did Carl have any sort of work after that?' he asked, replacing it on the table.

'Only bar stuff,' she said, 'and occasional messenger jobs. Nothing full-time.'

The detective pointed to her left hand, where gold and diamonds sparkled on the third finger. 'Did he give you that ring?'

'Yes, six months ago, to mark our being together for five years.'

'It looks a bit pricey. How could he afford that?'

She hesitated. 'He told me that he'd borrowed the money from his dad. I was surprised, since his dad's a miserable old sod. I only found out the truth a month ago. He borrowed it from a private finance company.'

'Do you know the name of the company?' asked McIlhenney.

'It was a man. A Mr Heenan. I found out about it all when he came to the house one night. He told Carl that with interest he owed him double the thousand pounds he'd borrowed, and that he wanted the interest paid within a week.' She paused, rubbing her throat absent-mindedly with the fingers of her right hand. 'He didn't make any specific threats, but I was scared.'

'What did Carl do?'

'I had a thousand in a savings account. I gave it to him, to give to Heenan. Then I arranged to borrow the other thousand from the bank. But Heenan came back last

Saturday and said that he wanted another eight hundred in interest and the capital sum repaid, all within a week. This time he had another man with him.

'Carl told him to fuck off. He said that he would get the thousand and that was it.'

'What did Heenan do?' asked Donaldson.

'Nothing. He just said "Within a week", and left. The loan came through from the bank on Wednesday, and Carl handed the money into his office in Peffermill Road on Thursday morning. In cash.'

The Superintendent looked at her. 'And you thought that was case closed, did you?'

He turned to McIlhenney. 'I guess, Sergeant,' he said, 'we should pay a visit to our old friend Mr Thomas Maxwell Heenan.'

'You know him? said Angela Muirhead.

'Oh yes,' said Donaldson. 'We know all the loansharks. We even know where most of them get their money. From the same guy that gave you and Carl your Christmas bonuses.'

35

'I'm sorry, ma'am, I was sure you said nine thirty.'

'It's all right, Sammy,' said Maggie Rose. 'I did. I've only been here myself for ten minutes. I'm still waiting for the system to boot up.'

'Is Inspector McGuire not coming then?'

She smiled. 'No. He's done his bit for the day.' The changing patterns on the monitor screen settled down and the retrieval menu for the information system came into view. 'Watch this,' she said, using the mouse to pull down the Find File command.

She frowned slightly as she keyed in the name, 'Evan Mulgrew', and clicked the 'OK' box to start the search.

A running man figure appeared on the screen. He ran and ran, for almost thirty seconds, and her heart began to sink. 'I doubt Mario's man can't have gone to jail after . . .' She stopped in mid-sentence as a file opened on screen. It was headed, 'Evan Mulgrew', and under the name there were two photographs, the traditional full-face and profile.

The Vulture stared out at the two detectives from the screen. By any standards, he was an ugly man, with small dark eyes and a bushy moustache which seemed to add emphasis to his leering expression. A long scar ran diagonally across most of his wide forehead, from the hairline down to his left eyebrow.

Rose clicked on to the next section of the file. She read quickly. 'He's three years into a twelve-year sentence, imposed in the High Court in Edinburgh for attempted rape. Pleaded guilty.

'Served six months for serious assault, eight years ago, previous convictions for assault, demanding money with menaces, and breach of the peace.

'Age thirty-nine, religion Roman Catholic, but divorced twelve years ago, therefore non-practising. Next of kin listed as a son, John Paton Mulgrew, age nineteen.

'Height five feet ten inches. Weight fourteen stone twelve pounds. Colour of eyes, brown. Colour of hair, red. Distinguishing marks; scar across forehead, large tattoo on right shoulder.'

She turned and smiled up at Pye. 'Got him! Your theory paid off, and Mario was right too. He'll be chuffed to bits when I tell him.'

Her grin grew even wider. 'There's one thing he won't like, though.'

'What's that, ma'am?'

'The Vulture's in Peterhead. Bang goes Mario's French Toast! Come on, Sammy, let's head up there.'

She switched off the terminal and headed for the door, a puzzled Detective Constable trailing at her heels.

36

Sergeant Masters was waiting in the Command Suite when Skinner arrived at headquarters at 11.35 a.m. He looked up, slightly startled when he saw her there.

It was the first time he had ever seen her in civilian clothes. She was wearing light blue jeans, which seemed to emphasise the curve of her hips, and a fresh, white cotton shirt. Her lustrous brown hair fell against its high collar, and her big eyes seemed to sparkle.

'Good morning, sir,' she said, with, still, a little uncertainty in her tone.

'Sorry I'm late, Pamela,' said Skinner, approaching. 'My son was at his most playful this morning. He's cutting some more teeth just now, and kept his mother up all night in the process. When I got there the Bonjela had done its work. He was as bright as a button, but Sarah was sound asleep.'

He stopped beside her in the corridor, outside his office door. 'Let me explain the layout to you. I'm in here, as you know, and ACC Elder's office, at the top of the stairs, backs on to mine.' He nodded to his left. 'Mr Whitlow, our civilian Head of Finance and Administration, is in there, then there's the Chief's secretary's room, leading into Sir James' suite.' He strode on up the corridor, beckoning to her to follow, and nodding to his right. 'Ruthie's in there, and beyond is your room.' He opened the door and stood aside, allowing her to enter a square, bright office, around half the size of his own, furnished with a beech desk, side table, a swivel chair, and two occasional seats. The outlook from the room was the same as that of the DCC, and Maggie Rose had positioned the desk deliberately so that she could always see the Chief Officer's car park.

'We'll settle you in here on Monday, but for now, come along to mine.' He led the way back and into his office, only to disappear immediately with the jug of the coffee filter.

'This place runs on coffee and adrenalin,' he said, as he returned, measuring out three flat measures of grounds, and setting the machine in motion. 'Oh,' he added, 'and paper; lots of paper.'

He ushered her, not to the desk, but to the low-slung leather chairs, set around the coffee table. As she sat down, as neatly and carefully as she had during their first meeting, he caught the scent of her perfume, not overpowering but apparent. He leaned back in his chair and smiled at her; a long, slow, easy smile.

'Since I've been in this office,' he began, 'yours has been occupied by Brian Mackie and Maggie Rose. Both of them are DCIs now. Before them there was Andy Martin. They and a few others are all part of what I like to think of as my team, the people upon whom, when things are at their toughest, I can rely on above all the rest to get the job done. When the really serious stuff happens, you'll find them involved. Welcome to the team.'

'Thank you, sir,' she said, flushing slightly as she returned his smile.

'Your job is to act as a barrier between me and the outside world,' he went on. 'As a rule, all the submissions, reports, correspondence and the rest which come to me, will be filtered by Ruth through you.

'Where necessary, I want you to write summaries of their contents. Where particular sections seem important, I want you to draw them to my attention. Where decisions are called for, then in time, once you've settled in, I'll welcome recommendations from you.

'As well as all that – and it's an onerous job, believe me – you'll find me using you as a sounding board. I'll let you into my thinking on some policy matters, to see if you agree with me. Sometimes I'll ask for your advice. In fact, I'll begin right now.

'We have to sell the concept of public participation in the crime prevention effort. I want you to look at our marketing in that area, tell me in general how well you think we're doing it, and give me a report on ways in which it could be improved.'

'How quickly, sir?' she asked.

'I don't want to overburden you in your first few days, so let's say six weeks from now. Oh, and be sure that your recommendations are costed.'

'What about funding from external sources, sir? Is that permissible?'

He smiled, again. 'It is now, if you think we can attract any.'

He paused. 'Going back to your role as a barrier, there are two exceptions, two areas in which Ruth will ensure that papers come straight to me. The first is material from the Chief. Anything coming up the ladder goes through you. Anything coming down the same way hits the top of my in-tray at once.' He paused, glancing across to check the state of the coffee filter.

'The other exception relates to my part-time job. In addition to what I do here, I am also security adviser to the Secretary of State for Scotland. Most of the time that doesn't involve much, but if there is a major incident or, say, a terrorist alert, it can mean a hell of a lot. In that role I am effectively part of an organisation known popularly as MI5.

'They, and the Secretary of State, contact me through a secure, unlisted telephone line. No-one else has the number, and you don't need it, but there's an extension on your desk. If it rings and I ain't there, answer, take a message and contact me pronto. I'll give you a list of the people who have the number. Every time you answer, ask the caller to identify himself, or herself. Okay?'

She nodded vigorously, her eyes wider than ever.

'Good,' he said. His eyes dropped to the table. 'There's one more thing I should tell you, since we'll be working so closely. Although you may have figured it out for yourself, given what I told you about calling in to see my son.

'Sarah, my wife, and I are living apart at the moment. We're not at daggers drawn, but . . .' he hesitated, '. . . things are not good. So until further notice, my off-duty contact number is the Gullane one on the list which you'll find in your office, not Edinburgh.'

She nodded, frowning. 'I understand, sir. I . . . I hope everything works out.'

'It will, Pamela. One way or another, it will.'

His attention seemed to wander for a few seconds, until he snapped himself back to the present. He jumped to his feet and poured two mugs of coffee from the steaming filter. 'No sugar, right?'

Returning, he placed the mugs on two coasters on the table. 'Let's get to the reason I asked you to come in today. Hold on to your seat while I explain it to you.' She looked at him, eyes widening again.

'Eighteen years ago, my first wife, Myra, was killed while she was driving my car. I won't tell you how, because it's too complicated a story, but recently, I've been faced with the possibility . . .' he stopped and shook his head, 'No, it's stronger than that. I've come to believe that she was murdered by someone who sabotaged my car, thinking that I would be driving.

'At the time, Myra's death was declared accidental. I've read the report to the Fiscal, and there's nothing there to help us. So what I have to do now is to go back through all the investigations which were running at the time, checking those in which I was involved, to see who it was that I upset so badly that he wanted me out of the way.

'When Myra died, I was a Detective Sergeant in the Serious Crimes Squad at Headquarters. I want you to help me check their files.

'As well as that, we'll need to check the photographic unit. The attending officers took pictures of the car at the scene. The prints will have been destroyed, by now, for sure, and the Mini went into the crusher eighteen years ago, but with a fair wind, we might trace negatives.

'Let's get down to the Records Office, and see what secrets we can uncover.'

37

'Aw come on, Tommy,' said Neil McIlhenney, 'don't play the poor innocent with us.

'It might say "Heenan Newsagent" over the door of this rat-hole, but we know the business you run out of this upstairs office. You are a loanshark, a tallyman, like they say in Glasgow, an illegal money-lender like they say in court.

'You are the sort of bastard that infests places like Craigmillar and Peffermill, where the poor people live, lending them money when no-one else will, then breaking their arms and legs if they can't meet your wicked interest payments, or if they won't give you their Giros and their Child Benefit, or steal, or prostitute their wives to pay you off.

'You know, if I wasn't a conscientious public servant, I'd wipe my arse with the likes of you, Pierre Cardin blazer and all.' He paused, eyeing the man fiercely.

'What was the rate of interest you were screwing out of Carl Medina? Twenty per cent a week, was it, at the end-up.'

Thomas Maxwell Heenan looked back at him, blandly. 'Who's Carl Medina?' he asked.

'Jesus, and this is a paper-shop too,' said McIlhenney,

sadly. 'Aged about thirty, five years or so younger than you. Lived in Slateford with his girlfriend. Borrowed a grand off you about six months ago. Last Saturday, you paid a call on him and told him you wanted the grand plus eight hundred interest within a week. You didn't say "Or else", but then you wouldn't, would you. You'd take it as understood.'

Heenan, tall, fair and well-groomed, smiled suavely. 'I don't know what you're talking about.'

'What we're talking about,' said Superintendent Donaldson, 'is the murder of Carl Medina in his home yesterday. The day after he repaid your thousand pound loan, and told you that you could whistle for the interest.

'Where were you yesterday morning?' he asked, suddenly.

Maxwell's mouth opened, then closed, then opened again. 'I was here,' he said at last. 'In my upstairs office. My wife was in the shop.'

Donaldson whistled. 'That's your only alibi? Your wife? Tommy, you're in the shit. We've got Medina's girlfriend at St Leonard's, looking through our rogues' gallery to pick out the heavy you had with you last Saturday. I think the three of us should join her, don't you?'

'Why did you kill him, Tommy?' asked McIlhenney, roughly. 'Normally eight hundred's only a broken-leg job. Was it because he told you to fuck off in front of your minder? Did you think you had to save face? Because if you did, your saved face is going to cost you a life sentence.'

Donaldson stepped up to Heenan and laid a hand on his shoulder, pushing him towards the door. Suddenly, with a quick sideways flick, the loanshark kicked the policeman just below the left knee, with the hard outside edge of the sole of his right shoe. As the Superintendent yelped with pain and collapsed to the floor, clutching his shin, Heenan dived through the doorway, and down the narrow flight of stairs which led out into Peffermill Road.

McIlhenny's way to the door was blocked by his fallen colleague. Awkwardly, he stepped over him, then crashed down the stairway, bouncing from wall to wall until he reached the door at the foot. In the street he looked first right, then left, where he saw Heenan's disappearing back, already almost thirty yards away.

It was another mild day and the midday crowds were gathering in Peffermill Road, most of them young men bound for an afternoon in the football grandstands. The natural instinct of many, witnessing a chase, might have been to stand aside for the pursued and impede the pursuer. But Neil McIlhenney, gathering pace, was a formidable object. The pavement throng parted before him, like fans before a Tour de France cyclist as he set off after Heenan. The few unfortunates who did not step aside were sent flying as the big Sergeant swept them out of his way.

McIlhenney, while a laborious runner, was quicker than he looked over a short distance, but he was able to make up little ground on the slimmer Heenan. He dug in, looking for his last yard of speed, but the cause seemed lost. The detective knew that if Heenan avoided arrest, then he would disappear and be swallowed up by the underworld in which he moved. He felt his thighs begin to tighten. He heard his breath begin to rasp. He saw Heenan, almost fifty yards ahead now and without slackening his pace, look over his shoulder, with the faintest of smiles.

And Neil McIlhenney smiled back. By the time it had dawned on Heenan to wonder why, it was too late. The child's plastic tricycle, which had rolled, seemingly of its own volition, out of an open doorway, was directly in his path. He tripped over it and fell headlong, rolling, tumbling across the pavement.

He scrambled on the ground, trying to regain his footing, but his disaster had given the big detective renewed energy. As Heenan stood up, McIlhenney, travelling at full speed, hit him with a flying tackle which was part Rugby League, part all-in wrestling.

The loanshark went down again, this time with all the Sergeant's weight bearing upon him. They lay there together, Heenan moaning, McIlhenney recovering his breath in great gasps.

'Tortoise and the hare, Tommy,' he wheezed at last, his forearm jammed across his captive's throat. 'You should have remembered. Fucking tortoise wins every time.'

38

It was as if the vulture was peering out at them. Evan Mulgrew sat across the table, shoulders hunched, in the interview room in the administration block of Peterhead Prison. His prison uniform shirt was unbuttoned almost halfway down, giving Rose and Pye a clear view of part of his right shoulder, and of the bizarre bird's head.

'Memorable, all right,' thought the Chief Inspector. The scavenger's beady eye stared out at her. From its beak a piece of bloody carrion hung loosely, red and horribly realistic.

Mulgrew caught her glance and smiled. 'Want to see the rest, hen?' he said, beginning to unbutton his shirt still further. At once, he was grabbed by one of two big prison officers who were flanking him. He was hauled roughly to his feet, and his arms were held pinned to his sides while the other officer buttoned his shirt tight, up to the neck.

As he was slammed back into his seat Rose smiled evenly across at him. 'Sunshine,' she murmured, 'I've seen better at home.

'D'you know,' she said, still smiling, 'my husband nicked you, Mulgrew. Three years ago. He said that when it came to it, you were a pure pussy-cat. Pity you don't have a cat's luck. It has nine lives; you attack a judge's daughter and get a twelve stretch.'

Mulgrew looked away from her and stared out of the barred window. Early Saturday afternoon in northerly Peterhead was much less mild than in Edinburgh, and thick globules of sleety snow were splashing against the glass. 'Aye okay,' he muttered. 'So what d'yis want?'

'When you were walking about on the outside, Mulgrew,' Rose began, 'you used to work out at the Commonwealth Pool.'

'Aye.'

'Do you remember talking there to a man called Carl?'

The Vulture scratched his chin. 'Youngish chap, fair hair?' Sammy Pye nodded.

'Aye. So what?'

'Do you recall,' asked Rose, 'telling Carl about a man named Douglas Terry, and about people who did odd jobs for him?'

Mulgrew's slightly bored expression changed suddenly to one of real concern. 'I might have done. I cannae remember.'

'Come on, Evan, Carl didn't make this story up. You were bragging to him, weren't you?'

The Vulture looked down at the desk and shrugged his shoulders, very slightly.

'You told Carl that you knew someone who did heavy work for Terry, and you mentioned specifically an attack on a Hearts footballer, Jimmy Lee.'

Mulgrew shook his head.

Sammy Pye took a chance. 'Come on, Evan. D'you want us to bring Carl up here? Now, why did you tell him that story? Are you just a windbag, is that it?'

The Vulture stared hotly across at him. 'You and me in a room, son, and we'll see wha's a windbag. I was trying tae sort out if Carl was interested in that sort of work. He said thanks, but he wisna.'

'So who was the man you knew?' said Pye.

Mulgrew's eyes narrowed as he looked at Maggie Rose. 'What's in it for me?' he asked.

The Chief Inspector raised her eyebrows and tossed her red hair. 'You're in for attempted rape, so it can't be much. But we can put a note on your file for the Parole Board. Then maybe, just maybe, mind, we can get you transferred out of this Godawful place, to somewhere like Shotts or Saughton.'

The prisoner sat silent for almost two minutes, fidgeting, chewing his right thumb-nail, glancing occasionally out of the window. At last, he looked across at the two detectives. 'Okay,' he said. 'Ah'll tell yis.

'The man I mentioned tae Carl was Ricky McCartney. He lives out in Craigmillar, and he works for Dougie Terry.'

'What do you know about Terry?' asked Rose.

'He runs a chain of betting shops and minicab companies.'

'What does McCartney do for him?'

'He puts teams together. Heavies. Like when somebody's out of order and needs sorting out.'

'Like Jimmy Lee, you mean?'

'Aye, like Jimmy Lee.'

'And how was Jimmy Lee out of order?'

The Vulture hesitated again. 'Saughton, right?' Rose nodded.

'The boy was a big gambler,' he went on. 'He was

intae Terry's betting shops for thousands. Terry sent Ricky to tell him that he'd let him off, if he fixed a game. The Jambos were playing some second division team in the League Cup, and the other team were great big odds against. It was an international thing, tied intae fixed odds gambling out in the Far East.

'If ye check the records of Terry's bettin' shops, ye'll find that he didnae take bets on that game.'

'We will,' said Maggie Rose, quietly. 'So what did Jimmy Lee say?'

'Nothing. Ricky wasnae giving him a choice.'

'What did he do?'

Mulgrew smiled, almost respectfully. 'The Jambos were a goal down wi' half an hour tae go. Jimmy Lee scored a hat-trick and they won three – one.'

'And that was why he was done?'

The Vulture nodded. 'That's right. A couple of weeks later, after a Saturday game.'

'Who was on McCartney's team?'

'Apart from Ricky himself, I dinna ken. I wis supposed tae be on it, but I twisted ma knee lifting a couple of days before.'

There was a pause and silence hung over the room. It was broken by Sammy Pye. 'Jimmy Lee always said that Hibs fans attacked him. Why would he do that?'

Mulgrew threw back his head and laughed. 'The boy's a true Jambo, son. A true Jambo would accuse the Hibees of bein' behind the Kennedy assassination.

'And onywey, he knew that if he'd said anything different, it would have been more than his knees that got broken. A true Jambo would rather die than fix a football match, but not if he had another option.'

'Tell me,' asked Rose, casually. 'In all this was the name Jackie Charles ever mentioned?'

The Vulture smiled again, with a trace of scorn. 'Miss, the name Jackie Charles is *never* mentioned. Nobody would be that daft.'

'Mmm,' murmured the Chief Inspector, staring at the ceiling. 'We'll see. We'll see.'

She looked back across the table. 'Where's Jimmy Lee now?'

'I can tell you that, ma'am,' said Sammy Pye, beside her. 'He'll be at Tynecastle. The club gave him a job on the commercial staff, selling sponsorship and shaking hands with the guests in the hospitality suites on match days.

'There's a home game this afternoon, against Rangers.'

Rose looked up at the wall clock. It showed five minutes past one. 'In that case,' she said, pushing her chair back from the table, 'if we put our foot down, we might just catch the second half.'

Mulgrew looked at the two detectives as they stood up, and as his guards pulled him to his feet. 'Saughton,' he said. 'Remember.'

Maggie Rose nodded. 'Okay, Evan. We'll get you back to Edinburgh. And who knows, maybe Dougie Terry and Ricky McCartney can share your old room here.'

39

Pamela Masters looked around the room, and pondered upon fate. It was Saturday afternoon and she was in the Royal Botanic Garden. After an hour of poring through dusty files, Skinner had called a lunch-break. Since the Senior Officers' Dining Room was closed for the weekend, and since the pubs would be crammed with football and rugby supporters, he had suggested the Garden Cafeteria.

Now he and his new assistant sat at a white wood table. He was demolishing his second chargrilled chicken and salad roll; she was hoping that her 'Dear John' message had reached her date, and that he would not arrive ahead of schedule.

'What school did you go to in Motherwell, sir?' she asked, as he finished eating.

He laughed. 'When I was a lad in Motherwell, that question meant, "Are you a Protestant or a Catholic?" That's if they couldn't tell from the handshake.

'The answer is that I didn't. I went to Glasgow High. Myra was at Dalziel, though.'

'Me too,' said Pamela. 'When did you leave Motherwell?'

'When I was twenty-one, as soon as I graduated. I did an ordinary Arts degree at Glasgow, to please my dad, then I applied to several police forces. I could have joined Lanarkshire or Glasgow, as they still were in those days, but Myra and I both fancied the idea of Edinburgh. So here I am.

'Maybe I've been here long enough.'

She frowned, and looked at him quizzically. 'Ach,' he said, 'don't listen to me. I love it here still. It's just that sometimes, everyone has to make a choice.

'How about you? What if you had stayed married? Would you still have joined the police?'

'I'd like to think so,' she said, her smile restored. 'But I'd probably have had the regulation two point four weans, and that might have made it difficult.'

'Do you want to have a family some day?'

She pulled a face. 'With the right man, probably I would. But I'm not obsessed by the idea. Just as well, because time's a-passing, and there's no sign of the right man. For a while I thought Alan might have been, but we just didn't gel.' She paused, and leaned back in her seat.

'You've got a child, sir. Do you recommend parenthood?'

He held up his right hand, palm outward and extended the first two fingers. 'Two. I have a daughter as well, Alexis. She's only about ten years younger than my second wife, and she's a law graduate. If you didn't know, she's engaged to Andy Martin.'

Pamela's big eyes widened expressively. 'Making it a family business, eh.'

He chuckled. 'Yes, and to cap it my wife's a police surgeon. That's how we met.' As he said the words, a pang of sadness ran through him, as he recalled the ecstatic early days of his relationship with Sarah, and the laughter left his face.

'To answer your question, as far as parenthood's concerned, I can recommend it. As for marriage, right now I'm not so sure.'

'Do you think the two necessarily go together?' she asked, matching his change of mood.

'I brought Alex up as a single parent,' he replied. 'I did my best, but she missed out on a lot. Right now, in fact, she's finding out just how much.'

She frowned again, but before she could ask him what he had meant, his mobile phone rang. He took it from the pocket of his soft, brown leather jacket, and pressed the receive button.

Brian Mackie's voice sounded in his ear. 'Can we see you, sir? Urgently. We've got something to report.'

'Sure,' said Skinner. 'It's half one now. My office at two fifteen. Okay.'

He picked up a hint of disappointment in the Chief Inspector's, 'Very good, sir.'

The DCC grinned. 'I know you, Thin Man,' he said into the phone. 'You were hoping to be at Tynecastle by then, weren't you?'

'Well . . .'

'Okay, then. Look, Pamela and I are up in the Botanics coffee shop, and it's quiet as a church. It's only two minutes away, so get yourselves up here now.' He ended the call and laid the phone on the table.

'More local knowledge, Pamela,' he said. 'DCI Mackie is an incurable Hearts fan. But then he can't help it. He's from Edinburgh.'

They sat and waited, admiring the garden outside,

which was edging gradually into its spring colours. After less than five minutes, they saw the slim figure of Mackie and the heavier frame of Detective Inspector Mario McGuire as they strode up the slope towards them. They moved outside to meet them, towards one of the patio tables, well out of earshot of the few other diners.

As Skinner introduced his new assistant, they arranged themselves around the table. 'Right, Brian,' said the DCC. 'What's so urgent?'

Impending football matches or not, Mackie was always brisk and businesslike. 'We did the check you asked for, boss. It isn't complete yet, but a plum fell out of the tree that we thought you ought to know about. I'll let Mario explain.'

McGuire nodded. 'I had just started the check, boss, when I was called by my oppo in Birmingham. They've been keeping a very close watch on a gang of Brummies with interests in protection, prostitution and gambling. In fact, they've got a man planted on the inside. These people aren't part of the Magic Circle that Jackie's in, but they're pretty heavy, nonetheless.

'Three months ago, the team's accountant vanished, and a hell of a lot of money went with him. By the simple means of torturing his wife, they managed to trace the guy, to a place in Spain called Palafrugell. They placed a contract on him, through Dougie Terry, and two guys were sent out to take care of the matter.

'They duly did. The accountant was found stabbed to death in the apartment he was renting. Terry's guys brought back the cash, but they brought it up to Edinburgh. Then the Comedian called Birmingham and told them that his boss had said that the fee on offer for the job,

206

forty grand, was too low, since the guy had pinched four hundred thousand, not the two hundred the Brummies had claimed.'

Skinner shook his head, gravely. 'You can't trust these Midlanders, can you. Go on.'

'He said,' continued McGuire, 'that since they had been pikers, they could have back the two hundred thou. He told them that Jackie was going to keep half, that their dough was in the left luggage at Waverley Station, and that the key was in the post.'

The big DI grinned. 'It turns out, sir, that these people aren't just cheats. They don't have a sense of humour, either. This morning two guys with shooters, and a driver, left Birmingham in a blue Ford Scorpio, registration M 22 FQD, with instructions to visit Jackie Charles at home at midnight tonight and ensure that he and his missus have a double funeral.'

The DCC looked at McGuire, then across at Mackie. 'Did you say a plum, Brian? This is a bloody pineapple. If we can manage to nab these guys and get them to talk, we'll have something to lay at Jackie's door at last. You can go to Tynecastle, Thin Man, you too, Mario, if you want . . .' McGuire, a Hibs fan, made an expression of distaste. '. . . But report to Andy Martin at Fettes at eight o'clock.

'Before you go though, arrange for armed people in plain clothes to watch Jackie's house from now on, in case these Brummies can't tell the time.

'But tell them to be discreet. I don't want Charles to have the faintest idea that something's up, until the visiting team appears, and we have them in the bag.'

40

'I want these people taken completely by surprise, gentlemen.' Andy Martin tapped the street map of Edinburgh spread out on the conference table in the Head of CID's office.

Dave Donaldson leaned across to follow his pointing finger. Alongside him stood Skinner, with Pamela Masters, who was doing her best not to be overawed.

'The entrance to Jackie's house is here,' said Martin. 'The visitors are coming from the south, so it's odds that they'll approach from the east, from the city end of Ravelston Dykes Road.

'I want a car here, waiting in this gateway just beyond Jackie's place, and another in position in Murrayfield Road. You, Dave, plus Mackie, McGuire and McIlhenney, will be across the road, out of sight in the bushes. I will be hidden in Jackie's garden, with night-glasses, at a point from which I can see the approach of the car, whichever direction it comes from.

'We'll have spotters parked here,' he tapped the map twice, 'and here too, just in case we're wrong about the direction of the approach. Their job will be to give the alert as soon as the Birmingham car appears.'

He leaned back. 'The road narrows at the entrance to

Jackie's place. As soon as the target vehicle gets into that area, our two cars will move out, on my command, and block it in, front and rear. They'll have high-powered wide-beam floodlights, two mounted on each vehicle. As soon as the Brummies are blocked in, we'll hit their car with light, blinding them but letting us see what we're doing.

'We will all be carrying, and wearing protective gear, and there will be armed officers in the two police cars. I want a very heavy show of force, to discourage any thought by these guys of shooting their way out.

'It's very important that we take these men alive. However, if anyone inside that car points a gun at any officer, then he goes down, no question. If the others are hit in the process, that'll be just too bad.' He looked across the table.

'You clear about all that, Dave?'

Donaldson nodded. 'It's understood. Do you want me to brief Mackie and McGuire?'

'No, I'll do that when they report at eight. Meanwhile you ensure that the people in the support cars are our very best shots. I don't want any Wild West stuff.'

'Okay, I'll get on with that now. I'll see you back here at eight.'

'Fine.'

Donaldson nodded to Skinner, with an informal salute, and left the room.

'Ever seen him under fire?' the DCC asked, after the door had closed.

'No,' said Martin, 'but he's well qualified. When he was a DS he took on two armed bank robbers in bad light, and bluffed them into dropping their weapons by aiming a truncheon at them.'

'Mmm. Yes, I recall that. Still, when you have your team meeting tonight, you'd be well-advised to order that if it comes to shooting, everyone follows Mackie's lead, or yours. You two are the best shots we've got and you don't hesitate, either of you. Make sure that you and he are on either side of the vehicle so that between you you can see everything that's going on inside.

'These people will not be Kamikaze pilots, but like you said, if any one of them offers a threat with a weapon, shoot him. Fill the fucking car with bullets if you have to.'

He looked down at his personal assistant and saw her face go pale. 'Shocked, Pamela?' he asked, his tone suddenly gentle. 'Of course you are, listening to us talking about shooting people. But it's part of the job. I've had to do it, Mr Martin's had to do it, so has DCI Mackie . . . yes, Sergeant, big quiet Brian could shoot your eyes out at four hundred yards.

'None of us wants to, but it's important that the people on the other side know that if they as much as present firearms at us, then we will, without a second's hesitation, shoot them dead. That way, they won't take the chance.

'You'll see, tonight there'll be lots of light and lots of noise, but no shooting. That's how it works out, nearly always.' He glanced at Martin and gave a short, grim, laugh. 'Except when I'm around, of course. Some daft bastard always has a go then!

'But don't worry, Andy. I won't be there tonight. I'm taking myself out of the firing line for a while. And anyway, I've got other things to do.'

He made towards the door, then stopped. 'Oh yes. A thought occurred, Chief Superintendent, about the Carole Charles murder. Are we still trying to find her friend, the woman Donna, that Jackie mentioned?'

Martin frowned. 'She's not at the top of my list, boss. We're still trying to trace anyone who was passing the scene and might have seen the killer arrive or leave. We've had people coming forward, but nothing so far that's stood up. We're looking into all Jackie's business records. Plus we're checking through his properties, trying to trace the ledger Medina claimed to have seen.

'On top of that, we've had Medina's death to deal with – although that may be cleared up – and now there's this Birmingham lead. Maybe the Brummies were behind last Wednesday's fire. Who knows?'

'We'll find out when you arrest them,' said Skinner. 'Still, Donna's a loose end and she should be tied up. I'll tell you what, since your resources are so stretched, I'll put Sergeant Masters on to it.'

He looked at his PA. 'Pamela, I'll carry on alone for now with the check through CID records. I want you to go up to Marco's leisure club in Grove Street. They run a Yoga class twice weekly, and Carole Charles, last Wednesday's murder victim, was a regular attender. Have a look at the club's membership records, and see if you can put a surname and an address to this woman Donna that her husband spoke about.

'It's probably of no consequence. It's just a piece of information that we don't have, and us coppers, being curious, like to know everything, about everything. It's what being a detective's about, really.'

41

Neil McIlhenney's feet were killing him. They hurt from the pounding of his chase after Heenan. Now they were slogging up and down the stairs and along the corridors of the big block of flats in Slateford in which Carl Medina had lived and died.

On top of that, his trousers were torn at the knee, and his shoulder was starting to hurt, both consequences of his tackle on the fugitive. Still, he smiled inwardly in pleasure at the force with which Heenan had hit the ground, and at the satisfied expressions on the faces of several of the bystanders who had seen his downfall.

He had knocked on the doors of seventeen flats so far, from the top floor down, and had shown his warrant card, and a newly taken Polaroid photograph of Thomas Maxwell Heenan, to twelve householders, noting the numbers of the five who would require return visits.

He knocked on door number eighteen. After a few moments a light went on behind the obscured glass panel, and an old woman's quavering voice called out, 'Just coming.'

The door creaked open. McIlhenney read the name on the panel. 'Mrs Smith?' he asked.

'Miss,' said the old woman, abruptly.

'Sorry,' he said quickly, producing his warrant card once again and holding it up for her to see. 'I'm Detective Sergeant McIlhenney. I'm investigating the death of a young man yesterday, on the third floor of this building, that's one above you.'

'Mr Medina,' she said. 'Nice young man, considering. They weren't married you know,' she added, conspiratorially, 'him and that young woman Angela.'

McIlhenney shook his head. 'That's the way it is these days, Miss Smith.'

'Not in my world, Sergeant! Now what can I do for you?'

He produced his Polaroid. 'I'd like you to look at this, and tell me if you saw this man around midday yesterday, in or near this building.'

She took the photograph and peered at it through her heavy-framed spectacles. After a few seconds she stepped out into the corridor, holding it up to the stronger light. At last she looked up at him, handing the Polaroid back.

'Do you know, Sergeant, I believe that I did. I was looking out of my front window yesterday, just before twelve.' She smiled. 'I do that quite a lot. It overlooks the entrance, you see. There was a tall, well-dressed, fair-haired man. He walked up to the front door, pressed the buzzer and went in.

'This looks like him.'

McIlhenney beamed. 'Miss Smith, you have made my day.

'Would you be prepared to attend an identification parade down at the St Leonard's police station? You needn't worry about anyone seeing you. We'll ask you to look at a line of men, but you'll be behind a one-way glass panel.'

Miss Smith nodded. 'Yes,' she said. 'I think I could do that.'

'That's great. I'll send a car for you once it's arranged. Meanwhile, is there anything else you can remember about this man?'

She thought for a moment. 'Not really,' she muttered, almost to herself. 'Only that he was carrying a Safeway bag.'

42

It was almost 2.30 p.m. before Inspector Shields returned Skinner's phone call. The photographic unit at the Howdenhall Lab was closed for the weekend and its head had been on the golf course.

'You were looking for me, sir?' boomed the cheery voice.

'Yes, George. Thanks for calling back. You sound as if you had a good day.'

'Can't grumble, sir. I shot a net 66, off 16 handicap. I should win the medal with that, unless there's another bandit still to come in.'

Skinner laughed. 'Good for you. Listen George, I want to ask you about your negatives, and what happens to them. I know that where major criminal investigations are concerned, they go to the files and are stored there. But what about the others?'

'What others, sir?' Shields sounded puzzled.

'Photographs from accident scenes, to be specific.'

There was a hiss of air from the other end of the line as the Inspector thought about the question. 'Mostly, sir, they're disposed of once it's clear that they're no longer needed. Do you have a specific accident in mind?'

'Yes. It happened eighteen years ago.'

'Then I'd have binned the negs, sir. Chances are they were destroyed long since . . .' He paused, '. . . unless of course, Sergeant Whatnot took them.'

'Who?'

'You remember, sir, Tam Whatling. He worked in the photographic unit for years. Everyone called him Sergeant Whatnot. He kept a lot of the negs once they were done with. He was always going on about writing his memoirs.'

'I remember Big Tam well,' said Skinner. 'He retired didn't he, last year? I made the presentation to him in the Chief's absence. Where is he now, d'you know?'

'He retired to a pub across the river in Lower Largo, sir. It's called the Travellers' Inn, I think. He also does photography: weddings and the like.

'If the negs you're after still exist, then the only place they'll be is with ex-Sergeant Whatnot.'

'In that case,' said Skinner, 'it looks as if I'm going for a pint in Fife tomorrow.'

43

Pamela Masters had never been to Marco's before. She practised her aerobics at the Edinburgh Club, just off London Road, where she was a member. The reception area was thronged when she arrived and so, while it cleared, she took a walk around the rambling building, looking in on the sweaty glass-walled squash courts and at the lines of snooker tables, a green baize archipelago in the midst of a dark sea.

Eventually she found herself back at the reception desk, from which the queue had disappeared. Showing her warrant card, she asked to see the duty manager.

'That's me,' said the girl on the desk, offering her hand as she stepped out of her cubicle. 'Sheila King. How can I help you?'

Sergeant Masters shook the outstretched hand. 'It's to do with a death which occurred on Wednesday,' she said. 'Mrs Carole Charles. You may have read about it.'

The manageress nodded. 'Yes, I did. That was awful. Poor woman.'

'I'm led to believe that Mrs Charles was a member here, and that she attended a Yoga class twice a week?'

Sheila King's mouth dropped open in a gasp. 'No! Was that her? I'd never have known from the picture in the

217

News. Blonde woman, late forties but really good looking and fit for her age. We just knew her as Carole; it's first name terms in my Yoga class.'

'You take it yourself?'

'Yes, Mondays and Thursdays, eight till nine.'

'Was Carole Charles a regular attender?'

'We-ell.' Sheila King paused. 'If you call about once or twice a month regular. She certainly didn't take every class. No-one does that.

'Fit woman, though, as I say. And no kids.'

'How did you know that?'

'The bum, dear.' She glanced down at Masters' mid-section. 'Tight, like yours. Pelvis hadn't spread.' She slapped her own backside with both hands. 'Nothing you can do about it. I've got two, and look at mine. Dead giveaway.'

Pamela smiled. 'I understand that Mrs Charles had a friend at the class, a woman called Donna. Is that right?'

The yoga teacher looked puzzled. 'Donna? No Donnas in my class. I'm certain of it. I've got Eileens, Aileens, Irenes, a Bernice and a few Maggies, but no Donna.'

She beckoned the Sergeant to follow. 'Come on through and we'll look at the membership records, but I can't remember a single Donna.' She led the way into a small back office where a computer sat on a table switched on. Quickly she keyed in 'Donna' and pressed the search button. The machine buzzed for about twenty seconds, then flashed up a message: 'No Donna found.'

Pamela Masters frowned. 'How strange. Did Mrs Charles have any other friends at the club?'

The mother-of-two shook her head. 'No. She wasn't

a mixer. Friendly enough, but she didn't invite conversation. Once the class was over, she didn't hang around, just showered, changed and out the door.'

'Hmm,' said the Sergeant. 'A mystery woman. Two of them in fact, her and Donna. My boss isn't going to like that. Not at all!'

44

'See if you can get an ID parade set up for six o'clock. I want to show Heenan to your old lady while that picture is still fresh in her mind.'

McIlhenney laughed. 'We could hold off for a week and my Miss Smith would still do the business. Old folk like her never miss a trick. She's probably a nosy old bat and a pain in the arse to her neighbours, but to us, she's a Godsend.'

'Still,' said Donaldson, 'let's take no chances. We don't want her to fall off her perch before she's fingered Heenan for us.

'Did the Muirhead woman pick the muscle who was with him out of our mugshot library?'

The big Sergeant nodded. 'Aye she did, and that's another cracker. She identified Ricky McCartney. I sent a car round to his house to pick him up, but he wasn't there. We'll get him, though. He's pretty obvious, is our Ricky.'

'That he is,' said Donaldson. 'Mind you, I don't know what we'll be able to put to him. According to Angela Muirhead's story, he never said a word while he was in the house with Heenan.'

'No,' said McIlhenney. 'He just kept eyeing up the

220

furniture as if he was deciding what he would smash first. But he didn't demand money, or offer violence.'

'Ricky doesn't have to offer violence. He *is* violence.'

'Fine, but try putting that down on a charge sheet: "Mr McCartney is charged with giving Miss Muirhead's sideboard a threatening look." As my Olive often says, I think not!'

'I know. Chances are he's heard already that we've picked up Heenan and he's gone to ground for a few days. But let's keep looking anyway.'

Donaldson stood up from his chair and walked to the window of his second-storey office. He gazed out towards Holyrood Park and the Radical Road. 'You handle the parade on your own, Neil. I want to brief the armed officers about tonight's operation.'

'I thought Mr Martin was having a team talk at eight.'

'He is, but he told me to handpick the people.'

'Mmm. Okay, sir. I'll look after Miss Smith.' He turned to leave, but as he did, there was a knock and the door opened. A WPC from the main reception area looked round. 'Excuse me, sir,' she said to Donaldson, 'but PCs Bridger and Fisher are downstairs. They're one of the Panda teams. They say they have to see you right away.'

The Superintendent frowned. 'They have to see me, do they?' He paused, then went back to his desk. 'Okay, send them up. But this better be important. Stay for a minute, Neil, will you.'

The door closed on the WPC. A minute later, there was another knock. 'Come!' shouted Donaldson. PCs Bridger and Fisher seemed to slide into the room. They looked nervous and uncertain as they stood before Donaldson's desk, caps in hand.

'Well?' said the Superintendent, sternly.

'Well, sir,' began the older of the two. McIlhenney recognised him as Bridger. They had worked together once. 'We were called in to help at Slateford last night, on yon boy's murder.'

Donaldson nodded. 'So?'

'Well. I heard the wee doctor say that the time of death was late morning.' Bridger hesitated.

'So?' It was almost a shout.

'It's like this, sir,' said Fisher, coming to the rescue. McIlhenney could tell that bad news was about to break, and that the task was beyond Bridger. 'We heard that you've picked up Tommy Heenan for the murder.'

'That's right. We've got an eye-witness too, who says she can put him at the scene, just before twelve.'

Fisher sucked in his breath. 'Ahh. That's a problem, sir. The thing is, Malky and I were on patrol in Peffermill Road yesterday in the Panda. We saw Tommy Heenan going into his office at quarter to twelve. No way could he have killed the boy Medina.'

Donaldson sat bolt upright in his chair. McIlhenney pushed himself off the wall against which he had been leaning. 'You sure about that?' he barked, as the Superintendent glared at him.

'Come on, Neil,' said Bridger, finding his voice at last. 'We've known Tommy Heenan for years, and we were no more than ten feet away from him.'

'Bugger it!' cried the big Sergeant furiously. 'I was dead certain we had the bastard. I'd have loved to put him away for murder.'

'But if it wasn't him, why did he leg it?' said Donaldson.

McIlhenney shrugged. 'He thought he was done. His wife would have been worse than useless as an alibi, and there's no-one in Peffermill would lie in the witness box for him. I reckon he must have panicked.'

The Superintendent looked up at the two Constables, at that moment the least popular men in St Leonard's. 'Okay. You can go.' As the door closed on them once more, he looked up at McIlhenney.

'Of course,' he said, slowly, 'we could always tell Bridger and Fisher that they were wrong, and go ahead with the ID parade.'

The Sergeant gazed back at him, trying to read his expression. 'No, sir,' he said quietly. 'Not *we*. I couldn't tell them that, when I know they're not.'

With a sigh, Donaldson nodded. 'In that case, Neil, get a photographer up here to take a shot of the bruise on my leg. If I can do nothing else, I'll charge the bastard with police assault and stick him up in front of the Sheriff on Monday morning. With his record that should earn him six months.'

'Small consolation,' muttered the Sergeant.

'It's the best we're going to do. But maybe we'll get a result with Ricky McCartney. Maybe your Miss Smith will identify him.'

McIlhenney shook his head. 'McCartney's a gorilla, sir. No, the old lady saw someone fair-haired and well-dressed, carrying a Safeway bag, which contained, no doubt, a binliner and four other Safeway bags.

'She didn't see Tommy Heenan, okay. But she did see someone who looks bloody like him.'

45

The roar of the crowd in the rebuilt Tynecastle engulfed them as Maggie Rose turned off grey-tenemented Gorgie Road, and parked in the enclosure towards which she had been directed by a uniformed officer. It rose and fell, a joining of two giant voices each singing out its alarm, expectation, disappointment and exultation.

As they reached the entrance to the main grandstand the sound rose in a crescendo and became a single, sustained shriek of joy. 'Somebody's scored,' said Sammy Pye, a closet Rangers supporter.

There was a lone policeman on duty at the gate, together with a security guard employed by Heart of Midlothian Football Club, or the Jam Tarts, as they are known by the entire population of Edinburgh; some friends, some foes, very few indifferent.

Rose and Pye showed their warrant cards. 'We're looking for Jimmy Lee,' the Chief Inspector said to the doorman.

'Ye'll no' get him till time up, hen. He'll be up in his seat among the Willie Bauld Restaurant guests.'

Maggie fixed him with the special steely glare which she reserved for men who called her 'hen'. 'If I want him, I'll get him,' she said, then paused. 'But we'll wait till full-time. How long is there to go?'

'About thirty-five minutes,' said Pye.

'On yis go through and watch the rest,' said the steward. 'There's no seats, but if yis go through that door on the left,' he pointed through the entrance hall, 'it'll take ye out on to the pitch. Yis can watch the rest frae the entrance tae the tunnel. Yis'll find Superintendent Johnston there.' Rose nodded. Fred Johnston was commander of the police division which took in Tynecastle.

'S'a great game so far. The Jambos have just gone one up.'

'How do you know who scored?' Maggie asked. 'You've never left the door.'

'Listen,' said the man, putting hand to ear.

Inside the stadium, the great single voice of Jambo support boomed out an anthem.

> Can ye hear the Rangers sing?
> Cannae hear a fuckin' thing,
> Nana Na Na Na Na!

'Ahh,' said the Chief Inspector. She and Pye followed the steward's directions. A narrow passageway led them past two rooms from which emerged an overpowering liniment smell, then round to the right and up a slight incline towards the field.

As they emerged into the open air of the arena, floodlit even in the daylight hours, the atmosphere sent shivers through them. Opposite and on either side the three newly-built cantilevered grandstands towered a hundred feet above their heads, each packed tight, blue colours

225

predominant on the left, maroon on the right. Behind them, the crowd in the old stand bayed for more Rangers' blood, as on the field, Hearts pressed home their advantage against the league leaders, looking to spoil a million football-pool coupons and fixed-odds betting lines.

As Rose and Pye stood there, suddenly overwhelmed, a tall uniformed man, carrying a walkie-talkie and wearing an overcoat and silver-braided, peaked cap bore sternly down upon them. His expression softened as he recognised the red-headed Rose. 'Hello, Maggie,' he said. 'What brings you here?'

'We need to interview someone called Jimmy Lee. The doorman sent us through here to wait for time up.'

'Fair enough,' said Superintendent Johnston, leaning close to make himself heard. 'But you can't stay here.' He pointed to his left, past the Rangers management team in their technical area, who were leaping, jumping and gesticulating manically as they urged on their players. 'There are two seats down beside the ambulance men. Sit yourselves down there. Go back to the entrance at full-time and I'll have Jimmy Lee brought to you.'

'Thanks,' said Rose. 'Has it been a good game?'

'Wouldn't know,' said Johnston. 'The game's the last thing I can watch.' They realised for the first time that the man was as tense as a drawn bowstring. 'I've got about eighteen thousand people in here, most of them hysterical, and they'll all be funnelling out into tight exit roads at the end.

'Rangers need at least a point out of this game, and if they don't get it, I'll have ten thousand very unhappy Bluenoses to control.'

'I'll keep my fingers crossed for you,' shouted the

Chief Inspector, over a sudden scream as the Rangers goalkeeper pulled off a seemingly impossible save.

They settled into their seats beside the first aid team, who were Hearts supporters to a man. As the game wore on the home side continued to press their advantage, looking for the game-winning second goal. The champions' rock-solid defence seemed on the verge of collapse several times, but on each occasion, as if heeding the cries of their support, they simply refused to surrender.

Gradually, as the Hearts players began to tire, they began to command more of the ball. But the home-bred Tynecastle defenders were as heroic as their cosmopolitan counterparts, and they dug in desperately to hold on to their winning lead.

The referee's whistle was almost in his mouth to blow full-time when the ball was swept out of midfield and down the right towards the Gorgie end and Hearts goal. Danish, Dutch and English genius combined. A perfectly weighted cross curved towards the far post, where, defying both age and gravity, Rangers' legendary striker rose, leaping and hanging in the air like a salmon fighting its way back to its spawning ground against the river's flow, to send a header bulleting into the back of the net for the equaliser.

Half of the crowd leapt up, waving colours in triumph, screaming their joy across the floodlit stadium. The rest sank back into their plastic seats, howling their disappointment and wringing their club colours between their hands.

The restart was a formality. As soon as the ball was in motion, three loud blasts of the referee's whistle ended the game. Rose and Pye stood with the rest and applauded as the drained, exhausted players left the field, shaking hands as professional colleagues, the animosities of battle forgotten.

Maggie turned and looked up, for the first time, into the main grandstand. She scanned the crowd until, in the central area behind the directors' box, she caught sight of Brian Mackie. He looked more sombre than ever.

As Fred Johnston had instructed, they made their way back to the entrance, past the closed dressing-room doors, through which the managers' voices could be heard. They waited there for almost ten minutes before a slim, dark-haired figure made his way towards them, wearing a maroon blazer with a crested badge, a white shirt and club tie. He was led by a uniformed woman officer.

Rose and Pye stepped forward. 'Mr Lee?' asked the Chief Inspector. The young man nodded. He was in his mid-twenties, slim and strikingly handsome. The heavy limp with which he walked seemed entirely out of place.

'DCI Rose and DC Pye. We need to talk to you. Can we go somewhere quiet?'

Jimmy Lee looked around. 'This place is bedlam. All the function suites will be full. Let's go across to my office.'

He led the way, slowly, out of the grandstand and across to a small single-storey building which housed the Hearts shop and commercial offices. As he walked, stopping occasionally to acknowledge a fan or return a handshake, the two detectives could see how badly he was handicapped.

Finally they reached the entrance door to the office suite. Lee opened it with a key, and showed them to a small room at the back. 'In here,' he said. The room was furnished with a desk and four chairs. Against one wall cardboard cartons marked, 'Away strips', were piled almost to the ceiling. In the far corner, stood two metal elbow crutches.

'D'you still use those?' asked Sammy Pye, pointing.

'Most of the time. Not on match days though. I don't like the punters to see me like that.' Lee settled awkwardly into the chair behind the desk as the police officers took seats facing them. 'So what's this about?' he asked, in a quiet, articulate voice.

'Do you know a man named Evan Mulgrew?' asked Rose.

The former footballer smiled. 'No, I can't say I do. Mulgrew isn't a common name among Jambos. Why?'

'Because we interviewed Mulgrew today in Peterhead Prison. He made allegations about you, a man named Ricky McCartney and another man named Douglas Terry.' Briefly but graphically she repeated Mulgrew's story.

'Was Mulgrew telling the truth, Mr Lee? Was that what happened to you?'

The young man's face had gone chalk white. He winced occasionally, as if recalling the agony of his attack. At last he looked across at Rose and Pye. 'Yes,' he whispered.

'Tell us about it,' the Chief Inspector said, gently.

Lee leaned back in his chair, composing himself. 'No point keeping my mouth shut now, I suppose,' he said.

'It was the life, you see. Players train in the mornings, and unless we've got businesses outside football, the rest of the day's our own.

'We get bored. You can only go to the movies so often. And anyway, we're sportsmen. So some of us go to the bookies and play the horses. A few of us get out of control. We think we're infallible because we're young and famous, with a few quid in our pockets. But we find out that we're wrong.

'I was down a hundred grand.'

Pye whistled. 'To which bookie?'

'The John Jackson shop just along the road. The fact is I didn't really know one end of a horse from another. When it came to winners I couldn't pick my nose. Eventually, Dougie Terry – he runs all the Jackson shops – came in one day and told me that I was barred, and that he wanted my tab paid off in three months.

'I told him that if he waited till the end of the season, in six months, I'd ask for a transfer and settle up with him out of my signing on fee. Not that I wanted a transfer, mind. I only ever wanted to be a Jambo. A few months before that Rangers had offered one and a half million for me, but I'd turned them down. Pissed the chairman off no end, I'll tell you.' He grinned at the recollection.

'But Dougie Terry said, no, three months it is.

'I did the best I could. Every bonus went straight to Terry, but after two and a half months I was still eighty thousand down.'

He paused and took a deep breath. 'One day, I was leaving the ground after training, and Ricky McCartney stopped me. I knew him from around the betting shop.

'He said that Terry had sent him to make me an offer.'

Rose held up a hand. 'He actually said that Terry had sent him?'

'Yes. He said that Terry's boss – I don't know who that is – had been approached by a Malaysian gambling syndicate. The Jambos were drawn in the cup against some non-league team from Melrose. They had got there on merit but the odds on us to win were astronomical. McCartney said that Terry wanted me to make sure that we lost. I was to get our goalie in on the act and we were to fix it. If I did that, my tab was clear.'

'And if you didn't?'

'McCartney made it clear that it wasn't a request. He said that if I liked being a footballer, I'd better make it work.'

'So what did you do?'

'You must know what I did. I never said a word to our goalie, but he had a bad day and let one in in the first half. I got a dead leg early on, and it took me about an hour to run it off. But once I was moving freely it was easy.' He smiled, sadly. 'I was quite a player.'

'You never considered letting the game go?' she asked. 'Not even when you were a goal down, and you were injured, and no-one would have known.'

Lee gasped audibly, and looked across at her with genuine shock on his face. 'I'm a Jambo, Miss Rose. And I'm . . . or was . . . a professional footballer. Ours is the most honest game in the world, and this is one of the oldest and finest clubs in the world.

'It's unthinkable that any footballer would try to fix a game. That any Jambo would . . . I just can't find the words.'

The Chief Inspector nodded. 'I believe you. But why didn't you report it to us?'

Lee smiled again, ruefully. 'Because if I had, the truth

about my gambling would have come out, and the fans would never have forgiven me. And because I was scared of Ricky McCartney.'

'Yet you went ahead and won the game?'

'Yes. I suppose I thought that I'd get away with it, that I was untouchable, and that after all, Terry would wait for me to get a transfer. I was wrong again.'

'What happened, Jimmy?' Maggie rose asked, gently. 'On the night.'

Lee drew in his breath and furrowed his brow. 'I was going home after a game. My last game. I still lived with my parents in Wester Hailes. I was nearly there when a guy stopped me and asked for an autograph. The place was deserted as usual. We were just chatting, when I was jumped and dragged off behind the building.

'There were five of them. Ricky McCartney and four others. I recognised one of them – his name's Barney something – but not the others. They were all wearing Hibs hats and scarves, and the other three had them over their faces.

'McCartney said to me, "You made a big mistake, son. Dougie Terry's boss had to pay off those Malaysians. Now you're going to pay him off." Then they set about me.' He closed his eyes, and leaned back in his chair. He was trembling.

'McCartney shoved a Hibs cap in my mouth, to stop me screaming. The other three used baseball bats, but he and Barney had big hammers. The three guys concentrated on my legs. McCartney and Barney battered my knees and my ankles with the hammers.

'I fainted after a while. When I came to, they were gone. And so was I, as a footballer. I nearly lost both legs.

I would have, but for an absolutely brilliant orthopaedic surgeon up at the PMR. I've got plastic knees and metal braced ankles now, but at least I can walk after a fashion.'

'Why did you say it was Hibs fans who attacked you?' asked Pye.

Lee shook his head. 'I never did. I just said that they were wearing Hibs scarves, which was true. I just didn't identify McCartney or Barney, that was all.'

'Why not?' asked Rose.

'Because I was terrified, that's why.'

'Was that the end of it?'

'Like hell! I got a hundred and fifty grand from my insurance, and Dougie Terry took the lot. But the club gave me a testimonial and that raised another eighty-five thousand. The organisers had that put in Trust, so they couldn't touch it. The Chairman gave me a job on the staff too, so I could still be a Jambo. I always will be.'

'We're going to arrest McCartney,' said Rose. 'Will you identify him now?'

Jimmy Lee looked at her, as if making a decision, then nodded. 'If you can guarantee me protection from him, I will. There's no point in keeping my gambling secret any longer. Who's to care? I'm just another ex-player on crutches.'

'About Barney, the other man,' said the policewoman. 'That was almost certainly Bernard Cogan, a known associate of McCartney. He was killed in a pub fight about two years ago. It would help if we could identify at least one of the other men involved. How about the man who stopped you? Can you describe him?'

Lee nodded, emphatically. 'Definitely. He was heavy

built, with a big moustache and a scar across his fore-head.' He drew a finger diagonally from his hairline down to his right eyebrow. 'He was a real poser. It was cold, but he was wearing a maroon vest. He had a big tattoo on his right shoulder. A vulture, I think.'

Rose laughed in triumph. 'Evan Mulgrew! We know where to find him, and I'll bet that he'll sing like a bird.'

She slapped the desk. 'Come in Douglas Terry, your time is up. Or rather, it's only just beginning!'

46

'I'm a tidy bloke, Pamela. I like all the ends tied off, and everything neatly in place.' Skinner sighed and scratched his head in exasperation.

'I was expecting that you would come back with a statement from Donna somebody about her friendship with Carole Charles, and that would be it. Instead, you've discovered that Carole was lying to Jackie about her Yoga class, most of the time at least, and quite possibly, since we can't find any trace of her, about the pal she was supposed to be meeting.'

'Where does that take us, sir?'

He smiled at her across the dusty table. 'You're a woman. You tell me?'

Masters gulped. 'Well, the obvious question, if not conclusion, is, was Mrs Charles having an affair? A middle-aged, attractive woman, maybe bored with her husband after twenty-five years – I was bored with mine after two, to tell the truth – with plenty of money and time on her hands.

'She has a mystery pal whose second name her husband doesn't know, and whom he's never met. I'd say that she was at it. She had a boyfriend stashed away somewhere.'

Skinner nodded. 'Or a girlfriend,' he grunted. 'These days you never know.

'But yes, a man on the side; that fits with what we know of Carole. It ties in with Carl Medina's story of the pass she made at him and with my own recollection of the woman from twenty years back.

'It's a bugger, right enough. It throws everything up in the air with Mr Martin's investigation.'

'Why's that, sir?'

'Because it puts Jackie back in the frame, for all his show of grief and shock when we told him about the fire. Maybe it *was* all an act. Maybe he realised what had happened with Medina. Maybe he found out about the boyfriend. And maybe, he just had enough. Except . . .' He hesitated.

'Jackie Charles loved that showroom of his like an only son. Even if he had decided to have his wife killed, I find it hard to believe that he'd have had it done that way. He'd just have arranged for her to have an accident.'

As he said the words, a shiver ran through him. He stopped short and gazed at the wall. 'Are you all right, sir?' asked Pamela Masters.

Skinner shook himself. 'Oh yes, I'm all right. Someone just walked over my grave, that was all. Except, if things work out in a certain direction, I'm going to walk over his.'

She stared at him, puzzled, and a little frightened by his tone.

'But back to today's business,' he said abruptly. Files were stacked high on the table in the CID Records Office. 'I've been through all these and only two offer any live possibilities.

'One is Jackie Charles, aforementioned.' She looked at him in surprise. He nodded. 'Yes. Jackie lived in Gullane at the time, and he knew that he was under suspicion of being involved in serious crimes. I was a gung-ho member of the squad, newly promoted Sergeant and out to make my name. Our paths had crossed before and he knew that I was after him. He knew what I drove and where I garaged it, plus he was in the motor business.

'And yet . . .' He stopped for a moment, and shook his head.

'At the time, we weren't within a mile of nailing Jackie, and he knew it. The fact is that apart from two abortive tips about where he kept his records, we've *never* been within a mile. Also, I was low down the CID food chain at the time. The man he really had to fear was Gillespie, my boss.

'Jackie's a calculating little bastard. As far as we've been able to tell he never has anything done unless there's a real need for it. And there was no real need on his part to kill me, or even to give me a fright. He had the means, and the opportunity, but I can't see any credible motive.'

'Who's the other live possibility?' asked Sergeant Masters.

He smiled grimly across at her. 'Actually, he's dead. Which may be just as well for him.

'Does the name Tony Manson mean anything to you?'

She thought for a moment, and a memory came back. 'Wasn't he murdered about a year ago? He was a gangleader, wasn't he?'

He shook his head. 'No. Tony was a businessman. Only his business was drugs, pubs and prostitution. He was a Field Marshal; other people led the common gangs. At

237

the time of Myra's accident he was my squad's number one target. We had a street-level drug dealer in our hands, facing twenty years inside and he was ready to talk.

'My job was to find someone who would corroborate his evidence that Tony Manson controlled the drug trade in Edinburgh. I was turning the city upside down at the time looking for that one brave soul. None of Tony's places were safe from me. I caused him so much aggravation that he had to shut down his drugs network, and stop his girls selling sex on the side in the saunas.' He chuckled, grimly. 'He even had to make the go-go dancers in his pubs keep their bras on.

'During that period, I, a humble newly-promoted DS like what you are now, personally cost Tony Manson a hell of a lot of money. But then Myra was killed and I was away from the job for a time. While I was off, our informant was found hanged in the toilets in the remand wing at Saughton, and the whole investigation collapsed.'

'But, sir,' asked Masters. 'With Manson dead, how will you ever be able to prove that he had your car sabotaged, if it was him?'

'I never will, Pamela. But I know a man who might be able to tell me, and if it *was* Tony, who might be able to give me the name of whoever it was cut that brake pipe for him. I'll go and see him on Monday. There'll be no point in you coming with me, though. If this bloke talks, it'll be to me alone.

'Anyway, that's enough for today.' As he picked up the files on Manson and Charles, there was a knock at the door, and Maggie Rose came into the room. He was surprised to see that she was grinning.

'They said I'd find you here, boss,' she said, giving a slight look of surprise when she saw Pamela Masters.

'Sammy and I have had a busy day. I've just given Mr Martin some great news, and he said I should tell you too, in person, so that I could see the smile on your face.'

'Sounds good. I'm ready for a laugh, so on you go.'

Five minutes later he was beaming from ear to ear. 'What a numbtie this Mulgrew must be, assuming that Lee would have forgotten his face, or his vulture. You're sure he'll talk?'

'I'm certain, boss. As soon as he sees he's in a corner he'll rush to do the best deal he can.'

'Then you and Sammy get back up to Peterhead tomorrow, and tell him from me that if he doesn't he can forget his transfer to Saughton, but that if he can give us the name of those other three guys who attacked Lee, I'll arrange for him to have the best room in the house!

'Get a wanted signal around on McCartney too, if Donaldson hasn't done it already. Description, car registration, the lot. And make it national. I want that man arrested wherever he is.'

Rose nodded and left the room, still grinning.

'That's Maggie's weekend taken care of,' said Skinner. 'Mine too, come to think of it. I'm off to Fife. If you're not doing anything, I'll take you with me to meet ex-Sergeant Whatnot.'

As she looked at him, puzzled, he glanced at his watch. It showed seven fifty, too late to visit Jazz again. 'Come to think of it,' he said, 'if you're not doing anything tonight, how about dinner?'

47

Andy Martin, crouched in the shrubbery at the foot of the villa's long sloping garden, whispered into his walkie-talkie. 'Brian, you can see the house from your position. Is there any sign that Charles knows we're here?'

'No, sir, nothing's changed. The light's still on in the downstairs hall and in a room to the side. What can you see?'

Martin peered through the night-glasses, looking eastwards along Ravelston Dykes Road, then down the hill where it swept up from Queensferry Road, the north-western approach to the capital. He could just glimpse the top of one police car, hidden in a lay-by. The other was out of his sight. 'Bugger all,' he replied at last. 'Let's hope these boys are punctual. They should be here any minute now.'

The team had been in position since 10.30 p.m., awaiting the appearance of the reported assassins from the Midlands. Wearing hard-hats and flak-jackets, they had moved in silently, from vehicles tucked away in the car park of Murryfield Golf Club, making sure that no residents, and particularly not Mr John Jackson Charles, were aware of their arrival.

They had sat and they had waited, for an hour and

twenty-nine minutes, alerted by the passage of each car along the road, but given no signal by their watchers, hidden out of sight three hundred yards away in either direction.

The flash of headlights from the side street meant nothing to Martin; at first. But suddenly, a distance away, he heard an engine roar into life, and a squeal of rubber as it took off.

He swung up the night-glasses, just in time to see a long car pull directly out into the path of another vehicle heading towards him along Ravelston Dykes Road. Behind that, he was sure that he could make out the shape of a third vehicle, but without lights.

The first, intruding car slammed on its brakes. Through the glasses Martin saw the shapes of two men as they jumped out, and on the evening breeze, he fancied he heard borne towards him, the cry of 'Armed police!' He could see little else for the obstructing vehicle, which he now recognised as a Jaguar, long enough to block the entire carriageway, but he fancied that he saw more movement from the car bringing up the rear.

He sat there, momentarily frozen, until the flash in the night and the bang of the gunshot hurled him into action. 'Move, move, move!' he yelled into the walkie-talkie. 'Murrayfield Road vehicle, head east along Ravelston Dykes Road, fast! The other car block this driveway! There's something going on along there. Come on everyone.'

He vaulted over the low wall of the Charles villa and sprinted up the slope and round the curve, towards the Jaguar, following his men in the Ford Granada which had been parked out of his sight. As he ran he could hear, above the noise of the braking police car as the blockading Jaguar's width brought it to a halt, a heavy engine roar, and tyres squeal as it reversed, spun round and raced off into the night.

Martin reached the scene just after the men from the Granada, who had jumped from their vehicle and taken up firing positions behind the Jaguar. He switched on his hand lamp and shone the broad brilliant beam on to the vehicle beyond, drawing his firearm as he did.

As he had thought, the third vehicle was gone. But facing him, he saw the nose of a blue Ford Scorpio, with its rear doors lying open. He directed the beam on the registration plate and read, 'M22 FQD'.

'Bugger!' he said, softly.

He swung the light back up, playing it around the vehicle. He could see no-one outside, but on the roadway, his eyes caught a reflected flash from broken glass. As Mackie, Donaldson, McGuire and McIlhenney arrived at the scene, panting from the sprint, he walked slowly around the Jaguar and shone his torch into the ambushed car.

The driver was slumped across the passenger seat, prevented by his belt from falling across it. Where his right eye should have been, there was instead a multi-coloured, glistening mess from which blood was pouring copiously on to the fabric of the upholstery. On the floor, in the foot well on the passenger side, Martin could see a pistol. The man's right hand was still twitching, the fingers clenching as if trying to pull a trigger.

He stood up and turned away wearily. 'Call an ambulance, someone,' he called, as the others came round the Jaguar to meet him. 'There's a guy in here, and he's still alive . . . technically. As for the others, I reckon that, technically, they're as dead as he's going to be soon.'

'Jackie's intelligence network must be as good as ours. His guys have beaten us to it.'

He looked at the watcher who had been nearest to the incident. 'Did you get a good look at what happened?'

'Not really, sir. I was trying to verify the number of the Scorpio when the Jag pulled out. I just saw a lot of rushing about, then I heard the shot.'

'Did you get a look at the third vehicle?'

'No, sir, my view was obscured. I could see two men being hustled into it, then it did a reverse turn and made off. I never saw the number or the model type, only that it was a big light-coloured vehicle.'

'That's something at least. Dave,' Martin called, 'radio in and order patrols to look out for a large light-coloured car with at least four, probably five men in it. Tell them to treat them as armed and dangerous, and to do nothing other than keep them in sight.'

On impulse he swung up his night-glasses and trained them on the villa which they had been guarding. He studied the upper windows straining to see if anyone was there watching them. There was no-one there, not as much as a shadow on a curtain, but instinct told him that, if there had been, Jackie Charles would have been smiling.

48

It had been a long day for Alexis Skinner, immersed in her exploration of her mother's past.

She had devoured the diaries slowly, line by line, trying to think of herself as their author, rather than read them as a stranger, objectively. Each time she had finished a volume, she had put it down and had taken something else from the trunk.

There had been the shoes, black, suede, with three-inch heels. She had tried them on, and found them to be slightly wide, but otherwise a perfect fit. There had been the costume jewellery, most of it plastic or carved wood, but some of it gilt. She had found a heavy imitation gold choker, with matching earrings, and had sat wearing them and the shoes as she made her way through the next diary, doing her best to be her mother.

Then there had been the clothes: the black, high-lift bra she had felt through the wrapping of its parcel; a suspender belt with black nylons, still in their box; a pair of frilled black panties cut high at the hip and narrow at the crotch; a black dress in sheer satin with a neckline which plunged enough to allow the bra to be at its most effective, and a short, square-shouldered matching jacket.

She had carried them all to her bedroom, where she had undressed completely, and had put them on, one by one. The 38C brassiere had felt slightly more comfortable than she guessed it might have to her mother, and the dress had been a little loose at the hips, but otherwise everything had fitted so well that she might have shopped for it herself. The hem of the skirt sat just above her knee, fashionable eighteen years before, fashionable again in Alex's era.

She had taken off the dress and jacket, and her own engagement ring, and had sat down at her dressing table with an enlarged colour photograph of her mother before her, the last taken before her death. As first she had done years before, as a teenager, she had copied her make-up; her blusher, her eye-shadow, the way she applied her lipstick. Using styling mousse she had teased her hair as best she could into her mother's fashion. Then she had put on the dress and jacket once more, and the costume jewellery, had taken the small black patent handbag from the trunk, and had gone out, into the day.

At 4 p.m. on a March Saturday, the image of Myra Skinner had walked again in the city in which she had attended college almost thirty years earlier, and in which her boyfriend had been a student.

She had walked along Woodlands Road, past the same pubs and shops, many of which had been altered only slightly by the years, down to its junction with Sauchiehall Street, at Charing Cross; stepping confidently, hip-swinging in her high heels, eye-to-eye with many of the men she passed, and looking down on more than a few. She had walked down Sauchiehall Street, along the pavement until she had reached the pedestrian precinct.

As she had made her way, she was aware of the heads turning, of the eyes fixing upon her in a way in which they seldom had before. Not only men, but women too, some with approval, some frowning, a few with looks of open hostility.

In Marks and Spencer, a young man in his twenties, shopping alone, had smiled at her. She had been unable to stop herself. She had returned the smile; not in her normal open, friendly Alex way, but with an added curl of the lip, and a slight raising of the eyebrow. He had approached, and she had known that he was completely in her power, that she could have done with him what she would. Excitement had swept over her, a pulse-raising thrill. She had felt a sudden burning pang deep inside.

Had she not been Alexis Skinner, she might have followed the feeling to wherever it would have taken her. Instead she had smiled again at the man, her normal Alex grin this time, and had turned on her heels and left the shop.

The presence of Myra had gone, completely, and her daughter's earlier excitement had turned to self-consciousness. The languid walking pace at which she had set out had given way to shorter, more rapid strides; she had felt awkward in the shoes and uncomfortable in the clothes. Pulling the jacket tighter across her thrusting breasts, she had turned on impulse into Sauchiehall Street's multi-screen cinema, and had brought a ticket for a film, any film, just to be out of sight, and to recover herself.

It had been dark when she had emerged, and she had taken a taxi home, throwing off the jacket and unzipping the dress almost before the door had closed behind her. She had showered again, and pulled on her most comfortable jeans, then bra-less in a sweatshirt, had gone across the street to her favourite Indian restaurant, back into her own world as if seeking reassurance.

Now she sat again with curtains drawn and the reading lamp shining over her shoulder. On her lap, she held her mother's seventh diary, her record of the year in which she had turned twenty-one.

The page was headed December 31. Silently Alex read the final entry of the year.

'Afterwards, we sat up in bed and ate Spaghetti Bolognese off big white plates. Now that, Robert, is what Myra calls bringing in the New Year with a bang!'

Alex closed the diary, put it back with the rest, put out the light, walked barefoot through to her bedroom, threw off her sweatshirt and her jeans and fell into bed. And there, alone in the darkness with her mother's ghost, she cried, as if she would never stop.

49

He leaned down to kiss her, smiling. She made to pull away, but he held her head firm between his hands and did it anyway, a big wet one in the middle of her forehead.

She stared up at him puzzled. 'What's put the spring into your stride?' Sarah asked, as she stepped newly-dressed into the garden where Bob had been playing with his son. 'Got a new woman or something, or maybe an old one?' For a second a shadow flickered across her face at her poor joke.

'Sorry,' she said, quickly. 'No more cracks about Myra, I promise. It's just that you seem happy, and I don't think I like that.'

His smile vanished. 'You don't?'

'You know what I mean.'

'Do I?' he asked. 'Do you mean that I'm supposed to wander around like a lost sheep, just because you and I have got a problem?'

'No,' she said, 'I mean that I hoped you'd still be missing me a bit, rather than coming in here looking like the cat that got the canary.' She gazed across the back garden at Fairyhouse Avenue, where Jazz stood in a playsuit, supported by a baby walker on wheels. It was a sunny morning, but there was a chill in the air which suggested that winter might be preparing a rearguard action against the change of seasons.

He looked sideways at her. 'Whatever happens to us, I'll always miss the way we were. Who knows, maybe we'll get over this. But if we don't nothing can take away how it was between us. Or can it?'

Still staring across the garden, she shook her head, very briefly.

'The reason I'm smiling,' he said, carrying on, 'is because I've finally got my Mission, or Crusade, whatever you want to call it, under way. Yesterday, I had a look for the people with an interest, eighteen years ago, in killing me or getting me out of the way. I've narrowed it down to a very short list.

'Today, I'm off on the track of hard evidence to support what I believe I saw in the car. If it exists, I know where to find it.

'The thing is, now that I'm finally under way, I feel more focused than I have in months. I don't think I'll ever be able to prove anything, or bring a prosecution. Yet knowing will be enough; it'll have to be if, as might be the case, the man behind it is dead.' His face grew suddenly very dark. 'Maybe that's why I look happy. Maybe I'd rather have a dead culprit than have to live with the knowledge that whoever did it is still walking around. Maybe I couldn't take that.'

He looked at the ground. 'I've read the post mortem report. Myra was pregnant when she died. A boy.'

There was a long silence. Sarah walked across the garden and lifted Jazz out of the baby-walker. 'Bob, I'm sorry. I can't talk about this. It's not just part of your past, but of your life today that I can't be involved in.

Call it jealousy if you like, but I can't take that. I feel just
as I would if you were having an affair. So if we have to
talk, let's make it about something else.

'I heard noise last night up in Ravelston Dykes Road.
What was it? Do you know?'

He nodded. 'Andy called me at Gullane. We had a tip
that some people were coming up from the south to kill
Jackie Charles. We had the place staked out, but someone
beat us to it. One of the visiting team was shot, and died
on the way to hospital. The other two were abducted.'

She gasped with alarm. 'None of our people was hurt,
were they?'

'No. They were too far away to be involved.'

'What about the two men who were kidnapped?'

'I don't think they were going to a dinner party in the
Caley Hotel. My guess is that sometime soon we'll find
two stiffs in Birmingham, gift-wrapped as a warning.'

'That's horrible! How did someone manage to beat you
to them?'

He smiled, grimly. 'That's a good question. The God
of the criminal works in devious and mysterious ways.

'But there's good news too. While we're no nearer tracing the fire-raiser from last Wednesday, we have learned
a few interesting things about the victim. And the net's
closing in on Jackie Charles too. Maggie and young Pye
are going up to Peterhead today to put the frighteners on a
witness who might help us nail his gopher, Dougie Terry.

'If we get something on him that could earn him fifteen
years, I'm hoping that Terry will give up Charles.'

She walked towards him, carrying their wriggling son.
'That's your real world, Bob, isn't it. That's where your
heart lies.'

He reached out and ruffled James Andrew's hair. 'No Sarah,' he said, sincerely, 'but right now it's all I feel that I have.'

'What about him?'

'He used to be ours. Now he's yours and mine . . . big difference. Soon, like Alex, he'll be his. That's the way it is.'

50

'Do you know what my Boss said, Evan?'

Maggie Rose smiled calmly across the table at the Vulture. They were in another room, on their second visit. This time there were no windows. This time Mulgrew had no chair. Instead he stood shackled, a menacing officer on either side of him and another in the doorway.

'He said, "If that bastard doesn't make a formal statement about the Jimmy Lee assault, and if he doesn't give us the names of the other three men in McCartney's team, I'll make sure he does the rest of his time on Devil's Island, or as near to it as I can get."'

'He also said that if you do help us, he'll try to find you a bedroom in Saughton with a sea view.'

Her eyes narrowed. 'Your choice, hard man. What's it to be?'

Mulgrew stood stock still for a second. Finally, he nodded very briefly.

'Very sensible. Now, you admit that you were the decoy who stopped Jimmy Lee, although you took no part in the assault.'

'Aye.'

'But you saw it and you can say who was there?'

'Aye.'

'Okay. Name all five men in the team.'

The Vulture took a deep breath as if he was about to dive into a very deep pool. 'There wis Ricky McCartney, Barney Cogan – though he's deid now – Willie Easson, Willie Macintosh and Willie Kirkbride.'

'An attack of the Willies, you might say,' muttered Sammy Pye. Rose shot him a look.

'When McCartney asked you to act as a decoy, what did he tell you? I mean Jimmy Lee was a local hero.'

'He told me that Dougie Terry wanted him sorted. That he owed him money, and that he'd double-crossed him in that game he was supposed to fix. He said that Terry had had to shell out a lot of money to the Malaysian folk that wanted the game sorted, and that Lee was to get the message. Hero or not.'

'He didn't mention anyone else?'

'No, miss.'

'That's Chief Inspector, Mulgrew. Were you paid for acting as decoy?'

'Sorry, miss. Aye, Ricky gave me three hundred in cash.'

'And you watched the attack take place?' Rose asked.

The Vulture nodded. 'The three Willies had baseball bats. They broke his legs. Ricky and Barney smashed his knees and ankles wi' big steel hammers. Ricky had a foot on his chest tae hold him down, and he had shoved something in his gob, tae keep him quiet. The boy passed oot eventually. They kept on for a while after that, then we all legged it tae Ricky's motor. It was parked round the corner.'

'Did anyone say anything after the attack?'

Mulgrew nodded. 'Aye, in the motor Ricky laughed

and said that the boy should get his players' insurance money after that.'

Rose stared up at him, coldly. 'You're not going to renege on what you've just told the tape, Evan, are you? Because if you did, we wouldn't be able to keep you segregated.'

'No, miss . . . sorry, Inspector. Ah'll swear to that in court, if Ah have to.'

'Good.'

'Dae Ah get to Saughton now?' asked the Vulture.

'Not yet,' said Rose. 'We'll keep you here under close guard until we have McCartney and the three Willies in custody, and until they've been interviewed. After the trial we'll move you down, once they're on their way here.'

She nodded to the guards. 'Take him away.'

As the thick door closed, and they picked up their notes and unplugged the tape recorder, she looked up at Sammy Pye, her laughter bursting out. 'An attack of the Willies, indeed!'

51

Pamela Masters was waiting in the street when Skinner arrived to collect her, in the spot at which he had dropped her off after dinner the night before. She lived in Leith, in one of the many warehouse conversions which had sprung up along the river-front which ran through Edinburgh's port.

Over dinner in Vito's they had talked mostly of work, Skinner telling his new assistant most of the stories behind his more recent high profile investigations, and she telling him something of her career in marketing, before her life had taken its change of direction.

He had enjoyed the meal, with its fellowship, more than any since his return from the States; in fact, he mused, as he cruised to a halt beside her on the pavement, as much as any he could recall in a long time.

She was dressed informally once again, in well-cut fawn trousers and a close-fitting cream sweater top, with a black blazer, and a cavernous bag slung over her shoulder. She smiled as she slid into the BMW's front passenger seat. 'Afternoon, sir,' she said. He glanced at the clock. It read 12.13 and he had told her to be ready for midday.

'Sorry once again, Pam,' he said. 'I'm not used to

this visiting parent routine yet. You haven't been stood outside since twelve, have you?'

She shook her head. 'No,' she lied, 'only for a couple of minutes or so.'

He swung the car around in the cul-de-sac and headed out on to the road which led to Granton and Newhaven, turning left towards Ferry Road, the most direct route to the Forth Road Bridge.

'I called Sergeant Whatnot before I left,' said Skinner as he swept through a green light and on to the A90. 'He's got a christening to photograph at three o'clock, but he'll be expecting us in the pub from around one.'

The Bridge traffic was light for a Spring Sunday, and there was no tailback at the tollbooth. With time to spare, Skinner might have taken the route through Aberdour, Burntisland and Kirkcaldy, but instead he headed up to Halbeath and down the new dual carriageway which had cut the time of the journey from Edinburgh to north-east Fife by around a third.

Without breaking a single speed limit, they rolled down the hill from Lundin Links and into the beachside village of Lower Largo just after 12.55 p.m. The narrow street was full of cars, lined down one side, most with the Glasgow or Edinburgh registration plates of weekend home-owners, and so Skinner had to drive for almost half a mile into the ribbon-like village before he found a parking space.

As he and Masters strolled back towards the Travellers' Inn, they passed a house with a statue of a ragged figure over the front door. 'Who's he?' asked Pamela.

'Alexander Selkirk,' said Skinner. 'The real-life model for Robinson Crusoe. Born here, but spent years as a castaway on a desert island, with only illiterate tribesmen for company. Bit like being a policeman, really.'

Tam Whatling, Sergeant Whatnot to his colleagues for many years, looked up as they entered his pub. It was busy, warm and welcoming. Most of the customers were congregated around the windows set into the bright western side of the bar, and a mixture of Glaswegian, Edinburgh and Fife accents struggled for domination in a dozen discussions. The DCC and his assistant moved towards a table in the far corner, away from the throng.

The grey-haired, rotund Whatling followed them down to the end of the bar. Skinner reached across to shake his hand. 'Good to see you again, Tom. This is my PA, Sergeant Pamela Masters.'

'Good to see you too, sir. And you, Sergeant. What'll you have? On the house, of course.'

'I'll have a pint shandy, and Pamela'll have . . .' He looked at her.

'Beck's, please.'

'. . . and a couple of filled rolls if you have them. But we'll pay our way. I've come to ask you for a favour, not drink away your profits.'

Ex-Sergeant Whatnot poured the drinks and laid four ham rolls on red-trimmed plates, but firmly rejected the ten pound note which Skinner pushed across the counter. 'No thank you, Mr Skinner. I'm on quite a good pension, you know. You and the Sergeant take a seat at yon table there, and I'll join you once my wife comes in to take over the bar.'

Skinner and Masters had just finished the ham rolls when Tom Whatling sat down beside them, carrying a steaming mug of tea. He turned his left wrist towards the

DCC showing the gold watch with which he had been presented on his retirement.

'There you are, sir. Still going strong. The gold hasn't begun to wear off yet either.

'Now, what can I do for you?'

Skinner looked at him, straight in the eye. 'I'm looking for some photographs, Tom. They were taken eighteen years ago, by two officers who attended a fatal road accident in East Lothian. The victim was my wife.'

Whatling's jolly face grew solemn as his heavy eyebrows knitted together.

'I've spoken to George Shields, and he told me that negatives of that sort of occurrence would normally have been destroyed by now. But he said that you salvaged quite a few of them . . . for your memoirs.'

Whatling nodded. 'That was what I said, and that was what I meant at the time. But Christ, with the pub and with my photographic work, I'm busier now than I've ever been. I think I'll be retiring again in two or three years, the way things are going.'

He looked across the table at Skinner. 'There was another reason for keeping those negatives. I love photography, but I value it too. I think that fire, the wheel, the printing press, photography and penicillin are the five most important discoveries that mankind has ever made.

'Photographs are a record of history, good or bad, and I think that it's a crime to destroy even a single one. It's like drowning kittens because you can't find homes for them. If you try hard enough, you can *always* find a home. I worked in the photographic unit for twenty years. Nobody realised it, not even George Shields, because I made light of it, but during that time I rescued as many negatives as I could that were marked for destruction.

'I didn't get them all. When I was on holiday, or on courses and the like, some would go into the fire. But if the pictures that you're looking for aren't on file anywhere, there's a fair chance that I'll have them.'

He paused, the frown returning to his big bluff face. 'But tell me one thing, Mr Skinner. Suppose you do find what you're after. What do you expect to get from it, after all this time?'

'Satisfaction, Tom,' said the DCC quietly. 'Evidence that my wife died because the car had been sabotaged in an attempt to get me. Either that or the peace of mind of knowing that I'm completely wrong.'

Whatling nodded, and drained his mug. 'Okay. Come on with me.' He stood up and led the way out of the busy pub, Skinner and Masters following at his heels.

Next door to the Travellers' Inn was a small shop, with an array of lavishly framed wedding photographs displayed in its single window. Whatling produced keys from his pocket, unlocked the door, disabled the alarm, and stepped inside. 'Over there,' he said, pointing to three high, grey, roll-down storage cabinets. 'Everything's in there.'

He stepped across to the cabinet on the left, knelt, and rolled up the front. Inside, negatives were suspended row upon row. 'Eighteen years ago, you said. If I've got them, they'll be somewhere in the lower half of this cabinet.' He reached in and drew out a metal bar, from which hung a dozen strips of negative, each with twelve frames. 'That's how they're stored,' he said, holding it up to the light. 'At the top of each strip you'll find a number. That's the file number of each incident, and that's how you identify the negs without looking at them. Not the most helpful system in the world, but that's the way they did it.'

Skinner sighed. 'Oh bugger! I've left the report at home, and I've no idea what the number was. We'll need to look at the lot.'

'Don't panic,' said Whatling. 'It's not quite that bad. Each reference includes a series of letters telling you what sort of incident it was, like HB means house-breaking, ASS means assault and FA means fatal accident.'

He opened a door beside the filing cabinets and, beckoning them to follow, stepped through to another room. It was bigger than the shop, and full of equipment. 'This is my processing room. What you should do is sort out all the FA negatives, then feed them through this viewer. Look.' He took one of the strips from the rack which he held and fed it into a slot at the side of the machine. He threw a switch and an image of a negative frame appeared on a small flat screen above, magnified around twelve times.

'It's difficult to make out detail in negative,' said Whatling, 'but with luck you should be able to tell when you've found what you're after . . . if it's there.'

He withdrew the negative strip, leaving the screen shining silver, stepped through to the shop and replaced the metal bar in the cabinet.

From behind the shop counter, he picked up a huge canvas bag. 'I've got to get to the old Kirk in Upper Largo to set up for my christening, so I'll leave you here to get on with it.

'I'll be back at five. If you've found what you're after by then, I'll do you some prints. There's the key, in case you need to step out for some air.' He stopped in the doorway. 'Tell you one thing,' he said, with a grim smile. 'I'd rather have my afternoon than yours, any day.'

As the door closed behind Whatling, Masters looked up at her boss. 'What did he mean by that?'

Skinner's eyebrows rose. 'He meant, Sergeant,' he said, unsmiling, with nerves clutching at the pit of his stomach, 'that looking through photographs of fatal accident scenes, even in negative form, is no-one's idea of a fun time.'

He looked down at her. 'I should have thought of that, Pamela. Look, you don't have to do this. It's above and beyond the call. If you like, you can go for a walk; or wait in the car, or in the pub.'

She smiled up at him, dropped her bag to the floor, slipped off her blazer and threw it across the counter of ex-Sergeant Whatnot's shop. She shook her head, the neon tubes above picking out highlights in her hair.

'Come on, then,' he said. 'Let's get to it.'

52

'I have to tell you, lads,' said Andy Martin, 'that I'm not finding all this very funny.'

The Head of CID was renowned as the least flappable man on the force. His qualities complemented those of Bob Skinner and made them into what contemporaries in their constabulary and in others regarded as the perfect team. Where Skinner was mercurial, and volatile, Martin was even-tempered and invariably cool-headed. No-one with whom he worked could recall ever hearing him raise his voice.

With that in mind, Brian Mackie and Mario McGuire, sat at the conference table in the DCS's office, each read his remark as a savage reproof.

'Your tip about the Birmingham team was reliable, all right,' he said, quietly. 'Too bad it wasn't exclusive.' He looked at McGuire. 'I take it that you've been raising hell with your oppo in Birmingham, Mario.'

The swarthy Inspector nodded. 'All kinds of hell and damnation, sir.'

'Have they given you any excuses, or theories?'

McGuire shrugged his wide shoulders. 'They think that there must be a second informant in the team, working either for Charles or for one of his criminal pals in London.'

'That's pretty bloody obvious.' Martin shook his head and laughed softly. 'Christ, can you imagine if we'd all turned up in the same place at the same time, all of us armed! It would have been like Buffalo Bill's Wild West Show.'

'Little chance of that,' said Brian Mackie. 'Jackie wouldn't have wanted them taken out right in his driveway.'

'I don't know, we were within sight of the buggers. Still, I suppose that was as far away as they could risk.' Martin sighed. 'I wish I'd thought to charge straight up to Jackie's door last night. I'll bet he had a back-up team in the house, just in case the roadblock didn't work.'

He glanced at Mackie. 'No word, I take it, on the missing men?'

The DCI shook his shiny head.

'Maybe they'll just give them a good talking to and send them home on the bus,' said Martin, his voice even, but heavy with irony.

Dave Donaldson's chuckle was silenced by a glance from the Chief Superintendent. 'Don't think that I'm amused by you two either.' Neil McIlhenny shifted uncomfortably in his seat. 'It's been four days since Carole Charles went up in flames, our only lead's been butchered under our noses, our prime suspect for that murder is alibi-ed by two of our own patrolmen – and incidentally, Dave, if you do press assault charges against Heenan, you're going to look a right fucking Charlie if he pleads Not Guilty and the case goes to trial – and it takes the Boss's new PA to find out that Carole might have had a bit on the side.'

He paused. 'Could do better, gentlemen, or am I being . . .' the telephone on his desk rang, '. . . unkind?' He stepped across the room and picked up the receiver.

'Martin. Yes? Excellent.' The four detectives saw a smile spread across his face. 'Yes, hold them there, please. I'll be down to pick them up myself.' He put the phone down.

'Game on, lads, at last. Ricky McCartney's been arrested in Northumberland. He's being held at Alnwick police station. His car was spotted by a patrol coming out of Haggerston Castle Caravan Park. He did a runner when he saw the blue light, but the chasers radioed in and there was a roadblock waiting a few miles down the road. They ran right into it. We got a bonus prize too. McCartney had a pal with him, one Willie Kirkbride, one of the three that Maggie told me about when she called from Peterhead.

'At least one line of investigation is going well. With any luck, we'll be able to arrest Dougie Terry within the next couple of days.' He waved his four colleagues to their feet.

'Let's get moving. Neil, you come with me down to Alnwick, to pick up McCartney. Dave, you work on picking up the other two Willies. Brian, Mario, you concentrate on plugging the hole in your network.'

Donaldson, Mackie and McGuire each nodded and left the room, without a word.

'Give me a second, Neil,' said the Chief Superintendent, as they went. 'I'd better give Alex a call. D'you want to phone Olive, and tell her you'll be late again?'

McIlhenney smiled, grimly. 'I think not, sir. You can, if you like.'

'Hah!' Martin picked up the phone again and dialled Alex's number. He waited for a dozen rings, before hanging up.

'Not in,' he said, as he slipped on his jacket. 'Let's get going. I'm looking forward to a chat with Mr McCartney.'

53

Alex laid the ninth diary face down on the floor beside her chair, and leaned back wide-eyed. She took a deep breath, blinked hard, then nodded, a decision made.

She jumped from her chair and ran through to her bedroom. Ten minutes later, the reincarnation of Myra Graham emerged once more, smoothing the dress against her thighs, flexing and thrusting out her breasts in the brassière, which was fastened at its tightest notch, and giving the suspender belt a final adjustment.

She stepped out into Woodlands Road and looked around. The pubs in the area were peaceful and friendly, fine for Alex, but not for Myra, and not for the dress. She walked towards the City Centre for a few minutes, until a taxi came towards her, its orange sign lit up, and she hailed it. 'Maitland Hotel, please.'

Barely three minutes later, the black cab pulled up outside the high-rise, five-star hotel. She paid the driver and strode confidently through the automatic doors. Inside, the foyer was plush and inviting. She looked around, selected an available table and sat down. As she lowered herself into the leather chair, the black dress rode up, revealing thigh almost up to the top of her nylons.

She glanced across at a waiter, summoning him with

a faint smile and a flick of an eyelash. As he strode briskly across the room, almost at a trot, she felt a surge of exultation. 'Yes, miss?' he asked, a little too eagerly.

'Gin and tonic, please.'

He returned, within a minute, with her drink and a bowl of potato crisps, setting them before her with a flourish, which turned into a bow as she told him to keep the change from the five pound note.

She sat there, sipping her drink and looking coolly around. The foyer bar was far from being at its busiest, but even late on a Sunday afternoon, it was alive with guests. A few of them were women, all accompanied, but mostly they were single men.

She spotted her target at once. Even seated she could tell how big he was from the size of his shoes and the length of his legs crossed in front of him. His reddish-blond hair was cropped tight and the yellow-tanned pallor of his skin marked him out as an American. She had sensed him watching her as she had swung, long-legged, into the hotel.

Slowly and deliberately, she turned her eyes around to look at him. She held his gaze for a few seconds, smiled briefly, then looked away. She picked up her drink, took a sip and looked over her shoulder, around the rest of the big area. When she turned back to replace her gin and tonic on its mat on the table, he was standing over her.

'Good evening, ma'am,' he said, in a light Texan drawl. 'Mind if I join you?'

She glanced towards the door. 'Well,' she said, 'I was late arriving. So I've either been stood up, or my date's given up on me. Sure, go ahead, sit down.'

She watched as he lowered himself into the seat

opposite her. He was around thirty, at least six feet six and running slightly, but not unacceptably, to fat. 'What a well filled lunchbox,' she thought to herself, as he sat down.

'Been in Glasgow long?' she asked, almost casually.

'Two days,' said the American. 'My name's Randall. Randall Garland, a lonely man from Austin, Texas.' He held out a hand.

She shook it, looking him full in the eyes, and holding it for just a second longer than necessary. 'Myra,' she said. She grinned, with a lift of that right eyebrow. 'Myra Graham, a friendly lady from Glasgow, Scotland.'

54

Tom Whatling's warning had been well placed. Many of his salvaged negatives bore an FA heading, and even in negative form, many of them were harrowing to see.

There was a two-car pile-up outside the Cramond Brig Hotel, in which Skinner and Masters counted eight bodies, before the DCC ripped the negative from the viewer. There were shots of pedestrian accidents, most of them involving children, but one of a man, his head and upper body protruding from beneath the double front wheels of a heavy vehicle. Not all the deaths had been road casualties. There were scenes of a family of three burned to death in a house fire, bodies shining white in the negative image. There was film from another incident on a railway line, in which they could make out a woman's severed torso beside the track.

Three times, Skinner asked Pamela to leave him to the grim task, and three times she refused, saying that if he wanted her to leave he would have to order her. Each time, smiling at her tenacity, he had pulled out another rack of negatives.

They had been surveying the grim scenes for almost three hours when they found the negatives which they were beginning to fear had been lost after all. There were four strips each bearing file number FA 4782. As soon as Skinner fed the first image into the viewer and switched on the back-lit screen, he knew. They had learned to read colours in negative, and when the DCC saw the light-brown shape of a tree, he stiffened and recoiled slightly.

It was a long shot, taken from the other side of the road, but the shapes of the car against the tree, and of the figure inside were clearly visible. All of the photographs on the strip had been taken from a distance, recording the crash from all around the vehicle, most of them showing the direction in which the Cooper S had been travelling.

Skinner withdrew the strip and fed in the next. The first frame, the second, the third and the fourth showed, from different distances and angles, deep tyre tracks in a patch of mud on the road. He pulled the strip through to the fifth photograph.

Pamela Masters cried out in horror as it appeared. It had been taken through the shattered windscreen and showed a close-up of Myra's body in the car, the steering column through her chest, her eyes staring wide at the sheer surprise of her last second of life.

Bob Skinner sucked in his breath and looked away. Suddenly he was back in his dream, thrust back into the depths of his recovered memory, seeing everything, hearing everything, smelling everything.

'Come on,' he said, thickly, to Pamela. 'This is what we came for.' He forced himself to look back at the screen, ripping images through quickly, one by one, looking for the right angle, hoping against hope that it was there.

It was the eighth shot on the fourth strip. The attending officer had taken the photograph from the exact point at which Skinner had looked into the car. The field of vision of the lens seemed to replicate his memory exactly.

He picked up a small magnifying glass which he had found in the studio, and held it close to the bottom right-hand corner of the negative image, searching, millimetre by millimetre. Suddenly, he stopped. His left hand shot out and grabbed Pamela's arm. 'There, Pam, there. Look.' He leaned back, holding the glass steady to allow her to see the spot upon which it was trained.

'I can't make out detail from this, but I'll swear that's the brake fluid pipe. You can see, it's been broken.

'When Tam gets back, I'll have him make me a print of this section, big as he can. Then, pray God, I . . . we'll . . . have what we need.'

55

The drive down to Alnwick took just over two hours: because Martin, driving his swift silver Mondeo with McIlhenney in the passenger seat, did not wish to suffer the embarrassment of tripping one of the many speed cameras on the A1; because behind them came a dark blue Ford Transit with black barred windows, and six burly uniformed policemen inside; and because, for the first time in several days, there was, simply, no need to rush.

Martin had never been to the old Northumbrian town before, but street signs took him, without difficulty, to its police station, past its castle and its prison.

Leaving the escort officers outside in the Transit they announced themselves to the Sergeant in reception, and were greeted within seconds by a uniformed Chief Inspector. 'Howay, gentlemen,' the forty-something man said, cheerily, 'I'm Frank Berry. Hope we didn't spoil your Sunday, but my lads were very pleased at catching your fugitive for you. They couldn't wait for me to tell you about it, in fact.'

'You didn't spoil our Sunday, Chief Inspector,' said Martin, with a grin. 'In fact you made it. We've had a parade of cock-ups in our investigations this weekend, so we were needing a break like this.

271

'Where are you keeping McCartney and Kirkbride?'

'We've got them banged up in separate cells. McCartney's already been charged with failing to stop for a police signal, and with doing almost a hundred and thirty trying to get away from my guys. We'll want him back for our magistrates on both those counts.'

Chief Inspector Berry shook his head in wonderment. 'You wouldn't have thought one of those big old round-bodied Rovers could go that fast, but it did. We only just got the roadblock in position in time. Just for a second, my lads thought they were going to try to crash through it.'

He looked at Martin as he led the two Scots through to a room behind the reception desk. Its window overlooked the station's secure car park. 'That's the flying machine across there,' said Berry, pointing to a big white Rover 3500s, reversed into the far corner of the yard. Its registration bore an A prefix, and in another era it might have been a police vehicle.

'What do you want to do with these two?' the Chief Inspector went on. 'You'll want to caution McCartney formally and arrest him on the attempted extortion charge. You can interview him here if you like, or you can just lift him straight away. I assume we'll just let his mate go. We've nothing to hold him on.'

Martin smiled and shook his head. 'Oh no, Frank, we want Willie Kirkbride too. We've got another matter to discuss with him and McCartney, one that's far more important than a wee bit of half-hearted intimidation for a loanshark. Let's have a word with them both now, if we may.'

'Okay, sir.' Berry opened the door and barked an order to the Sergeant on reception. One minute later, the door opened once again and two men were bustled into the room, each in the grasp of two Constables.

Ricky McCartney was just under six feet tall, and built like a barrel, with black greasy hair and heavy brows, over dark, brooding, threatening eyes. His jutting jaw was black with a day-old stubble. Beneath his crumpled grey jacket he looked to be massively built, with long arms, which lent a simian look to his overall appearance. His companion, Kirkbride, was an inch or two taller. His pinched face was unshaven like McCartney's, with a greying beard which looked as long as the remaining hair on his bald head. He had mean, nasty eyes which darted all around the room, save at Martin and McIlhenney.

The escort officers shoved both men down, roughly, into seats at the interview table. McCartney, a heavy hand on each of his shoulders, looked up at Martin, briefly, then across at McIlhenney. 'You!' he said, with a snarl. 'I might have known you'd show up.'

The big Sergeant nodded. 'Bet on it, Ricky. I've never forgotten that time I broke your nose, see. I'd go anywhere for another shot. You're all right, guys like you and Tommy Heenan, with someone you've got outnumbered, or you know you can lean on. But you never fight in your own weight division, because you haven't got the fucking bottle.'

'Heenan?' said McCartney, 'What about Heenan?'

'Come off it, Ricky,' said Martin. 'You know damn well. As soon as you heard that we had lifted Heenan for Carl Medina's murder, you did a runner. Because you were with him last weekend at Medina's house when you went to give him an eighteen hundred-pound message, and because you knew that we'd be after you too.'

The thug looked at him. 'Don't know what you're talking about,' he said, shiftily.

Martin smiled, as he and the Sergeant eased themselves into seats facing the two men. 'Of course you do, but it doesn't matter. Heenan is no longer a suspect in the Medina case. You would be, only you don't come anywhere near fitting our eye-witness description of the killer.'

McCartney sat in silence, staring down at the desk. Kirkbride continued to gaze shiftily around the room.

'Well, Ricky?' asked the Chief Superintendent. 'Aren't you going to ask us what it's all about.'

McCartney's vicious eyes looked up at him. 'Aye, okay. What is it then?'

'It's about some work you two did for Dougie Terry.' Across the table, both men flinched, taking Martin momentarily by surprise. 'A few years back,' he went on. 'You and Barney Cogan, now deceased, Willie Easson, and Willie Macintosh, with Evan Mulgrew as lookout, beat up and crippled a young footballer named Jimmy Lee. You did so on the orders of Douglas Terry.'

McCartney's eyes seemed to go completely blank. Beside him, Kirkbride slumped back in his chair, breathing heavily. Martin stared at them both, his confusion gathering. He had expected the usual denial and bluster, not this.

'Dougie Terry's a great singer,' said Neil McIlhenney. 'Now we want to hear what sort of a voice you've got. You're going to sing for us, Ricky.'

McCartney nodded, without looking up. 'Aye okay then,' he muttered. 'Get us up the road then, and we'll tell you about it.'

Andy Martin leaned back in his chair and had a vision: through night-glasses, of a suddenly-appearing Jaguar, a Ford Scorpio and, behind it, a big, light-coloured, indistinct shape.

He sat bolt upright, a huge, triumphant, exultant smile spreading across his face. 'You're in a tearing hurry to get out of here, aren't you?

'Chief Inspector Berry,' he asked, his eyes not leaving McCartney and Kirkbride for a second, 'have you searched that Rover out there?'

'Well, no sir, not yet. In fact, we were waiting for you.'

Martin cut him off. 'Get the keys, then, and come with us. And bring these two.' He jumped up from his seat, and led McIlhenney and the rest out of the room. He looked around until he spotted the exit to the yard, then marched outside, across to the Rover, and round its long nose, to the boot.

He stood there, staring at it, waiting, as Berry ran towards him waving two big car keys, and as McCartney and Kirkbride, ashen-faced, were dragged outside by the four Constables across the car park.

Martin was smiling still as he bent over the tailgate of the big hatchback car, unlocked it and swung it open.

'Jesus Christ,' gasped Chief Inspector Berry, as he looked inside. Involuntarily, he took two paces backwards.

The two bodies were crammed into the boot space, their knees forced up to their chest, and their hands tied behind them. Their eyes bulged like organ-stops and their tongues protruded from their mouths.

Andy Martin leaned over the cadavers. 'Strangled,' he

275

said in a calm, even, almost friendly voice. 'Garrotted with wire. Very effective, very colourful.' He looked around.

'On our way to Birmingham, were we, gentlemen? To make a special delivery?'

McCartney struggled briefly in the hands of his escorts, then gave up. Kirkbride slumped in a half-faint, staring transfixed into the boot.

'I think we should have that discussion about Dougie Terry, don't you?' said Martin. 'Only now we'll widen the agenda. Come on, Neil, let's take them back north.'

Chief Inspector Frank Berry gulped. He was faced with one of those rare decisions on which a career could hang.

'I'm sorry, sir,' he said, hesitantly. 'I can't let you take these men anywhere. There have been two murders committed on my patch, and I have to hold McCartney and Kirkbride for questioning.'

Martin frowned at him. 'But man, these two stiffs were abducted from a car in Edinburgh last night, in which a third man was shot dead. We know where they're from and why they were killed, and I'll bet the PNC will tell us who they were as soon as we feed their prints into it.

'It's our active investigation, not yours.' But he was playing poker with no cards in his hands, and he knew it. So did Frank Berry.

'No, sir, I'm sorry,' said the Northumbrian, 'but you can't take the prisoners anywhere unless you can prove to me that those men were actually killed in Scotland, or unless my Chief Constable says otherwise. In fact, you can't even speak to them. It'd be more than my job's worth.' It was the traditional and unmistakable sound of a pension being protected. Martin and McIlhenney knew they had lost.

Berry turned to the four Constables, his arms flapping and pointing all around. 'Take McCartney and Kirkbride back to their cells. Get the duty CID people out here, pronto. Have this area roped off. Call the Medical Examiner.

'And call the photographers. We must have photographs!'

56

They were waiting in the Travellers' Inn when Tom Whatling returned from Upper Largo Kirk, and from his christening engagement. Skinner had spent almost half an hour studying the same small section of the image in the viewer, until Pamela had persuaded him to take some time out from the agonising task.

'Any luck?' asked Whatling.

Skinner nodded. 'I've found the negative I was after. Sergeant Haig and PC Orr did a good job. They took three identical shots from most angles just to be on the safe side. Let's hope that at least one of them was in focus.

'Tom, can you do me a print?' The ex-policeman nodded. 'Can you isolate a single section of an image, and blow it up?'

'Yes. I can't guarantee what the resolution will be like – the cameras were often too complicated for the police photographers in those days – but we can only try it and see. Come on.'

He led them out of the pub and back to his shop. In the studio he switched on several pieces of equipment before turning back to Skinner. 'Let's see what you've found, then,' he said quietly, switching on the viewer, in which the negative strip still lay. He winced as he looked at the shot.

The DCC handed him the magnifying glass. Pointing at the screen he traced a line with his finger around the lower right quarter of the rectangular image. 'There, Tom, that section is what I need. In the middle of it, you'll see a thin pipe, part of the hydraulics that were forced into the car by the impact. See it?'

Whatling peered through the glass. 'I see it,' he said. 'It's been burst open in the crash.'

Skinner shook his head. 'No, not burst open. Cut half through, before the crash. That's a wire braided, hydraulic brake fluid hose; good for 100,000 miles and virtually unbreakable in any impact. It might be ripped loose from its connection in a crash, but it would never go in the middle like that.'

He waved a hand towards the next room. 'You've got hundreds of accident shots through there. You look through them all and I guarantee you that you won't find another pipe that's fractured in that way.'

'Tell you what, sir,' said Whatling. 'I'll do that. I'll look through a selection, and I'll make prints. If your theory's right, that might help you prove it to a jury one day. Meantime, though, let's print up this section and see how sharp we can get it. I'll start with an eight by six. Highest I can go is about fourteen by eleven, but I don't know if I'll be able to keep the resolution at that size, on my equipment.'

He withdrew the negative strip. 'Look, before I can isolate your section, I'll have to study the whole image in positive form. You don't need to see that, so why don't you and Miss Masters go back to the pub and finish your drinks, if my wife hasn't cleared them up.'

Skinner smiled, sadly. 'You're a kind man, Tom. The truth is that for the last four months, I've seen that image every time I've closed my eyes. And you're right, the last thing I need is to see it while I'm awake.'

He led Pamela back into the Travellers' Inn, where the Sunday evening crowd had gathered, many of them specifically to watch Manchester United tackle Liverpool in the day's televised football match. Collecting their drinks from the table, the two police officers stood and watched with the rest, groaning or roaring with every passage of play, swaying as if they were back on the terraces of Fir Park, the ground where each had watched football as a youngster, ten years or so apart.

The match had been over for almost an hour before Whatling returned carrying a large flat envelope. Skinner and Masters were back at their fireside table, nursing a half-pint of shandy and a gin and tonic, as he crossed the room to sit down beside them.

Looking over his shoulder to make sure that there were no eavesdroppers, he laid the envelope on the table. 'Sorry I was so long,' he said, 'but I had to wait for these to dry.

'I've done you eight by six, ten by eight and fourteen by eleven, and I've focused in on the pipe as tight as I can without losing quality. The fourteen by eleven's a bit fuzzy, but I think the ten by eight gives you what you're after.'

Peering into the envelope, he withdrew an enlarged photograph and laid it on the table in front of Skinner and Masters. The damaged brake pipe leapt out at them, everything else distorted and out of focus by comparison. The print was so sharp that the camera's flash could

be seen reflected in the strands of severed wire braid-
ing.

The cut had been made laterally, clean and straight
across the top, not quite halfway through the diameter
of the pipe, to a depth at which the fluid would have
escaped under braking pressure gradually, rather than all
at once.

Staring at the enlargement, Skinner realised that he
was holding his breath. He blew it out in a great sigh,
his shoulders sagging and his head dropping like a
cross-country runner at the end of a race. 'You've found
it, boss,' said Pamela. She grasped his hand in her
excitement. Unconsciously, he squeezed hers, and held
it tight.

As he stared at the image again, a flat, empty, feeling
gripped the pit of his stomach, overwhelming him. With
a final quick squeeze, he released Pamela's hand, stood
up from the table and walked quickly outside. She made
to follow him, but Whatling put a hand on her shoulder.
'Give him a minute, lass. There's nothing you can say to
him just now.'

He was back in five minutes. 'Sorry,' he said quietly,
as he slipped into the bar and rejoined them at the table.
'I just needed some air.' He smiled at Masters, but she
frowned at him, at the pallor of his face.

'Tom,' he said, as briskly as he could. 'I can't thank
you enough, but what I can do is pay you for your time and
materials.' Whatling shook his head and held up the wrist
on which his gold watch shone in the pub's even light.

'You did already, sir. Anything I can do, ever, to help a
former colleague, I do with pleasure.' He paused. 'Listen,
that's the best I could manage with my equipment, but

if you ask the boys at the lab, they have computer-aided gear that can get it a lot finer than that.' He replaced the enlargement in the envelope and pushed it across the table. 'The negative's inside.'

Skinner took it and stood up. 'Thanks again, then, Tom. I'm not sure where this will lead me, but without you I couldn't have taken a step further.' With a final wave, he ushered Pamela Masters out of the Travellers' Inn, and into the Lower Largo evening.

The gloaming was giving way to darkness. They stood on the pavement listening to the lapping of the waves against the harbour wall, Masters gasping slightly at the sudden chill which had swept down from the north-west. Skinner nodded across the road, to the brightly-lit Crusoe Hotel.

'I need food, Pam,' he said, softly. 'What would you say to supper before we head back?'

She smiled up at him in the darkness. 'I'd say it was getting to be a habit, sir.'

The Crusoe's dining room was empty, the weekend residents having gone back to Glasgow and to Edinburgh, but they were welcomed nonetheless. They followed the waiter's recommendation of crab soup and roast beef salad, and chose a bottle of Findlay's mineral water to wash it down.

Sipping the clear bubbling liquid, Skinner smiled across the table at his assistant. 'You know, Pam . . . Sorry, Pamela . . . we've come this far in two days yet I haven't told you the story behind this mission of mine.'

She grinned back at him, her big eyes smiling too. 'Pam's fine. It's just Polly that I couldn't stand. Made me sound like a bloody parrot. Yes, I like being a Pam.'

The smile vanished, as quickly as it had appeared, and was replaced not by a frown but by a look of concern. 'So what is the whole story, sir? Why have you suddenly launched this investigation after eighteen years?'

He paused, as the waiter served the crab soup, adding a little crème fraiche, and left.

'A few months back,' he began, 'I was stabbed.'

'I remember. Everyone on the force was worried about you.'

'I would have been too,' he said quietly, 'if I'd been conscious. The fact was, I nearly died. After my surgery, I experienced a reaction under sedation which made my consultant, and my wife, decide that I needed investigative hypnotherapy. So they called in a guy named Kevin O'Malley; the best in the business, so they say.

'Kevin put me under and led me back to incidents in my past life, leading up to Myra's death. He discovered . . . we discovered . . . that the experience of turning up at the scene of her death, and of what I saw there, had caused a traumatic amnesia.

'Kevin took me back to the scene and, under hypnosis, I saw everything I'd seen before – including, I believed, that cut brake pipe.

'Yet there was always a chance that I was wrong. Kevin admitted later that while the experience was real, he couldn't be one hundred per cent certain that I didn't add in that detail because of my own guilt . . . guilt because, as I told you, Myra was driving *my* car.

'Now I know I wasn't wrong, that I didn't imagine any of the details.' He looked, gloomily, down at his soup, stirring in the crème fraiche.

She looked up at him. 'Then why are you so down?' she asked quietly.

He sighed, long and deep, and tapped his chest. 'I suppose it's because, in here, I hoped that I was mistaken. What we got there wasn't the answer I wanted, not in my heart of hearts. Until now, it's been a theoretical exercise. Most of me wanted it to stay that way, for it to be stopped at the first hurdle, so that I could get on with my life, duty done.

'Now I have my evidence and I have to carry on. The trouble is, the process is having side effects.'

'Such as?'

'My marriage, for starters. This thing has changed Sarah, just as it's changed me. It's made us different people. I can't explain it any better than that. It has driven us apart.

'It's affecting Alex too. She's now finding out things that I've held back from her since she was a child. That part's a bonus, though. It's time she found out for herself what a terrific woman her mother was.'

'So what do you, we, do next?' asked Pam.

'I go to Shotts Prison tomorrow, to see that man I told you about. A remarkable man: a multiple murderer, but a remarkable man nonetheless. Our paths have crossed before. In fact he tried to kill me, once. His name's . . .'

In the pocket of his jacket, slung over the back of his chair, Skinner's mobile phone rang. He took it out and switched it on. 'Yes?'

'Boss, it's Andy. I've been trying to get you for hours.'

'Sorry, I was busy. The phone was off. What's the panic?'

'I'm in Alnwick,' said Martin. 'The police here pulled in Ricky McCartney for failing to stop and for speeding on the A1. Big Neil and I came down with a team to collect him. When we got here we found we had a bonus: our two kidnapped tourists from Birmingham, dead in the boot of McCartney's car.

'Now I find myself in a tug-of-war over him and his partner, Willie Kirkbride. The Northumbrian police are being difficult. They've found a caravan up on the Haggerston Castle site, and they're assuming that the Brummies were killed there.

'I've done my best to persuade them to let me have McCartney and the other fellow, but they're digging their heels in. I've been right up to the Chief Constable himself, but he's playing it by the book.'

'Whose book?'

'His own,' said Martin, wearily. 'Yet I have to get these two back home. As soon as I can take statements from them I can arrest Dougie Terry on a lifetime's worth of charges, including, I'm sure, setting up these three murders.'

'Bugger that,' said Skinner. 'Leave it with me. I'll ask Proud Jimmy to speak to their Chief Constable first thing tomorrow morning. These guys are ours and we're having them, even if I have to come down to collect them myself. For now, you and McIlhenney get yourselves home.

'Meantime, Andy, keep a veil over this. I don't want anyone outside the team to know what's happening, until the moment that our hands feel Dougie Terry's collar. After that, it'll be next stop Jackie Charles!'

57

Sir James Proud's great grey head nodded slowly and sagely as he stared at the loudspeaker phone on his desk.

Skinner, Martin and Pamela Masters were seated in armchairs well away from the instrument's sensitive microphone.

'I quite understand, Chief Constable Clark, your view of the situation,' he said. 'These bodies were found in your area. Where a murder is committed on your patch your duty is to investigate and report to the CPS.'

'That's right,' a tinny voice boomed in reply from the speaker.

'In that case, Hugh, please try to understand my view. The chain of events in this crime began in Edinburgh, when these men were abducted from a car in which a third man was shot dead. The men you are holding are prime suspects in that and other crimes.

'My duty is to pursue investigation of these men with all vigour, wherever it leads me. As I understand it, you have found no proof as yet that the two men found dead in the Rover car were actually killed in England. Is that correct?'

The loudspeaker coughed. 'Yes it is. However we

have found a caravan belonging to McCartney on the Haggerston site. I've got specialists at work there now.'

'Indeed?' said Proud Jimmy, ingenuously. 'When did you first make that discovery?'

'At around six last night,' the Geordie voice replied.

'Ah. So you've been looking for over fifteen hours and you still can't say that the crime was committed on your territory.'

'No, but . . . Come on, Jimmy, these things take time.'

'Yes, but not forever. Which brings me back to my duty. The way things stand, I've got no choice but to go to our Supreme Criminal Court and ask the Lord Justice General for an order requiring the return to my jurisdiction at once, of McCartney and Kirkbride, plus the bodies of the two victims.'

A spluttering sound came from the speakerphone. 'This is England, Jimmy, not Scotland. Your court order wouldn't work here.'

'I disagree. It would be effective unless you could produce a counter from your highest criminal court. Even then, it's possible that our Lord Justice General would issue a warrant for your arrest on grounds of contempt, to be effected by any Scottish force when next you set foot in Scotland.'

He shook his silver mane, a dolorous expression on his face. A few feet away Skinner and Martin struggled to keep their laughter in check, while Pam Masters stared open-mouthed, astonished by the goings-on in her new professional circle.

'Very embarrassing, Hugh, very embarrassing,' said Proud. 'I think that before it got to that stage, I'd have to ask my deputy, Bob Skinner, who's an adviser to our

Secretary of State, to contact his opposite number in the Home Office, to get a ruling from the Home Secretary himself.'

He smiled, easily, as if he were addressing someone across the desk, rather than a box upon it. 'I can do that right now, in fact, without even going to the court.'

The conference telephone sat silent.

'Tell you what,' said Sir James at last. 'Let's do a deal. You keep the stiffs, for as long as it takes you to establish where they were actually killed . . . if you can. I've got more than enough bodies to be going on with up here at the moment.

'In the meantime, though, you hand over McCartney and Kirkbride to me, so that my investigations can proceed. My people need to take statements from them today. Once that's done, if you want to charge them with murder in Northumberland, you can have them back, and we'll let the Crown Office and the CPS argue about who tries them first. I don't care where these chaps serve their life sentences. It's the people above them in the chain that we're after.

'How about it?' He looked across at Skinner, Martin, and Masters, with a wide smile of victory.

'All right,' said Chief Constable Clark, at last, wearily. 'You send people down to Alnwick for four o'clock and we'll hand them over . . . unless we do find something at Haggerston and have to charge them and hold them for court.'

'Mmm,' the Chief Constable muttered. 'I don't know about sending people to Alnwick. We've done that once already. Best that you hand them over at the border . . .

for appearances' sake. Shall we say three o'clock? That'll give you another four hours to work at Haggerston.'

'Okay, Jimmy, okay. I'll have them there.'

'Good, good,' beamed Proud. 'Pleased about that. Now is there anything that you have discovered that might be of help to our investigation?'

'We found two handguns in the Rover's glove-box,' Clark replied. 'One had been fired recently, so we ran tests on McCartney and Kirkbride. We found residue on McCartney's clothing which indicates that he had discharged a firearm within the last forty-eight hours.

'I'll give you the guns, when we hand over the men. They're not linked to anything in England. We've run a ballistics check though the PNC.'

'Indeed,' said Proud. 'We'll run our own ballistics tests, but I'll bet we can establish a link with our murder on Saturday night. We've identified the victim as Eddie Chang; half Chinese, half Brummie.'

'Interesting,' said Clark. 'The other two were Irish gentlemen, named Maloney and O'Flynn, both with Birmingham addresses. The PNC gave us their details from fingerprints this morning. Maloney did twelve years for attempted murder in Belfast.'

'He didn't succeed this time either,' said Proud, with an irony that was unusual for him. 'The sentence was a lot tougher, though.'

'Yes,' the Englishman chuckled grimly. 'I don't think he'll attempt any more. See you, Jimmy. An ordeal doing business with you, as usual.' A loud buzz filled the room as the line went dead. Sir James pressed a button to switch off the speaker box.

'There you are, lady and gentlemen.' He beamed,

hugely pleased with himself. 'Tact and diplomacy. Amazing what it can secure.'

'That's right,' laughed Skinner. 'But it's nothing compared to what you can secure through naked threat. Christ, did you hear the intake of breath when you mentioned arrest.

'Thanks, Chief, objective achieved.' He stood up and led Martin and Masters from the room by the side door.

'Wonderful,' said Martin, outside in the corridor. 'I'll send McIlhenney down there with a team to take possession. Two transport vehicles, though: I want those guys kept apart from now on.'

As she looked at the Head of CID, Pamela Masters could sense that he was buzzing with excitement. 'Do you want to be in on the examination of McCartney and Kirkbride?' he asked Skinner.

The DCC shook his head. 'No, I've got other fish in the fryer. You do it, with Donaldson and with Maggie Rose. Let Sammy Pye sit in on it too. He and Mags have done some bloody good work, so he deserves to be in at the kill.

'But listen, the way the weather's looking, that won't be until six tonight, at the earliest. We're still no further along in the Carole Charles investigation, with which, after all, we started out. McCartney and Kirkbride won't be ready for interview until six at the earliest. While you're waiting for them, give that another push. We don't want it to stall.'

Martin grunted as he followed Skinner and Masters into the DCC's office. 'Yes, boss. I'll do that. I did hear before I came up that there's a taxi driver who wants to see us about a pick-up he made last Wednesday. Mind you, we've had a few of those so far, all of them a waste of time.'

He paused. 'These other fish of yours. Anything to do with . . . ?'

Tom Whatling's envelope lay on Skinner's desk. The DCC took out the print and handed it to Martin. The Chief Superintendent's green eyes widened. 'This is it?'

'Yeah. That's my Mini Cooper, or at least part of the wreckage. You can see for yourself . . .'

'It's been cut. By a hacksaw, I'd say, or maybe a Stanley knife.' He looked up with a smile, green eyes shining. 'You've done it, Bob. You've proved that you were right.'

'Bully for me,' said Skinner, glumly. 'So the story goes on.'

Martin shrugged. 'It must. That's evidence for a culpable homicide prosecution at the very least, and the Crown Office would probably go for murder. On the basis of that, stretched resources or not, I'll open a full, formal investigation.'

'No. Don't do that. Leave it to me. I've already done some checking. My likeliest candidate seems to be Tony Manson, and we'd have a hell of a job bringing him to trial, on account of his being dead.'

'So what are you going to do?'

'Well,' said Skinner, 'while Pamela is taking that negative out to the photo unit, to have the technicians give us the cleanest print they can, I'm going to take a drive out to Shotts nick, to see my old sparring partner, Big Lennie Plenderleith.'

58

'Quinn. My name is Willie Quinn.'

'Thanks for coming to see us, Mr Quinn,' said Andy Martin. The taxi driver nodded a quick, 'No problem,' glancing nervously around at the same time. The Chief Superintendent suspected that this man had years of experience of not looking policemen in the eye.

'For the record, how old are you?' he asked.

'Forty-nine.'

'And your address?'

'Number ten, Glenfiddich Walk, Southhouse, Edinburgh.' Martin nodded, imperceptibly, to Neil McIlhenney, standing at the door. Quietly, the big Sergeant slipped out of the room.

'Who do you drive for, Mr Quinn?' asked Dave Donaldson, seated beside Martin in the modern airy interview room, directly beneath his office in the St Leonard's station.

'Snap Cabs,' said the small, grey, shifty man.

'Who's your boss?'

'Hard tae say. Ma controller's a woman called Marilyn Snell, but the guy that collects the money, that's a Mr Terry.'

'When you phoned this office, you told an officer that

292

you had information for us about the Carole Charles murder,' said Martin. 'So, what have you got to tell us?'

Willie Quinn shifted uncomfortably in his chair once more, like a man experiencing a culture shock. 'Last Wednesday, I made a pick-up in Seafield Road. About quarter to nine.'

'Where, exactly?'

'Just before the roundabout at the King's Road. Outside the Balti House.'

'Okay, go on.'

'It was a man. Marilyn told me that he'd called because his car had broken down, and he needed a quick pick-up. He had tae be somewhere for nine o'clock.'

'Can you describe him?'

Quinn screwed up his face, as if the act was an aid to memory. 'Youngish bloke, in his thirties. He was fairly tall, and light-haired, I think; but mind youse, it was dark, and pissing down.'

'Anything else?'

'He wore a big overcoat. Like I said it was raining, so he had the collar turned up.'

'Where did he ask you to take him?'

'Tae the Jewel, up across Milton Road, through the roundabout where the tyre place is.'

'You don't remember the address.'

Quinn looked sheepish. 'No. The guy was giving me directions once we got past the roundabout, but I missed a turn. He said that it was okay where we were, then he paid me, got out of the car, and legged it up one of the side streets.'

'Do you remember what time it was by then?'

'A couple of minutes before nine.' Quinn looked over

his shoulder as the door opened behind him, and Neil McIlhenney stepped back into the room. He was holding a sheet of paper which he handed to Martin.

'One thing I don't get, Willie,' said the Chief Superintendent, amiably. 'Why's it taken you five days to come forward?'

The shifty man shrugged, looking embarrassed. 'Well, I don't read the papers much, see. Someone telt me about the murder over the weekend, and I mentioned that pick-up to Marilyn, when I started my shift last night.

'She came on the radio later on, and said that Mr Terry wanted me to speak tae youse.'

Martin's green eyes widened. 'Mr Terry?' He glanced at the sheet of paper on the desk.

'D'you always do what Mr Terry asks?'

'Too right. Not that he asks me for much, mind.'

'Willie, we've done some checking on you since you got here. This says that you have eleven convictions, for theft, housebreaking and shoplifting.' Quinn's eyes dropped. 'You're not a very honest bloke, are you.' The man said nothing.

'So tell me, is your story exactly as it happened, or has Mr Terry embroidered it for you in any way?'

'No!' The voice rose. 'What I told you, that's just how it was, like. Honest.'

Martin smiled at this final assurance. 'Okay. When you were in Seafield Road, do you remember seeing anything else?'

Quinn's eyes narrowed again as if from the effort of racking his brain. 'As I was pulling away a big fire engine came tearing round the corner, heading in the other direction. That was all.'

Martin nodded. 'Nothing else?'

'No.'

'Right, I want you to wait here with the two Constables and set down what you've told us as a formal written statement. Once it's been typed up and you've signed it, you can go.'

He stood up and strode out of the room, followed by Donaldson and McIlhenney. 'Yours, Dave,' he said, heading for the stairs.

'What do you think of that?' he asked, as the door of the Superintendent's office closed behind them.

'It'd be a first all right,' drawled McIlhenney. 'A murderer making his getaway in a minicab owned by the intended victim.'

'Sure,' said Donaldson, 'but what if his car really did break down?'

'Then he'd hardly have buggered off and left it at the scene, sir. Unless it was stolen.'

Donaldson shook his head. 'Every vehicle in the vicinity of the fire has been accounted for.'

'After the event,' said Martin. He looked at McIlhenney. 'What would your Olive do if your car broke down on a rainy night in Seafield?'

The Sergeant pondered the question. 'Apart from giving me a severe tongue-lashing, she'd phone the RAC.'

'And if she'd to be somewhere in a hurry?'

'She'd tell them where it was, leave the keys in it and get a taxi.'

'Right. So let's follow this through. Neil, you and Sammy run a quick check with the motoring organisations, and with the garages around town who do emergency rescue services. See if any of them picked up a car from Seafield Road last Wednesday.

'If they did, I want to know who owns it and where he lives.'

'Unless it's my Olive,' said McIlhenney.

Martin smiled and shook his head. 'No, even if it is. I'm ruling no-one out of this investigation!

'This might not be a hot lead, exactly, but it's the only one we have and we'll follow it to the finish.'

59

Like most modern prisons Shotts is not built in a suburban environment. It sits on the edge of a small town, on a plateau approximately halfway between Edinburgh and Glasgow, but definitely not on any tourist route.

A few relics of its mining past are scattered around the landscape, but in the modern era the Department of Social Security is its principal paymaster.

Winter was unleashing the icy sting in its tail as Skinner drove through the double gates of the jail. Snowflakes were falling and beginning to lie on the ground as he parked and walked across towards the administration building.

Charles Hall, the Governor, was waiting for him in his office, coffee at the ready.

'Welcome, Bob,' he said. 'Long time no see. Good to see you looking so fit and well after what I read about you a few months back. Fully recovered, yes?'

The policeman smiled. 'Just about, thanks, Charles. My family had a hell of a fright at the time, but once I was through the first couple of days, the physical side of it was stabilised. It was just a matter of recuperating, then working at getting back into shape.'

He smiled. 'How's things with the Prison? I haven't

heard anything of you recently, so I take that to mean that all's well.'

The bright-eyed young Governor shook his head. 'Fingers crossed, but yes. The place seems to be under control these days, and as far as I can tell, it's me who's running it, not the prisoners.'

Skinner laughed. 'That's good to hear.'

'The man you've come to see may have a lot to do with that,' said Hall. 'He's an awesome figure among the inmates. He keeps himself very much to himself, reading, studying – writing now I hear – but you sense that no-one would dare to do anything that they thought Lennie might not like. And so far he's been a model prisoner.' He paused.

'He was intrigued to hear that you wanted to see him. He agreed to it at once. I've set up an interview room in this block, so that none of the other prisoners see you together. I'll have two of my biggest lads sit in with you.'

Skinner laughed again, even more heartily. 'Two! Double it and it still wouldn't be enough.

'No, Charles. Big Lennie and I have had our go at each other. He won't want a return match any more than I do. I'll see him alone if you don't mind. What I want to talk to him about has to be off the record.'

Hall stared at him, doubtfully. 'You sure?'

'Absolutely.'

'Well, in that case . . . he's waiting for you now.' He led the way out of his office and down a short corridor, stopping outside a brown varnished door. He rapped three times with his knuckles and stepped inside, Skinner following behind.

Lennie Plenderleith was standing at the window, looking out at the snow, his back to the door. At least Skinner assumed that there was a window there. Big Lennie lived up to his nickname so well that he blocked it out. He was six feet seven and built like an elephant. The strapping guards who flanked him looked puny by comparison.

He turned at the sound of the door opening, and smiled: the slow, contented smile of a man at peace with himself. 'Hello, Mr Skinner,' he said. 'What brings you here on such a bloody awful day?'

He offered out his right hand and Skinner shook it, awkwardly, since Lennie was handcuffed.

'Take those off, please,' the policeman asked the Governor. 'There's no need for them.' Hall nodded, and one of the guards unlocked the cuffs. 'That's good. Now if you'll leave us alone . . .

'Sit down, big fella,' said the DCC as the door closed, taking a seat himself, with his back to the window so that his companion could still see the day outside, putting himself deliberately at a disadvantage by leaving the prisoner between him and the door. He looked across at the giant and smiled. Lennie Plenderleith, multiple murderer, convicted the year before of three killings, including that of his wife. Lennie Plenderleith, millionaire, heir to the fortune of the late Tony Manson. Lennie Plenderleith, hooligan turned intellectual, Open University graduate and now doctorate candidate. Lennie Plenderleith, the only criminal Skinner had ever met for whom, against all his basic instincts, he had formed a genuine liking and respect, the only one in whom he had ever recognised a code of honour similar to his own.

'The Governor tells me you're writing now, Lennie.'

'That's right.' The huge man's voice was soft and gentle, in complete contrast to his physical appearance.

'Am I going to be in it?'

'Maybe. It's a book about Tony's murder, what led up to it, and what followed it. But I haven't decided yet whether to write it as my memoirs or as a novel.'

'It should be a best seller,' said the detective, 'whether you do it as fact or fiction. If I can help with anything, you only have to ask. I know the story too, from the other side of the road, so to speak.'

Lennie smiled. 'That's kind of you, Mr Skinner. I'll take you up on that.'

'Done. Listen, the name's Bob. Our professional dealings are behind us.' He paused. 'You all right, in here?'

'Sure. I've been here before, remember. This time, I'm philosophical about it. Tony left me all his money. The things I did to get in here I see as having done to earn it. I regard it as a pension fund, and when I'm released from here, I'll still, hopefully, be young enough to enjoy it.

'I've never had a chance to say this, but I'm grateful to you for persuading the Crown not to ask the judge for a minimum sentence. That gave me a chance of seeing the outside again.'

He looked across at Skinner. 'Why did you do that?'

The detective returned his frank stare. 'Between you and me? Because I didn't think that what you did was all that bad. Your wife committed a form of suicide in my book. As for the others, I'd have put them away for life. You put them away for good. Part of me wanted to let you go, you know, to let you walk away.'

Lennie guffawed with sudden laughter. 'Too bad about the other part,' he chuckled at last.

'Now, Bob. What's brought you out here?'

'Okay,' said Skinner, 'let's get to it.' He reached into the pocket of his jacket, produced Tom Whatling's eight by six print and handed it across to Plenderleith. 'Know what that is?'

The giant peered at the picture. 'It looks like a broken fluid pipe in a crashed car.'

'Not broken, Lennie. Cut. Eighteen years ago. My Mini Cooper. My car, but my wife was driving at the time. They hadn't even taken her body out of the car when that was taken. The photo's been hidden since then, for all those years. Now I've found it, and I have to know who cut that pipe, who it was that killed her.'

Plenderleith looked across at him, genuinely stricken. 'Your wife? Instead of you? That's awful, for both of you.'

Skinner grimaced, as he nodded. 'I've been checking the investigations that I was involved in around that time, and in the period leading up to it. From those files, the name that jumps out highest is Tony Manson. If it was him, he's dead, and he can't answer for it. But that doesn't matter; I still have to know.'

He paused. 'This thing may have happened before you went to work for Tony, but I have to ask you this. Did he ever mention anything to you afterwards, about me, or about this? And if he did, will you tell me now?'

Lennie Plenderleith closed his eyes and threw his head back, so that his thick brown hair fell on his shoulders. He sat like that for almost three minutes, as if he was searching his memory, or weighing up a decision.

At last he looked at Skinner once more, full in the

eye. 'This is between us, Bob, yes? No hidden mikes or anything. Nothing leaves this room?'

'On my honour.'

The great head nodded. 'Okay then,' he said. 'You got your timing wrong as far as I was concerned. In fact, eighteen years ago, I had just gone to work for Tony. Eighteen years ago you were indeed giving him grief. Everything was shut down, the girls, the drugs everything.

'One day Tony called me in to see him. He said that he had had an ultimatum from his major drug supplier in London. Reopen the market or else, the guy had told him. Tony told him that he should sit tight, that the informant who was spilling his guts to you would be taken care of, and that you would run out of leads and patience. But the London man said no. He told Tony to have you killed, or else.'

Lennie smiled. 'Tony Manson had very definite views about things, you know. He wasn't as powerful in those days as he became, but even then, no-one threatened him, or gave him "or else" orders. Also, he had very definite views about harming policemen in general, and you in particular. He knew that if you were hit then there would be nowhere for him to hide; no, not even him.' He paused. The smile faded and he took a deep breath, as if he were about to dive into a very deep pool.

'Tony gave me my instructions. He sent me to the man in London to make him see sense. So I went down there, I followed the man home one night, I broke his bodyguard's neck, and I made him see sense, the fool who had threatened Tony Manson, by driving a big knife right through his brain.' He reached across and tapped the left side of Skinner's head. 'Right here.

'I felt like a million dollars. I was just a lad, and Tony had trusted me that much, to give me such an important job.'

Skinner sat, motionless and silent, as Big Lennie in his soft voice, finished his story. 'Tony Manson didn't try to kill you, Bob. He saved your life. Between the two of us, you have my word upon it.'

It was the policeman's turn to throw his head back. He hissed out a long sorrowful sigh. 'Sssshit!' he whispered. 'This doesn't get easier.'

Lennie frowned. 'You believe me, don't you.'

'Hah!' said Skinner. 'That's the trouble. I do. It's just that for the second time in as many days, I haven't had the answer I wanted. I was hoping that it was Tony, and that I could have closed the book on it.

'Now, I have to go on, and I'm left with only one obvious alternative. My problem is, I can't make myself believe that it was him either.'

60

'Sorry to bother you, sir, but I can't raise DS Donaldson, and I felt I should pass this on for further instructions.'

'That's all right, Maggie,' said Andy Martin, into the telephone. 'What have you got?'

'Two of my Detective Constables have just finished the check of Jackie Charles' property company, the one that owns the flats. It looks as if we've got a problem with the theory that Charles might have used one of them to store any records relating to his illegal business.'

'How come?'

'Because all the flats are occupied, sir. By legitimate, *bona fide* tenants with no obvious connection to Charles. They're all managed by a reputable agent, all the tenants have rent books and tax is paid on the net income.'

'Ah well,' sighed the Head of CID, 'another chased hare goes to ground. I must admit I didn't think that Jackie would leave himself as exposed as that again, not after those two earlier tip-offs that we had.'

'That's one point that did emerge from our search,' said Rose. 'The records showed that each of the flats we raided had been untenanted for a considerable period leading up to each raid, but that both were let immediately afterwards. That does sort of hint that the theory could

304

have been right, up to that point; at least so far as to indicate that Charles did keep flats for his private use.'

'Mmm. Could be. That is the only property company that Charles owns now, right?'

'Yes. He used to have three, but he rolled them into a single company a year or so back. For tax reasons, I think.'

'Okay, Maggie, thanks for letting me know. I'll think it through to see if there's anything else we can do to keep that line of enquiry alive. Meantime, you concentrate on Douglas Terry. Have you found the other two Willies yet?'

'Macintosh is in London, we believe, sir, but we've arrested Easson. I haven't interviewed him yet. He knows why he's been picked up, but I've left him to sweat on it, until we get McCartney and Kirkbride back up here.'

'Could he have been part of the team that snatched the Brummies, d'you think?'

There were a few moments of silence on the line. 'I don't know, sir, but the people who lifted him said he seemed scared shitless. Maybe that was why.'

Martin smiled grimly to himself. 'Time will tell, Mags. Time and maybe Willie Easson himself.'

He paused. 'Listen, are you using young Pye for anything just now?'

'No. Why?'

'Send him up here, then. I'm going to see a man, and I need company. You've heard the story we were told by Quinn, the taxi driver, about picking up a hire in Seafield Road, a bloke who said that his car had broken down.'

'I heard that, yes.'

'Well, McIlhenney's come up with a name through

the AA. Dominic Ahern, 32 Mountcastle Gardens. I've decided to see him myself, so have Sammy here inside half an hour, as my back-up.'

'Very good, sir.'

Martin replaced the telephone and stared out of the window. The skies were even more ominous than before, heavy and with the purple tinge of snow clouds as they moved steadily eastwards. Outside a few flakes fluttered to the ground.

Suddenly Martin sat bolt upright and picked up the telephone, dialling an internal number. 'Pamela?'

'Yes, sir.'

'The Boss isn't back yet, is he?'

'No. I don't expect him for a while yet.'

'Good, because I'd like to commandeer you for a while. There's a search I want made, in a fair old hurry. I know that Mr Skinner will approve, so if you come along here, I'll brief you. When he gets back I'll let him in on the secret.'

61

'This is Mountcastle Gardens, all right, Sammy, but I'm damned if I can see number 32.' Pye, at the wheel of his white Peugeot 205 peered out of the window, as he cruised slowly along.

'Well look, sir, that's 26, then there's the church, then there's . . . number 34.' His voice tailed off in puzzlement.

'Hold on,' said the Chief Superintendent. 'Got it. That must be it, set back from the road. You can hardly see it for the trees.'

Pye swung the car in a U-turn and parked in front of the long, tree-lined path which led up to 32 Mountcastle Gardens. As he climbed out of the car, a strange feeling of unease came over Martin, deepening quickly into frustration. His brow furrowed as he and Pye walked up the long pathway, up to the big red stone villa at the end, with its brown-painted door and guttering, and its austere brown velvet curtains.

When Pye's ring of the doorbell was answered by a severe woman in a wrap-round overall, with her grey hair tied back in a bun, the Chief Superintendent's gathering suspicions were confirmed. 'We're from the police,' he said. 'We'd like to see Father Ahern; Dominic Ahern.'

The woman glared up at them for a second, then beckoned them inside. Pye looked bewildered as she ushered them, without a word, into a dull room off the hall, with heavy old-fashioned furniture that had seen better days. 'How did you know, sir?' he asked.

'The church next door. It's called St Magdalena's. And this is the Chapter House, where the priests live. It takes one to know one, Sammy. Why d'you think I joined the Edinburgh force, rather than Glasgow?'

There was a cough from the doorway behind them. They turned to see a tall fair man, in his early thirties, in a black shirt and narrow clerical collar. 'Yes, gentlemen?' he said, in a light Irish brogue.

'DCS Martin, DC Pye. We're sorry to call unannounced, Father, but this has come up at rather short notice.'

Father Ahern frowned, but said nothing.

'Last Wednesday,' Martin continued, 'you called the AA to report that your car had broken down in Seafield Road, just after eight thirty. You also called a minicab company and were picked up ten minutes later by a taxi driver, a Mr Quinn.'

'Yes,' said the priest slowly, and, the detective sensed, faintly apprehensively.

'You may not have been aware of it then, but at that time a car showroom in Seafield Road was set ablaze. In that fire a woman died.'

'I learned of it later,' said Father Ahern.

'Did you pass close by that showroom?' asked the detective.

'I did.'

'And did you see anything?'

'I saw a man leaving in a car.'

'Did he see you?'

'Yes.'

Something in the priest's tone seized Martin with expectation, and seemed to prompt his questions. 'Did you recognise that man?'

'Yes.'

'What was his name?'

'I cannot say.'

'You mean you can't recall it?'

'I mean I cannot say.'

'What sort of car was he driving?'

'I cannot say.'

'Is it because you don't know?'

'Chief Superintendent, I cannot say. Do you understand me? I cannot say.'

Martin nodded. 'I understand.' His mind whirled as he searched for his next question.

'Did this man recognise you, Father?'

The priest gave a tiny gasp, hesitated for a second then nodded his head. 'Yes, he did.'

Martin looked at him, fixing him directly with his piercing green eyes. 'Is this man one of your own parishioners, Father?'

Dominic Ahern gazed back, weighing the consequences of his answer to the simple question. 'No, he is not,' he said at last.

The detective grunted. 'Thank you, Father,' he said, 'for your help, insofar as you were able to give it. We'll see ourselves out.'

As the heavy brown door closed behind them with a thud, Sammy Pye could contain himself no longer. 'Sir, if you don't mind me asking, what the f . . . was all that about?

'What help did he give us in there?'

'A hell of a lot, Sammy,' said the Chief Superintendent, 'as much as he could without breaking sanctity. He told us that he saw and recognised the murderer as he left the scene of the crime, and that the murderer saw and recognised him.

'He told us that, before Father Ahern knew of the fire or of Carole Charles' death, the murderer, although he attends another church, sought him out and made confession to him, securing his silence for ever.'

'But what does that do for us, sir?'

Martin stopped, his hand on the roof of the Peugeot. 'For a start, Sammy, it eliminates about seventy-five per cent of the male population of Edinburgh from our enquiries!'

62

'Holy Mother of God – if I may say so – Andy! So all we've got to do is trawl through all the Catholic males in Edinburgh one by one, till we find our killer.'

'Not quite. You can forget McGuire and me for a start, and you can rule out any parishioner of St Magdalena's.'

'Can the PNC help, I wonder?' Skinner mused. 'Why not ask it to give you all Roman Catholic males with criminal form in the Edinburgh area, aged, say, between twenty-five and forty?'

'Priorities, boss,' said Martin. 'Where am I going to find the manpower to follow it up?'

'Okay, fine it down a bit more. Add in the old lady's description of the Slateford killer. See what that gives you.'

'But there's no evidence, not even circumstantial, that Carole Charles and Medina were killed by the same person.'

'Doesn't mean it didn't happen,' said Skinner. 'It's only computer time, Andy. Get the data and follow it up when you have people available.'

He fell silent. 'A thought strikes me about Father Ahern,' he said at last. 'Maybe he was trying to tell you something else.'

'Such as.'

The DCC shook his head. 'It's only a thought, and you've got enough on your plate. Anyway, it's an area where we might need to call the Chief back into action, with the tact and diplomacy of which he's so proud. Leave that to me.'

Martin nodded, turned to leave the office, then stopped. 'I almost forgot. How did you get on at Shotts?'

Skinner sighed, and sat back in his chair. 'Well. Too well. I can't go into detail, because I swore that our conversation would be as privileged as Ahern's confessional, but if you believe Lennie – as I do, implicitly – then far from being out to kill me, Tony Manson was my guardian angel.'

'Which leaves you with . . . ?'

'As far as I can see, with only Jackie Charles. Yet Jackie never did a stupid or reckless thing in his life, and for the life of *me*, I cannot comprehend why he would want to do anything as daft as that.

'There has to be someone else, Andy: someone else who cut that pipe. Only I can't see who it was.'

'So why not leave it at that, Bob?' said Martin, softly.

Skinner looked up at him. 'Believe me, Andrew, with all my heart and soul, I wish that I could. But I have to go on until I find all the answers, even though I have this scary feeling that I'm never going to find the one that will let me live in peace.'

He pushed himself up in his chair and grabbed a file from his in-tray. 'Still, this life goes on. Ask Pam to look in on me as you leave, will you.'

'Ahh,' said the Head of CID. 'Something else I have to tell you. I've borrowed her.'

Skinner's eyebrows rose in an unspoken query.

'I've had a car take her up to Companies House, up in Saltire Court. The search of the Charles property company drew a blank. Only it did seem to confirm that, at one time, he did use his properties for private purposes.

'So I thought to myself, suppose, after those two raids, Jackie decided that was too risky. A little while back he rolled three property-holding limited companies into one. But suppose there's a fourth company, one that we don't know about, in which neither Jackie nor Carole Charles is listed as a director. That's what I've sent Masters to investigate.'

The DCC nodded. 'I follow your thinking. But couldn't he simply have bought another property for cash, without forming a company to do it?'

'He could have, but that's not the way he works. He always takes the corporate route, winding everything back to a holding company offshore.'

'Just like Tony Manson did,' said Skinner. 'So that even if he had been caught and imprisoned, we'd never have been able to seize his funds.'

'That's right. Anyway, I've checked the register of properties. Neither Jackie nor Carole Charles are listed under their own names as the owner of any residence or office. Even the Ravelston Dykes house belongs to the property company. In theory, Jackie's his own landlord, and his own tenant.'

Skinner nodded. 'You could be right, then. If you are, Pam'll find them out. One thing I know about her already: she doesn't stop until the job's done.'

'She could answer another outstanding question for us, too,' said Martin. 'Where did Carole Charles go when she wasn't at her Yoga class?'

63

'Ricky, Ricky, Ricky. What's come over you?' the Chief Superintendent laughed. 'Yesterday you were so keen to get away from Alnwick that you were singing like a bird.

'Today we can't get a fucking note out of you.' The bull-like McCartney sat there, glowering at the wall. 'Of course, the song sheet keeps changing. Yesterday it was Jimmy Lee – Know that one? Aretha Franklin does it brilliantly – today, there's a blues number as well. Three murders and you're bang to rights for them all.

'Do you know how long you're going to get? What age are you, again? Let's see.' Martin picked up a criminal record sheet from the interview-room table.

'Forty-five. Jesus, Ricky, do you know what that means?' He walked across to the interview-room door, opened it for a few seconds, then closed it again with a bang. 'You never think of an unlocked door as a luxury, do you? At least I don't. But you . . .

'Three murders, abduction, a vicious, brutal, crippling attack on a successful young footballer: the most liberal judge on the bench would give you at least a twenty-year minimum sentence for that lot, and God knows what some of the hard ones would do.' He sat down on the corner of the table and looked down at McCartney. Then he picked up a photograph which had been lying face-down, turned it over and thrust it under McCartney's nose.

'That's just part of what you're going down for. His name's Eddie Chang, and on Saturday night you blew his right eye and a chunk of his brain out through the back of his head. We've recovered the bullet, and you know we'll match it to the gun found in your car, a gun which those tests carried out in England can prove you fired.

'Ricky,' said Martin, heavily, 'you will never be alone again in an unlocked room from this day on, until you're at least sixty-five years old. Maybe you never will be. As a free human being, you're history. You're just as dead as Chang, Maloney and O'Flynn are . . . only it'll be a few years before they bury you.

'That's the consequence of playing the silent hero. Whatever you think that Dougie Terry might pay you, it won't be enough. My guess is that he won't pay you anything. It'd be cheaper to have you killed in jail than put your family on a pension.

'It'd be relatively easy too. How can we arrange for special protection if you just sit there and carry the can yourself?'

McCartney looked up at him, doubt invading his defiance.

'You can't see any other way, Ricky, can you?' He paused, letting his words do their work.

'Well I can,' he said at last. 'Yesterday you were ready to tell us all about Jimmy Lee, just to get away from that Rover. Its contents have caught up with you, but the remedy is still the same. Talk to us, tell us the whole story, and we'll do what we can to help you.

'But don't keep us waiting. Even as we speak, DS Donaldson is leaning on your friend Kirkbride. Once we've got his statement we might not want yours. Sergeant McIlhenney here, he doesn't want to offer you any deal at all. I tell you, it's just as well for you I outrank him.' McIlhenney smiled across the table at McCartney, and nodded his head, slowly.

The thug stared from one detective to the other. Finally his eyes settled on Martin. 'Okay then. What sort of a deal are yis talking about?'

The Chief Superintendent nodded and sat back in his chair. 'Common sense at last! Here it is then.

'You plead guilty to the culpable homicide of Eddie Chang, the driver of the Scorpio. You'll claim that the gun discharged accidentally and we'll accept that. You'll also plead to being involved in the assault on Jimmy Lee. We'll close the book in Scotland on Maloney and O'Flynn, and we won't single you out as the leader of the team that did Lee. You'll get time, about twelve years I should think, and you'll probably do the lot, but that's better than the alternative.

'This is a once-only offer. To qualify, you have to give us, locked up tight, the man behind the Lee attack and behind Saturday night's job. Of course, for a conviction it'll take more than your evidence alone. We'll need a duet, not just a solo.'

Martin paused. 'Now. Who gave you your order to have Lee crippled?'

'Dougie Terry,' said McCartney, quietly. 'After the boy crossed him over fixing a Hearts game.'

'And who ordered the killings on Saturday?'

'Dougie Terry.'

'Why?'

'He said that he had information that a team was coming up tae do a friend of his. He told us where they would be and when, and that he wanted it done as far away from his pal's house as possible.'

'Did he mention the source of his information?'

'No.'

'Did he ever mention by name the person who gave him his orders?'

'No, but we all know.'

'That doesn't matter, Ricky, unless you can prove it. Again, did he ever mention his boss by name?'

'No.'

'Right, now the question that could decide whether you draw your old age pension as a free man. Was anyone else present on each occasion when Terry gave you your orders?'

McCartney nodded vigorously, as if with relief. 'Willie Kirkbride,' he said. 'Both times.'

'This gets better. All you need to do now is hope that Kirkbride tells the same story as you.'

Martin stood up once more and walked to the window. 'While you're in this frame of mind, Ricky, is there anything else you can clear up for us? You know who we're really after. Can you tell us anything that might help us nail him?'

Suddenly and surprisingly, McCartney's big brutish face broke into a smile. 'Them, you mean, not him.'

'Eh?'

'Same deal right? Ah plead to those two charges and that's it?'

The detective nodded.

'The Indico job. Twenty-something years ago. Ah was on that one. Tony Manson called me in and said that this lad had come to him with a proposition, looking for money and muscle to back it. Tony had agreed, but on condition that the lad was involved in the action himself.'

Martin sat back in his chair. Beside him, Neil McIlhenney leaned forward, expectantly. 'So,' asked the Chief Superintendent, quietly, 'who was on the team?'

'There was five of us on it. Me, Barney Cogan, Dougie Terry, Jackie Charles and Carole Charles.'

The two policemen stared at him. 'Carole?' said McIlhenney, incredulous.

McCartney nodded. 'Aye. Ah'll swear to it. She drove the getaway car. Dougie Terry drove the other one, that we used tae block in the van. Jackie didn't want her on the team, but she didn't give him a choice. As far as I could see she never gave him a choice about anything. It was okay in the end, though. She was a great driver.'

'One of the security guards was shot,' said Martin. 'Who did that?'

'Jackie did it. Dougie Terry got careless, and turned his back. The bloke was about to brain him with a pickaxe handle, but Jackie blew his leg off. That's why the pair of them are so close. It all goes back to that.

'Jackie Charles shot that guard, and saved Dougie Terry's life.'

64

'We've got him, Bob, by the balls. McCartney and Kirkbride have each given us independent statements, taken separately, implicating Douglas Terry in the Birmingham murders, and the Lee attack.'

'Brilliant, Andy. Let's hear the bastard joke his way out of this one.' Skinner smiled at his friend's delight, evident even over the telephone, yet he sensed that there was something else.

'Ah but there's more,' said Martin, confirming his feeling. In the background Skinner could hear the distinctive sound of Neil McIlhenney's laughter. 'He's given us the key to Jackie Charles' cell as well. All we have to do is force Dougie Terry to turn it.'

Quickly, he related McCartney's account of the Indico robbery. When it was over, Skinner sat silent for a while.

'I've waited twenty-three years for that,' he said, at last. 'Listen, no-one knows we've got McCartney and Kirkbride locked up, do they?'

'No, we've had a news blackout over the whole thing. So have the Northumbrians, at our request.'

'That's excellent. In that case you can choose your moment. You could pick Terry up now, if you like.'

'What would you do?'

'Guess.'

Martin scratched his chin and smiled. 'I reckon you'd knock up the Fiscal and get a formal arrest warrant,' he said. 'Then you'd pay a call on our funny friend first thing tomorrow morning, at his home, and invite him to give us a special performance.'

'Spot on,' said Skinner. 'Where does he live? Torphichen, isn't it? Say around seven thirty. Late enough for him to have had his last breakfast as a free man. Light enough for our people to see. Still early enough for there not to be too many neighbours around to get in the way. That's what I'd do.'

'Good enough for me,' said Martin. 'Let's have him, then, and let's see how he reacts when he finds himself looking at thirty years.'

'Don't let's build our hopes too high, Andy. I spoke to a man today who'd happily have done life for his friend . . . in a sense he is. If Terry doesn't talk, we may get him, but we don't get Charles.'

'He will, though; I feel it in my bones. Terry isn't in the same league as his gaffer. Do you want to be there?'

'No, son. It's your show. You don't need me around. Take no chances though. When you pick him up, go in armed. We're lifting him for ordering three murders, after all.

'Let me know as soon as you've got him.' He smiled. 'And if you need me to come into the interview and terrify him, just ask! I'd enjoy that. Good luck.'

He hung up and looked at his watch. It was five minutes past seven, and he was alone in the Command Suite. He picked up the phone again and dialled the number of the mobile which had been issued that morning to Pam Masters.

'Yes?' She sounded hesitant.

'It's okay,' he said, 'it's me. Where are you?'

'Still at Companies House,' she said. 'No luck so far though, sir.'

'Got much still to do?'

'There are a few things I can try.'

'In that case, I'll come up and help you.'

Outside, the snow which had been teasing the city all day had finally made up its mind to get serious. The BMW snaked sideways momentarily as he eased it down the white-blanketed driveway, but his reaction, and the car's own systems, straightened it up at once. He chose the least hilly route to Companies House, relocated from George Street to plush new premises in Saltire Court, a showpiece office building in Castle Terrace. By the time he parked before its high-pillared entrance, sat in the shadow of the Castle Rock's great bulk, the car's clock showed 7.29.

Saltire Court is home to major law firms, accountancy practices, fund managers and others as well as to the Scottish Register of Companies, and so the building was ablaze with light as he walked into the first of its two atriums, and showed his warrant card to the doorkeeper. As he reached the lifts, one of them slid open and a round-faced, blue-suited man stepped out. 'Hello, Neil,' said Skinner, recognising a lawyer friend from East Lothian. 'Knocking off early tonight?'

'You're not, I see,' said the man with a smile. 'You don't need our services, do you?'

'I hope not,' said the policeman, suddenly grim, 'but if it turns out that I do, I'll give you a shout. Cheers for now, though. Watch yourself on the way home. The roads are pretty bad.'

As the lawyer looked after him, frowning, puzzled by his off-the-cuff remark, he strode off in search of his assistant.

He found her in a glass-walled office, accompanied by a registrar. He could tell at a glance that the man was clearly not enjoying his enforced overtime.

'Hello, boss,' said Pamela. 'Just in time for the final act, I fear.' She shifted in her seat, adjusting the skirt of her tight-fitting two-piece grey outfit. 'I think I've run out of ideas. Mr Shaw and I have covered every company registered in the last twenty-five years and still trading. There's nothing with John Jackson Charles, Carole Charles or Douglas Terry listed as a director that we didn't know about before.

'We've looked for every combination of those names that we could think of. Carole Jackson, Charles Jackson, Terry Douglas, the lot; no joy. Except that Terry Douglas is a director of a toffee manufacturer in Inverness, and Charles Jackson is on the board of a computer firm in Glasgow. I'm coming to the conclusion that this is one very wild goose.'

Skinner sat down beside her. 'Sounds like it.' He scratched his chin, racking his brain. Suddenly his eyebrows rose. 'There is one other outside possibility,' he said. 'Try looking for the surname Huish, Mr Shaw. Spelled H-U-I-S-H. Carole Huish.'

The man sighed with undisguised impatience, adjusted his spectacles and bent over a computer printout, his untidy black hair dropping flakes of dandruff on the pages as he searched through its leaves.

At last he looked up. 'There's no Carole Huish listed,' he said. 'Only one person with that surname, in fact. Jacqueline Huish, sole director of a company named Thirty-First Nominees, registered three years ago, registered office, 31a Rankeillor Street.'

'Pull its records for us, Mr Shaw, then we can all go home.'

The man disappeared, unsmiling. 'Heavy going, isn't he,' said Skinner, quietly, as he left.

'His boss made him stay with me,' said Masters. 'Not a happy man.'

'He's a bloody fool, then.' Her big eyes, and a sudden surprised smile, flashed up at him.

Mr Shaw returned within three minutes, holding several photocopied sheets. 'It seems to be a holding company,' he said. 'Very small. It lodges a balance sheet every year, for minimum compliance with the law. It seems to have nothing but fixed assets, depreciated over different periods. That usually means that it's a device for holding property.'

Skinner stood up. 'Just the device we were after, Mr Shaw. Thank you for being so patient with us. Come on, Pam.' He took the photocopies, shook the man's hand, and ushered Masters out of the office.

'Yess,' they hissed in unison, outside in the corridor.

'Jackie Huish,' said Skinner. 'Pretty obvious if you know the key. Carole's maiden name, Pam, in combination with his Christian name. And she's a sole director. I wonder if even Jackie knows all the details of this company.'

'Surely he would, boss?'

'Not necessarily. Not if he felt he didn't need to. Or maybe, not if Carole felt that he didn't.'

'Tomorrow we'll look at the property register to find out what Thirty-First Nominees actually owns.'

He glanced at his watch. 'But that's tomorrow. Tonight I'm bloody starving. The Atrium Restaurant's in this building. Some say it's the best in town. Fancy a bite?'

She laughed, and laid a hand on his arm. 'Boss, I can't let you feed me all the time. I've got food in the fridge, and you're going home to an empty house. Come home with me, and I'll make us both dinner.'

He looked down at her, doubtfully, for a few seconds, pondering her invitation. 'What the hell,' he said at last. 'Why not? You're on, Pam.'

Three inches of fresh snow had fallen on his car in the half-hour they had been in the building, and it was growing deeper by the second. He swept it away from the front and rear screens and from the side windows, with a cleaning blade which he took from the boot. As they slid into the car the snow created a fantastic winter scene as it swept through the yellow beam of Edinburgh Castle's floodlights, high above them.

'March can be a demon of a month, can't it just,' he said as he drove off, slowly and more carefully than ever. 'Every year, when we think it's spring at last, it chucks this sort of stuff at us. Remember how mild the weather was at the weekend too.'

He reached the lights at the foot of Lothian Road, and turned, into the clutches of Edinburgh's notorious one-way system. 'I would like to take the buggers responsible for this maze and lock them away for a very long time indeed,' he muttered, almost to himself. 'I told Jimmy we should oppose this tooth and nail, but the Police Board is stuffed with sympathisers of the sods who dreamed up this nonsense.'

In the darkness, she smiled, amused by his frustration.

Even with the car's state-of-the-art steering, the treacherous crawl down Leith Walk was a nightmare. But at last they reached Pamela's flat in one piece, and parked in a vacant space outside. The snow was heavier than ever, almost blinding. Skinner looked out from the shelter of the doorway as his assistant fumbled in her bag for her key.

'I should really head for home,' he said. 'Trouble is, I doubt if I'd make it as far as Portobello.'

'It'll ease off,' she said, opening the door. 'And if it doesn't,' she added, cheerily, 'I've got a spare room.'

She paused, as they stepped inside. 'Or would that embarrass you?'

Bob smiled down at her. Had he thought about it at that time, he would have realised that for the first time in months, he did not feel completely alone. 'I'm going on forty-six,' he said. 'All my life, I've been too easily embarrassed. Too old for that now. Whether it would be appropriate, though, that's another question.'

The flat was on the attic floor. She showed him into a spectacular loft-style living area, perhaps eight metres square, with two large windows set into the wall looking for all the world like at inverted 'W'. A large green leather sofa sat, facing out towards the blizzard, with a single matching armchair beside it, both set before a Sony television set. The floor was sanded, varnished beech, with small rugs strewn about here and there.

'Make yourself at home, sir,' she said. 'I have to change into my cooking gear.'

'I will if you stop calling me "sir". I hope I'm here as a friend, not a senior officer. "Sir"'s for out there.'

'What will I call you then?'

'In here? Anything you bloody like.'

She grinned. 'Okay, Eagle.'

'What?' He laughed, surprised. 'What's with Eagle?'

'Because that's how I think of you. When I was in marketing, the consultancy hired a personnel development consultant. Part of her technique was to make us see everyone in our group as the particular creature which they most resembled. It was a team-building exercise . . . I think.

'I still play the game, for my own amusement. I see you as an eagle. A great big bird, flying high, watching everything. Always ready to swoop when you see something wrong, and when you do, unstoppable.'

He was still laughing as he took off his jacket and threw it across the back of the sofa. 'Hey, hold on a minute; an eagle's a bird of prey, a ruthless hunter-killer.'

She nodded. 'I know. That's how I see you. And I'll bet that's how you've looked to some of the people you've put away.'

She grinned again. 'What about me? What animal do I make you think of?'

He gazed at her, appraising her; studying her tumbling hair, and her big, round, smiling eyes. And suddenly, for the very first time he realised, consciously at least, of whom she reminded him: a wild creature at times, but human. Every time he looked at her, at the back of his mind he thought of Myra.

He played the game, nonetheless. 'Okay. I see you as a panther. A big, sleek cat,' he laughed, 'with a purr like thunder.'

She whistled. 'Wow! I'm flattered. A panther. What makes you see me that way?'

'I knew another panther, once.' He loosened his tie and grinned again. 'Now, what did you say about dinner? This is one hungry eagle.'

Six doors opened off the room. She disappeared, with a wave, through the one closest to the window, on the left. As he waited for her return, he stood and looked out of the great uncurtained 'W'. Although the central heating radiators kept the room at a comfortable temperature, a rim of ice had formed on the glass outside, and the snow had turned the waterfront into a belated Christmas card. It was piled high on the rigging of the floating night-spot, which was moored against the east embankment of the Water of Leith. It lay like icing on the pointed roof of the Malmaison Hotel, transformed from its earlier state as an abandoned customs house. There was no more traffic. The blizzard had won, and was rubbing in its triumph.

Pamela's cooking gear turned out to be a blue and white apron, worn to protect a plain white teeshirt and baggy cotton trousers with a pattern which reminded him of the waiters in a certain beachfront Spanish bar. She showed him how to operate the television remote, but instead he followed her into the kitchen.

'How can I help?' he asked her.

'If you're serious, you can wash and cut up the peppers and stuff.' She pointed to an assortment of vegetables, lying on a chopping board, and handed him a broad-bladed knife.

'Would you like a drink?' she asked. 'Sorry I've none of that Spanish Eagle beer, but there is some San Miguel.'

He glanced out of the kitchen window. 'Appropriate or not,' he said, 'your spare room looks inevitable, so I might as well. Not beer, though. I could murder a vodka and tonic.'

Pam nodded. 'Good choice. Me too.'

They sipped their drinks as they worked, Bob preparing the vegetables for the wok and washing the rice, Pamela defrosting a brick of frozen fish soup in the microwave and cutting chicken breasts into strips. Gradually their meal took shape, until, as they finished their second vodka and tonic, Pamela pronounced it ready.

There was a tall uplighter in the corner of the room, but in spite of it Pam lit two candles on her round dining table. They ate, mostly in silence as they concentrated on their food. The fish soup was followed by the chicken, stir fried and served over the rice with a robust tomato, courgette and pepper sauce, all with a bottle of strong, smooth Argentinian red wine to wash it down.

'Pam,' said Skinner, as he forked up the last of the rice, 'ten days ago I had a slap-up dinner in the best restaurant in Los Angeles. It wasn't a patch on that.'

She smiled back, almost coyly, through the candlelight. 'Thank you, sir . . . sorry, Eagle. Food's always at its best when you're really ready for it.' She drained the last of the Echart from her glass. 'There's no dessert, I'm afraid, but . . .'

She skipped through to the kitchen, returning a few seconds later with a tray bearing cups and saucers, a jug of steaming black coffee and a bottle of Bailey's Irish

Cream liqueur. 'Try this,' she murmured, as she poured the coffee and topped it off with the Bailey's, added as if it were milk. 'Irish coffee, the Pamela Masters way.'

Intrigued, he picked up his cup and took a sip. His eyebrows rose. 'My God, that's indescribable. Why have I never done that myself?'

They emptied the jug and much of the Bailey's. Finally Pam produced goblets and a bottle of Hennessy cognac. 'What's the good of being a single woman if you can't indulge yourself,' she said.

With their brandies warming in their cupped hands, they sat on the green leather sofa, looking through the window at the falling snow, Pamela at one end, with her legs curled under her, Skinner at the other. On the table, the candles still guttered, but the uplighter was dimmed, and the only other light in the room spilled in from the waterfront outside.

'Who was she, then?' she asked at last, in its silver glow, 'Your other panther?'

He looked down at her, settling into the sofa, feeling warm, muzzy, replete and very comfortable. 'It was Myra. She was quite a bit taller than you, but . . . Your eyes, the way your hair is, the way you move: you're different, you understand, but in a way I can't pin down, you're very like her.' He smiled.

'And what about me. Who do I remind you of?'

'No-one,' she laughed. 'You're an absolute one-off.'

There was a long silence as they sat gazing out of the window at winter's last shout, sinking deeper into the leather cushions. It was Skinner who broke it. 'I'm thinking, Pam,' he began, 'that I should really phone Fettes and have one of the Traffic Department Landrovers pick me up and take me to Fairyhouse Avenue. There's a spare room there as well.

'You could bring the BMW in in the morning, if the roads are okay by then.'

She nodded. 'I will, if that's what you decide. But can you trust the Traffic boys?'

'What do you mean?' He looked at her puzzled.

'Can you trust them not to put two and two together and make seventeen, when they pick you up from my flat at going on for one in the morning?'

He laughed. 'That is a very cynical view of the loyalty and discretion of your average Traffic Department colleague. And it's absolutely spot on. It's a fair bet that the news would be on the canteen grapevine before the current shift was over.' He paused. 'Of course, I could always threaten them with crucifixion if they breathed a word.'

It was Pamela's turn to smile. 'That would really start them thinking, wouldn't it.'

'Yes, I suppose you're right. If they hadn't been picturing the worst, that would do it for sure. Okay. Your spare room it is, then. And it's time I was off to it. We've got a big day before us tomorrow.'

He stood up, reaching out a hand to help her to her feet. 'Thanks a million, Pam. It's been a smashing evening, and it's done wonders for me. I was getting pretty doomy, without knowing it. I really needed to relax, and I'm grateful to you for helping me do it.'

She looked up at him. 'It was a pleasure. With one thing and another, you must be having a tough time just now.'

Bob shrugged his shoulders. 'Maybe so, but no-one's

immune from problems, and no-one can assume that any marriage, any relationship is so strong it's fireproof. Maybe too, if I was honest about it, I'd see that some of my problems are of my own making. Yes, maybe.

'But for Christ's sake, Pam,' he burst out. 'How are you supposed to react when you feel betrayed by someone you love?'

65

She sat up in bed, her legs pulled up under her chin. It had been a long time since her parting from Alan Royston, and since a man had spent a night under her roof.

The heating had been on all night and, despite the winter outside, the room was hot, so she had thrown back the heavy quilt. She was still thinking as she had been when she had fallen asleep, of his surprising vulnerability, and of his obvious helplessness in the face of his split from his wife. She knew the feeling herself, having been through divorce, and she knew that it was an area too personal and subjective for her to lend any more support than a sympathetic ear.

She jumped when the bedside telephone rang, and looked automatically at the alarm clock. It showed 7.19 a.m. Wondering who the early morning caller could be, she picked up the phone. '3179,' she answered.

'Pamela.' A clear voice, familiar to her already, came down the line. 'It's DCS Martin here. I don't suppose the Boss told you where he was going last night, did he? I need to contact him, but I can't raise him at Gullane, and his mobile's switched off. He's not at his Edinburgh number either.'

She gulped, and hesitated for a second, before making

332

up her mind. 'Actually, he's here, sir,' she told the Head of CID. 'He drove me home last night, then got snowed in. Hold on, I'll call him.' She jumped out of bed and slipped on her robe, then skipped across the living room.

'Boss,' she called out, loudly, rapping on the closed door of the spare room. 'Telephone. It's Mr Martin. You can take it in the kitchen if you like.'

'Okay, Pam, thanks,' came the voice from within. 'I heard it ring. I'm just coming.'

A few seconds later the door opened and he stepped out, barefoot, with a black shadow around his jawline, and wearing the trousers of his suit. He smiled at her and headed for the kitchen. As he passed, she could see, showing red and vivid still, the scar of the surgery through which his life had been saved a few months earlier.

Skinner took the phone from its cradle on the wall. 'What's the matter, Andy? Did you lift Terry earlier than planned?'

'We never got to Torphichen, Boss. We picked up a treble-9 call forty-five minutes ago from the cleaner in his office in Stafford Street. That's where I'm calling from. I think you should get up here.

'The Comedian won't be turning the key on Jackie Charles for us, I'm afraid. At least not without the aid of a medium. His brains are all over the floor, and he isn't getting the joke at all.'

66

Skinner showered, then shaved, using a razor and foam left months before by Alan Royston. He was barefoot, but otherwise fully dressed when he rejoined her in the kitchen. She had thrown on jeans and a sweatshirt. Two mugs of coffee, a plate of buttered toast, and another of sliced tomatoes were set out on the breakfast bar.

He looked at her and smiled. 'Royston didn't leave any socks behind, did he? I hate wearing the same pair twice running.'

She shook her tousled head. 'No, he didn't. He never wanted to move in . . . not that I'd have let him, mind.'

'More fool Royston,' said Skinner, taking her by surprise. 'Sound man, Alan. He's good at what he does, but he lacks imagination. I expect he'll be on the scene at Stafford Street.'

Pam frowned. 'It's a big blow, isn't it, losing Douglas Terry?'

'Yes it is, in terms of getting Jackie Charles. We're not just back to square one, we're right off the board. Terry was our best hope of a lead to Carole's killer too. I tell you, Pamela, it's worrying.'

She handed him his coffee. 'It's not the end of

the world. Something else will turn up to incriminate Charles.'

He peered into the mug. 'There's no Bailey's lurking in here, is there?' His half-smile vanished as quickly as it had come. 'No, lass, that's not what's worrying me. It's the way the little bastard's been ahead of us every step of the way. It's getting to me.'

'Terry was murdered, I take it.'

'Unless he smashed the back of his own head in, yes he was.'

She grimaced. 'You sure you don't want me to come with you?'

'Senior copper's tip number one. Never volunteer to go to a murder scene. No, you go to the office as usual, check the incoming paper, then make an appointment for the two of us to check the register of property titles. We've got Thirty-First Nominees Limited to follow up, remember.'

She laughed, as he straightened his tie. 'You're really chuffed with yourself for turning up that company, aren't you. Jackie Huish, indeed.'

Placing his mug back on the breakfast bar, he looked at her, almost conspiratorially. 'Listen,' he said quietly, 'even a Deputy Chief Constable can still get a kick out of being a smart-arse. Only . . .'

'. . . No-one loves a smart-arse!' They laughed in unison, until Pam picked up the toast and tomatoes. 'Come on, let's finish this lot next door.' She headed back through the living room, back to the green leather sofa, while he went back to the spare room to put on socks and shoes. Then, with the plates on the cushion between them they shared breakfast and drank their coffee, looking out of the window at the new day. The snow had stopped and the temperature seemed to have risen. As they watched, a great bank of snow slid off the Malmaison roof and crashed to the ground.

She grinned up at him. 'Well, at least you're not snowed in any more. We're back in the real world.'

'Still,' he said. 'I enjoyed last night. It was good to find someone else that I can talk to. There aren't many people in that category, I can tell you. Four, apart from you . . .' He hesitated. 'Sorry, make that three.'

'So your problems don't look any better in the daylight,' she said, softly.

He shook his head. 'I just don't know, Pam, and that's the God's truth. But I can't lose this feeling that the Sarah I loved isn't there any more, and I guess she feels the same about me.'

She looked down at her coffee and frowned. 'Maybe you'll find each other again.'

'Maybe we will, Pam. Maybe we will. But right now, neither of us knows how to go about that . . . or even if we want to start. I never believed it could happen, but our marriage has broken down.'

'I know it has,' she said. 'Otherwise last night you would have called the Traffic boys without a second thought.' She reached across and tapped his chest. 'In here,' she said. 'Each of you has to start searching in here. Maybe those other people you spoke of haven't gone away; maybe they're just hiding.'

She frowned at him, suddenly. 'D'you love Sarah?'

He hesitated. 'Look . . .'

'Sorry,' she said quickly. 'I'm going too far.'

He sighed. 'No, Pam, you're not. To be honest, six

months ago I'd have said, "Yes, with all my heart." But I have a big hang-up over trust. To me, it's everything. So I fear you hit on the answer just a few seconds ago. If I still loved her, surely I wouldn't be sitting here now. Last night, I would indeed have called the lads. Or better still, I'd have called Sarah and asked her to get her four-wheel drive out of the garage and come and get me.

'It certainly never occurred to me to do that.'

Bob stood up and stepped over to the window. Looking out, he said, 'The way that things are between Sarah and me makes me feel indescribably sad. It's like bereavement. You're divorced. You should understand that.'

Pamela stood up and came to his side. 'Yes, I understand it. But the only advice I can give you from my experience is not to throw away the keys to any door you've locked behind you, until you're absolutely sure that you'll never want to walk back through it.'

'Okay,' said Bob. 'But maybe there's a new complicating factor.'

'What's that?'

'Ah, I can't tell you that. Not just yet. Maybe it's there, maybe it isn't. I'll know in time.'

'Ah well,' she sighed. 'If all else fails, you can do what I did after I left David. You can throw yourself into your work. At least Fettes is a constant.'

'Don't be so sure,' he said with a grin, and started to head for the door.

'What do you mean?'

'Never mind. I still have some secrets, even from my PA.

'Thanks yet again for last night, Pamela. But now I'd better head up to Stafford Street. Dougie Terry won't keep for ever.'

67

The Comedian was smiling . . . or so it seemed as Skinner
bent over the body, in the cramped little attic office.
Douglas Terry lay face-down, with his head turned to
the side, and the corner of his mouth turned up in a
grinning rictus.

The back of his head was indeed smashed in, a red,
black and grey mess of blood, hair and brain tissue, with
bone chips mixed in.

The scene of crime squad had finished its work and had
gone, but Arthur Dorward remained behind. He, Andy
Martin and Dave Donaldson, were the only other people
in the room.

'Do we have the weapon?' asked the DCC.

'Yes, sir,' said Inspector Dorward. He held up a clear
plastic bag, containing a short-handled hatchet, with a
heavy iron head. It, and most of the wooden shaft
were caked with blood. 'The DIY stores sell hundreds
of these every week, quite legally. The perfect murder
tool, effective and untraceable.'

'Effective is an understatement. What happened, Arthur?'

'It seems pretty clear, sir. Terry walked into his office
and someone was waiting for him, there behind the door,
out of sight. One blow would have been enough, but our

338

man made sure. He must have hit him half a dozen good wallops as he lay on the ground. There's blood and brains all up the desk there, see?'

'Time of death?'

'The ME estimates around ten o'clock last night. She came up with that description of the murder, and I agree with her, as always. A tall man, she said. Slightly taller than Terry at any rate.'

Skinner looked round at Andy Martin. 'She?'

He nodded. 'She's just gone.'

'Was she here when you called me at Pam's?'

'That's how I knew you weren't at Fairyhouse Avenue,' he said, wincing. 'I never expected . . .' He left the sentence unfinished.

'Magic,' Skinner whispered ironically, then turned to Dorward once more. 'Anything else, Arthur?'

'Yes, sir. This.' He stepped across to a corner of the room, picked up a steel wastebin, and held it out for the DCC to inspect.

Skinner looked inside. The walls of the rectangular bin were scorched, and on its base lay a tangled, shapeless black and white mess. He sniffed.

'We'll need to test it of course, but I'd reckon that it's a binliner and plastic bags.'

'Burned,' said Skinner. 'This bugger gets more thorough every time.' He turned to Donaldson. 'It's a bastard, Dave, is it not?' he said vehemently. 'We've been trying for years to land this guy. At last, McCartney hands him to us on a plate, then this happens.

'How did Charles know?'

'McCartney must have had an arrangement to call someone, boss,' said the Superintendent. 'When he didn't, maybe Terry reported it to Charles, and maybe Jackie decided that it was getting too close and that he'd have to play it safe.'

Skinner looked down at the body. 'It doesn't get any safer than that,' he growled. 'Bang goes our chain of evidence leading up to Charles. With Terry dead, he's probably out of business, but that's small consolation if he's still walking around as a free man.'

'Maybe he won't be out of business, sir,' said Donaldson. 'What if the guy who did this is ready to take Terry's place?'

The DCC laid a hand on the Superintendent's shoulder, and looked at him, earnestly. 'You really know how to cheer a man up, Flash, don't you. If you're right, then it's up to you to go out there and catch him.' He nodded at the corpse on the floor. 'There's no way that Jackie did this himself. He's two or three inches shorter than Terry, and if my wife said that the killer was taller than him, you can take that as gospel.

'McCartney and Kirkbride are in the nick, Barney Cogan's dead, Willie Easson's been lifted and Willie Macintosh is out of town. So who the hell else is there? And what's the link that ties all the murders together?'

He gave Donaldson's shoulder a final pat. 'You're the man on the ground, Dave. I'm counting on you, above all, to give us the answers.'

68

The Roman Catholic Metropolitan Cathedral of St Mary
is probably the most understated seat of any of that
Church's British Archbishops. Dwarfed by its neighbours, the St James Shopping Centre and the monstrous
New St Andrew's House, it sits in relative anonymity,
looking out at Paolozzi's massive bronze sculptures,
across Picardy Place, past the statue of Sherlock Holmes,
over the seemingly eternal gap site and on to the northern
slopes of Calton Hill.

Unlike its Episcopalian namesake a mile and a half to
the west, it has no impressive spires, no tower of bells,
nothing other than a flight of wide steps leading up to its
ever open doors.

Morning mass had just ended as Sir James Proud
stepped out of his car, picking his way around the
puddles and the heaps of fast-melting snow, and climbed
the stairway, past a trickle of departing worshippers. He
was dressed, as was almost invariably the case during his working day, in full uniform, complete with
black military belt. Automatically he swept off his cap
as he entered the cathedral, looking round until his
gaze fell upon a young curate. He advanced upon the
priest.

'I'm looking for his Eminence,' he said. 'He is expecting me,' he added, to quell the surprise in the young man's eyes.

'In that case, sir, if you'll follow me.' He led the Chief Constable up the aisle, making a blessing at the altar, before turning across the nave, and heading for a side exit. They stepped into a small corridor, on the far side of which was a heavy oak door. The young priest rapped hard with his knuckles, and opened it, on a muffled shout from within.

Sir James nodded his thanks and stepped past him into the room. 'Hello, Gilbert,' he said, smiling and offering his hand. 'Good of you to see me at such short notice.'

Cardinal Gilbert White, acknowledged leader of the Roman Catholic Church in Scotland, crossed his spacious study, greeting him warmly. 'Nonsense, Jimmy. We are princes, you and I: you of the City, I of the Church. A simple courtesy between us which you would have extended to me also.'

The small eyes twinkled beneath the round red skullcap. 'Besides, you fascinate me as always. "A very delicate and confidential matter," you said. These sources of yours never cease to amaze me. But how did you know this time? It was only confirmed yesterday afternoon.'

Proud stared at him, confused. 'I'm sorry, Gilbert, but I don't think I know what you're talking about.'

'Ahh. Have I let the cat out of the bag? You're not here to ask me about the Papal visit?'

'No indeed, although it's nice to have advance warning. When is it?'

'In October. He's addressing a Special Assembly of the Church of Scotland.'

The Chief Constable clapped a hand to his forehead. 'Oh no. He isn't, is he? The policing of that will be a nightmare. Couldn't you talk him out of it?'

'I tried, Jimmy, believe me, but I understand that the idea was suggested by the Leader of Her Majesty's Opposition during a recent audience.'

'Then I hope that the irresponsible fool loses the next election. We'd better waste no time on this. I'll arrange for Jim Elder, my ACC Ops, to meet your people, and the Church of Scotland, as soon as possible.'

Cardinal White nodded, ushering his guest towards two red armchairs on either side of a gas-fuelled open fire. 'If that wasn't it, then what is your delicate matter, may I ask?'

'It's something that Bob Skinner asked me to raise with you,' said Proud.

The Cardinal's eyebrows rose. 'The famous Mr Skinner. What have we done to attract his attention? How is he, incidentally? Recovered from that incident, I trust?'

'More or less, yes. He's back in harness. The thing is, our CID people are investigating a murder. It happened in a car showroom in Seafield last Wednesday. During the course of our enquiries, we discovered that one of your clergy, Father Dominic Ahern, had been in the area at the time.

'When we asked Father Ahern if he had seen anything near the showroom, he said that he had. We then ran into an area of difficulty. Father Ahern felt unable to tell us any more.'

'Ahh,' said the Cardinal, hunching his shoulders beneath his dark robe, 'I think I understand. A matter of confessional sanctity?'

'Yes.'

'In which you realise I cannot intercede?'

'Of course not, Gilbert. I must tell you at once that Father Ahern has behaved with absolute propriety in this matter. But in the light of the limited responses which he felt able to make to our questions, I have a couple of things to ask you.'

Cardinal White nodded. 'Go on. I'll see what answers I can give you.'

'The first is easy. Before Father Ahern became parish priest at St Magdalena's, what was his posting?'

'That's easy indeed. He was priest of St Teresa's, one of our smaller charges, in Morningside.'

'Right. Now can I ask you, does each of your churches keep a record of its parishioners?'

The Cardinal laughed. 'Too right we do. And the archdiocese keeps an overall record, centrally.'

'Then I'll come to the point. Gilbert, we have deduced, not from anything Father Ahern told us, but from what he didn't, that the man we want for that murder is likely to be a Catholic.

'Purely as a speculative exercise, you understand, and on the basis that nothing you let us see would be required as a production in evidence, would you be prepared to let us look at the list of male parishioners of St Teresa's?'

Cardinal White looked at him in surprise, his small eyes widening in his puffy face. 'St Teresa's? Not St Magdalena's?'

'That's right.'

The churchman stared into the fire, considering the question. 'Purely speculative, you say?'

'That's right.'

'There'd be no attempt to call Ahern as a witness, or interview him further?'

'None. Plus, no-one but Bob Skinner would see the material you gave us, and it would be returned to you or destroyed as soon as it had been assessed.'

The churchman looked at the Chief Constable, long and slow. 'With all those provisos, yes,' he said at last.

'How long will it take you to make it available?'

Cardinal White laughed again, merrily, as he pressed a button beside the fireplace. 'About five minutes. This is very nearly the twenty-first century, Jimmy.' The study door opened, and the young curate entered. 'We keep all our records on computer these days. I take it that a three-and-a-half inch floppy will be okay.

'You can just wipe it when you're finished.'

69

Feeling uncomfortable in yesterday's clothes, Skinner walked along to Frasers, at the West End of Princes Street, and bought a shirt, socks and underwear.

He changed into the fresh items in the small private room behind his office then buzzed through to Pamela. 'A word please, Sergeant,' he said. A few seconds later, the door opened. She was dressed, as the day before, in a fresh white blouse and in her close-fitting grey business suit. He smiled as she entered.

'Hi Pam. Look, I've got something I'd like you to do for me as a priority, involving the lab, before we go to check on Thirty-First Whatever.'

'Okay, boss,' his assistant replied. 'But first, the Chief called a minute ago, from his car. He said I should tell you that his visit was successful and that he has what you asked for.'

'Good; that's good.' He sounded a shade distracted.

'How was Stafford Street?' she found herself asking, as she turned towards the door.

'It was messy, very messy. You may have heard the term "hatchet job", but believe me, you don't want to see one. Every murder scene I've ever visited has been one too many, but some are worse than others.'

She grimaced. 'This priority thing you want me to do? Has that got anything to do with it?'

The depth and sincerity of his sigh took her completely by surprise. 'I hope not, Pam. I really do hope not.'

70

The General Register of Sasines conceals behind its grand
and mysterious title the details of most of Scotland's
property ownership. To avoid the chancy business of
parking in the back streets off London Road, Skinner
and Masters arrived at its slightly drab entrance in the
police car which had ferried Bob to and from his regular
lunchtime visit to Jazz.

'How was your son?' Pamela asked, at last, as the car
drew up outside the flat uninteresting bulk of Meadowbank
House.

'In fine loud form,' Bob smiled. 'His mother was
absent though. Deliberately, I think. I'll call her later.'
For an instant, he considered telling Pamela that Sarah
knew where he had spent the previous night, but their
driver's presence made him think better of it.

They jogged up the steps, and were given clear
directions by an attendant which led them to an office,
modern but quite unlike that in which the Register
of Companies was maintained. It was dull and dry,
smelling of crisp paper and old, oiled leather bindings.
Glass-fronted bookcases lined the walls of the big room,
in which a man and three women worked at old grey
metal desks.

One of the women rose and came towards them. 'Yess?' she asked in the tentative tone of one who hoped that whatever the enquiry was it would not be too taxing.

'Good afternoon,' said Pam, brightly. 'I'm Sergeant Masters. And this is Deputy Chief Constable Skinner. I called this morning to make an appointment for two fifteen, with Miss Brittle.'

'Ahh yes.' The woman sounded relieved. 'Mary,' she called across the room. 'Your two fifteen!'

Miss Brittle rose from behind the furthest desk and wound her way towards them. She was as grey as her desk, as grey as the carpet on the floor, as grey as the city on a wet November day. Her hair was drawn up in a tight bun, and she walked with a slight stoop, her spine curving beneath the embracing wool of her twin-set, which was, of course, grey. She looked at least sixty. In fact, Skinner thought to himself, she looked as if she had been sixty for ever.

'You're the police lady,' she said in a clear, shrill tone.

'Yes, and this is my boss, DCC Skinner.'

Mary Brittle gazed up at him, severely. 'What's this about then? We're not used to police traipsing in here, asking for information. You didn't need to call personally, you know.'

'I know,' said Skinner, doing his best to charm the dragon, 'but we thought that it would be easier for you if we did. There is a degree of urgency, as well.'

Her glower softened, almost as if it were starting out on the long journey towards becoming a smile. 'Oh well,' she said. 'What is it you want?'

'We need to locate all properties owned by a company, registered in Scotland, called Thirty-First Nominees Limited,' said Pamela. 'There's nothing in the company's returns to indicate where they are, and we believe that its sole director may have died.'

'Won't the death have been registered?' asked Miss Brittle.

'We've checked. This person's birth isn't even registered. The name in Companies House is an alias.'

'Hmm. Very mysterious. Hold on then, and I'll check. Thirty-First Nominees Limited, you said.' Pamela nodded.

'It'll take a wee while. There's a display on downstairs: why don't you wander round that and come back in fifteen minutes or so.'

Leaving Pamela to tour the exhibition of old Scottish Feudal charters, Skinner stepped out of the building, walked up the few steps which led up to London Road, and took out his mobile phone. He dialled in his Edinburgh home number: Sarah's number now, he reminded himself. It was Tracey, the nanny, who answered. 'Hello, Mr Skinner. Yes, she just came in.'

'Hello, Bob.' His wife's tone was so frosty that it chilled him to the bone. 'I suppose I should sing, "Who Were You With Last Night?", shouldn't I?'

He had been expecting her to say something, but still a great flame of anger swept through him, obliterating the chill and stopping just short of lighting his notoriously short fuse. 'I got snowed in,' he said curtly.

'If you say so. I got snowed in too, with our son.'

He sighed. 'Listen, Sarah, I think we should talk to each other, about the situation, about where we're headed. Can I visit you tonight? I'll bring supper with me.'

'No thank you.'

'You come out to Gullane then. Leave Jazz with Tracey.'

'Oh no!' Her voice was vehement, her upstate New York accent as pronounced as it was when first they had met. 'I'm not coming back to the haunted house! Listen, I'll decide when we meet, and where. If we meet, that is.

'As for tonight, I'm sure you'll find that your evening's occupied.' Abruptly, she hung up.

He felt another blaze of anger. He pressed the 'Redial' button, but caught himself and stopped the call. Instead, he took three deep breaths, to calm himself, then called his office.

'Ruthie,' he said, calmed at once by the sound of his secretary's friendly voice. 'It's me. Is the Chief back from his lunch yet?'

'Not yet.'

'Okay, when he comes in, tell him that I've reviewed the material he secured for me, taken what I need from it, and wiped it as agreed. Tell him too that if the ball spins the way it might, I may need a very private meeting with him tomorrow afternoon.'

'Yes, sir.' She paused. 'Mr Skinner, don't mind me asking, but are you all right? It's just that I've never heard you sounding so stressed out.'

'I guess that's because I never have been.' He chuckled, and that was a relief in itself. 'But don't you worry about me. Stress can be a stimulant, they say.

'D'you have anything else for me?'

'Yes, one thing. Alex phoned. She said she wants to

see you tonight, at Gullane. She said to expect her at eight thirty.'

He laughed again. 'That sounds like an order, not a request. I'll look forward to it.' He replaced the phone in his pocket, stepped back into the building, reclaimed his assistant from the exhibition, and headed back to the formidable Miss Brittle.

Pam climbed the stairs a couple of paces ahead of him, her hips rippling in her tight skirt as she took the steps. For some reason Bob thought again of Sarah and the chill in her voice, and suddenly felt ashamed of his angry reaction.

Miss Brittle was waiting for them as they stepped back into the big room. This time she showed them to a desk and invited them to sit.

'That wasn't too difficult at all,' she said, with a slight air of smugness. 'Thirty-First Nominees owns three tenemental properties, all in Edinburgh. Here are the addresses.' She pushed a handwritten note across the desk. '31a Rankeillor Street, 5c Westmoreland Cliff, and 59 Stalbridge Colonies.

'Titles to all three properties were registered within a six-week period, three years ago. None of them are encumbered.' Miss Brittle's smile surfaced at last, weak and watery, as she looked across at Masters. 'That means that none of them are mortgaged, dear.'

Skinner threw a quick sideways glance at his assistant. Only a sudden clenching of the muscles at the base of her jaw as she forced a smile in return betrayed any reaction to Miss Brittle's patronising.

'Indeed,' she said. 'Do your records show who acted for the company in the acquisitions?'

The grey woman nodded. 'Watson Forbes, Solicitors, of Falkirk; a small firm. I was surprised. I don't usually see their name involved with corporate work.'

'Thank you very much, Miss Brittle,' said Skinner, rising from the desk. 'You've given us what we were after. We're very grateful.'

'We are here to serve,' said the elderly lady, fixing him with a sudden gaze so perceptive that it almost made him start. 'I can't imagine what this is about. But it must be very important, to demand the personal attention of a Deputy Chief Constable.'

They walked side by side from the building, in silence, and down the steps to their waiting car. As Skinner opened the back door for his assistant, a slow smile spread over his face. 'A right cunning old bird that was,' he muttered.

He stopped, his hand on the roof of the car. 'Pam, drop me off at Fettes, then head on out to Falkirk and find this Watson Forbes firm. See what they can tell you about their mysterious client. Meantime I'll speak to my pal the Fiscal and get entry warrants for these three properties. I'm sure I can find grounds under the Companies Acts.

'Once I've taken care of that, I'll be going out to Gullane. I've been bidden to meet with my daughter, and I can only hazard several guesses as to what it might be about.'

71

He was waiting for her, watching from behind the curtains of his darkened bedroom, as she drove up the Green, and as her headlights swung off the road and turned towards the cottage. She was five minutes early.

He had opened the front door, beneath its welcoming light, before she had even switched off the engine. He looked on as she pulled her long coat tight around her, and climbed out of the car, more awkwardly than usual. He watched from the doorway, as she took a holdall from the boot. He stood back in surprise as she walked up the path towards him, but without looking at him, then swept past him, into the hall.

He had no time to register details, only his own surprise. He followed her into the living room.

Alex dropped the bag in the centre of the floor, threw off her coat in a single sweeping motion and turned towards him. He gasped in surprise and stood frozen in the doorway.

'Hello, Bob,' she said, in an accent that was not her own. She was wearing the black dress, the tight thrusting bra, the high heels. Her hair was teased, and her make-up was applied perfectly. She stood and faced him, the dress riding up her right thigh as she bent her knee, slowly, rubbing her foot against the back of her left calf.

And then she was Alex again.

'You wanted me to get to know my mother, Pops. I did. Both sides of her.

'I read the diaries. In there I found my mum, and your wife. But I found someone else too: a woman you didn't know existed. The woman who wore this dress, these shoes . . .' She pulled up the dress quickly, revealing the catch of the suspenders and the top of the stocking, '. . . this underwear.

'You put all these things in the trunk, Pops, but you didn't know what they were for. I guess you remember her wearing them, but you never for a second understood why she did.'

She walked across to the doorway and hugged him, briefly, as he stood there, bewildered. 'My mum loved you, Pops. And she loved me, and she loved her job. All that was very clear, all the way through. But there was another side to her that only her diaries knew about. Only the diaries and the men.

'There was another person inside her: a bad, wanton person, one that she kept hidden from you all your life together. She suppressed her for as long as she could, but gradually her urges took a stronger and stronger hold of her. If she were here today, I think she'd say that she was compelled to do these things, and that she couldn't stop herself. But there was more than that to it; there was the danger too. She seemed to love that.'

She led him into the living room, and tugged his arm until he sat on the couch beside her. His face was dark, disturbed.

'Myra . . . I can't call that part of her Mum . . .' said Alex, 'realised from the start that she had a power over men. She even thought she could use it to snare you, when you were both sixteen, only she fell in love with you. You were strong; without knowing it you kept her devilment in check for years. But Myra's wanton side was strong too, and it couldn't be suppressed for ever.' She paused.

'She had affairs, Pops.' Her voice dropped to a whisper. 'Not long-term, not serious – until the end – but quick, dangerous liaisons. Gradually, the more dangerous they were the better they became. The other Myra spent her life searching for the ultimate sexual excitement, and risk had to be associated. She was addicted to it. It's all there, Pops, in the diaries. I'm sure that simply keeping them, under your nose, with the possibility that you might get curious and pick one up, was the biggest risk of all. Yet she did it. She knew you too, obviously, and was confident that you would respect the only privacy she asked of you.'

Alex looked down at her clothes. 'This dress I'm wearing, these clothes, were a weapon. Pops, some nights while you were working late and someone was babysitting for me, she'd get dressed up in them and go to a hotel in town, one of the good ones in the city centre, looking for a man on his own. For her, it was easy.

'My University friends and I, we laugh about it. We call it sharking. Pops, in terms of sharking, Myra was a Great White.' She paused. 'After a while, just to add to the thrill, and the risk, she got round to taking money. Fifty pounds, sixty, a hundred pounds once.'

Bob sprang to his feet. 'No!' he exploded. 'Fantasies,

356

girl, that's all these diaries are. The fantasies of a woman with . . . with . . . an imaginary friend, to act out her bad thoughts.'

Alex stood up too. She dropped her head slightly and looked at him from beneath hooded eyebrows. 'Oh no,' she said quietly, a smoky edge to her voice. 'I wore these clothes, Pops. I went out in them. I became Myra.

'And I was overwhelmed by what I could do, by the power I had, by the danger I could put myself in, and by the sheer depth of the thrill it made me feel.

'I went out to a hotel in Glasgow, Pops. I met a man, an American. I pulled him, just like that. He'd have given me three hundred quid, for me to take this outfit off. I took myself, almost literally, to the bedroom door. I said okay, sent him up ahead of me in the lift, then I jumped into a taxi and I got the hell out of there.

'I was terrified, Pops.' Tears welled up in her big blue eyes and ran down her cheeks, through her make-up, destroying her mascara. 'Not by the man or anything about him, but by me, and what I could do.'

She pointed to the bag on the floor. 'The adventures in those diaries are not fantasies, believe me. They may have begun that way, but Myra acted them out, every one of them.' She wiped her eyes with the back of her hand.

'Now I have to get out of these clothes. Because they scare the life out of me.' She strode from him, quickly, through to her bedroom. When she reappeared in five minutes, she was Alex again, in sweatshirt, jeans, and flat shoes, her eyes clear, her face scrubbed clean, her hair bouncing in its usual shape.

'I've left them through there, Pops. I don't want them.

357

When you've read what's in those diaries, I think you'll want to burn them.'

She stepped up to him and hugged him, as she had when she was small.

'When I had finished,' she said, quietly, 'I didn't know what to do. Should I keep them to myself, should I leave you with your memories of your Myra? Or should I show you what was in them, and risk breaking your heart?

'I called Sarah this morning, to ask her advice. She chopped me off. She said she was the last person I should talk to, and hung up the phone, more or less. I couldn't talk to Andy; that wouldn't have been right, telling him and not you, and anyway, I'm not ready to come clean with him about all of my weekend. Maybe I never will be.

'So at last, Pops, I decided you had to know. Especially because of the end, and what's there.'

She picked up the bag and put it into his hands, heavy with the weight of the fourteen volumes, heavy with what they contained. 'Don't read them all,' she said. 'That'd be too much, even for you. No; especially for you. I've marked the pages that I think you have to see. They're all in here, in order.

'I'm going to leave you to it. You've got the strength to read them alone. If you want to speak to me when you're finished, I'll be at Fairyhouse Avenue for a while. I feel, at least part of me feels, defiled. I need to encounter purity. So I'm going to visit my brother. And to talk to Sarah while I'm at it, whether she or you like it or not.

'After that, I'll be at Andy's. Even although he doesn't know it, he deserves some reassurance. And I need to be reminded of who I really am.'

She picked up her coat, then turned and walked out of the cottage, leaving him standing in the silent room, staring at where she had been, with the heavy bag in his hands.

At last he sat down on the sofa, and took out the diaries. They were still bound together, in order. Two pieces of blue marker paper protruded from the second volume, others from the eighth, from the twelfth, from the thirteenth and several from the last.

He took out the second diary and opened it at the first page which his daughter had marked. It was Myra's account of the day of her sixteenth birthday, April 21. The first cold shaft of desolation shot through him as he read of her seventeen-second coupling with Campbell Weston on the living-room carpet. Then he came into the narrative himself; suddenly he felt like a time-traveller, spectating at the events which the diary described. He saw his own face twist in pleasure at the flattening of Campbell, and his overt disappointment when Big Zed backed off. He saw the exultation in Myra's eyes.

He turned to the next marked page, and read, pictures coming clear into his head.

April 28. At Home.

Afternoon with Alice, getting ready for the big date. She's taken it really well, all things considered.

Met Bob outside the Rex at seven o'clock. He paid. It's dark in there, especially in the back corner of the circle. It was a British film, with some guy named Roger Moore. I didn't see much of it, though. I spent most of the time with my tongue down Robert's throat and with his hand up my jumper. He caught on quick.

We went straight back to his house afterwards. He said his mum and dad were away at some place called Chirnside, visiting friends, and wouldn't be back till Sunday night. I asked if we could have a drink, gin or something, but he said no, we didn't need it. It was the first time he's ever refused me anything. Instead we went straight up to his bedroom.

I don't know why, but all of a sudden I felt a wee bit frightened. He left the curtains open and the light out, and he took my clothes off in the dark. He undid the bra-clip first time, too. I was shivering, lying there, watching him undress, until he lay down naked beside me, and touched me, between my legs. That's when I knew that Alice had been wrong. It was like being with a man, not a boy like Campbell. His muscles were hard . . . but not as hard as . . . ! He just lay there for a while, kissing me and touching me, until I couldn't wait any longer and I pulled him over and into me. Right away I found out what an orgasm means. It went on and on, then I could feel him starting too. He was going to pull out, but I held him there, with my legs wrapped around him, until he shot it all, hot and sticky, way up inside me.

As he lay there on top of me, with the pair of us sweating, I told him that I loved him, and he said that he loved me. Guess what, diary? We both really mean it.

We did it again, with a Durex this time, (he had

them in his bedside cabinet) then we got dressed
and he walked me home. He doesn't know it, but
I'm going back round there tomorrow morning!

He smiled as he closed the book. In fact, Alice had been
right, but from his and Myra's first kiss at her party, he
had been thinking about the moment. When it had come,
he had simply known, instinctively, what to do.

He picked up the next diary in Alex's sequence and
opened it at the next marked page.

July 17. Estartit.

I don't know what made me do it. It must have been
the heat, that's all I can think of. It's not that I'm
not getting enough; Bob and I have been at it two
or three times every day since we got here.

But it happened, nonetheless. I had gone up from
the pool to the apartment for a pee, since I don't like
the toilets down there. I did it, and I was coming out,
when there he was, Dougie Fiddes, in his swimming
trunks, going into his studio across the corridor. He
gave me a smile, friendly, just like he does at the
pool. I gave him a grin back, only something in me
took over and it became a bit more than friendly.

The urge just swept over me after that, and I
couldn't stop myself. I kept grinning at him as I
walked across the hall. I pushed him back, into his
apartment. The bed wasn't made or anything but I
didn't care, I just shoved him down on it. I tore his
trunks off, then my bikini bottom, and I jumped on
him. I did all the work. It didn't take long, but I

came like a train and so did he. I'll never forget his face beneath me, tongue out and bewildered, all at the same time. I'll never forget the thrill, the scariness, the excitement.

When I went back down to the pool and saw Bob, looking so fit and tanned, and happy and sexy, a funny thing happened. All of a sudden I wanted him, really wanted him, more than I think I ever have. I grabbed his hand and yanked him away from the pool, up to our apartment, up to bed.

Dougie's terrified now in case Bob finds out. I must admit I'm a bit scared myself, because I'm never sure what he might be like if he really got mad. But then I'm not going to tell him, am I. And Dougie certainly isn't, that's for sure. Still, it's as well we're off home tomorrow.

Bob closed the diary and stared at the wall, gasping, his heart pounding. Dougie Fiddes: his best friend at the time. And his fiancée, for he and Myra had been engaged then. By her account, she had raped him, virtually. A week later, Dougie, his wife, and their baby daughter had died in the wreckage of their plunging plane.

Fighting away images of Dougie Fiddes' last thoughts, he picked up the next marked entry, and he read on. And on.

An hour later, he closed the last diary and sat on the sofa, his face suffused with rage. Then with a roar like a bull he leapt to his feet and threw the volume against the wall, smashing it and sending pages flying everywhere.

Something unstoppable drove him through to Alex's room. The black dress and underwear lay on the bed, the

362

shoes and stockings on the floor. He gathered them all up and strode out to the back garden, grabbing a newspaper and a box of matches on the way.

He tore the funnelled lid from the garden incinerator and threw the clothes inside, mingled the sheets of newspaper among them and lit a match. Replacing the lid, he stood back as the fire took hold, watching like an onlooker at a witch-burning as the relics of a woman he had never known were consumed and rose in a column of smoke and sparkling ashes, up and away into the darkness of the night.

Gradually his rage began to abate, until he was able to walk back into the house; he was quiet, calm, and infinitely sad.

He thought of phoning Alex, but realised what she had suffered over the weekend, and that she deserved to be left alone with Andy. He thought of phoning Sarah, but could think of nothing to say to her. He thought of phoning Pam, even of going to see her, but knew at once that it would not be fair of him to visit her in such a mood. Indeed, some instinct within him warned him that it could be dangerous for both of them.

Instead, he turned off the light. In the darkness he sat, as a coldness swept over him. Staring at nothing, he thought of all of the day's revelations, and he planned.

72

'How did you get on yesterday at Falkirk?' he asked, as soon as she stepped into his office.

Something in his voice made Pam look at him across the rosewood desk. It was barely noticeable, but there was an edge of weariness to it. His eyes gazed back at her with their usual warmth, but deep down in their blue pools, and in the creases around them, she saw traces of pain.

'Very well, boss,' she said, forcing herself to be brisk. 'It couldn't have gone better. I saw the senior partner of Watson Forbes, a Mr Jenks. He said that he was approached three years ago by a woman calling herself Jacqueline Huish. She said that she had come into some money, and wanted him to set up a company for her so that she could invest it in property. There and then she gave him two hundred and ten thousand in cash.'

Skinner's eyebrows rose. 'She didn't show him any ID?' he asked.

'No. Mr Jenks just accepted everything at face value, especially, it seems, the money. He admits that he made no attempt to check where it had come from. He went ahead as she instructed, bought a shelf company from a legal services firm and registered it, with Jacqueline Huish as sole director and secretary.

'She came back, gave him a list of half a dozen properties she had looked at, and told him to buy any three of them, within budget. He did, completed the conveyancing, and gave her a fee note. She settled it from the money that was left, and took the balance away.

'I did a check with the Edinburgh City Finance Department. The Council Tax on the three properties has always been paid in cash. The taxpayer for each is listed simply as Thirty-First Nominees, of the Rankeillor Street address.

'Mr Jenks never saw Jacqueline Huish again . . . until I showed him a photograph of Carole Charles, that Alan Royston got for me from the *Evening News*. Then he nearly fell out of his chair.'

Skinner beamed at her. 'That's excellent,' he said. 'The Fiscal said he'd agree to search warrants if I could satisfy him that Carole Charles and Jacqueline Huish were one and the same person. I was a bit concerned about that, but you've cracked it. Good work, Sarge.'

She flushed, and smiled. 'It was just luck.'

'No. Having the nous to show him the photograph wasn't luck. That was good police procedure. Right, I'll speak to Davie Pettigrew and secure those search warrants. You call McIlhenney and have him here at two thirty. Don't tell him what it's about and tell him to say nothing to anyone else.'

She looked at him, puzzled. 'McIlhenney?'

'Of course. Deputy Chief Constables don't go kicking doors in as a rule, and I wouldn't ask you to do it.'

'Glad about that!' She stood up, but paused, and her grin left her. 'How did you get on last night? Or shouldn't I ask?'

He motioned her back to her seat and leaned across

the desk. 'Pam, you're a friend as well as a PA,' he said quietly, looking deep into her eyes. 'You have a perfect right to ask, not just personally, but professionally too. In that respect, I can tell you that Skinner's Mission is accomplished. I know who tried to kill me, and why.

'Very soon I'll settle that account. But first, there are some other ducks that have to be got into a row.'

He paused. 'Personally, my life is taking a new turning. I'll explain it all to you once the smoke clears. All I'll tell you now is that last night we had an exorcism at the haunted house.'

Her frown deepened, so dramatically that he laughed. 'That's whetted your appetite, I can see. I want you to do something for me now that'll puzzle you even more. I want you to go to personnel and pull a complete service record file for me.'

'Right away. Whose?'

His smile vanished. 'Robert Morgan Skinner. Deputy Chief Constable.'

73

McIlhenncy thumped on the door of number 31a Rankeillor Street with the side of his clenched fist.

'Let's count to thirty-one, for luck,' said Skinner. The three stood on the doorstep of the basement flat and waited, until finally, the DCC nodded.

McIlhenney picked up the big black battering ram by both handles and heaved it, as smoothly as he could. With hardly any splintering of wood, the door gave and swung open violently.

'I didn't hit it *that* hard,' said the Sergeant, puzzled. He looked at the doorjamb and at the keeper of the five lever lock, and turned to the DCC. 'Sir, I'd say that someone's been in before us, with a crowbar. The door was just held on the Yale, and barely at that. It's a wonder it didn't open when I knocked on it.'

Frowning, Skinner led the way into a dark hallway. He ran his hand along the wall until he found a light switch and flicked it on.

Three doors led off the hall, all of them closed. He opened each in turn. 'Bathroom. Pam, you check in there. Living room, kitchen off. Neil, you take that. This must be the bedroom. I'll look in here.

'Remember, don't touch anything for now. We're

looking for ledgers, files, correspondence. If someone's beaten us to it they won't be here, but you never know what else we might find.'

The bedroom, like the rest of the flat, as far as he had seen in his snap look round, was furnished for functionality rather than comfort. A continental quilt, with a cheap cover and white cotton pillowslips lay on the double divan bed. He bent over the pillows and looked closely, a strange smile on his face.

The wardrobe, chest of drawers and dressing table were made of light pine, matching the headboard. A number of cosmetic items and a tall tube of hair spray lay on the dressing table, on which a thick film of dust had gathered. There were three drawers in the chest. He opened them one by one. The first was half-filled with female underwear. Skinner took out a pair of panties and held them up. He shuddered as he was reminded of the garment which Alex had worn the night before, and which he had consigned to the flames.

He closed the drawer quickly, and opened the next, revealing a few tops and sweaters, of varying weights. The bottom drawer was empty, save for a large box of condoms. He picked it up. 'Twenty-four at a time,' he muttered to himself. 'Randy bugger, eh.' He looked in the box. It was full '. . . Or did she buy them?'

Skinner opened the wardrobe. Inside he saw, hanging neatly to the left of the rail, half a dozen dresses, three pairs of slacks, and a tracksuit. The right side of the wardrobe was empty.

He sensed Pam behind him before she spoke. 'Nothing in the bathroom, boss,' she said. 'Nothing at all. It's been scrubbed clean.'

'So has this, in a way. I'd guess that there were men's clothes here, recently, but not any more. One drawer's empty, and half the wardrobe. And look here.' He picked up one of the pillows. 'The sheet's been stripped from the bed, and these pillow-slips; there isn't a single hair on them.

'The bastard's been thorough,' he said with feeling.

'Ahh, but . . .' Masters reached down and felt the coverlet of the quilt, then, slowly and carefully, turned it over. 'Not that thorough,' she said. 'Nobody, but nobody can get all the hairs off a nylon duvet cover.'

She smiled up at Skinner, brightly. 'That's why I use cotton.

'Look, here. And here. And here. And here.'

Skinner went to the door. 'Neil,' he called. 'Through here, with those plastic envelopes for forensic samples.'

He turned back towards his assistant, as McIlhenney's heavy tread sounded in the hallway. 'Pam, call in for a car to pick you up and get out to the lab as quick as you can, with these strands of hair for matching and checking. The report's for my eyes only, like before.

'Meanwhile, Neil and I will check the other two flats. Let's just hope that our friend didn't know about them.'

74

It took three blows of McIlhenney's siege hammer before, finally, the door of 5c Westmoreland Cliff yielded and burst open.

The Sergeant examined the wreckage of the two locks. 'No-one's been in this one before us, sir,' he said. 'Not without a key anyway.' He led the way inside. The flat was more or less the same size as the one in Rankeillor Street, but far more spectacular in its outlook. Every room, except for the bathroom, looked down upon Dean Village and along the narrow, tree-lined valley which the Water of Leith had carved through the centre of the city.

There was no furniture in the house, nothing other than, in the living room, a cheap desk, an electric typewriter, a shabby chair, bought from a secondhand shop or from a downmarket warehouse, and a grey four-drawer filing cabinet, similar in shape to the blackened shells which had stood in the ruins of Jackie Charles' showroom.

'Keys,' said Skinner absentmindedly. He took out his mobile and dialled a number. 'Inspector Dorward, please,' McIlhenney heard him say. 'Arthur, amongst the mess last Thursday morning, did you find any keys close to the body, or anything that could have been a key?

'You did? Good. Have them sent round to my office at once.'

He put the phone away. 'Carole had three flats, Neil. One as an illicit nookie nest, old habits dying hard and all, one as an office, and the third, I'll bet, just as a bolthole, in case this one was compromised.'

He tugged at the top drawer of the filing cabinet. To his surprise it slid open.

'My God, she must have been confident, to leave this unlocked.' He looked in the drawer, and saw, nothing. He frowned and slammed it shut. When he found the second drawer was empty also, a scowl began to gather on his face, but it vanished as he opened the third. It was lined with green sliding folders, each packed with documents. He took out a handful at random and flicked through them. They were carbon copies of typewritten letters, none of them carrying a destination address, but all of them dated.

He held one up and read it aloud:

November 11, 1993

This is to confirm the substance of our conversation by telephone this morning. The business which we discussed will be completed as scheduled next Saturday afternoon. I am assured that the agent involved knows his position, and that he will co-operate in securing the desired outcome. Therefore it is safe to make your investment.

Skinner frowned, and flicked through the papers in his hand, until one in particular caught his eye. He read it to McIlhenney:

November 17, 1993

I understand your concern at yesterday's unexpected turn of events. Since the mishap occurred at this end, I will of course make full restitution of your lost investment, plus one hundred per cent as a sign of good faith. Be assured also that the agent involved will suffer the consequences of his failure to carry out his commission.

However I think you will agree that our experience this weekend has taught us all that this is not the most suitable country in which to attempt to arrange such transactions.

'No salutations and no signatures,' said the DCC, 'but if you look at the dates, these could relate to the business that earned Jimmy Lee his broken knees. When we match these letters to Carole's typewriter, we've got the start of a chain of circumstantial evidence. If Telecom can tell us whether Jackie Charles made any international calls on November 16 or 17, 1993, it'll get that bit stronger.

'We're on to something, Neil. This lot's going to Special Branch. Sure it's all circumspect and circumstantial, but if they can compare references and dates with crimes around the country, you never know what picture we might be able to paint for a jury. Remember that serial killer whose conviction hung on the fact that he bought petrol with a credit card eight years before his arrest?

'With hard work, nothing's beyond us.'

He replaced the documents, then tried the fourth drawer. At first he thought it was empty, like the first two. The book was black-bound, and obscured by shadow. He was on the point of rising to kick the drawer shut when it caught his eye.

He picked it up, feeling it thick and heavy in his grasp, and opened it. It was a cash ledger, a record of payments received, and payments made, each one dated, kept meticulously in ink, each entry in the same firm hand. He flicked through it. On each page there was a third column showing a positive cash balance, running into tens, sometimes hundreds of thousands of pounds. He stopped at one point and traced the columns backwards, pausing then continuing.

'Jesus, Neil,' Skinner whispered. 'This is it. The Charleses' criminal treasury. A cash pile building up, then being reduced by regular transfers, out of the country I'll bet. There's millions in this book.'

He looked at the first page, and saw that entries began in 1984. Sitting down at the desk, he began to pore through it, describing it to McIlhenney as he went. No names, Neil. Just initials. Most of the incoming payments are marked 'DT'. That'll be loanshark money, protection money from minicab drivers, all channelled through Dougie Terry.'

He paused and pointed. 'That's interesting. Here's an outgoing payment, made on June 29, 1989, fifty grand to TH. I wonder if that was stake money advanced to Tommy Heenan. My, but this book's going to make a lot of people very uncomfortable.'

He flicked through the pages until he found November

1993, then scanned its columns. 'See here. An outgoing payment on November 18, of one hundred and fifty thousand pounds, made to a destination shown as KL. Kuala Lumpur, I'll bet.' He whistled. 'No wonder Jimmy Lee's on crutches.'

Skinner would have closed the book then, and taken it back to his office, but the next entry caught his eye. An outgoing payment of five thousand pounds, made to someone with a single initial. Hazarding a guess, he turned to February 1994. Three months on, to the day, a further five thousand. He went back six months. Five thousand.

At last he closed the ledger. 'Jackie himself didn't know about this place, Neil. If he had, these things would not be here still. No-one knew about Westmoreland Cliff. Not even Donna.'

75

Pam was waiting at the door of Skinner's office as he turned into the Command corridor. She had seen the BMW as he had parked it beside the Chief Constable's modest Vauxhall Vectra.

'Come in,' he said grimly, holding tight to the ledger until he laid it on his desk.

'Well,' he said, as he poured them coffee from the filter machine. 'Any news from the labs?'

She nodded, as she took her mug. 'The samples match, boss. All of them.'

'Ahh!' he sighed, throwing his head back as if he had been hit, and slamming his palm down on the ledger on the desk in a sudden violent movement, which made her jump. 'That tears it, then.

'Pam, I want you to ask Mr Martin to call a meeting of the whole Charles investigation team, in half an hour, in his office. I want to brief them all, every one of them, on the arrest of Jackie Charles.

'But first, I have to talk to Proud Jimmy.'

Pamela looked at him as he headed for the door, at the mixture of emotions written on his expressive face. 'Who is it?' she asked, quietly.

Because she was who she was, and because he knew already that he could rely absolutely on her loyalty and discretion, he told her.

375

76

'So there it is, ladies and gentlemen. Jackie and Carole Charles' entire illegal business, since 1984 at least, all wrapped up in there. I'm sure that there are other records going back before that period. I'd guess that, wherever the money is, that's where we'll find them.'

As Skinner spoke, Andy Martin closed the ledger and passed it to Dave Donaldson, seated beside him.

'But there's nothing solid, boss,' said the Chief Superintendent. 'It's all initials; there isn't a name in it. We'll never convict anyone with that, because it doesn't incriminate anyone.'

Skinner grinned. 'Oh yes it does. It incriminates Jackie Charles, right up to his nuts. We'll prove that every entry in that book is in Carole's handwriting. We'll show that there are gaps in the entries which match dates when she and Jackie took their holidays, taking with them, as the variations in the balance indicate, great chunks of cash.

'Then we'll do him for tax evasion. A couple of million, at a rough calculation.'

As he looked around the table, from face to face, they all looked up at him as he stood by the window. Andy Martin, Dave Donaldson, Maggie Rose, Sammy

Pye, Neil McIlhenney, Brian Mackie, Mario McGuire, Pamela Masters: his team, Skinner's people.

His smile embraced them all. 'Ladies and gentlemen of the Jury, I ask you. When Jackie gets up in the witness box and says "I never knew. My late wife obtained and disbursed all that money illegally and salted the balance away overseas, and I never knew," which one of you is going to believe a word he says? Who could believe that a man could be so ignorant of what his own wife is doing?'

As the words left his lips, his voice tailed off, and he turned to look out of the window, so that no-one, not even Andy or Pamela, could see his face. For he knew that he was the one person in the room who could give credence to the only defence open to Jackie Charles.

He mastered himself and turned back to face them. 'Right now, Jackie's sat up there, in his unprotected villa in Ravelston Dykes thinking that he's as safe as houses. Terry's dead, and so there's no chain to link him to McCartney, the Birmingham murders or the Jimmy Lee attack.'

He pointed to the ledger. 'But he doesn't know we've got that. He didn't even know where it was himself, because that's one thing Carole didn't tell him. She didn't tell him about the three properties she bought as Jackie Huish, maybe for added security, or maybe just because she didn't want him to know where she and her so-called pal got up to whatever it was they got up to when Carole was supposed to be at Yoga.

'Jackie doesn't know that we've got his records, and he doesn't know what that book can do to him.' He paused and resumed his seat at the table, beside Martin.

'So tonight, he can stay where he is, while Pam, Sammy and I do some more work on that ledger, and while Brian and Mario check the dates and hints in that correspondence against robberies, murders and other assorted events around Britain.

'He can stay there until ten o'clock tomorrow morning, when you, Mr Martin, and you Mr Donaldson, with Sergeant McIlhenney's strong arm beside you, will call at Ravelston Dykes and pick him up.'

He took the ledger from Donaldson. 'Once we've got him, and he sees this, then just like Ricky McCartney, to earn himself a few years less in the pokey, I'll bet he puts a name to every initial in this book.'

He stood up. 'Pamela, Sammy, you come with me. The rest of you, I'll see you all here, 9 a.m. tomorrow.'

77

They stepped to the left of the monoblock driveway, crossed the foot of the lawn and made their way up through the trees, until they were almost at the villa.

Since the line of their approach kept them out of sight of its sensor, the security lamp over the garage stayed dark. There were no lights showing in the house itself, only the cream globe over the door, and the strong blue metal glow from the big television set in Jackie Charles' private cinema.

Silently, they took the last few steps up to the front door. A black-gloved finger pressed the bell, which rang out loudly inside. They stood and waited. Eventually, a light shone in the big hallway. Eventually, the door swung open, silently.

Jackie Charles stepped back in surprise at the sight of Sir James Proud, in full uniform, standing on his doorstep, the light shining on the silver braid on his epaulettes and his cap. Quickly, he slipped something into the right hand pocket of his red, velvet-trimmed smoking jacket, and ran his hand over his neatly cropped hair.

'John Jackson Charles,' the Chief Constable boomed. 'We are here to arrest you on charges of tax evasion.' Then he glowered, fiercely. 'But first, my deputy, Mr

379

Skinner, would like a word in private about another matter.'

He stepped aside, and Skinner swept into the hall like a Mediterranean thunderstorm, dark and crackling with unleashed fury. In a flash he seized Charles by the lapels, bunching them in his right fist. The other hand went to the right-hand pocket of the smoking jacket and took out a slim automatic pistol.

'Not completely certain, Jackie, were you?' he said, showing the gun to the Chief behind him without looking backwards, then slipping it into the pocket of his own jacket. 'That's something else we can do you for. There's no way that gun's licensed.'

He propelled the struggling man before him, towards the television room, and thrust him inside, closing the door behind them and moving quickly to pull the heavy curtains.

'What's all this . . . ?'

Crack! Skinner's backhanded slap took Charles off his feet, in mid-protest, and sent him sprawling across one of the red chairs, and down to the floor. As he lay there shaking his head, as if to clear it, the policeman hauled him upright, lifted him to eye level, and butted him hard between the eyes, before hurling him into one of the two chairs, like a discarded garment.

Bleeding heavily from the nose, his eyes wide with shock and terror, Charles stared up at his assailant, helpless. His mouth opened, revealing a twisted dental bridge. Before he could speak, Skinner's right index finger shot out, warning, threatening.

'Not a word, Jackie. Not a single fucking word. Just think back to eighteen years ago, you little shit. That's what this is about. You were afraid of me then, were you? Oh, by Christ, but what I'm going to do to you now!'

Bloody words started to bubble from Charles' lips, until they were silenced by a single ferocious look.

'Myra kept a diary, Jackie,' Skinner snarled. 'Every day of her adult life. I never read it while she was alive, because she told me that it was the one thing she wanted for herself alone. After she died, it stayed unread. Until last night, that is, when finally, I started looking for answers.'

He reached into his inside pocket and took out two folded sheets of paper. 'It's some read, Jackie, I'll tell you. Hot stuff. Listen to this.'

January 17. Gullane.

I know I shouldn't have, with Bob away on his course. If he had been home we wouldn't have been there. But my old devil grabbed me, so I asked Lindsey to babysit, I put on the glad rags and I went to Bill and Gerrie's party.

He was there as usual, that little slimeball Jackie, with his tart of a wife. I remember the way she tried to come on to Bob last year at Linda's, and how he froze her. So that's what happened tonight but the roles were reversed. Jackie, half-pissed, comes on to me, grabs me up for a dance, cheek to cheek, chest to chest, crotch to crotch, or it would have been if he wasn't so short. Then he starts whispering rubbish in my ear. Well, the red mist came down. I danced him into the hall, with no-one looking, and into the big cloakroom. He started playing with my tits, until I said to him, 'Look Jackie, just fuck me, okay.' I heard him gasp in the dark. I'm sure he wanted to get out of there but I stepped out of my shoes, unzipped him, took the puny thing out, and grabbed him by the unmentionables until he performed as best he could.

Skinner paused, then read on silently, actually finishing the page for the first time. The night before he had stopped halfway, numbed with shock.

All of a sudden, while he was doing it, a strange thing happened. It was as if there, in the dark, I was up in a corner of the cloakroom, looking down at myself and at the sweaty little pervert. Out of my body, I thought of Bob and I thought of my wee Alexis, and I realised what I've always known, that they are what I love more than anything in life. Yet here I was again, doing my level, wicked best to lose them both. For sure, I value them more than me. I detest the woman I can become, with her urges and her need to dominate men. I think I understand now, that all of that has been a reaction to the power which Bob, without even trying, holds over me. But why should he not, because I, the real me, love him more than life itself?

And so I pushed the gasping, shrivelling, little wretch aside, stepped back into my high heels, and walked out of the cloakroom, out of the party and back home, to my lovely little daughter, and to pine for my man while he's away. The glad rags are in the wardrobe now, and that's where they'll stay.

His stomach came up into his throat as he read Myra's confession, knowing that it was what Alex had wanted him to see most of all. Then he saw Jackie Charles staring up at him, terrified, and his grief fuelled his anger.

'You screwed my wife, you little bastard,' he snarled. 'Or rather she screwed you, for you wouldn't have been up to it on your own. A real party animal, aren't you. But it backfired on you, didn't it.'

He held up the second sheet of paper.

March 23. Gullane.

Jackie phoned me at school today, in the interval. How could he do something so stupid! I told him that he'd better accept it, that there's no doubt that I'm pregnant. I told him that I'd been to the clinic and that they can't do anything for me. To get a termination I have to see my own doctor first, and that just is not an option.

I can tell that the wretch is shitting himself stiff about what Bob will do when he finds out that I'm expecting and figures out eventually, as he must, that he was away at the time. I have to say, diary, that I'm more than a little nervous myself on that score. But Jackie, dear Jackie, he keeps saying, not to worry, not to worry, that he knows what to do to sort the problem out, and that everything will be all right.

Why should I believe a word he says? What am I going to do?

On a happier note, Alexis won a prize for singing at playgroup today. I called Mum and told her, she was dead chuffed. Bob came home late, and said he wants the Triumph tomorrow. George the mechanic is going to service it for him in his lunch-hour. That means I get to drive the flying machine. I wish I could drive it straight at Jackie Bloody Charles.

Skinner shoved the pages into his pocket. 'Jackie will sort the problem out,' he said, in a cold, hard, razor-edged voice.

'You bastard! You broke into the garage that I rented then, behind Hopetoun Terrace, didn't you. You took a hacksaw, and you cut the brake pipe of my Mini Cooper. You were in the motor trade. You must have known what happened to those things in an accident. That was your solution, wasn't it? Only I didn't drive the Mini next day, did I?

'You didn't care about Myra's problem, not at all. But you were terrified of me, so you decided to kill me. You murdered my wife instead, but that didn't really matter did it? Either way, your problem was solved.'

Towering over the man, Skinner's fury turned into a cold, hard, killing rage. If Proud Jimmy had been in the room and had seen him, he would have been as terrified as Charles. He reached down to pick him up.

'No,' his victim howled. 'It wasn't me!'

His voice, given a lisp by the twisted bridge, was so pathetic, and his twisted face was so terrified that together they seemed to break the spell that had engulfed Skinner. He straightened up.

'It was Carole,' Jackie Charles moaned. 'She did it. And she wasn't trying to kill you.

'It was Myra she meant to get, all along.' He paused

and looked up at Skinner as if he was pleading for his life, as indeed he might have been. The policeman glared down at him, his disbelief showing.

'Honestly, Bob,' the broken man cried. 'It was Carole!

'The night before the accident, I told Carole that I had had a fling with someone and that she was pregnant. She knew someone who could fix these things, a bent doctor, I think. I tried not to tell her who it was that was expecting, but she made me. She said she wouldn't give me the abortionist's name otherwise.

'When I told her it was Myra, she just went quiet. Then she gave me the doctor's name.'

He paused to wipe a trickle of blood from his mouth. 'Next evening, I heard that Myra had been killed.

'Remember the funeral, Bob? The whole village was there, just about everyone. I was there, though probably you didn't see me. But Carole wasn't. I asked her to come with me but she just glared at me and said no.'

He wiped his mouth again. 'When I got back from the cemetery, she told me about it. She was out with the dog that morning, very early, around six. She saw you drive away in the Triumph. She knew that Myra would have to take your Cooper S. She had seen her drive it before, and she knew that she always went too fast.

'Carole knew all about cars. We used to rally together, but she was far better than me. She went home and got a chisel and broke into your garage. Getting into the car and opening the bonnet was easy for her. She was a good mechanic; she knew which pipe to cut, and how far to cut it.'

He paused and looked up at Skinner, as if pleading for his life. 'She was infertile, Bob, you see, but wouldn't ever accept it. She always blamed me for us not having kids. When she heard that I had made Myra pregnant, she just snapped.'

The detective stared down at Charles for long, tense silent minutes. Then he stooped down and seized the man's head in his powerful hands, digging his thumbs under his chin, gripping him like a vice as he gazed into his eyes.

'You're telling the truth, Jackie, aren't you,' he said, dispassionately. 'Yes, I guess you are. I knew Carole too. She was capable, even more so than you, and I saw that in her from the off. Maybe I should have guessed.

'Mind you, you little shit, you still more than earned that burst mouth.'

He gave a great sigh, and looked down at the man who had been his quarry for more than twenty years. 'I could have killed you tonight, Jackie. Or I could have sat back and left it to someone else.

'I guess you've figured out by now who murdered Carole, and Medina, and Dougie Terry. I guess you were pretty sure too – despite that precautionary gun – that, since Carole's ledger is buried deep, so deep that not even you know where it is, there was nothing to link you and the murderer, and that you were both safe from each other. You wouldn't shop the killer, so doing you in would be an unnecessary risk.'

Skinner smiled, cruelly. 'Wrong, Jackie. We've dug up the ledger, and the other records. They'll put you away, for sure. From the killer's viewpoint, that means that you have to die after all, before you can talk.

'The murderer is coming tonight, for you. Be sure

of that. It's just as well, then, that you'll be some-where else.'

He stepped across and opened the door. 'Pam, Sammy,' he said quietly. Masters and Pye, who had been following Skinner and the Chief through the garden in the darkness, stepped into the room. 'Mr Charles is in custody. Caution him formally, then take him to Fettes, and lock him up. Go in the back way, and don't let anyone see you, other than the duty officers.

'Oh, and tomorrow you might call in Mr Lockie to look at his teeth. He seems to need some bridge work done.'

78

Jackie Charles' giant television set glowed against the darkness of the room, shining out into the night through the uncurtained window. The stereo sound of a crowd filled the room as highlights of that evening's football were played out on screen.

The grey-templed man in the chair sat, watching the action. He watched for an hour, then for another, as the clock display in the top right corner of the picture counted out the minutes. Twice he changed channels, from sport, to news, to a late-night movie.

He sat, focused, seemingly, on nothing but the huge screen, as at last the handle of the heavy door turned, and as it opened without a sound. He did not react to the odd, faint rustling noise, as the shadowy figure advanced towards him, or catch the television's light reflecting on the long blade in its hand. The figure stopped and tensed . . .

Then, suddenly the room was ablaze with light. The intruder spun round to see Bob Skinner stood in the corner, his hand still on the switch. In the armchair, Sir James Proud looked round at last.

The figure tensed again. It was grotesque, with its body encased in a black binliner, plastic bags on feet and hands like great galoshes and gloves, and another, smaller and with a wide eye-slit, over its head as a makeshift hood.

There was nothing grotesque, though, about the blade as it was held towards the DCC, waving, jabbing, threatening.

Skinner dropped his hand from the light switch, and took Jackie Charles' pistol from his pocket. 'If you come at me with that knife,' he said, his voice flat and emotionless. 'I will kill you. Stone. Fucking. Dead.'

The assassin hesitated, and stopped edging forward.

'I mean it,' said Skinner, 'and you believe it, don't you.'

He raised the small pistol, pointing it at the centre of the intruder's chest. 'Drop it. Now. Or do you really want to die?'

There was a moment of deadly silence. Then the threatening hand was lowered, and the knife fell to the ground.

Pocketing the gun, the detective stepped quickly towards the figure; grasping by the left arm, twisting upwards, violently, stretching shoulder tendons, swinging round, slamming hard, brutally, face-first, against the wall. His lips curled up in a grin of savage pleasure as he heard the cry of pain, and felt the body sag in his grasp.

He swung his captive round, and, still holding the plastic-clad figure pinned to the wall, ripped off the makeshift hood.

Detective Superintendent Dave Donaldson screwed up his eyes involuntarily as they were caught directly by one of the five bright spotlights in the ceiling above.

'Why, Dave?' Skinner hissed. 'Why?'

He jerked him round and sent him flying, crashing,

into the second of the red leather chairs, facing the Chief Constable.

'Why man?' said Proud Jimmy, his face ashen.

Donaldson sat between them like a great plastic scarecrow, looking from one to the other. 'How?' he snarled. 'How come you were waiting?'

Breathing slightly heavily from his brief exertion and with his face twisted in disgust, Skinner looked down at the man, with a glare so full of hatred and contempt that Donaldson sank back into the chair, and lowered his eyes.

'How come we were waiting?' the DCC repeated, savagely. 'Give us some credit for being good coppers, Dave. And give the Chief and me a bit of credit too for being able to face the unbelievable: the fact that one of our senior officers might have been selling us out.'

He paused, allowing his breathing to return to normal. 'I've had a niggle for a couple of years that the Charleses were being fed information by someone close to us. Those raids on the flats, the ones that went wrong. You know what they say. "Once is bad luck, twice is enemy action."

'Then, when the guy who gave us the tip-offs about the two flats had a fatal accident at work with a forklift truck, that smelled more than a bit off.

'Like I say, I thought it, but I never dreamed that the leak could be that close to me. I thought it might have been a civilian staff member, talking too much to a pal off duty. I never thought for a second that it could have been one of my team, one of Skinner's anointed.' There was pain in his voice as he spoke.

'It began to come home to me when Medina was killed.

I just couldn't buy the idea of Jackie putting us on to him, and then knocking him off. There had to be another reason. It was then that I twigged about the ledger, and about Medina's notes. If that book existed, and if there was someone on the inside, then perhaps he might be afraid that it would incriminate him. In that case he couldn't take the risk of Medina producing those notes.

'The fact is that Jackie never knew that Medina had seen the book. As far as I could determine, the only people who did know about that were those involved in the investigation.

'So it was smart thinking on your part to look for another motive for Medina's killing,' said Skinner. 'You must have thought all your birthdays had come when you nearly nailed Tommy Heenan for a murder that you did yourself. If it hadn't been for those two Constables he might have gone down for it at that.'

He paused. 'The binliner and bags made me think, you know. They made me think that maybe this wasn't just someone who didn't want to get all bloody. I mean, the killer could have cleaned himself off in the flat before he left. No, I thought, maybe, just maybe, it was someone who didn't have *time* to get all bloody, because he had to be back at work . . . or on duty.' Idly, he stepped across to the television set and switched it off.

'The next thing,' he went on, 'was the Birmingham team. Sure, Jackie could have had his own source of information down there.

'But alternatively, someone could have set those men up to be killed just to keep Jackie alive, to keep the secret intact. Because still there was the ledger that Medina had mentioned, and Jackie's inside man didn't know where it was, or what was in it. But he must have been scared that if Jackie had been bumped off, all of his secrets would come to light.'

He looked down at Donaldson. 'It was when you burned the second set of binliners in Dougie Terry's office that I began to narrow the list down. As I said, I was sure by then that it was an insider. It was clear to me that Terry was killed because McCartney had put him in the frame, and because he could incriminate the informant, if not directly, then by shopping Jackie and spilling the beans on the whole thing.

'I suppose you just called him and said you wanted to see him at his office. Waiting behind the door, were you?' he asked. Donaldson stared up at him, mute.

'When I saw that second set of bags and binliners, all burned up,' Skinner went on, 'I realised that the killer had got wise to the danger of leaving a DNA trace. I guessed that he was one of the very few people – just two, in fact; you and McIlhenney – who knew that we had found a hair in the first set of plastic bags, and had been sure not to make the same mistake twice.' He leaned down and looked the man close up, dead in the eye.

'So Dave, right there in Terry's office, I palmed a hair off your jacket. Remember, when I patted you on the shoulder? That was when I did it. I had it tested, without anyone knowing whose it was. Believe me, I really was gutted when it matched the one found at the scene of Medina's murder, in the binliner. Sometimes I really hate being a clever bastard.' He took a deep breath, shaking his head.

'That wasn't proof enough for me, though, or for any court; how could it be? Your obvious defence would have been that a hair from your head had simply fallen into one of the bags at the scene. If that had been the only evidence, then I, as well as the jury, would have given you the benefit of the doubt.'

He smiled, without humour. 'It was your old parish priest that made me absolutely certain. He saw you leaving the scene of Carole Charles' murder, and he recognised you. So you did a very smart thing. To be sure, you sought him out at his new church, St Magdalena's, and you made confession to him. You went into one box to keep him out of another one.

'It was just an extreme precaution, of course. You didn't think for a moment that we would actually trace him. But you didn't know that his car had broken down and that he would take a taxi, or that we would find him through his motoring organisation. When we did, he kept your faith. He told us nothing, but Andy Martin did trick enough information out of him for us to check the roll of his *last* parish. It's a small charge, Dave, and your name leapt right off the page at me.

'With that I knew beyond doubt, but it still wasn't proof enough. We didn't have that until Pam and I found out about Rankeillor Street. You did a thorough job cleaning up there. Thorough indeed, but not perfect. The place was as clean as a whistle . . . apart, that is, from all the body hair still stuck to the inside of that nylon quilt cover.

'I'll tell you something funny. It didn't come to me until then about you and Carole. Donna, Donaldson: so bloody obvious, too. Jackie never twigged either, not that he could have done anything about it anyway. But once we matched one of the hairs from the bed with the other two, we had completed a nice circle . . . although even then, not one that would have meant anything in court.

'You must have thought you were in the clear when you couldn't find the ledger at Rankeillor Street. You must have thought that it was buried deep, or that Jackie had burned it. But Carole never told you about Westmoreland Cliff, did she? You thought she only had one secret hiding place. But we found the other one, and we found the book.'

He stood in front of Donaldson, sat in his chair. 'When I briefed you about the ledger with the rest of the team, when I let you see it, I knew that I was telling you to go and kill Jackie. Because without his evidence, that book would have meant nothing.

'Well, we've got it now. We've got him now. And we've got you. By the balls, for life, and then some.'

He shook his head again. 'But there's one thing I still don't understand. Why the fuck did you kill Carole in the first place, to set this whole thing in motion?'

Donaldson shook himself free of the plastic bags on his arms, and, in an odd gesture, rubbed his face in his hands. Then as Skinner and Proud stared at him, with bitter, undisguised contempt on their faces, he began to tear off the rest of his black body covering. At last he looked up at them.

'It was Carole all along,' he said, with an expression, and in a voice, that neither knew. 'She got me into it. I met her and Jackie at a Charity do a few years back. She made a pass at me and like a mug I followed it up. She was a good looker for her age, you know. Most men would have been tempted.' He gazed at Skinner, as if expecting some understanding, but finding not a sign.

'Anyway,' he went on, 'I saw her once, and again. Before I knew it we were having an affair. Then she asked me. She said that Jackie had a feeling that someone was talking to us. She told me to find out who it was, and to pass back everything that he fed us.

'I told her she was crazy. She told me that if I didn't, she'd send a video to my wife, and to the Chief.'

'A video?' said Skinner, incredulous.

He nodded. 'We filmed ourselves once. We were drunk, acting daft. Carole set the thing up. I'd forgotten about it, but she'd kept the tape.

'So I gave her what she wanted, and as a sweetener she gave me five grand every three months. I thought, "If I'm hooked, I might as well get something out of it." So I took it and banked it. In a building society, using my wife's maiden surname. It's all there still. I'd been meaning to transfer it to a foreign account.'

'Did Jackie know where the information was coming from?'

'Oh yes, for sure,' said the turncoat, bitterly. 'He knew because Carole told him. She even brought me a handwritten note from him once, saying thanks.'

'So why did you kill her, Donaldson?' barked Sir James. 'After all that.'

The cornered man looked across at his Chief. 'Because I wanted out. I told her I didn't want any more danger, or any more being afraid of being found out. She showed me my way out. She told me that I was to kill Jackie, and that afterwards she and I would disappear. She mentioned the Cayman Islands. I think their money might be there.

'Like before, she didn't give me any choice. She threatened me with the video again, and she gave me two weeks to make it happen, to get rid of Jackie. Implicitly, what she was saying was that I would be her captive for the rest of my days.' He smiled, wickedly. 'She'd have dragged me away from my wife and kids, whether I wanted to go or not. But I didn't, I didn't.' His eyes flashed.

'So, instead of Jackie,' he whispered, 'I killed her, the evil cow. We had a date last Wednesday. She told me that she was going down to Seafield to look over the books, and that she'd meet me at Rankeillor Street at nine thirty. I went to the showroom instead. It was unlocked and she was in the office. "What the fuck are you doing here?" she said. "You," I said. And then I hit her. Bang. Right on the chin. Laid her out for a while.

'By the time she came to, I had tied her hands and feet with rope that I had soaked in petrol, so that it would burn off in the fire. Then I filled the cans from the pump at the back, placed them all around, and laid the rope fuses. When everything was set up right, I lit them.

'All the time I was setting the thing up Carole was screaming at me, lying there in the office, cursing me, calling me for all the bastards in creation. I could hear her as I drove away. I could hear her for hours afterwards.

'This morning, at breakfast, with my wife and kids, I could still hear her.'

He looked up, with blazing eyes, and for the first time, Skinner could see the depth of his rage. 'That should have been it. And it would have been, but for Medina, and McCartney, and Terry. And most of all, but for you, you bastard.'

Sir James Proud shook his silver head. 'How could you, man?' he said, sadly. 'You were a fine officer, in the prime of an outstanding career. You've got a lovely wife, lovely children. How could you do all that wickedness?'

'Easily, Jimmy,' Skinner murmured softly, dreamily, distantly. 'We've all got wickedness in us. Most of us can keep it in check, but there are some in whom it will always surface. That's all there is to it.'

79

She lay along the sofa with her head on a cushion, replete from the dinner he had cooked for her, and relaxed by the wines he had poured. She was barefoot, and her white blouse was open at the neck. He sat cross-legged on the floor in front of the fire, in a polo shirt and chinos. The dinner dishes lay piled in the kitchen ready for the dishwasher, and his chef's apron hung behind the door. His Caithness tumbler, with the smoky Lagavulin, was warming in his big hand, while hers was balanced on the crest of her belly.

The desperately sad voice of Maria Callas filled the room around them, matching his mood, and hers, after the story which he had set out for her over dinner.

'What'll happen to him?' she asked at last.

'He'll plead guilty to the murders of Carole, Medina and the Comedian.

'As for the others, we'll keep our promise to McCartney and Kirkbride. The pair of them will do their twelve years each and think they're the luckiest men alive.

'Jackie Charles will plead guilty to tax evasion, up to an agreed amount, and will pay his dues, plus fine and interest, out of his Cayman Islands money. He'll do about two years, and then he'll disappear, off to the Caribbean, never to return.

'There will be no trials, no evidence led in detail, no cross-examination, no verdicts for juries to deliver, no stinking linen washed in public. There will be no public chronicling of all the betrayals of trust and loyalty that my team has managed to uncover over the last few days.'

'But Donaldson,' she repeated. 'What about him?'

'He'll be sentenced to a minimum term, not less than twenty-five years. He'll expect to serve it mostly in solitary, for his own protection. But somewhere along the line, a man with a blade and a grudge will get close enough to him. Or maybe, he'll tear off a strip of bedsheet and do the job himself. I don't think he'll ever breathe free air again.

'I saw him this afternoon. I interviewed him formally, with Andy and the Chief, for more than four hours. Davie Pettigrew, the Procurator Fiscal, sat in on it as well, and Hamish Lessor, the best solicitor we could find to act for him. He confessed to everything, in detail.

'Lessor will have him examined by psychiatrists. So will Pettigrew. I guess that there's a possibility that he'll be found insane and unfit to plead. But I doubt it. He knew exactly what he was doing, all the way along the line, from the moment he fell into Carole Charles' honey-trap until the end, when he squared up to me with that blade.'

His head dropped down and he hissed, aloud. 'Ahh, what a traitor. Everything we stand for in this job. Everything I've ever believed and tried to teach, he betrayed. I've encountered some cold and ruthless people in my time. Indeed, if I was to be honest, I'd apply that description to myself. But Donaldson's the worst I've

ever met. His only motive was self-preservation. He had
no guiding principles, no cause: only himself. For his
own interests alone, he killed, or had killed, half a dozen
human beings.

'God protect his poor wife, and his poor kids. But God
damn him to a hundred hells.'

She propped herself up on an elbow, and looked down
at him, solemnly. She understood that the blow which he
had suffered from Donaldson's treason was only one of
a series, physical and mental, that had torn his life apart.
When he had called to ask her to join him for dinner
at Gullane, and as he had prepared their meal, she had
sensed the depth of his hurt, and had known the flood of
feelings that he was holding back.

She wanted to hug him, to comfort him, to make him
realise that trust and loyalty are not always repaid in
kind. She wanted to, but instead she simply reached
down and stroked his cheek. He looked up at her and
smiled, weakly.

'Forget Donaldson,' she whispered. 'He's just another
criminal you've caught. The point is that you did catch
him. You alone found him out. And at last, after all this
time, you've got Jackie Charles, and he's going to jail.

'Most of all, perhaps, you've solved the mystery of
Myra's death.' She smiled at him, as he took a sip of
his malt.

'What you have to do now,' she said, 'is to draw a line
under it all, and get on with your life, and your career.
Now that you know everything.'

He looked at her and grinned, but very sadly. 'Know
everything? Know that my wife had a secret side, that she
was two personalities, the classic mother–whore image

acted out?' He reached up and ruffled his hair, and in the instant, his mood seemed to lighten.

'I'll tell you what I do know. I know that, when Myra died, the whole village turned out in grief to bury her, because they knew and loved the same Myra I knew and loved: the one who was there for nearly all of our lives together, apart from the odd occasion when being Bob Skinner's wife got too much for her.' He laughed. 'Myra was big-scale. When she kicked over the traces she kicked them good and high.

'She's dead now, and properly put to rest. Her diaries and her glad rags are ashes, and the person who killed her . . . well, one way or another, she died by much the same sword. No tears for Carole Charles, except perhaps from Jackie, although I wouldn't bet the house on that.'

He smiled, looking, all at once, very, very tired.

'Get on with my life,' he chuckled. 'Okay. Let me tell you about that. I've made a decision. A few weeks ago I was asked by someone very important if I wanted to be considered for a very senior job. I told him I'd think about it.

'I have done, for over a month. This morning I went to see him in St Andrew's House and I told him yes, that I do want my name to be in the frame. It would be a big jump, and I probably don't have the command experience to be a serious contender, but even to be in the running is a huge compliment.

'What I was really saying, really deciding, I think, is that having closed the book on the first half of his life, Bob Skinner is looking for new motivation. Maybe it'll be in Edinburgh, maybe down South, maybe somewhere else, but he'll find it . . . trust old Bob to do that.'

He sighed, and looked up at Pamela, into the warmth of her eyes.

'After I'd made my call, I went to see Sarah, to tell her what I'd done, and to see how she would react. She wasn't there. Instead I found this.' He reached out and picked up a letter from the low table beside the sofa, handwritten, on plush cream note paper. He began to read, aloud.

My Dearest Bob,

This is to say I'm sorry, for what I did with Jimmy, and for the way I've behaved since you rediscovered how Myra died. Now, at last, I can tell you why I acted like I did.

Alex came to see me the night before last, in something of a state. She told me the whole story about you giving her Myra's diaries, about her reading them, about wearing her clothes, and about learning the whole truth about her. I understood why the poor kid was so upset. Because you see, I've read those diaries too, from cover to cover. I knew about Myra, her affairs and her secret pregnancy by Jackie Charles, before either of you.

Understand me, I tried not to look in that trunk, after you told me what it was. But it was a hell of a temptation, and I just wasn't strong enough to resist it. So piece by piece, whenever I was at Gullane on my own, I read my way through Myra's life story. I almost tried on the clothes, just like Alex, but something held me back. Finally, when I was done, I tied all the diaries in yellow twine and put them back in the trunk, hoping against hope that you'd never read them; until I realised that once you started on your precious mission, inevitably, you would.

So you see, Bob, I have a secret side too. I'm not just the jealous manipulative woman you fell out of love with. I'm someone else who can give in to temptation. Only I found I couldn't handle the consequences.

When I came to Gullane last week, after you had gone from here, it was to throw myself at you, to spill the beans and to make a last effort to rescue things. But when I saw you watching that cine film, I knew it was too late, and I realised how deeply Myra, dead as she was, still had you in her grasp.

If I'd been honest with you when it mattered, maybe it would have been all right. If I had confessed to you at once that I had looked in the trunk, and shown you what was in it, I guess you'd have had the strength to handle it. But I wasn't honest. I wasn't honest about that, or about my job. I wasn't frank with you about one or two other things either; like for example about my being less than content to be settled in Edinburgh for the rest of my life.

The reason I couldn't talk to you when it mattered was because of your shell, the wall that you have around you. It's built on foundations of trust. You bestow it on people without question, and you expect unstinting loyalty in return, from all of us who carry it. That loyalty includes honesty and frankness.

The one thing you can't handle is betrayal of that trust. I've seen how much that hurts you, and how fiercely you can react. That's where the cycle of conflict came into being. I couldn't bring myself to tell you about Myra's life of betrayal, because I knew that it would devastate you. Yet in trying to save you from learning what I knew, in your eyes, I wound up betraying you myself.

That's why you don't look at me any more like once you did. Because, just like Myra did all those years ago, without your knowing it, I've failed the Bob Skinner loyalty test, and Bob Skinner doesn't hand out second chances. The reason I look differently at you now is because I can't penetrate your shell any more, or carry the weight of your unspoken expectations.

I heard about Donaldson. Andy called in this morning to tell me. I've never seen him really angry before, but I think that if he could have got his hands on him he'd have killed him. He understands that you and Jimmy had to play it so close because it was so sensitive, but I think it would be a good idea if you explained that to him anyway.

Given the beliefs that you hold, and that make you what you are, I know how it must have hurt you, to find that you had a traitor in your midst. So I'm sorry to pile on this last piece of betrayal. I have decided that the way things are, I can no longer stay in this house, in this city, in this country.

So I am taking Jazz today, and flying to the States, to be with my folks for now. They deserve a visit from their grandson. Time will tell where he and I go from there.

I don't want anything from you, Bob, other obviously than your love and support for our son as he grows. If you want anything from me, you know where I am. For now at any rate.

Love from the heart

Sarah

He leaned back and gazed at the ceiling. 'So there you are. I don't have much luck with wives, do I. Nor they with me. I can't live with secrets being kept from me, Pam.' All at once he looked at her, with a helpless expression. 'How can I when my job, my life is dedicated to rooting them out?'

'But look, there are two sorts of secret, surely,' said Pamela. 'There's the kind you keep because if they're uncovered they'll hurt you, then there are the others, the ones you hold on to so that they don't hurt someone else.'

He grunted, ironically. 'Sarah's right, isn't she. I don't give an inch.

'Pam,' he said, 'I am riddled with guilt. Guilt over having such a hold over Myra that she became a whore, just to seek respite, guilt over Sarah being afraid to talk to me when it really mattered, guilt because I promoted Donaldson even as he was selling us out . . .'

He shook his head. 'I am one very contrite polisman, believe me.'

She leaned back, smiling. 'You've nothing to be contrite about, Big Bob. You're only human, like the rest of us. It's a hell of a thing, isn't it,' she murmured, 'when you realise that you're not perfect. It came as a shock to me when it happened, I can tell you.'

Bob laughed, softly. 'And when was that?'

'Tuesday. Around midnight, when I realised that I didn't really want you to sleep in that spare room.'

As he looked at her, astonished, she swung herself off the couch to sit alongside him on the floor, and took the letter out of his hand. 'Let's see, shall we, what Sarah is really saying to you.' She read quickly, then reread the final section.

'She's confused, she's guilty, she's hurt, she's bitter and she's angry with you,' she murmured, as she read, 'but through it all, you know what she's saying, don't you?'

Bob gazed at her, still slightly stunned by her frankness, and shrugged. 'You tell me.'

'She's asking you to knock down your wall, to put everything else to one side, and to go out there and get her!'

'But am I like she says? Do I have that impenetrable wall around me?'

She looked at him appraisingly. 'Maybe you do, but I can't see it. When I look at you, all I see is the Eagle. I see you. I'm a little in awe of you, but I'm not afraid that if I touch you I'll break.'

'So where should the old war-bird land, do you think, Pam?' he asked her, hesitantly. 'Should it be America?'

'I'm not the one to tell you,' she said. 'Only you can answer that question.'

He reached out and took her hand. 'I know that, Pam, love, I know. But the trouble is, I don't know if this Eagle can fly that far.'

'Maybe, for his own sake, he has to try,' she said, smiling, as their eyes met, and locked.

'But it doesn't have to be tonight.'

Now you can buy any of these other bestselling books by **Quintin Jardine** from your bookshop or *direct from his publisher*.

FREE P&P AND UK DELIVERY
(Overseas and Ireland £3.50 per book)

Thursday Legends	£5.99
Gallery Whispers	£5.99
Murmuring the Judges	£5.99
Skinner's Ghosts	£6.99
Skinner's Mission	£6.99
Skinner's Ordeal	£6.99
Skinner's Round	£6.99
Skinner's Trail	£6.99
Screen Savers	£5.99
Wearing Purple	£5.99
A Coffin for Two	£6.99
Blackstone's Pursuits	£5.99

TO ORDER SIMPLY CALL THIS NUMBER

01235 400 414

or e-mail <u>orders@bookpoint.co.uk</u>

Prices and availability subject to change without notice